International acclaim for Jody Shields's

The Fig Eater

"Suspenseful....A chilling tale of detection, betrayal, and failed ratiocination. . . . Ms. Shields gives the reader a palpable sense of fin-de-siècle Vienna. . . . In turning Dora's story into a murder mystery, she has managed to write a gripping psychological thriller while capturing the nervous mood of a city preoccupied, like one of its most famous residents, with sex and death."
— Michiko Kakutani, *New York Times*

"An elegant, intricately crafted puzzle that fairly bursts with history, personalities, and sensory details as well as suspense."
— Glenda Winders, *San Diego Union–Tribune*

"Vivid....A beautifully written book.... *The Fig Eater* takes readers, with mesmerizing clarity, to Vienna in 1910. . . . Ms. Shields flashes dazzling stereopticon slides of a city floating between opposites: the fading nineteenth century and the bustling twentieth, the analytical male point of view and the intuitive female, the scientific and the superstitious. Ms. Shields has a powerful gift for poetic and painterly imagery. Her startling scenes, rich in metaphor, linger long in memory."
— Tom Nolan, *Wall Street Journal*

"A lushly developed entertainment.... *The Fig Eater* is cleverly written."
— Edna Stumpf, *Philadelphia Inquirer*

"*The Fig Eater* adroitly mines the fertile tension between morality and passion that provided such rich material for Freud himself. . . . Rather than tantalizing readers with the usual proliferation of suspects and red herrings, Shields sustains our interest by delving deep into the minds of her detective-protagonists. . . . What makes this novel compelling is its eerily atmospheric depiction of Vienna and its account of the cunning machinations its female detectives must enact to pursue their covert investigation. . . . *The Fig Eater* is one of those novels whose aura stays with you even after the details of its plot are forgotten."
— Leslie Haynsworth, *Denver Post*

"Shields evokes the beautiful but decaying Vienna of the last days of the Habsburgs with a rich, sophisticated structure as simple and complex as the labyrinthine Ringstrasses the characters traverse in their quest for the solution. I'm looking forward to recommending this to my customers."

— Susan Avery, Ariel Booksellers, New Paltz, New York, *Book Sense 76*

"A story of obsession, superstition, and sexual secrets.... *The Fig Eater* is an atmospheric period piece in the tradition of Caleb Carr's *The Alienist*. . . . A vivid portrait of coffeehouse society in turn-of-the-century Vienna, as well as the sinister and sordid underbelly of a seemingly civilized society."

— Kathleen Parrish, *Denver Rocky Mountain News*

"Shields's debut work works — mostly because her cool, precise narrative style lets readers supply their own flourishes to the story."

— Isobel Montgomery, *Guardian* (UK)

"We are carried along by the book's magnificent, elegant creepiness. Shields paints a gorgeous portrait of turn-of-the-century Vienna. . . . Even after Dora's murder is solved, we can't escape the feeling that what Erszébet was really investigating was human nature."

— Melanie Rehak, *Harper's Bazaar*

"As a thriller, *The Fig Eater* works expertly well, with an intelligence and care that make it a pleasure to read."

— Lesley McDowell, *Herald* (Glasgow)

"Immensely engaging.... With a feeling similar to Penelope Fitzgerald's *The Blue Flower*, the brief snapshots of scenes and moods tease readers into wanting more. This absorbing book is practically impossible to put down."

— Christine Pappas, *Lincoln* (Nebraska) *Journal Star*

"A hypnotic, voluptuous mystery that not only envelops the reader in turn-of-the-century Vienna but creates a powerful central character — the police inspector's mysterious wife."   — *More*

"An atmospheric thriller. . . . Shields's Vienna is a wonderfully realized creation."   — Mark Rozzo, *Los Angeles Times Book Review*

"While the whodunit plot is first-rate, readers who aren't fans of the mystery genre will still enjoy this tale.... Miramax was smart to pick up the movie rights; this book has the potential to be a beautiful, suspenseful film."　　　— Rebecca May, *Lebanon Co. Weekender*

"Shields's knowledge of period Vienna is quite astounding. She offers detailed botanical descriptions, depicts the era's rage for curious tuberculosis treatments, and conjures opulent visions of the Viennese carnival season. 'Your investigation is like the telling of a dream,' the inspector's wife tells him one night as they lie together in bed. Such, as well, is Shields's poetic book."　　　— Nancy Lemann, *Mirabella*

"A stylish murder mystery.... Shields's contribution is to transpose Dora's story into a pop genre, a thriller, and to give a cinematic immediacy to the sentiments that color the popular response to her today — anti-Freudianism, anti-Austrianism, and the desire to rehabilitate women's intuition."
　　　— Judith Shulevitz, *New York Times Book Review*

"A very unusual murder mystery — elegant and cerebral.... The pace of the writing is swift.... *The Fig Eater* works as a historical whodunit. But it's also entertaining as a complex game played with Freud's work."　　　— Scott McLemee, *Newsday*

"Shields paints an intricate picture of early 1900s Vienna, filled with dark secrets, shocking medical practices, and tons of suspense."
　　　— *Reader's Edge*

"A glorious maze.... Sometimes gruesome and highly mysterious, *The Fig Eater* is an exciting new brand of detective story."
　　　— Jessica Berry, *Spectator* (UK)

"What if not psychoanalysis but another of our modern secular religions, criminology, were brought to bear on the mystery of Dora? That's the premise of Jody Shields's hypnotic first novel, and she pulls off the switch with impressive elan.... The novel abounds with sensual pleasures.... Shields expands our way of seeing."
　　　— Maria Russo, *Salon.com*

"A dark, seductive novel.... An addictive and sinister read."
　　　— *Scotland on Sunday* (Edinburgh)

"An unusual and intriguing tale. . . . *The Fig Eater* resounds with vitality. . . . The layered mystery is revealed slowly, with Shields's evocative prose exploring the crossroads of scientific and superstitious belief." — Adam Woog, *Seattle Times*

"Evocative. . . . The dance between [the Inspector and his wife] as they pursue their separate inquiries is as intriguing as the murder mystery itself." — David Tarrant, *Dallas Morning News*

"A stylish literary thriller. . . artful and evocative. . . . Shields's Vienna is rich in the texture of corruption."
— Lisa Appignanesi, *Independent* (UK)

"Suspenseful, atmospheric, and highly intelligent: Jody Shields focuses a brilliant light on the murky world of imperial Vienna and Freud's famous patient Dora. There is a sense of intellectual daring such as, in a different way, we find in Freud's case studies."
— D. M. Thomas, author of *The White Hotel*

"Hypnotic in effect. . . . Certainly it's one of the most original historical novels we've read lately." — *Denver Post*

"Astonishingly original and vivid. . . . One of the chief attractions of *The Fig Eater* is the laconic and elegant style. . . . Understanding and judging the motives of the characters is, with brilliant effectiveness, left to the reader." — Charles Palliser, *The Good Book Guide*

"Every word in *The Fig Eater* is a brush stroke, every brush stroke reveals a detail, every detail reveals a color, a light, a shadowy image of the story. . . . Shields offers fascinating portraits of turn-of-the-century prejudices toward women and minorities, as well as a frightening look at the de rigueur but deadly medical treatments used for syphilis and tuberculosis. Those fascinated by botany, early photography, and all things Viennese will find *The Fig Eater* hypnotically entrancing. . . . It rushes to a savage, bizarre conclusion that's well worth the wait." — Carol Memmott, *USA Today*

The Fig Eater

A Novel

JODY SHIELDS

LITTLE, BROWN AND COMPANY
Boston · New York · London

Originally published in hardcover
by Little, Brown and Company, March 2000

First Back Bay paperback edition,
March 2001

The characters and events in this book are
fictitious. Any similarity to real persons, living or
dead, is coincidental and not intended by the
author.

Excerpt from *Hungarian Folk Beliefs* by Tekla
Dömötör, translated by Christopher M. Hamm.
Copyright © 1981 by Tekla Dömötör. Coedition
Corvina–Indiana University Press, 1982.
Reprinted by permission of Corvina Books,
Budapest.

Shields, Jody
    The fig eater : a novel / Jody Shields. —
1st ed.
        p. cm.
        ISBN 0-316-78564-4 (hc) 0-316-78526-1 (pb)
        I. Title.
        PS3569.H4836F54   2000
        813'.54 — dc21   99-37048

10 9 8 7 6 5

Q-FF

Printed in the United States of America

For Kathleen Bishop
Richard Jay Kohn
John Owen Ward

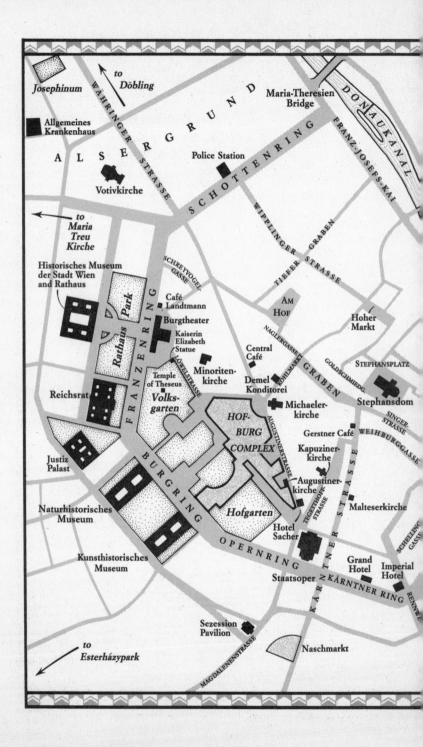

to
Augarten
Park

N

VOLKS-
PRATER

HAUPT ALLEE

P R A T E R

DONAUKANAL

WOLLZEILE

STUBENRING

Museum für
Kunst Industrie

GARTENBAU
PROMENADE

P A R K R I N G

Stadtpark

Kursalon

VIENNA
1910

Miles

0   1/4

Meters

0   300

to Belvedere Garten,
Botanischer Garten, and
Zentralfriedhof

© A. Karl / J. Kemp, 2000

But an Investigating Officer must never and under no circumstances allow himself to follow the paths along which he is pushed, be it designedly or accidentally, by the various witnesses. Apart from the fact that the reconstitution of the crime for oneself is the only effective method, it is the only interesting one, the only one that stimulates the inquirer and keeps him awake at his work.

—HANS GROSS,
System der Kriminalistik, 1904

The Fig Eater

CHAPTER 1

E STANDS UP NEXT TO THE girl's body. He looks down for a moment, then carefully steps over the narrow boards lying around it. He walks across the grass and joins the three men, waiting like mourners. No one speaks. The body is poised like a still life waiting for a painter.

Now they watch the photographer edge his way over the boards, his equipment balanced on one shoulder. He stops and gently lowers the legs of the tripod into place, then steadies the bulky camera directly above the girl. Without looking up, he snaps his fingers. The men silently move aside, shifting their lanterns as a boy passes between them, moving with a sleepwalker's strangely certain gait, eyes fixed on the frail pyramid of white powder he carries on a tray.

The boy stands by the photographer, nervously waiting while he adjusts the dials on the camera. The photographer ignores him. He hunches behind the camera and pulls a black cloth over his head. In that secret darkness, the camera lens tightens around the dead girl's mouth. The photographer mutters something unintelligible, then his hand blindly works its way out from under the cloth. The instant his fingers snap, the boy strikes a match and holds it to the powder on the tray.

A blinding flash lays transparent white light over the girl's body, her stiff arms and legs, the folds of her dress, transforming her into something eerily poised, a statue fallen on the grass. There's shadow, a black space carved under her neck, in the angle where her head is bent toward her shoulder, and below one outstretched arm. Her other arm hides her face. The light vanishes, leaving a cloud of odor. Burned sulphur.

The Inspector keeps this harsh image of the girl's sprawled figure in mind even later, after her body is cut open, becoming curiously tender and liquid.

She lies in the Volksgarten, near the seated stone figure of the Kaiserin Elizabeth. The statue faces a fountain pool in the center of a bosquet of low flowers, and behind it is a curved wall of bushes nearly twelve feet high. The park is a short distance from Spittelberg, Vienna's notorious district where the *Beiseln* offer music, drink, and women.

The Inspector points at a crumpled piece of white paper or cloth near the girl's body. Two of the policemen nod and begin to pick up the boards. There's no haste in their movements, even though it's getting late. They set a board on top of two rocks to make a walkway over to the cloth. If there are footprints on the ground, the boards will protect them.

During another investigation last year, the spring of 1909, the Inspector temporarily preserved footprints in the snow at a crime scene by placing a flowerpot over each one. There are other ways to keep prints left in sand, soft dirt, or dust.

While the photographer's boy patiently holds a lantern over his head, the Inspector squats on the boards, close enough to see that the cloth has been roughly smoothed over some small object. A rounded shape. There are flies around it and a sweet, foul odor. He takes tweezers from a leather pouch and pinches a corner of the fabric. It sticks slightly. When he pulls it off, the fabric has a dark smear on the underside, and he has a shock of recognition as he drops it inside an envelope. Someone has murdered a young woman and defecated next to her body.

When the Inspector stands up, he realizes he is sweating. His shirt is damp; his suspenders are wet stripes over his shoulders. The humid night air has also weighed the girl's clothes down over her body. It is hot, unusually hot for the end of August.

They prepare to take another picture. Egon, the photog-

rapher, drags the tripod over. He sets it up and cranks the camera down and down, stopping it two feet above the soft excrement. One of the men raises a lantern over it so he can see to
focus. The Inspector steps back and turns his head away, waiting for the whispered sizzle of the lightning powder as it ignites. In a minute, the lantern's light is eclipsed by the
explosion. Days later, when he looks at the photograph, the
grass around the body appears as stiff as if it had been frozen,
not burned into the film on the glass plate in the camera by the
explosion of light.

When the boards surrounding her are removed, the girl
looks frailer alone on the ground. They find no objects, no
other obvious clues around her. The thick grass masks any
footprints. They'll search the area again tomorrow during the
day, when there's better light.

Invisible in the dark, the Inspector stands on the marble
platform next to the Kaiserin Elizabeth's statue. He's a tall
man and can reach nearly as high as her head. He gently
touches the statue's shoulder. He never would have permitted
himself this trespass at any other time, but he's unsettled by
the extraordinary discovery of the girl's body near the memo-
rial. Kaiserin Elizabeth was the wife of Franz Josef. She was as-
sassinated in 1898, stabbed in the heart by a madman with a
blade so wickedly thin it left only a speck of blood on her chemise. It is said her dying words were *"At last."*

He wonders if there is some connection between the
statue and the location of the girl's body.

In front of him, the men move quietly in the circle of
light made by the lanterns, and between their dark figures, he
can glimpse the whiter shape of the girl. Just beyond the park,
the wing of the Imperial Palace is faintly visible. From behind
the trees, there's the occasional, isolated sound of an unseen
carriage proceeding around the Ringstrasse.

According to police routine, a sketch is always made before a description of the crime scene is written. Closely trailed
by the boy holding a lantern, Egon paces out a rough square
around the girl's body, three hundred and sixty paces, and
transfers this measurement onto a graph, drawing the kaiser-

in's monument as a dash, the sign used on survey maps. Without disturbing the dead girl's hair, he pushes the end of a tape
measure into the ground at the crown of her head and measures one and a half meters to the base of the monument. Her
right arm is bent over her dark face, so he unspools the tape
from her shoulder to the same point. A distance of almost two
meters. Finally, he pulls the tape from the left heel of her white
canvas boot over to the path, just over one meter. When the
sketch is finished, he signs and dates the paper.

Now her body has been remade as the center point on a
graph. Lines radiate from her head, arms, and legs as if she
were a starfish or a sundial, pinning her exactly in this place at
this hour.

Before the dead girl is moved, the Inspector gently removes her pearl earrings. He cuts through the strap of her
watch, uncoils it from her wrist, and seals the objects in an isinglass envelope. He asks for more light, and now with two
lanterns above him, he kneels over her, shifting his weight, balancing himself on one hand. Careful not to touch her, he uses
the point of the scissors to delicately manipulate her thin cotton dress. Occasionally he asks for a magnifying glass. His eyes
filled with the harsh white of her dress — a dazzling field —
he forgets the body under the fabric until he accidentally
sets his hand on her bare arm. Although he instantly jerks it
away, the impression of her cool skin stays on the palm of his
hand, as if he'd touched a liquid. He rubs his hand against his
trousers.

He knows the other men noticed his spontaneous reaction. He forces himself to touch her again, to break the spell,
pushing her thumb down hard against the ground. It's slightly
stiff, and he estimates she's been dead at least four hours. The
heat makes it hard to calculate, although rigor mortis affects
the small muscles first.

He discovers a pale hair under the collar of her dress, and
his assistant, Franz, wordlessly holds out an empty glass vial to
receive it. No bloodstains are found on her clothing. However,
the back of her white dress is stained when they lift her off the
ground.

When they flop her onto a stretcher, Egon vomits. The

other men look away. The Inspector also ignores him, but he understands his distress. It's the movement of the body that sickened him, its parody of motion. He orders one of the policemen to stay at the site for the few hours remaining until daybreak.

As soon as it is light, Franz goes over the kaiserin's monument, checking for fingerprints. First he dusts the statue with powdered carmine applied with a fine camel-hair brush. The second time he uses charcoal dust. The same fingerprint powders are also applied to the ornamental urns and the marble gateposts at the entrance to the Volksgarten.

Franz reports that all the stone is too rough to hold any impressions.

The afternoon of the same day, the girl's body is in the morgue at the police station on the Schottenring. The men smoke in the morgue during the autopsy to cover the smell of decay and formalin. The ceiling fan cools the room, but it also sucks up the odor of the cigarettes they exhale over the metal table where she lies. They work in the body's stink as if it were a shadow.

Franz takes scissors in slow strokes down the sides of her dress and across her shoulders, then lifts it off. He cuts the thick canvas corset from her waist with a heavy knife after slashing through the laces. It probably took her longer to get into the corset, he jokes to the man leaning across the table, a doctor in a white jacket. The older man is as blond as Franz, but his hair is thinning. His pink head hovers over the girl's discolored face. The doctor nods without looking up. I think she's about eighteen years old, he says. The bare room doesn't hold conversation well.

Her clothing is dissected, the labels removed. Everything was purchased at good *Bürger* shops, Farnhammer, Maison Spitzer, Ungar & Drecoll in the Kohlmarkt.

The unidentified girl is now naked, her head propped up on a wooden block. Her eyes are flat and bloodshot, and her tongue partially protrudes between her lips. The upper part of her chest is the same livid color as her face, and darker blotches stripe the sides of her red neck. The underside of her body is a blurry-edged patchwork of stains. Uncirculated blood has seeped from the veins and settled here, sagging under its own weight, ripening into the deep violet and green of decaying flesh. Over her body, a mirror-lined lamp shade reflects these colors in its distorted curve, an obscene chandelier.

"She's been strangled?" Franz asks.

The doctor nods.

The Inspector walks in and stands at the opposite end of the table. He imagines the girl's body is carved from stone and he looks down on it from a great height. This exercise helps him think about her without emotion.

He watches the doctor wrap a cloth around her head and under her jaw to contain her tongue, close her mouth.

"How will you fix her skin?" he asks.

"I can bleach it. Remove her hair, make cuts on the back and sides of the skull and leave it in running water for twelve hours. That will lighten the greenish color."

The Inspector tells him to wait. There must be a less drastic way to make the body presentable. He anticipates a mother or father — or perhaps a close relative, since the dead girl wears no wedding ring — will come to identify her.

Later, the Inspector and Franz smoke cigarettes in the hallway.

"Thirty years ago, when I was an assistant policeman, I had to take care of the head of a corpse on my own," the Inspector says. "There was a murder in a remote village, and no refrigeration or ice was available. I put the head in a perforated box and set it in a stream. But first I covered the head with a net to protect it from fish."

Alone in the morgue, the doctor removes gray sludge and pieces of more solid matter from the dead girl's stomach, fiercely slopping the liquid into a metal basin.

A few rooms away, Egon dips his sketches of the Volksgarten and the girl's body into a pan filled with a solution of stearine and collodion. The paper will dry in fifteen minutes without changing color. The solution protects it from moisture and the dirty hands of the witnesses and jurymen who will handle the papers in court.

Later that day, Egon returns to the Volksgarten. The area he paced off is surrounded by stakes linked with string. The excrement next to the body has been scraped up and replaced by a rock with a number painted on it.

The policeman on duty nods at Egon and idly watches him unpack his equipment. The young man works quickly, with the skilled sleight of hand that comes with long practice. He takes out a small wooden box, a device called a Dikatopter. He doesn't trust technical devices, although he sometimes straps a pedometer on his boot to measure the distances he paces out, especially on hilly ground.

He stands with his back to the stakes, looking into a black mirror inside the open lid of the Dikatopter. Fine threads are pulled through holes in the mirror, dividing it into fifteen squares. Holding the box in front of him, he moves forward a half step at a time, watching until the path and the kaiserin's monument are visible in the web of threads, so he can calculate the position of the girl's body against these landmarks. He's pleased with his work, the fugitive images captured in the box like butterflies.

In the bottom of the box, there is a paper divided into a graph identical to the one on the mirror. He draws an outline of the girl's body on the paper from memory, and the monument and the path exactly as they are reflected in the mirror above his hand in the lid.

Light shines through the holes in the dark mirror, and the penciled outline of the body is suspended below these bright dots, as if it had been connected from a constellation of stars.

The Inspector didn't sleep the night the girl's body was discovered. He stayed at the police station, and went home the following evening.

The first time he describes the girl's body, his wife, Erszébet, creates her own image of it. She imagines the men standing around the body as if it were a bonfire, a radiant white pyre, its light shining through their legs as if they were alabaster columns in a temple. The dead girl fallen inside their circle.

Erszébet asks the girl's name and age.

"She's unidentified. The doctor guesses she's about eighteen."

"Why was she in the Volksgarten?"

"That is the mystery."

"She must have been from Spittelberg. Why else would a girl be in the park at night?"

"She may have been killed earlier in the evening. Judging by her clothing, I believe she's from a good family. Her murder would seem to be a misadventure or a *crime passionnel.*"

"Have you discovered any suspects?"

"None yet."

She nods and doesn't question him further. She's satisfied with his limited information since it allows her to produce her own theories. The girl's body has punched a hole in the safe space that was the park.

Two days after the body was discovered, the Inspector talks about the girl during dinner, although it isn't his custom to mention the dead at the table. He asks Erszébet to come to his office tomorrow and bring her paints. This is the first time he's asked her to help him in this way.

That night, when Erszébet can't sleep, she thinks of the nameless girl who has died, whose face she will paint tomorrow. In Hungary, there's a custom of dressing unmarried young women and girls in white for their funerals, as death transforms them into brides of heaven. The deceased girl is given away by her parents with the same words as a wedding ceremony. Tomorrow, she'll silently recite an old verse over the girl's unclaimed body. *While I live, I'll dress in black. When I'm dead, I'll walk in white.*

Franz walks in front of Erszébet down the hallway in the police station. He lets her enter the morgue ahead of him. The girl's body is on a table, a cloth covering everything except her head. Her face is still blotchy, the skin as dull and opaque as beeswax, and her eyes have sunk into their sockets. The cloth around her chin has been removed, and her mouth is slightly open. Her long pale hair is tied back with a piece of string.

It seems that all the cold in the room presses down against the still face, bitterly sculpting her profile, making it sharper than it had been in life. For a moment the total passivity of the body seems peculiar to Erszébet, until she remembers the girl is dead.

That's all Erszébet notices before she turns and presses a handkerchief to her nose. Later, the odor in the room will sometimes return to her, an unbidden ghost, the smell of decay. This morning, she prepared for painting by heavily dousing herself with perfume, touching the bottle's glass stopper to her wrists and the fleshy nape of her neck. Her hair was secured in its upswept coil with extra pins.

Now she strokes red, yellow, and brown pigments into a thick smear of white lead paint on her palette until it turns a pale flesh color. Venetian pink. She adds linseed oil and soap so it will adhere better to the cold surface of the girl's skin.

She asks Franz to loosen the cloth from around the girl's neck. First she paints the darkest parts of her face, around the mouth and nostrils, stopping her hand just before she blends the paint into the dead face with her finger.

She's been working on the body for nearly an hour when a man walks in carrying a bowl filled with a white paste. He casually sets the bowl down on the girl's stomach. Remembering Erszébet is in the room, he courteously moves it to the table.

"I'm Doctor Pollen. Have you finished?"

She nods and steps aside. He begins to vigorously knead the thick mixture in the bowl.

"This is my own modeling formula. Ten parts white wax and two parts Venetian turpentine melted together. I add potato starch to make it sticky."

"What are you going to do with it?"

"You could say I re-create the crime in a positive fashion. I can make what's absent. Someone shoots a gun into a wall, my modeling wax goes in the hole. Then I pull out an impression of the bullet's passage."

She asks if the same technique works for bodies.

"Yes, but I use cigarette papers. When they're wet, they're so fine they pick up the smallest impression, even a knife scratch on skin. To fill deeper holes, like stab wounds, I glue something slightly heavier on top of the cigarette papers. Toilet paper works best."

He digs around under the cloth and pulls out the girl's hand. Because her hands had been so tightly clenched, a small incision had been made at the base of each finger to loosen it for fingerprinting. Now he easily bends back a damaged finger, sticks a little ball of wax over the cold fingertip, and begins to work it down.

"I've made waxes of ear wounds, missing teeth. Even the stump of a tongue that had been bitten off. Mice love this mixture. I keep all my wax models inside a glass cabinet to keep them from being eaten."

He curls his hand around the girl's finger to warm it, then continues to pinch the soft wax up to her second joint.

Erszébet is unable to move away or even avert her eyes. She stares at his hands, engaged in their task as routinely as if he were writing a letter.

"Why are you copying her fingers?"

"I'm not making a copy. First I cleaned under her nails with a bit of paper. The wax just picks up anything left under there. Hair, dust, a thread. Sometimes there's nothing but their own skin. Or dried blood, if the victim fought their attacker. I suspect that's what I'll find here, since she probably struggled to pry the murderer's hands off. See, she has scratches down both sides of her neck."

His fingers press the wax too firmly and it bulges over the girl's knuckle. Finished with her hands, he sticks a finger into her mouth, careful not to disturb the paint on her lips. With his other hand, he delicately presses a wad of wax over her teeth.

Erszébet didn't realize she'd made any gesture, but suddenly Franz is next to her, guiding her into the next room. The light wavers, and there's a round buzzing pressure in her head just before she abruptly sits down.

Egon quickly moves his equipment into the morgue to photograph the girl. Someone draped fabric over the block under her head and the metal table to disguise it, and he calculates how his camera can disguise her immobility.

Later, Erszébet visualizes the strange fragments in the doctor's cabinet, objects as mysterious and dumb as fossils, reverse images of damage done to a body. There's a delicate X shape, molded from a double knife wound in a man's chest. A whitish tube, thick as a finger, cast from the passage made by a bullet into someone's back. A rough, V-shaped wedge documents a stick's impact in the muscles of an arm. These are the soft interiors of bodies turned inside out, turned solid.

She's familiar with the wax charms and effigies that work magic at a distance. Gypsies twist wax or unfermented, uncooked dough into tiny figures and stamp them with incomprehensible markings, aids made to win love or wreak revenge, for good or ill. To make the spell more powerful, nail parings, pubic hair, menstrual blood, urine, and perspiration are kneaded into the soft mixture. At one time, the lives of the French kings had been endangered by these *vols* models. In Germany, *Atzmann* figures were used as evidence in witchcraft trials.

When she was a child, she remembers a girl burned a

scrap of her own dress, which was saturated with her sweat. The ashes were secretly fed to a boy whose love she hoped to win.

Erszébet knew the boy. When he unknowingly ate the ashes, she watched his face convulse with astonishment and disgust as he realized what had been done to him, what was the bitter taste in his mouth.

CHAPTER 2

HREE NIGHTS HAVE PASSED since the girl was discovered in the Volksgarten. The Inspector and Franz prepare to take her photograph to the park to see if anyone recognizes her, can give them a name.

Then a well-dressed man comes to the police station to report his daughter is missing. Without questioning him, the Inspector leads him into the morgue.

The body lies on a table in front of them, covered with a cloth. The Inspector gently unveils the girl, nesting the cloth around her head, exposing her painted face. The man stares at the floor. His body doesn't immediately betray him with any gesture, neither fear nor anger. Only when he steps away from the body does the man look up. The Inspector can tell he's studying the cloth around the girl's neck, obviously confused about where to rest his eyes. Since hers won't look back.

"Do you recognize her, sir?"

"Yes. Her name is Dora." He could hardly answer. He closes his eyes.

"Is she your daughter?"

The man nods and blinks. He has full whiskers on the sides of his face, muttonchops in the style of the elderly Emperor Franz Josef, although he is probably forty years younger. His fingers nervously touch his nose and stroke his whiskers. The Inspector doesn't take his eyes off him, even when he turns his face away. It is necessary that he observe the motions of the man's grief. He never anticipates that a stranger's expression of sorrow will surprise him. He is surprised that he continues to find these intimate encounters so unsettling. Pliny the Younger is a comfort during these encounters, and he recites his words like a prayer. *Est dolendi modus, non est timendi.* Grief has limits, whereas apprehension has none.

Erszébet had recently returned to Vienna after spending the hottest weeks of the summer in Hungary, on her family's estate. During her visit, two of the servants had been stricken with cholera and died in a few hours. A laundress, a young unmarried woman, was also infected, and Erszébet insisted she would nurse her back to health.

The girl was quarantined in a wing of the house in a bedroom stripped of most of its furniture and carpeting. A dozen sheets soaked in a solution of carbolic were hung in the room. The odor of the disinfectant was strongest just after midday, when the bedroom was stifling. Because of the heat, Erszébet stripped off all her clothes except for her chemise and petticoat. In this intimate undress, she felt light, free, on equal terms with the sick girl.

Erszébet watched her patient night and day, only occasionally relieved by two nuns. The girl was delirious, heavily dosed with opium. When it appeared she was recovering, Erszébet fed her a spoonful of sour milk every quarter of an hour. She watched the clock, holding a glass of milk in her hand. Even when the hungry girl moaned in protest, the dosage couldn't be exceeded or she would die.

Erszébet had no contact with the outside world except for the nuns. They gently reminded her to eat. Although she was never afraid she would become sick, after three weeks Erszébet's eyes began to play tricks on her. The numbers on the face of the clock became meaningless. The hours of the day were distinguished only by the intensity of the sun on the layers of fabric hanging up in the room. Once, the nuns opened the windows, and a breeze swept the sheets so that when

Erszébet entered, it seemed the entire room was in motion. She imagined she was on a ship with her mute companion and the sheets that surrounded them were ghostly sails. She was cradled in this white space, wordless silence, and the smell of the girl's sick body.

One night, she soothed the girl with a familiar healing incantation, reciting it over and over. *Let bone go to bone, marrow to marrow, vein to vein, tendon to tendon, blood to blood.*

When the laundress died suddenly, Erszébet walked out of the room. The hallway, the stairs, the rest of the house shocked her, its profusion of color and furniture, and she stumbled outdoors into a field. She remembered sitting down in grass. She must have fallen asleep, for when she opened her eyes, she was enveloped by a blackness as total as the whiteness of the sickroom.

When Erszébet saw the dead girl wrapped in sheets in the morgue, she felt as if time had slipped and this was her patient, returned to her. She was cold Lazarus.

It is still light outside when the Inspector comes home to find Erszébet in the kitchen, dropping *csipetke* into a pan of boiling water to cook. He sets his hands on her shoulders, and she shakes her head and moves away, smelling the disinfectant on him. Without a word, he goes to wash his hands, having carried the odor of the dead girl's body across the city to her.

When Erszébet smelled the disinfectant, the scent of the girl on his hands, she suddenly wished to possess her. To understand the puzzle of how her life led to her death. To know her. When she first heard the girl had died in the park, there was something — a needle prick of menace, a cruel loneliness — that was familiar. It felt true as a memory. This recognition startled her.

At that moment, Erszébet began her study of the murder. She assumed ownership of this second young woman whom fate had delivered to her. It was a private act, a secret pursuit that excluded her husband.

Months later, she will think of her actions as a dream that she witnessed but couldn't interpret or claim.

Tonight her husband has news about the investigation.

"We've found the girl's family," he says. "Her father, Philipp, came to the morgue and identified her. I told him she had been strangled as gently as I could."

"What is the girl's name?"

"Dora."

Without looking at him, she whispers the word. "Dora." She asks how he prepared the girl's body for viewing.

"I hid her bruised neck with a piece of fabric. I'm certain the paint you put on her face was a comfort to him, even if he didn't detect it."

He doesn't mention the unpleasant secrets he kept from her and Dora's father. The tiny spots that bled inside the girl's mouth. The fractured bone in her neck. An area of skin filled with red-brown-violet blood under her skirts. The material the wax pulled from under her fingernails, flakes of dried skin and dirt. Nothing he could identify.

When the Inspector examined the dead girl's watch, he found a minute dark smear on the crystal. To preserve the stain, he pressed a moist square of filter paper against it, waited a moment, then transferred the paper to a sheet of glass painted with gum arabic. When a sliver of the stain was immersed in a saucer of bezidene reagent, the opaque whitish liquid sluggishly turned blue, which indicated the presence of blood.

If he were lucky, further tests might identify the blood type. It had been only seven years since the professor at the Institute of Hygiene in Greifswald discovered that human blood could be distinguished from animal blood. However, not all magistrates would admit this as evidence in a murder trial.

After the clothing was stripped from Dora's body in the morgue, each garment was dropped into a separate paper bag. Franz glued them shut. Her clothing wasn't mentioned again until the Inspector handed Franz one of the thick paper bags in his office.

"Is this Dora's dress?"

The Inspector nods and walks across the room to get his walking stick. Puzzled, Franz watches as he comes back and stands in front of him, holding the stick like a club over his shoulder.

Now Franz, I want you to hold the bag steady in front of you, he says. Hold it away from your body. Hold it out a little farther. Don't move. He swings the walking stick and strikes the bag. He hits it again and again until the bag is creased and battered. Smiling, he thanks Franz and asks if he felt like William Tell's son. Franz's face fills with color; he has a blond's easy blush.

Mystified, he helps the Inspector spread huge sheets of white paper over the carpet. They cut the bag open and gently lift out Dora's dress, each of them holding a sleeve, as if they're dancing with a scarecrow.

"Shake the dress over the paper. Carefully."

Dust, threads, and tiny particles twirl and drift from the dress down onto the papers, a miniature windstorm. The Inspector kneels and gently folds up the papers, then slips them into a large envelope and seals it.

Franz raises his eyebrows. "Sir?"

"I'm collecting dust. It will reveal Dora's history while she wore the dress. Where she went, if she sat on a bench or the grass. If her skirt brushed against the roses in the Volksgarten. We'll scrape her boots later."

The Inspector used the same technique on a jacket found at another crime scene. A chemical examiner analyzed the dust harvested from the garment and identified it as finely pulverized wood, so it must have belonged to a carpenter or a sawmill worker. The Inspector requested a more detailed report. The second investigation showed gelatin and powdered glue mixed with the sawdust. The Inspector reasoned the jacket must have belonged to a joiner, and he was later proven right.

In 1898, the Inspector had traveled by train to Czernowitz, to attend the lectures of Professor Hans Gross, the author of a number of books, including *System der Kriminalistik,* the first psychological study of crime. Gross was also an associate of the renowned German psychiatrist Richard von Krafft-Ebing, director of the public insane asylum in Graz.

It was Gross's theory that a crime was a *scientific problem,* an *organization of facts* committed by criminals who were *morally shipwrecked.* Solving a crime required the Investigating Officer to determine *the error in the situation.* In his published works, Gross covered such topics as "The Self-Mutilation of Hysterical Criminals," "Arson and Homesickness," and "Experimental Contributions on the Fauna of Corpses."

At the Inspector's request, Franz continually memorizes paragraphs from *Kriminalistik.* The younger man recognizes this discipline as an important part of his training. Today the lesson from the book concerns the characteristics of an Investigating Officer.

> Tact — that faculty which nothing can replace — to light instinctively upon the best way to set to work, is a natural gift. Whosoever does not possess it will never make an Investigating Officer, though he be endowed a hundredfold with all the other necessary qualities; with the best intentions in the world, he will stumble against everything without discovering anything; he will intimidate the witness who wishes to give him important intelligence; he will excite the babbler to babble still more; he will encourage the impudent, confuse the timid, and let the right moment slip past.

Egon unpacks his camera in the Volksgarten, in the same place where Dora's body was found. He works quickly; it is almost dusk. At this hour, there are no sightseers or children in this secluded corner of the park.

Tonight he works without artificial light, since the image he wants to capture is too delicate.

He hopes the picture will reveal something magical, intangible, hidden from the eye. As an artist holds a mirror up to a portrait to find its unsuspected faults, which become obvious when the painted image is reversed. He hastily unscrews the camera tripod, tip-tilting the legs into the grass. Three short poles lengthened, made even. In secret, he'd marked the spot where Dora's body lay, hammering small sticks so deeply into the ground they're invisible. He presses his fingers into the grass, feeling for these guides, like broken teeth.

Now he aims the crossed lines of his lens between these sticks. Grass is the image on the glass plate, tight, tiny spears pinched into focus. He pulls the black cloth off his head and squats next to the camera, positioning himself so he can see what its glass eye sees, fixing his eyes on the ground. He waits, anticipating the dead girl will materialize. The grass will change color blade by blade, gradually transforming itself into her image, as a photograph develops in a tray. Or perhaps her last breath still hangs in the air, a ghostly vapor that can be captured in the same way a photograph freezes an invisible motion into a visible blur. A postmortem clue. Message in a bottle.

As he presses the shutter release in his hand, the lens opens and closes so slowly his heartbeat seems to expand, connected to the camera. An audible *click*.

There are spiritualist mediums in Paris and London who can call forth the dead during séances. He's seen harsh pictures of a female medium, her head thrown back in a trance, eyes vacant. The dead hovered behind her as a white light, a disembodied hand, and a sexless figure in translucent rags. In other photographs, invisible spirits that made their presence known as a cold breeze were documented as the blurred motion of a curtain, and the indistinct line of a woman's skirt. He sensed the photographer who took these pictures was uneasy, didn't know where to fix the camera, unable to anticipate which object might suddenly become possessed by a spirit.

From experience, Egon knows that rooms, houses, certain places in the landscape, retain an insidious presence if they have been the setting for a violent crime. Objects and clothing too. He's seen clothing taken from a murder victim shape itself into a mute gesture as surely as it stank with blood. The night he photographed Dora's body in the Volksgarten, the wind suddenly blew her thin skirt across her legs, even though he was certain he'd set a weight on the fabric to hold it down. Her clothing was blurred in several of his photographs. He was unnerved.

Once during a police search, a drowned body had risen from a lake exactly where he was looking. Believing he'd willed the corpse to surface before his eyes, he was so shaken he forgot to trip the camera shutter. Another time, he photographed a document — a suspected forgery — by gaslight. The finished picture showed two different values of ink, the original gray and the false black, which appeared similar to the naked eye. See, nothing can hide from the camera, he told the Inspector. This is just another type of ghost.

It is darker now. Twilight turns the trees and shrubbery around him hazy, and the same gray clouds his camera lens. He anxiously scans the ground, waiting, watching. Nothing. He swears the grass has a different quality where his lens is focused on it.

He puts the black cloth over his head and bends over behind the camera. The glass plate reflects a rectangle of grass, an upside-down image. A pair of white boots overhung with a skirt walk into the bottom of the picture frame.

"Get out of the picture." His shout is muffled by the cloth.

The skirt and feet float away. He cranks a knob on the side of the camera. In one motion, he plucks the cloth off his head, stands up, and squeezes the shutter release. There's a gratifying mechanical noise. *Click.*

A woman, a stout Viennese matron, watches him from a few feet away. She swings a closed parasol until the younger woman next to her gently stops its movement with her hand. She quietly says something to her; he can't understand her words. He nods at them, politely dismissive. He expects them to courteously vanish. They probably came to the Volksgarten to stare at the site where the girl's body was found. A homicide in Vienna is a rare and extraordinary event. When photographing other locations for the police, he has often worked in front of a whispering crowd, his presence sometimes the only perceptible proof of the crime.

The younger woman walks toward him. Her silhouette is ungainly; her clothing is oddly cut. Perhaps foreign. The veil of her straw hat is carelessly pulled back over the brim, exposing her face and her dark hair. She frowns at him.

"Why are you photographing the grass?"

"I'm documenting the site. Don't walk there, Fräulein. It's bad luck. Someone died on that spot."

"We know all about it."

Her accent is English. An Austrian girl wouldn't start a conversation with a stranger. She steps around the place where the girl's body had lain and stops next to his camera. He moves to guard it, the black cloth hanging off his shoulder.

"We wanted to see this place. What it was like. Erszébet can sense things," the girl says, gesturing at the older woman waiting impassively behind her. "Are you here on official business?"

"I work for myself."

He ducks back under the cloth to close the lens. It's no use working if women are around. He makes a strange figure, like a child hiding, his head and shoulders covered by the dark cloth, his two thick legs and the camera's three thin legs underneath. He asks if she was a friend of the dead girl who had been found there.

"Yes, I knew her. I'd rather come here than visit her in the cemetery. My name is Wally."

Wally lies. We could have been friends, she thinks. No, I consider myself her friend, since I'm trying to help her.

Irritated, Egon quickly unlocks the metal hinges of the tripod. The gleaming wooden legs snap together smoothly; it's an expensive instrument, French made. She senses his pride in the camera. It makes him seem older, even though his fair hair has been ridiculously mussed by his encounter with the camera cloth.

"You must be shocked about what happened to your friend. You aren't afraid to come here?" he asks.

She shrugs. "Afraid? Afraid of what? There's nothing

frightening here in the park. Nothing waits here. It isn't haunted."

The three of them walk through the Volksgarten, passing the Temple of Theseus and a pavilion where hundreds of couples waltz to a military band on some afternoons. Typically, the program includes *Schöne Edi* by Strauss.

They decide to have coffee in the pavilion. Egon moves awkwardly across the room, maneuvering his satchel and the tripod around the tables and chairs. He sits between Erszébet and Wally, his equipment occupying the empty chair at their table like a fourth guest. Both women smoke furiously, sharing Egyptian cigarettes, barely touching their *Indianerkrapfen* cake.

In this light, he's startled by the color of the older woman's eyes, a fierce and icy pale blue that gives her face a peculiar fragility, as if there is glass, not bone, beneath her skin. Erszébet makes him uncomfortable. She kindly asks what kinds of pictures he takes.

"I photograph landscapes, I take portraits. I do what pleases me. I have my own photography business in a studio near the Graben."

The women listen politely, but their eyes watch his hands grip the coffee cup. Half of the third and fourth fingers on his left hand are missing. The fifth finger on his right hand is also damaged. It has no fingernail, just a snug, dark welt, so the fingertip resembles a narrow flower bud.

He holds both hands out in front of them, very matter-of-fact.

"My lightning powder blew up when I was taking a photograph. I accidentally left a few grains of powder on the rim of the container. Sulphur and saltpeter, the same powders used for fireworks and bombs. When I screwed the lid on, the jar exploded. I'm lucky I didn't lose my entire hand."

He doesn't mind talking about it. He spreads his mutilated hands on the tabletop.

"I don't notice it much anymore. Although sometimes the missing parts of the fingers feel as if they're being pinched. It's strange, but in my dreams my hands are always whole."

Wally is fascinated by his damaged fingers. She doesn't look away, even when he addresses a question to her.

"Do you visit the park very often?"

"I'm a governess. The children I take care of come to the park with me nearly every day. They'd be here now, but they're in the country."

"Are you from London?"

"Yes."

Erszébet abruptly changes the subject. "Did you ever meet the girl who was murdered?"

He shakes his head, wanting to learn what she knows.

"Why were you photographing the place where they found her body?"

"Idle curiosity. What was the girl's name?"

"Dora. They said some strange animal may have attacked her." Erszébet watches him as she speaks, but the image she sees is Dora's face, colorless under the light in the morgue.

"She was attacked by animals? Surely this is impossible in Vienna."

His surprised reaction to her news is genuine. He imagines the girl's ravaged body, the marks left by animals in the soft skin underneath her skirts. He sees this picture in black-and-white. Sometimes he can visualize images without color, a strange talent his photography has encouraged. He knows there are people who have never seen a face without its color.

He smiles at Erszébet, catching her quick sideways glance at Wally before her eyes meet his. She reassures him that this information about Dora comes from a very good source. Her words don't dispel his misgivings. He senses something has been held back, as if he'd heard a door slam and then silence, no angry words or footsteps.

The next day he suddenly recognizes the older woman. He remembers her in a white room, wearing a white smock. Erszébet, the police inspector's wife. She was in the morgue painting Dora's face for his photograph. She didn't seem to recollect meeting him. He wonders about her relationship with her young friend, Wally.

After he left their table in the pavilion, Erszébet turned to Wally.

"You did well to lie to him about your friendship with

Dora. He'll be more useful to us if he believes that is our motive."

The girl is pleased by her praise. "I almost lost my nerve. He seems kind."

"Don't tell him too much. He thinks he's an artist."

The week after Dora's body was identified, the Inspector makes an unannounced visit to Dora's family. They live in Alsergrund, the Ninth District, a respectable section of Vienna.

He finds the house unlocked, although there is no concierge. He studies the stained-glass window set in the door before he cautiously opens it. Inside, his footsteps echo until he stops in front of an elaborate staircase that rises through the center of the house.

He senses something move. Two legs are visible on the third-floor landing. He cranes his neck and calls up to him.

"Good day. Is your mother at home?"

At the sound of his voice, the boy runs away. In a moment, he returns to the landing accompanied by a woman. All the Inspector can see are the flounces on the bottom of her long dark skirt next to the child's legs.

"I'm the Inspector from police headquarters. May I speak with you? If this is a convenient time?"

She doesn't answer but descends the stairs, the heavy trim on her dress trembling with each step.

When she sits across from him in the drawing room, he can see the shadows under her eyes and the curved lines beside her mouth, swags of grief. Although she possesses a grave self-sufficiency, her eyes are vague and unfocused. He believes it is terrible to study a stranger's mourning, but he must let this sentiment go in order to proceed. He looks her in the eye and puts pity out of his mind, everything except how she answers his questions. Sometimes as an exercise, he'll focus on the hidden patterns in a painting, squinting to cancel out the images so the hidden dark and light shapes will emerge.

He apologizes again for the necessity of his visit and begins the interview.

No, she says in answer to his first question, she didn't know Dora had left the house the last night of her life. Why would she have gone out? No, she didn't know whom she would meet at that hour. Dora had never done it before, yes, she is certain of it.

She is still angry at her daughter, as if she had run away. He knows her anger is a negotiation, a way of making their separation less bitter.

"But this is unbelievable. You're certain the body is . . . she is my daughter? There's no mistake?"

"Your husband positively identified her, yes."

"He told me it was Dora. He didn't explain to me how she died. She didn't suffer?" She clenches her handkerchief.

The Inspector speaks very slowly, giving her time. "He didn't tell you? Then I can reassure you, she died quickly. She looked peaceful when we found her." He hands her the isinglass envelope containing Dora's pearl earrings.

When the woman cries, her anger leaks out. Her shoulders sag, and her black necklace slips farther down on her bodice. She presses a handkerchief over her closed eyes and holds it there with her fingertips. The peaceful death is his customary falsehood, and he is never comfortable using this lie in front of Franz or another officer. But it relieves her enough to continue. He gently asks her who else lives in the house.

"My husband, Philipp. You met my boy, Otto. He's thirteen."

"I'd like to speak with him later."

She frowns. "There's nothing he can tell you. He's only a child."

"I'm sorry. It's police routine."

"You'll have to return another day. He's just gone to his tutor."

He strains at the impression her voice made on him, certain it had an edge of triumph. When he conducts an interview, he habitually strips down the person's answers, their accounts of events, to reveal a structure. This woman is somehow pleased her son has eluded him.

"I'll speak with Otto another time. Please tell me who works here in the house."

"We have a cook, Mizzi. She's been with us for years. She was visiting relatives in Bischofshofen that evening. We also have a maid, Nini Teleky, but she doesn't live in. She leaves in the afternoon. I don't understand why you would need to talk to them. They didn't know Dora. My daughter had no secrets from me."

The Inspector writes down their names in a small notebook. "It's not that Dora had secrets from you. They might have noticed something unusual. Or heard something."

"Dora was an obedient daughter. She did errands for me but she was always accompanied by her *promeneuse,* Rosza. She went out alone occasionally. She would attend lectures at the Akademische Gymnasium or the Museum of Art and Industry."

"Does the boy have a governess?"

She hesitates. "Fräulein Rosza also took care of Otto, since Dora was getting older. But she left us suddenly in March or February. It was not the best of circumstances."

He's careful not to show too much interest. He takes a slow breath, so his voice is easy when he asks about her disagreement with the governess.

"There was no disagreement. Fräulein Rosza was a meddler. She didn't know her place in this family."

"What did she do that made you so unhappy?"

"I'd had enough of her, that's all." Anger burns through her grief. The expression on her face doesn't change, but she gives herself away by picking at her handkerchief. "I'm not certain where you can find the woman."

He tries again, closing his book and leaning toward her. "Was Fräulein Rosza friendly with other governesses?"

"I wouldn't know about her friends."

"And do you know the names of Dora's friends?"

"Perhaps Dora had friends at the gymnasium, but I don't know their names. No one came to the house. Dora stopped going to school."

"Are there any relatives Dora spent time with? Perhaps a cousin?"

"Two cousins live in Merano, but we haven't seen them in years."

Although the woman responds to his questions, her resistance is strong. Her words are flat. Her recollections are weighed down by anger and grief, which prevents any true memory picture from emerging. Still, this can change over time.

"Any friends of the family?"

"Dora was close to Herr Zellenka and his wife. She took care of their children from time to time."

"You can put me in touch with them?"

She nods and looks down at her lap, reluctant to involve anyone outside of the family in the shame of her daughter's death.

"Dora had no admirers?"

"No. I certainly would have met any beaux. I was a good mother to her. I don't know anything else that could help you, Inspector." She quietly starts to cry.

This is the Inspector's situation, the recognition of a paradox. How can this woman give him information she cannot bear to know? It is a familiar stopping point in an interview. He gazes down at his notebook, giving her time to calm herself, use her handkerchief, pretend he's only a guest in her house.

Her voice shaking, she begins to talk quickly, as if to move ahead of her own thoughts.

"My husband was at home that night. I remember it very clearly. Dora did nothing unusual. She seemed happy. We had dinner together, as we always do."

"Did you notice if Dora ate her dinner that night?"

"She never had much of an appetite. She was very thin."

He has a sudden memory of the girl's naked body, her skin slack over the sharp bones of her shoulders as the muscles decomposed. He blinks the image away.

"What did you serve for dinner?"

"I don't know. What does it matter?" She pinches her lips

and frowns down at her handkerchief. "I believe we had *But-ternockerln* and boiled beef with chive sauce."

He makes a careful note of her answer.

"After dinner, did your husband or Otto notice Dora leave the house?"

"No. I told you, she never went out alone at night. But as you see, this is a big house. She could have walked through this room to the side or the back doors."

He imagines Dora passing them, ghostly, silent, intent on her unknown rendezvous in the Volksgarten. He remembers her white canvas boots, discolored with dirt and grass stains when he found her.

"Who wanted to harm your daughter?"

She's motionless for a moment, then her face twists when she understands his words. In a moment, her cheeks are polished with tears. She bends over her lap, hiding her eyes. Some stranger. A foreigner, she whispers. *No one we know would hurt Dora.* It isn't possible. Without sitting up, she blindly grabs his hand.

"Don't tell anyone what Dora looked like when you found her. Please."

Ashamed, he nods. She didn't believe his lie about her daughter's peaceful death. After she's composed herself, he asks if he may search Dora's room. He makes the request as gently as he can.

She stares at him, uncomprehending.

"There might be something she kept in her room that can help us. I must look for it, don't you see?"

"But her room is untidy. It hasn't been cleaned."

She's closed off her daughter's room, an intact but now unimaginable space.

Reluctantly, she takes him upstairs. He enters the girl's bedroom and firmly shuts the door behind him. He can hear her pacing in the hallway outside.

He'll return later with his assistant and his equipment; for now, he'll just look around. Following his ritual method, he begins his search at the left side of the door and moves clockwise around the room. It's a chaste bedroom, almost masculine in its simplicity, with none of the frills or colors he'd expected in a girl's room. The bed is neat, the curtains closed. Nothing seems to have been touched. He wonders why she said it was untidy.

One of the men he trained with, a Slav, confessed he often thought of another woman when he made love to his wife. With practice, the Inspector found he could use the same transposition in his work. He tries it now.

Conjuring up the image of the dead girl, animating her stiff limbs, is easy. He's memorized her body, even though he's never seen it in motion. His memory is as intent and focused as a lover's as he imagines Dora here, standing before him, walking to the vanity, to the window.

Most clearly, he sees her lying on the bed, in the same abandoned posture she had in the Volksgarten.

Two policemen bring two Gypsies into the station for questioning. The men aren't charged with any particular crime; they had simply been loitering on the Opernring near the Hofgarten at a late hour. Gypsies have been persecuted for lesser infractions.

First they search the men. It is well known that Gypsies habitually conceal slips of paper inscribed with coded spells in their clothing. The hem of a sleeve or the heel of a boot may also conceal a crumb of sacramental bread, which protects the bearer from the police. Franz and Móricz, the youngest assistant, use scissors and tweezers to take apart their trousers and jackets, snipping open the seams, collars, waistbands, and pockets. Even the bands and the linings are carefully cut from their felt hats. Franz uses his scissors reluctantly, afraid of the clothing and its secrets. Móricz bends over the table, examining the fabric with a magnifying glass, looking for suspicious threads or hairs. He reminds Franz that the Gypsies steal children, especially *Bolo hameshro,* those with flame-colored hair, which they believe brings good luck. Dora had light-colored hair, blond almost red.

Franz tosses the two men coarse new clothing, since their own garments were ruined when they were cut apart. The *dilko,* the small bright scarves the men customarily wear around their necks, aren't replaced.

The Inspector is secretly drawn to the Gypsies and he always watches for them on the street. They appear fantastical, mocking, improper. Once in broad daylight, he saw a Gypsy man wearing a ragged cloak over a jacket with silver buttons and a pair of scarlet embroidered breeches. His scarf was a scrap of lace. Even in Vienna, all the Gypsy children and some of the men are barefoot. They always walk together in a group, talking loudly, the color of their clothing and their dark skin intensified by the gray buildings. The proper *Bürger* nervously move out of their way, afraid of the evil eye.

An outsider has no chance of deciphering their beliefs or customs. Even their language, Romany, is a mystery. Erszébet is slightly familiar with the Gypsies and she helps her husband read through an old Romany grammar book that was written in Hungarian — her first language — by the Archduke Josef. The Gypsies have a long and conflicted history with the Magyars, who at one time sold them as slaves. There is a proverb, *Give a Magyar a glass of water and a Gypsy and you'll see him drunk.* Gypsies are called *Cigány* in Hungarian, or *Fáraó népek,* pharaoh's people, as it was believed the Gypsies originally came from Egypt.

The first time the Inspector interviewed Gypsies about some matter, he was astonished to discover that they were congenital liars. This confirmed tales he'd heard as a child. They lied constantly and flamboyantly. They lied even when it wasn't necessary. None of their answers were ever direct. This was their manner of treating *gaje,* everyone outside their circle. It was reported that Gypsies would claim to be converted Catholics to please a Catholic, and Protestant to please Protestants. He was familiar with the old saying, *The Gypsies' church was built of bacon, and the dogs ate it.*

The Inspector interrogates the two Gypsy men in a bare room down the hall from his office. He moves behind Franz and asks the men to stand; perhaps he means to tire them. They shift their feet in their poor boots.

He asks the older man for his name.

He shrugs, "My true name is unknown."

"Your age?"

"Only my mother knows the hour of my birth."

"Why were you in the Hofgarten?"

"I'm a poor Gypsy, passing the time."

When the Inspector takes a step near him, or even takes his hand from his pocket, the man blinks and cringes. At other times, he looks at him with an exaggerated, imploring expression, almost pantomiming. The younger man glares at him without speaking or moving, his mouth a grim line in his brown face.

The Inspector becomes hugely patient. Even his speech slows down.

"Can you recollect where you spent Wednesday evening one week ago?"

"How would a poor Gypsy know the day?"

The interrogation is so long and tedious that Franz stops writing notes and rests his hand on the table. His expression is impatient and superior, until the Inspector catches his eye.

After nearly two hours of questioning, neither of the men has told them anything of importance.

In the morning, after the men were locked up overnight, Franz hands each of them a shallow enamel pan. Embarrassed, his face turning red, he haltingly answers the men's bewildered looks, instructing them to defecate in the pans.

Later, Franz covers the pans with a cloth and wheels them on a cart down to the laboratory. Slowly, so the soft piles don't shift.

He waits as Dr. Pollen compares the contents of the pans to the photographs of the excrement found next to Dora's body. There is nothing similar about their color or shape. The pans are placed in the refrigerator cabinet so the evidence can be measured and photographed when it is frozen, stable and odorless.

Egon photographs the Gypsies' excrement in the morgue. He fits a narrow metric scale, Bertillon's measuring device, inside the back of the camera. He explains to the officer assisting him that when the picture is printed, the scale across the bottom will show the exact size of the object. Otherwise, you can't tell the dimensions. It would look as if I'd photographed a mountain without the land around it, he says. They both laugh, self-conscious about their peculiar task.

Afterward, the Gypsies are released without an apology or a handshake.

Foreigners entering Vienna are required to pay a fee of four kreuzers for the upkeep of the paving stones in the streets. It is a city of pedestrians. From ten o'clock in the morning until midday, and from six to eight in the evening, the Viennese promenade in front of the grand hotels by the Staatsoper, along the Ring, and under the double rows of horse chestnut trees in the Prater. The upper classes do not walk on Sunday, when the streets are filled with workers on their day off.

In the heart of the city, the streets echo with the rattle of carriages and the shouts of their drivers, who pride themselves on the speed of their vehicles. Hearing the driver's loud warning *ho ho,* pedestrians quickly move off the street to the narrow sidewalks. Thick stone posts capped with iron line the sidewalks on the busiest streets to protect the buildings from the wheels of the fiakers.

It is the Inspector's habit to dismiss his fiaker and then take a tortuous route home from different points in the city. Sometimes he ducks into a narrow *Durchhaus* beneath a building, as if he were being followed. His wife never knows at what hour to expect him. They're accustomed to this rhythm, the uncertainty about his arrival, and neither of them wishes to change it. Although they have one of the few telephones in Vienna, it is rarely used. When it does ring, the noise is startling, an intruder in their home.

One evening, Erszébet hears the front door close. Then there's silence, and she knows her husband is setting his bowler hat and walking stick on the stand in the hallway.

What he does is put down his hat and then swing a small vial up to the light on the wall, as if it were a conjuror's prop, a glass wand. He shakes it, and the opaque, gray-brown material inside whirlwinds in the liquid. The vial contains a piece of one of the figs found in Dora's stomach.

Because of the undigested condition of the evidence, he calculated she probably ate the figs immediately before she died. Ate them ravenously, for large pieces of the fruit were intact in her guts. The remainder of her last meal was sludge, squeezed out of the slippery tube of her intestines into a white basin.

He considers the fig an oddity. He keeps the vial on his desk and picks it up from time to time, as some men toy with a paperweight.

When he hears Erszébet enter the hallway, he quickly slips the vial into his pocket before handing her his folded gloves.

In the first few days the vial with the fig was in the house, Erszébet twice asked her husband if he was certain the fruit had been fresh when the girl ate it. Yes, he answered, that's what the doctor's report said, do you want to read it? It's not very pleasant.

"Was the fig the last thing she ate?"

"It isn't definite. But I don't think the fig is significant. The girl wasn't poisoned." He shrugs. "Besides, Dora clearly had dinner at home."

Erszébet doesn't pursue the subject with him. She faultlessly meets his eyes, already conscious she's hidden her decision from him. She knows she can divine something from this evidence, this fruit he's discarded. She believes that what was left in Dora's body is a powerful talisman. If the fruit had just been picked, the tree is growing somewhere in the city. Who gave her the figs?

Later, she learns that some scholars believe the fig — not the apple — was the original fruit of knowledge. Another gift.

She doesn't tell her husband how greedy she is. Erszébet follows him into his investigation of Dora's murder as if it were a labyrinth. Her pursuit is shared only with Wally.

Erszébet believes painting is similar to divination by cards. When the tarot is read, each newly drawn card alters the interpretation of the one before it. Just as her hand will choose a color guided by some mysterious precedent.

Two days later, she unpacks her little enamel pans of paint, fills a jar with water, sets the vial with the fig inside on the kitchen table.

With the end of her paintbrush, she nudges the vial forward, moving it into a stripe of sunlight from the window. The clumsy brown fruit bobs in the liquid. It has a narrow, arched neck, swollen at the stalk end, and a bulbous, rounded body. The loose seeds spill like snow, as if the inside of the jar were free of gravity.

Her brush strokes brown paint inside the outline of the fig on the paper, as if her finger touched it through the glass. She transforms the fig's skin into velvet with a violet paint made from phosphates of cobalt. The dark place under the crook of the stalk is a richer shade, purple of Cassius, compounded from oxides of tin and gold.

Some watercolors have a fugitive character and fade or change when exposed to natural or artificial light, or even another color. Tools can also strangely alter colors. If cobalt violet is touched with a steel palette knife, it will be discolored. Even dark colors can be unreliable. Vandyke brown is made from earth, rotted organic and bituminous materials. If this paint doesn't dry quickly on the paper, it's an indication that it will lighten later.

Her painting instructor told her about a French artist, M. Drolling, who stole a number of royal funeral urns from the Abbey St. Denis in Paris in 1793. He softened the embalmed hearts of Marie Thérèse, the duchess of Burgundy, and Henriette d'Angleterre in oil and then mashed them into paint. Curiously, all of the women's hearts produced the same shade, a dark reddish brown.

She waits impatiently for her watercolor to dry, listening for her husband's returning footsteps. Her painting is a small white rectangle of paper stretched and glued to a board. It gleams with water, like saliva on skin, turned luminous by the reflected light.

In secret, Erszébet makes the fig her object of study. She discovers that the edible fig, *Ficus carica,* is deciduous, growing fifteen to thirty feet high. Its rough, heart-shaped leaves are easily recognizable, deeply curved into three to five lobes. Locksmiths and armorers soak small pieces of the fig tree's spongy wood in oil and use it to polish metal.

The skin of the fruit itself ripens into a spectrum of colors, yellow white, dark yellow, green, green brown, purple brown, violet, and a dark purple that is indistinguishable from black. Off colors.

The tree bears three distinct crops of fruit. First, *figues fleurs,* or *florones,* which mature in May in warmer countries and in June in colder climates. *Figues ordinaires* are the second and largest crop, harvested in late August. *Figues automnales* remain on the tree over winter and are picked in spring. Dora had eaten *figues ordinaires,* a souvenir of summer's end.

The fig tree grows its flowers strangely inside out, concealed within the soft interior of the fruit. Erszébet imagines the fig's hidden fairy weight of seeds, grown in a sweetness that is also a darkness. Like a treasure in a cave. A tumor.

A midwife once told Erszébet of the *üszögös gyermek,* the stunted child, a premature fetus born alive, a scurrying, spectral thing with a rat's feet and ears. Unless the stunted child is immediately destroyed, it will return to its mother's womb. It is something monstrous, grown in secret.

As Erszébet reads by candlelight in the library, it seems that every wavering shadow could curdle into a blot, shape itself into one of these monstrosities and seek its unimaginable shelter.

CHAPTER 3

ORA'S FATHER, PHILIPP, RE-
fused to meet with the Inspector at the po-
lice station. His letter explained he had a
business conflict. The Inspector immediately sent a messenger with a second curt
letter demanding an interview with Philipp
and his son.

The next day, Dora's father waits for the Inspector in the
vestibule of his house. They shake hands, two cold palms. He
invites the Inspector into the *Herrenzimmer,* the study, and offers him a chair in front of his desk.

When he interviews someone for the first time, the Inspector uses as few words as possible, making his questions
and observations brief. He'll deliberately let the conversation
lag and fall into silence. He's found this often forces the other
person into hasty speech, filling the quiet between them with
nervous, disjointed words, as if they were throwing rocks in a
pool. Toss, then wait.

Philipp doesn't disturb the Inspector's calculated silence.
He offers him a cigar, an expensive Regalitas. Then he silently
watches the Inspector, toying with his cigar. The light from the
tall windows strikes the smoke suspended over his desk, turning it into a lazy, opaque drift. It is late in the afternoon.

Perhaps conscious of his duties as the host, Philipp finally
speaks.

"My wife has discussed your questions with me, and I'm
afraid I can't answer them. I don't know who Dora would have
met in the park or why she would have been there. It's not a

place she'd go, not at night. It's a complete mystery to me and my family."

The Inspector makes him wait while he leisurely prepares his cigar. His voice is mild, his manner easy. "Thank you for taking the time to meet me. When I work on a case, it's my method to learn all I can about everyone involved. Especially the victim. Please describe your daughter, Dora."

He knows men have difficulty depicting someone in a personal way. He intentionally asks this question first to make him uneasy, hoping he'll answer quickly to relieve his discomfort. He watches for any signs of emotion. Philipp frowns, and the Inspector notices there is something wrong with one of his eyes; it's slightly slower.

"Describe my daughter?" A long pause. "She was quiet. She never enjoyed good health."

"What did she enjoy? Did she have any interests?"

"What should a girl of that age enjoy? It's her duty to help her mother." After a moment he speaks more softly. "Dora liked to read. She wanted to attend the *Mädchenlyzeum,* but I decided it was better she stayed at home."

Another stretch of silence.

The Inspector takes a small notebook from his pocket and holds a pencil upright over its pages, putting Philipp on notice that he's waiting for him to speak. He continues to wait.

"Dora wasn't able to do much because of her ill health. She suffered from a chronic cough and shortness of breath. I remember when we walked in the woods near the sanatorium in Merano, she had to stop and sit down on the path."

"With her poor health, I imagine it was difficult for Dora to leave the house unescorted?"

"No. She sometimes went out without Rosza, her *promeneuse,* to accompany her. She argued with her mother about it. She was headstrong."

"And did you also argue with your wife about Dora?"

"Her mother and I discussed her behavior, yes. Dora could take care of herself. Or so I thought."

He touches his nose, his gesture unconscious. He suddenly leans forward over the desk.

"How much responsibility does a parent have? Is this my answer, the terrible thing that happened to her? Is it my fault she died?" His voice is angry.

The Inspector knows better than to express sympathy. Social formalities always change the atmosphere. He notes that Philipp slips and becomes emotional only when he speaks about himself. He's certain this will be the most revealing exchange they'll have. The man is too self-conscious and controlled to show him such honesty a second time.

Philipp stares at a fountain pen in its stand.

"Where were you the evening of Dora's death?"

"At home. I had dinner with the family."

"What is your memory of the dinner? Did Dora seem distracted, uneasy in any way?"

Philipp rests his hand on a stack of papers, as if he were swearing on a Bible. "Dora wasn't feeling well that night, nothing unusual. She had a cough. She left the table early."

"Did you stay in the house after dinner that night?"

Dora's father carries his cigar across his desk and taps it in an ashtray. "That night? Yes. I was at home the entire evening."

The Inspector makes note of the timing of his gesture. "You're quite certain?"

Philipp nods and then looks out the windows into the garden. *Avoids my eyes,* the Inspector writes. The light has dimmed outside, and the window gives back a reflection of the room, the carpet a dull red square next to the bulky desk, the Inspector's face expressionless and slightly distorted behind Philipp's silhouette.

"I have the impression Dora's health kept her from any kind of pleasure. Even friendship, perhaps?"

"She wasn't without friends. She was close to Frau Zellenka and her husband. And she was fond of their children, almost like a mother to them. She spent time with her *promeneuse.*"

"I believe her name is Rosza?"

Philipp says yes, and obligingly spells out her last name. When the Inspector asks if he knows Fräulein Rosza's whereabouts, he hesitates before shaking his head. No, he has no idea where she is. None at all.

"Did Dora have a beau?"

"There was no one. I knew everything that concerned her."

When the Inspector asks if Dora was happy, the man appears perplexed.

"We took her to doctors constantly. Sometimes they found a reason for her illnesses, sometimes not. Now I feel as if I wasn't sympathetic enough." He laughs, but without amusement.

The Inspector can tell he's dismissed the reasons Dora might have had for being unhappy, although the girl obviously made a relentless show of her ailments. It's interesting that he emphasizes her frail health but has never asked for specific information about her death, if she suffered.

Philipp clasps his hands together and takes a deep breath. "Once Dora threatened to kill herself. But she left the suicide letter where I would find it, so you see she wasn't serious."

"Why did she want to kill herself?"

"I don't know. Her health problems weren't serious. Nothing pleased her. Her letter said she couldn't endure her life as it was. As if I didn't give her anything. Believe me, I make certain my children have a comfortable life. Better than I had."

He shrugs and straightens a stack of papers on his desk.

Although he can tell this is the signal he's been dismissed, the Inspector pursues his questioning.

"Do you still have her suicide letter?"

"Of course not. I threw it away."

"When?"

"When? As soon as I found it."

"How long ago did she threaten suicide?"

"I believe it was early last spring. I'll ask my wife."

Writing during an interview sharpens his perceptions. He uses the pages in his notebook to hear the voice without the face. Philipp's responses have become so curt he knows there's nothing more to gain from their conversation. The man is a formidable opponent.

"I'd like to interview Otto in another room now."

"I'm afraid that's impossible. Otto has tuberculosis. He's in a sanatorium for the time being."

The Inspector notes the sanatorium's name and address. Philipp isn't sure when his son was admitted. He rubs his nose. "You don't think I had anything to do with Dora's death, do you?"

"I couldn't answer your question at this point."

"A stranger killed her. It couldn't have been anyone else. I'm certain some Gypsy kidnapped her. Dora wouldn't have gone to the Volksgarten alone. She was taken there. You waste your time talking to me and my family."

"Everyone connected with this tragedy will be thoroughly investigated. It's police procedure." The Inspector slips the notebook into his pocket.

Dora's father abruptly stands up, crosses the room, and opens the door.

"If there's anything else I can do for you, please let me know." He doesn't hide the expression of relief that relaxes his mouth.

"Thank you. Good evening."

As he walks away, the Inspector identifies Philipp's nervous gesture. His nose is slightly indented in the middle, a sign of tertiary syphilis. Eventually the bridge of his nose will collapse, the cartilage gone, rotted in his face. He waves ash off the end of the cigar he's still smoking, the scent reminding him of Philipp's study.

At the beginning of his career, the Inspector searched for a framework for his cases. How an action provoked an untimely death. The pivotal moment. A man swindles another man, and his sin is repaid with violence. A woman betrays her husband, and he strikes her, sometimes kills her. Although he was confident this straightforward analysis would solve a crime, Professor Gross taught him that the deciphering of motivation was a more subtle art.

Now he regards the event of the murder, the manner of death, the victim's relationships, the situation of his or her life, as equally important.

When he starts a case, he imagines each fact as an identically bright point of light, stars against a night sky. He does this to see a new pattern, to create a sense of incomprehension for himself. This state of unknowingness is the way he avoids organizing his information prematurely, or giving any fact the wrong importance. It is the most difficult task — living with this disorder — that he imposes on himself.

Sometimes he fantasizes that this state must be what a poet endures.

He senses that Erszébet exists in a state much like this, although he could never discuss it with her. He fears and admires her.

For the briefest moment when he enters a room where there has been an act of violence, he is overwhelmed by the incoherence of the objects around him, their hidden significance. Everything waits. An ordinary drinking glass could be marked with fingerprints, a stool may have supported the suicide's feet, a hair might be tangled around the knitting wool in a basket. Mirrors frustrate him, since the image of the event they've witnessed leaves no trace.

His wife treats objects with the same reverence, but she is motivated by superstition. She has a profound respect for bad luck and its prevention. A charmed object or a correct action can waylay devils and malevolent spirits, or stop a malignant event from unfolding. Resting a broom beside the door can avert a spell. Willow twigs can ward off *szemmelverés,* the evil eye. When there's been a death in the family, lighting a fire in the house or leaving a mirror uncovered will bring misfortune. Erszébet refuses to look into a mirror in the evening, for she believes this will bring the devil to her dreams. She constantly refers to an Egyptian book of dream interpretation, *A legrégibb és legnagyobb Egyiptomi Álmoskonyv,* which is kept on the nightstand next to their bed.

If she dreams of someone close to her who has died, she prepares their favorite foods the next day. This offering of a meal appeases malefic spirits, eases the dead. Still, he is always surprised when she serves these unannounced dishes, as if there's an unseen guest at the table. Her late mother's favorite dishes, *Fischbeuschelsuppe* and *Gänseljunges,* made with the offal of geese, are set on their dinner table at least twenty times a year. Once during a crisis in their marriage, she served it every day for a week. He sensed she was reproaching him with her mother's presence, but he couldn't confront her.

She once told him about the mysterious trampled-down places found in fields, which the peasants superstitiously call werewolves' nests. Coming across one of these sites, she fell to her knees and buried her face in the flattened yellow grasses, hoping to inhale the odor of a werewolf, a *csordásfarkas.* As if his scent was a charm. She smelled nothing but hay burned by the afternoon sun.

He seeks her opinion and has never considered it a weakness to confide in her. She can calculate and make the assumptions that he forbids himself. She can say what he struggles not to think.

Occasionally when his sense of separateness from her is too strong, he secretly studies the objects connected with her. The shoes she's worn tell him which market she's visited, her choice of hat reveals the importance of an errand, the angle of her comb and brush and the thin frost of talcum powder on the bureau indicate whether she hurriedly left the house, or even left the house at all.

Vienna is paved with cubes of gray granite, twenty centimeters square. Between midnight and four A.M., the streets are washed by a procession of quiet men who unroll hoses from huge wheels connected to water tanks. The Inspector is one of the few residents to witness this ritual, since he is out during these irregular hours. Most public events, even the theater and concerts, are over by nine P.M., so everyone can be home an hour later, when the *Hausmeisters* lock the front doors. After ten o'clock the city is as still as water.

When there's a full moon, its light pales the cobblestones and inserts dark cracks between them, so they appear to float in bottomless blackness. On nights when he comes in very late, the Inspector sleeps in a separate room. Silently passing his wife's bedroom, it seems the black shadow under her door is as deep and unfathomable as the space around the cobblestones outside, square lines infinitely repeated across the city.

In Hungarian, the word *wife* is a proper noun, which means *"my halfness,"* Erszébet has explained to him. She rarely says the word, and allows him to use it only during the moments of their deepest intimacy.

Once she whispered the three loveliest words in her language to him: *csillag, szüz, vér.* Star, virgin, blood.

Walking to work, he suddenly thought of the mirage they'd seen together on their honeymoon. The experience was one of the touchstones of their relationship. An illusory event.

A week after they were married, the Inspector hired a motor cab and a driver, and they traveled east from Buda Pest. In the Alföld, the region of the Great Plains, he witnessed his first mirage, the *délibáb.* Erszébet was aware of it before he was.

She suddenly told the astonished driver to stop, then pulled her husband out of the vehicle. Look over there, she said, and pointed in front of them. He saw nothing but grass, as flat and silvery as the horizon of a great sea. Erszébet took his face between her hands and gently directed it. There now, do you see it? she whispered. He did.

First a small blue lake appeared in the distance, just above the horizon. As he watched in disbelief, it spread rapidly, faster and more fluid than any earthly river. Then the pointed roof of a house floated upside down in the air above it, and cattle slowly made their way to the lake. A rounded shape was a well, which seemed nonsensical, as if it should absurdly spill its contents onto the ground below it. Suddenly, all of these liquid figures were broken by a shimmer of heat, as the shapes of their colors tilted and bled into each other, then vanished.

&

After his search through the city's servant registry failed to produce Rosza's name, Franz began to look for a contact to lead him to the missing *promeneuse*. He waited until a sunny day during the week to venture into the Volksgarten, when the park is an island of women and children. He walks self-consciously among them, a young man with police papers concealed in his pocket. It's after mid-September, and the weather is still so warm that jacketless boys in short pants and shirts chase hoops and balls. Girls in pinafores and hats take turns skipping rope or wander arm in arm down the paths. Their governesses sit complacently on benches and wire chairs, immobile as a choir, raising their voices only when their charges leave the paths for the grass or climb the ornamental marble balustrades.

Near the Temple of Theseus, he sees a girl he guesses is about the age of Dora's brother. No sooner has he asked her a question — did she know Otto and Rosza? — than a woman stalks over and indignantly yanks her away, without even giving him a chance to explain or produce his documents. Another girl rolls her hoop straight at him, and it bounces off the back of his legs. Now he's the object of everyone's attention, and his face heats until he believes it is a red balloon balanced on his neck. He senses the line of their eyes following him as he steps over the circle of metal fallen at his feet and walks to the temple, fumbling with a cigarette.

Later, he goes by the line of governesses twice before getting up the courage to approach them. A young woman at the end of the bench has a kind face, so he speaks to her first, introducing himself, pulling his official papers from a pocket. Her name is Eva. She squints at the documents, she probably can't read, won't admit it to a policeman. Flustered, she gives the papers to the woman sitting next to her. The papers are silently passed from hand to hand before they are gently returned to him.

As he explains his mission to Eva, he also addresses an audience, as all the women on the bench turn their heads to examine him, a row of skeptical faces below the larger ovals of their hats. Under their intense scrutiny, his face is rinsed with red into the pale roots of his hair.

Several of the women cross themselves when he mentions Dora, and yes, they had seen her in the Volksgarten, sometimes with her brother and Rosza.

Do you know where I can find Fräulein Rosza? he asks.

They shake their heads and excitedly debate his question. *Where is Rosza?* One elderly woman remembers her in the Hofgarten with two boys. Not today, not recently. They suggest Rosza may live with a family in the neighborhood. A governess usually has a small room at the top of the house. In less well-to-do homes, she might cook and clean the house, take care of the children, and sleep in the kitchen.

Does anyone know Rosza's address?

The interview isn't going the way it should; he can feel it slipping away from him, reshaped by their excited chatter. He's made a mistake. In a group, a single person will rarely volunteer information. To compose himself, he remembers a sentence from *Kriminalistik. "Tact. . . . Whosoever does not possess it will never make an Investigating Officer, though he be endowed a hundredfold with all the other necessary qualities."*

He offers his arm to Eva so she's compelled — giggling and blushing — to walk with him toward the temple. He then separately promenades and questions each woman in turn: Fräulein, do you know Rosza? What time of day would I find her here? Where does she live? Do you know anyone who was a close friend of Rosza's, of Dora's? Did you see Dora with anyone, a stranger, in the park? Have there been Gypsies around? May I speak with your children?

No one has a photograph of Rosza, and although she is described as pretty, their hesitant descriptions cannot print a picture of the woman in his mind.

With an exhausted little bow, he hands each of them an engraved business card and wishes them good day. Now he has enough information to realize Rosza will be located only by luck.

Franz makes similar excursions to the Augarten, Hofgarten, Stadtpark, the Belvedere, the Prater, and the inexpensive tea-and-milk rooms frequented by governesses, nurses, the caretakers of children and the elderly. Over the next few months, various women will approach him on the street in a familiar way, and he will stammer for a moment before remembering their encounter in one of the parks.

Franz walks all along the Franzenring, the street that borders the Volksgarten, before he turns on Volksgartenstrasse. He's spent the day interviewing the *Herrschaftsportiers,* the stout men in ornately decorated coats who guard the doors of the government buildings, hoping one of them might have seen Dora or observed something suspicious. The arrogant *Herrschaftsportier* on the steps of the Justiz Palast demands to see his identity papers and a police letter. After these formalities, he shows the man Egon's photograph of Dora. Her eyes are closed, and she appears to be sleeping. The paint and the cloth around her neck cover the bruises, the souvenirs of violence.

In spite of his official documents, the *Herrschaftsportier* looks at Franz suspiciously and turns aside his questions with curt words. No, he doesn't remember the girl in the photograph. Why should he? What he doesn't say, but Franz begins to understand, is that a girl is beneath notice for someone in his position. He guards the doors for men.

Franz receives the same response from the other *Herrschaftsportiers.* Discouraged but polite, he always thanks them.

His official papers are of no use at the Kinderklinik, where his request to meet with one of the patients — Otto, Dora's brother — is flatly rejected.

This is a tuberculosis clinic, the disdainful head nurse tells him. An interview with the boy is out of the question. And I wouldn't linger here if I were you, young man. Everyone here is contagious.

Franz thanks her even more briefly than the *Herrschaftsportiers* and makes his way to the door, his cheeks burning.

Fruit is stacked in great pyramids on rafts and floated down the Danube to Vienna, where it is delivered to the Hoher Markt. Peasants make half a day's journey to arrive at the Markt at two o'clock in the morning, their carts loaded with cheeses, mushrooms, truffles, all kind of meats and vegetables. Like an occupying army, they quickly fill the square, erecting canvas awnings to shelter their booths and tables. By sunrise the square is thronged with shoppers, mostly women, who maneuver their baskets around the tables, the great stacks of potatoes, beets, cabbages, and horseradishes, the rough heaps of firewood.

Erszébet buys melons and fresh duck from Hungary. Today there's also pheasant from Bohemia, and she selects two fine birds. Another stall sells nuts, dried figs, Turkish apricots, dates from Egypt. Are fresh figs grown here? she asks the owner. None that he knows of. It's too cold for the trees in Vienna. They won't survive the winter freeze unless they grow in a greenhouse. He waves his thick hands over his boxes, waiting for her to select something. There's plenty of other fruit, he says, try these sugared peaches. She buys a bulky wreath of dried figs, one hundred of them flattened, strung on reeds, and tied in a circle. They're shipped from Greece, the islands of Andros and Syros, he tells her as he wraps them in rough paper.

She edges through the Markt, closely followed by a uniformed *Dienstmann* who reverently installs her purchases in a little wooden cart pulled by a large dog. At other times, she has hired a *Dienstmann* to buy her theater tickets, deliver letters and packages, pack trunks, and even prepare fruit for canning.

In the kitchen, Erszébet snips the thread of reeds holding the figs, and they tumble loose on the table. They're heavy and dry, their wrinkled skins amber brown or gray violet, with the dull sheen of honey. Hidden inside is rose brown pulp and seeds small as grit. She arranges the figs in a silver bowl on the dining-room table.

Her husband says nothing about the figs but doesn't eat them. He watches her eating one fig, then two more, grinding the seeds between her teeth, the sound echoing in her head, perhaps the last sound Dora heard before there was the thunder of blood in her ears.

On another day, Erszébet talks to a genial woman with a fruit stall in the Naschmarkt near the river Wien. *Locoum* figs are considered the finest, she tells Erszébet, wiping her red hands on her apron. Imperials, London, Choice, and Prime are the four different grades. See, these figs are packed in the English way? She tilts the box to show her. The fruits have been shaped into squares and wedged so tightly together they're as precisely flat as a checkerboard. The box has eleven rows of five figs and weighs three kilograms. A layer of laurel leaves or *Calaminta nepeta* protects the fruit against insects. Erszébet buys a dozen boxes.

She asks the cook to prepare the figs into a pudding. Dried figs, chopped very fine, 450 grams. Four tablespoons butter, four eggs, 170 grams powdered sugar, half a liter of milk, 100 grams cake crumbs. The ingredients are mixed together, put in a bain marie for three hours. She serves it with whipped cream, *Schlagobers*.

Her husband enjoys the dessert until his teeth crush the fine seeds and he recognizes the fruit. He gives Erszébet a curious look. She smiles back.

Erszébet has the habit of taking up one obsessive pursuit after another. For a time, she constantly visited the exhibitions at the Sezession pavilion across from the Naschmarkt. She admires the building's peculiar ornamentation, a sinuous bas-relief of trees. The masks of three snake-curled women guard the portal over the door, a Medusa in triplicate. The building is crowned with a huge dome, transparent as filigree, which appears to be stitched together from gold laurel leaves. Certain wags call it "the cabbage." When a young Sezessionist artist who exhibited there was arrested for making pornographic drawings of his schoolgirl models and his work was burned before a judge, Erszébet was distraught for days. Later, her husband discovered all her souvenirs of the artist ripped to shreds in the bottom of a drawer.

At one time, she collected Venetian glass, filling the credenza in the dining room with shapes in molten colors like precious edible things, brittle candies. But she grew bored with them. They're pretty enough to break your teeth on, she said dismissively. When her husband pointed out the pale dust cloaking their shine, she only shrugged. Yes, I know they need cleaning.

Cracks and chips mysteriously appeared on two of the vases that she'd formerly prized.

He was relieved when she began painting again, although her search for subjects — landscapes, plants — took her away from the house. She gave only vague answers when he asked *where exactly* had she spent the day?

Once, he stroked her paintbrushes with the tip of his finger to see if they really were damp when she returned from one of her artistic expeditions.

Erszébet's capriciousness led her to hire and swiftly dismiss a succession of maids, none of them alike in their character or appearance. The new maid, a dour woman from Hajdúság in eastern Hungary, seemed to please her, although it irritates him to be left out of their conversations in their own language. He's uneasy in the maid's company but would never say a word against her. He understands that his tolerance of these servants somehow secures his own place with his wife. There are decoys working in the household.

Erszébet discovers references to the fig in mythology as well as in accounts of trade and horticulture in the ancient world.

The Greeks believed the first fig tree grew in Phykalos by command of the goddess Ceres, her gift to the inhabitants. In the regions of the dead, Tantalus was condemned to stand in a pool, forever grasping at the "pomegranates, pears, apples, sweet figs, and dark olives" just beyond his reach. According to Roman legend, Romulus and Remus were nursed by a she-wolf under a sacred fig tree.

Cato knew six varieties of fig. Two centuries later, Pliny cataloged thirty kinds of figs, their names taken from the places they grew or the individuals who cultivated them: Rhodian, Hyrcanian, Lydian, Herculean, Pompeian, and Livian figs.

Herodotus noted that Kroisos was warned to avoid war with "barbarians who knew neither wine nor figs." In his time, the fig had not yet reached Persia or Babylon. Later, the Arabs came to revere the fruit. According to Zamakhschari, an Arab scholar who wrote on the Koran, the prophet Muhammad said, "If I should wish a fruit brought to Paradise, it would certainly be the fig."

In the sixteenth century, Cardinal Pole brought fig trees from Italy and planted them in the gardens of the Archepiscopal palace at Lambeth.

The botanical classification of the fig remained to be discovered by others.

That winter, Wally had arrived in Vienna to work as a governess with no introductions except to the family who employed her. She met other governesses in the parks with the children but refused to socialize with them, spending her time alone in various *kaffeehäuser* around the city. She took lessons at the Military Swimming School & Bath near the Kronprinz Rudolf Bridge and traveled by rail to Baden for elaborate mineral-water treatments at Sacher's Helenental Hydropathic.

Because of illness, the family she was staying with had temporarily left the city in June, so Wally had time to explore. She'd take the Humber bicycle from the stable and wheel it to the Prater, where the Vienna C.T.C. had laid a winding track along the banks of the Danube.

At the highest point of the track, Wally would unpin her braids and hook her hat over the bicycle's handlebars, so it bounced crazily as she sped downhill, scarcely able to breathe with fear and excitement, the Danube a streak of silver at her side, solid as the wind on her face.

Moving this fast, she could barely sense the bicycle beneath her.

Wally believed she had been embraced by a community

of women when she discovered this secluded area of the park, since the *Bicyclistinnen* rode on the track. When the women approached each other on their bicycles, they would slow down, lift their veils, and exchange a greeting, as if they were coconspirators.

One hot day in July, Wally had stopped her bicycle at the bottom of the hill after a wild ride. Exhilarated, breathless, she thought she was alone. Suddenly, a woman stepped from the shadows at the side of the track, startling her. It was Erszébet, and she congratulated Wally on her riding skills. They gradually became friends.

Wally never bicycles on the streets, although there is less wheeled traffic in Vienna than London. Automobiles are rare, and she's noticed small carts pulled by ragged boys or muzzled dogs even in the heart of the city. When she first arrived, she was surprised to see pedestrians wandering freely on the streets — rather than the sidewalks — barely breaking stride for a speeding wagon or fiaker. Without lowering their parasols, women stepped blindly off curbs onto the cobblestones. She regards this as primitive behavior.

Heads will always turn for a nobleman's carriage. The families of Prince Trauttmansdorff, Prince Esterházy, Prince Auersburg, Count Pálffy, Baron Rothschild, and Princess Pauline Metternich keep their equipages in town, and when they tour the Haupt Allee in the Prater, their carriages are preceded by uniformed runners with silver walking sticks.

On state occasions, Emperor Franz Josef rides in a coach accompanied by ten footmen in white periwigs, forty lackeys, and eight marching *heiduques*. A member of the Hungarian Honor Guard stands at each side of the coach, a panther skin over the shoulder of his scarlet and silver uniform.

Wally arrives early at Gerstner's on the Kärntner Strasse and takes a table in the back. Everyone sitting around her is idle with newspapers or card games. It's just four o'clock. After too many critical eyes are directed at her, a young woman sitting alone, she pulls cigarettes from her reticule. She orders a *Kaisermelange,* black coffee with an egg yolk and brandy, and a sweet, *gebackene Mäuse,* which curiously translates into English as "baked mice."

When Erszébet arrives, Wally greets her loudly — in English — so the other patrons will recognize her as a foreigner.

Erszébet sits down and strips off her gloves. "I asked my husband if they found anyone who saw Dora that night in the Volksgarten."

"Yes?"

"They haven't found any witnesses. They questioned the chestnut seller and the lamplighter. There is also a Slav shoeshine man who always stands near the park entrance. When the police found him, he claimed he hadn't seen anything, even after they took his polishes and locked him up for two nights. The man claimed he never looked at women's faces, only their feet."

"Did they show him Dora's boots?"

Erszébet laughs. "The police didn't think it would be useful information. I'm not so sure. When I was a child, I saw the shoes of a saint. Do you have a Saint Lucy in your church? She traditionally appears on her namesake day, December thirteenth, to check children's behavior. One of our servants disguised herself as Saint Lucy in a long sheet with a sieve over her face. I remember she held a rolling pin, like this. She was frightening. She questioned me, Did I do my household tasks? Was I a good girl? When my mother pushed me forward to recite my prayers, I burst into tears and fell at Saint Lucy's feet. I was so astonished to see muddy shoes under her disguise I stopped crying."

The *Speiseträger* brings more coffee and glasses of water. They're quiet until he leaves the table. Then Erszébet reads from the notebook she's started on Dora's case. "A fresh fig was the last thing Dora ate. The murderer gave it to her. The fruit sellers in the markets have no fresh figs. Only dried ones are available. So the fig was grown here in Vienna. I can identify the variety of fig since I saw it in the vial. We need to find the tree."

"Maybe her family has a greenhouse. A fig could grow there," Wally suggests. That would be easy.

"It would be a clue hidden in the most obvious place."

"Not obvious to everyone. The murderer is the only one who knows about the fig."

"Yes. Unless there was someone else with Dora and her murderer in the Volksgarten." Erszébet smiles. "There are at least four people who also know Dora ate a fig. The murderer. My husband. You. Me."

Wally returns her smile.

Erszébet has carried the painted replica of the fig across the city in her satchel. Now she hands the watercolor to Wally.

"This is the fig from Dora's stomach?" Wally is fascinated by the painting. "It's wonderful, so precise. Like a photograph. How did you learn to paint?"

"My father hired an instructor. He taught botany, drawing, and painting."

Erszébet also grew up surrounded by the words of the old women helping her mother. They told stories, floating the household on a wave of superstition and omens. Days of the week and even some hours had a special significance attached to them that determined the activities of the house. No needles or scissors could be used on Monday or Friday. Tuesday, *Kedd,* was unlucky, a dangerous day to wash hands or comb hair. Every day at sunset, evil spirits gathered, reaching the height of their powers at midnight.

Erszébet props the watercolor up against her coffee cup. Although pleased by Wally's compliments, she would never praise anything she accomplished or owned. The girl doesn't understand Erszébet's belief in the magical power of words. A Magyar mother will call her unchristened newborn *the little ugly one* or *the little pagan one* to protect it from sorcery. Words guard the baby, disguise its perfection.

Although Erszébet doesn't acknowledge this to Wally, she knows they have collaborated on an irresistible story about Dora's murder. She chooses to discuss it only with the girl. If she confessed her pursuit of Dora's murderer to her husband — even though he values her opinion — it would give authority to his greater experience and wisdom. She cannot disclose her role without renouncing it. What is unspoken remains most powerful.

However, this secret pursuit has altered her relationship with her husband. She wonders if her new concupiscence is the result of frustration, and if it is shared by the others who circle around Dora's corpse, desiring an answer, a conclusion, resurrection.

Later, when they walk toward the Hofburg, Erszébet tells Wally about a legend she found in an old book. It sounds like a dream, she says.

> *If you fall asleep under a fig tree, you will be awakened by a spectral nun. She will offer you a knife. If you take the knife by the blade, she will stab you through the heart. If you grasp the knife by the handle, she must grant you good fortune.*

Wally doesn't smile at the story. She adopts the image as her own, as if she'd fashioned it in her dreams.

The night following their conversation, Erszébet dreamed of figs but not of good fortune. She saw a girl's face, white and still. A fig was split open over her closed eyes and mouth, like swollen brown lips, bruised genitals. Green brown violet, the colors of decay.

CHAPTER 4

THE CITY OF VIENNA IS INTI-
mately positioned over crypts and burial
vaults hollowed out under its churches, the
Kapuzinerkirche, the Stephansdom, and
the Michaelerkirche. A subterranean passage connects the Burg and the Augustiner-
kirche. Thousands of plague victims are interred in a deep pit
near the church of Maria Treu.

Now pneumatic mail tubes snake underneath the city,
avoiding these enclaves of the consecrated dead. Above
ground, they are marked by red postboxes.

The Inspector received a letter from Dora's father, delivered by pneumatic post. He'd like to discuss a matter that
concerns them both. In his office. Very little surprises the Inspector at this point in his career. Frequently, people connected
with a crime contact him months or years later, their memories
embroidered by guilt and fear. Suddenly an incident, a word, or
even a stray glance they've recollected becomes enormously
significant.

The same thing happens with individuals who were close
to a suicide. They blame themselves, assign their own behavior,
some selfishness, as the cause of the tragedy. Nothing usually
comes of it. He's convinced this phenomenon works like a superstition, just as a bloodred moon is later remembered as an
indication of the next morning's windstorm, and a dog's howl

or a magpie perched on a roof foretold a death. He doesn't
trust a rethreaded memory. It isn't a reliable guide.

The Inspector finds Philipp's office is located at a good address, and furnished in an expensive modern style. He welcomes the Inspector, pulls out a chair for him, and even leans
toward him over his desk, flatteringly attentive. He offers a Regalitas and then lights one himself. The man seems more at
home here than in his own study.

Behind a ragged cloud of tobacco smoke, Philipp says
he's been thinking about his daughter's case. There is some information he'd like to share. The Inspector silently quiets his
skepticism and doesn't take his eyes off the man's face or hands
as they maneuver his cigar. He watches him as closely as a lover.

"I suggest you talk to a friend of the family, Herr Zellenka. He might be able to help with your investigation."

The Inspector carefully puts his cigar down. He takes out
his notebook and makes a note about Herr Zellenka, identifying him in code as *Herr K.* This is the man Philipp's wife had
also mentioned.

"You believe he knows something of interest?"

"It didn't occur to me at first. But now, yes, I think so. I
noticed he had a strange manner when Dora died, and even
long before that. Until recently, he took a genuine interest in
Dora, gave her books, escorted her to museums. But I believe
they quarreled. In fact, she was no longer speaking to him
when she died."

"Do you have any idea about the reason for their quarrel?"

"I'm afraid I don't. You'll have to ask him."

"Herr Zellenka is happily married?"

"Yes. Of course, you'll want to speak with his wife, too.
She was also close to Dora."

"What is your relationship with him?"

"A fair question. He was an intimate friend of mine, but
we had an argument. I haven't spoken to him since Dora's funeral. Over three weeks now."

During their conversation, the Inspector is highly conscious of the man across from him. How he nervously jerks his chair forward. At what point he picks up and puts down his cigar. When he touches his face or raises an eyebrow. The Inspector tallies these silent gestures as well as what he says. For members of the *Bürgertum,* any show of emotion or flamboyant gesture is unmanly, unrefined. Even young men walk and talk carefully, slowly, like grandfathers, following this male code of respectable behavior.

"May I ask what your quarrel was about?"

"I assume it is necessary for me to answer?"

The Inspector notes he takes offense at the question, stalls his response. He struggles to keep from anticipating the man's answers. Keeping his face expressionless, he stares straight across the desk at him. Philipp idly watches the frail burned end of his cigar crumble.

"Very well. Our quarrel had nothing to do with my daughter. Perhaps *quarrel* is too strong a word. We just drifted apart. He'll give you the same story regardless."

"You're quite certain of that?"

Philipp leans back in his chair, lazily playing with his cigar. This action betrays his agitated state of mind. The Inspector senses he's furiously deliberating with himself. He wonders what memory pictures the man is recalling, possibly struggling to disavow. He makes himself remote from Philipp's process.

"I may as well tell you. We had a disagreement over a woman. Not my wife."

"Is your wife aware you're seeing this woman?"

"My wife doesn't exactly know about her, but let's say she understands. At any rate, I'm no longer in touch with this woman, and I don't wish to say anything more about her. She has nothing to do with my daughter's death. I won't reveal her name."

"I will note your refusal to give me the woman's name. You won't reconsider?"

"Her identity is a point of honor, although I don't imagine that's something you encounter very often in your work. I'm certain you'll be able to discover who the woman is by questioning Herr Zellenka or one of the other gossips employed by my wife to manage the house."

The Inspector wonders about Philipp's code of honor. He makes a show of closing his notebook and rises slowly from his chair. He retrieves his cigar. He waits. He knows not to leave before the subject of an investigation indicates he has finished. It's a mysterious signal; sometimes it doesn't happen at all. But occasionally a man or woman will blurt out something of interest, reveal themselves with a remark or a joke made in sheer relief the interview is over. It's always significant. There's an expression, *Herrschaften haben Zeit,* "Ladies and gentlemen never hurry."

Philipp pushes back his chair and gets up, shifting his cigar so he can offer his hand to the Inspector.

"I imagine you're a perceptive judge of men, so I probably don't need to explain this to you, but Herr Zellenka is not to be trusted. That is just my very biased experience, of course."

The Inspector allows himself an almost imperceptible shrug. Though Philipp made his comment in an offhand way, he detects an eagerness, as if his words were underlined. He nods absently, as if he hadn't heard him.

He thoughtfully taps his bowler hat down on his head and picks up his walking stick. He is halfway down the polished hallway before he realizes Dora's father has forgotten his claim that a stranger, a Gypsy, is responsible for the death of his only daughter.

Not for the first time, he wishes it were possible to truly share the intimate process of an investigation. To ease his isolation. He cheats when he takes his wife and Franz through the course of his deductions. Unconsciously, he tailors his sentences and his questions to each of them, trying to shape their answers. He also holds back certain uncomfortable or speculative ideas.

He recognizes uncertainty as part of the process of solving a case. There is always a waiting period, an empty time when nothing seems to happen and nothing seems connected. He can live with this state of unknowing. This is how he differs

from the author of *Kriminalistik,* who put a name to everything. Professor Gross's theory of crime has no blanks.

In his copy of *System der Kriminalistik,* the Inspector has
marked certain passages with pencil. He often turns to these
pages, like a man rereading poetry or the Scriptures for guidance.

Now he leafs through the *Kriminalistik* to the chapter on
"Orientation," although he knows it by heart.

> What above all is of importance in private life is to ferret out
> a motive for a lie. When a story about something has been
> related either to ourselves or others, false in some particulars
> which we only discover later on, we more often than not
> carry the matter no further, because it is of no importance in
> itself; but if we wish to gather a lesson therefrom we shall
> try — by a direct method for preference, as by frankly and
> honestly asking the question — to discover why the lie has
> been told.

When the Inspector studied with Professor Gross, he was
compelled to keep a notebook commenting on what he'd read,
his observations about others, and the nuances of his own
moods and desires. This mindfulness is a noble pursuit that
brings self-acceptance and pleasure, Gross told his students. It
may lead you to some truths about yourselves as well as criminal
types. In this way, he modeled the students' self-development
on the lessons of Epictetus, who believed men must vigilantly
test their thoughts against the highest principles.

The Inspector has religiously kept up this habit, so that
he is a watcher of men and himself. This training has enabled
him to work unencumbered by his emotions.

He also has the habit of creating a visual picture for the
crimes he investigates. When he thinks of Dora, he sees her
body spanned with threads, so she's roped and bound to the
ground like Gulliver. This is his image of the case right now.

He never imagines the face of the murderer. He does memorize the face of the victim.

On the street, gentlemen lift their bowler hats to friends, acquaintances, and unfamiliar attractive women. The police are less obliging, and treat all women with equal contempt in public. If a single woman is moving too slowly on the sidewalk, they loudly ask her what she's waiting for. Wally has noticed that some women will walk quickly past a policeman, averting their eyes or focusing on something in the distance, hoping to avoid his loud comments.

There is no ordinance forbidding women to smoke in public, and so even young girls defiantly enjoy cigarettes and small cigars on the street, in offices, and even on the electric tramways. In the most expensive restaurants and hotels, women are allowed to smoke and have dinner without a male escort.

One evening early in October, Erszébet took Wally to the Hotel Sacher on Augustinerstrasse, to celebrate her eighteenth birthday. The Sacher is considered the best hotel in the city, and several tables were occupied by women dining together. In a corner of the room, two elderly women relentlessly turned the air blue with their cigar smoke. A pair of American ladies waved the maître d'hôtel over. Tell them to put out their cigars, they ordered. I regret I cannot do so, he whispered, the smokers are the Princess Trauttmansdorff and the Princess Esterházy. *Aristokraten*. The American women silently folded their napkins and left the room to eat downstairs with the coachmen.

Archduke Otto, the emperor's nephew, disgraced himself in the lobby of the hotel when he appeared naked except for his sword and cap before a group of ladies.

Erszébet felt uneasy about two women visiting the Naturhistorisches Museum, so she selected her best hat, a deep-brimmed black felt with feathers and other pieces of bird snared in its veiling. She carries an umbrella. Wally wears her red cloak.

They meet in the headquarters for the licensed *Dienstmänner* on the Stephansplatz. Erszébet hires a *Dienstmann*, Andrásy, to escort them for the afternoon, paying him forty *Hellers*. He's stout, red faced, and outfitted in a scarlet leather cap and a uniform with a round, numbered medallion. This gives him an air of accountability.

A fiaker drives them the short distance to the Naturhistorisches Museum, a heavy half-Renaissance, half-Baroque building on the Burgring near the Volksgarten. The solemn *Dienstmann* sits up front with the driver.

Erszébet had written Herr Pietznigg, the chief botanist at the museum, in advance, using her husband's name. When they are ushered into his office, Pietznigg makes it clear he was expecting an official, not a woman. The *Dienstmann* waits by the white-tiled stove, his arms folded across his chest. His posture tells them he also believes this is no place for women.

Under their critical eyes, Erszébet calmly unwinds her watercolor of the fig from its silk wrapper and hands it to Pietznigg.

"We need this identified."

Pietznigg is very blond, and his spectacles are fashioned from such fine wire they're invisible on his face. The skin above his transparent eyebrows puckers in a frown.

"A fig?"

"What variety is it, please?"

"It isn't my habit to answer questions upon the instant. I will contact you with the information at a later date."

Erszébet makes an impatient clicking noise with her lips and narrows her eyes. "My husband, the chief inspector of police, would prefer an answer as quickly as possible."

Wally interrupts his protest. "We aren't gardeners. We're here on business. This is a police matter."

She's confident her English accent will excuse her aggressiveness. She's also afraid Erszébet will lose her temper. Wally knows that when Erszébet is provoked, she will never compromise her dignity by raising her voice. Instead, she'll become very quiet or excessively polite, and then suddenly make a provocative statement. Sometimes she even reacts violently, which seems to appear from nowhere. Once Wally watched as Erszébet plunged her parasol between the wheels of a fiaker, simply left it there after the driver cheated on the fare and she paid it without complaint. Thrilled and embarrassed, Wally retrieved the parasol and hurried after her.

Pietznigg backs down. "Very well, Fräulein."

His footsteps grow fainter as he disappears into a maze of bookshelves to search for information. The *Dienstmann* clears his throat and shuffles his heavy boots. In a few minutes, the botanist reappears, struggling with a huge book. The *Dienstmann* rushes to help maneuver it onto the table. Pietznigg obviously doesn't like the man's touching it, but he elaborately thanks him and makes a ceremony of opening the book. He reverently turns the pages, which mollifies him.

Erszébet notices the dark, rough-edged parchment, the dense Latin script.

"Your fruit in question would appear to be *Col di Signora Nigra,* a variety of *Ficus carica,* the edible fig. It is grown extensively near Roussillon, in France. Its second crop is edible, usually ripening in late August."

Wally asks if the fig can grow in Vienna.

"It could, although it's susceptible to cold and wind. The tree is buried in the winter."

He smiles at their puzzled expressions. "You dig around the roots to loosen them. Then you dig a fairly deep trench straight out in front of the tree. The branches are tied against the trunk, and the entire tree is lowered into the ground and covered with dirt."

"Exactly when is the tree buried?" Erszébet asks.

"I'd calculate sometime in November, depending on the temperature. You dig the tree up again in the spring. A botanical resurrection."

"Like Lazarus," says the *Dienstmann*.

His voice comes from the corner, startling them.

Pietznigg misunderstands the women's anxious looks. "There are plants that are even stranger. For instance, the trumpet flower and the mimosa are both pollinated by bats."

❦

Afterward Erzsébet pays the *Dienstmann* and they walk up Kohlmarkt to Demel Konditorei. The interview has tired them, and Erzsébet forgets to open her umbrella. They order two strong *Kapuziner* and share a *Streuselkuchen* and a *Guglhupf.* Wally has found Erszébet unfailing in her choice of desserts. They finish eating before discussing the subject that obsesses them.

They discovered an enemy in the Naturhistorisches Museum. Snow. Once the fig tree is laid under earth and snow, hidden away from their eyes, the murderer is safe.

"Maybe the fig tree is firewood by now." Wally wants reassurance.

"Why would the murderer go to the trouble of cutting down the tree? For all he knows, there's no reason to even be concerned about it. He believes the figs he gave Dora are safe inside her body. Already buried underground. We have a few weeks to find the fig tree."

"That's what we hope."

Erszébet shrugs. "Don't complain. We have nothing else to follow. No evidence. You see, we must be more cunning than the murderer. More cunning than my husband."

Wally waits.

"There's a way to predict when it will snow," Erszébet says suddenly.

"How?"

"There are signs to read. I can kill a goose and examine its breast meat while it is fresh. If the flesh is light colored, snow will soon fall. If it is dark, there will be a period of rain."

They have a space of time, although the weather has already grown chilly and twilight comes earlier every day. Erszébet has told her that by mid-November it will be so dark the lamps on the streets will be lit by midafternoon.

A week later, Pietznigg sends Erszébet an official description of the *Ficus carica,* copied by hand in an elaborate script.

Col di Signora Nigra. Medium-sized fig, 6 by 4 centimeters. Shape ovate pyriform, obtuse at apex: neck very

*narrow and long, curved and swollen toward the stalk
end. Rib markings are distinct on the body and on the
neck and stalk. Color, dark violet chocolate with a slight
greenish flush in the shade, the swollen part of the neck
close to the stalk being bluish-green. Apex dark violet
brown, with here and there a flush of bright bluish green.
Bloom thick, bluish white. Pulp very dark bloodred, of
exquisite flavor and sweetness: meat greenish yellow.*

Erszébet continues her research on *Ficus carica,* the edible fig. She decides the myths involving women are especially significant.

*The fig was worshiped in early Rome. During Bacchanalian orgies, men carried statues of Priapus carved from
fig wood. Women wore figs around their necks as symbols
of fertility.*

*Judas hung himself on a fig tree. For that reason, St.
Jerome claimed the fig was cursed, haunted by spirits,
"obscene monsters," he called them.*

Every morning Wally looks anxiously out of her window, *Has it
snowed?* She presses her hand against the glass, checking the
temperature outside.

Little winter light, and even less air, comes through the
tall French doors in her room. Her first winter in Vienna, she
was amused by the insulation installed in the windows. To keep
out drafts, a flat cushion — like a thin mattress — was fitted
into the bottom half of the windows between the double panes
of glass.

Wally still isn't accustomed to the light in the city, although both London and Vienna are located near the reflective
presence of water. Thick fogs are also part of Vienna's landscape, isolating streets and buildings as ably as a flood.

On certain streets, her eye always picks out the houses

painted yellow, which indicates the building once belonged to someone in the imperial household. The rest of Vienna's stonework, its statues, walls, and cobblestones, is a blur of gray-ness. She refuses to become familiar with the city, keeping a distance. This is her only acknowledgment of her homesick-ness.

Underneath Vienna, there is another kind of light. She's seen it, following a guide's faint torch into the Michaelerkirche crypt, where hundreds of corpses are visible in half-open coffins or stacked on top of each other, their shriveled flesh and fine clothing cold and intact for hundreds of years. Here, even the shadows have a different quality.

She found the darkness in the crypt seemed to have no depth, moving like a wash of ink over the nerveless hands, the limp neck ruffs, the innermost folds of the corpses' clothing, a steady black tide pushed back only by the weak light of their candles and torches.

After the guide's tour had ended and she stood in the nave of the Michaelerkirche, she discovered her gloves were stiff, completely covered with wax where her candle had melted.

As she listens to Wally's story, Erszébet realizes she's placed the memory of Dora's corpse and the young laundress together in a deep intimacy, a dark well that beckons and may engulf her.

After a moment, she asks Wally if the children she takes care of are afraid of the dark.

"Yes. I leave the door open when little Hans is in bed, so there's light in his room from the hallway. He cries whenever someone walks past, because their shadows fall on his bed. He used to be afraid of horses."

Erszébet remembers when she was very young and saw a photograph for the first time. The shadow of the man who took the picture was in the foreground. The image frightened her. It was like her book about Peter Schlemihl, the boy who sold his shadow to the devil for gold. She was fascinated by the book, reading it over and over. One engraving showed Peter Schlemihl looking the other way as the spiky black figure of the devil delicately peeled his shadow off the ground with pointed fingertips. Even after the shadow was taken from the boy, it still kept his shape.

Erszébet believes the evidence of the crime is Dora's shadow. If she peers into its blackness, she will be able to decipher the original shape that cast it.

Wally sent a sympathy note to Dora's mother. As Wally had hoped, she wrote back, inviting her to *Jause* at five o'clock.

Now Dora's mother ushers Wally into the drawing room, where a samovar, small sandwiches, and torten are arranged on a table draped with an intricate Turkish weaving. She motions to the sofa. Wally refuses her first and second invitations before she finally sits on the edge of a stiff cushion. Seating a guest is a ritual, and she has lived here long enough to understand its peculiar etiquette. She smiles sympathetically at her hostess.

Grief and sleeplessness have laid a dry hand on the older woman's face, hollowing her cheeks, clenching her eyes in wrinkles. She wears black, and her old-fashioned crepe dress absorbs the light. She is eager to talk and asks Wally how she knew Dora.

"We met at a lecture," Wally lies. "We were reading the same books."

"Dora always wanted to go to the *Mädchenlyzeum*. She loved to read, although her father didn't like her to attend lectures."

"Yes, she told me."

"He argued with her. She'd leave the house anyway. Now I think he was right to insist she stay home."

"You didn't know what would happen."

Dora's mother begins to ramble. "If I'd known she was going out that night, I would have stopped her. Last week, I woke up because I thought the front door opened and Dora had come back. I got out of bed and stood in the hall, but the door was closed. It was a dream."

Wally clatters her fork against her plate, sets her brittle cup down with a sharp *click* to bring back Dora's mother, who stares straight ahead, oblivious to everything in the room. Wally waits a moment before she speaks, making her voice light.

"Who would Dora have been meeting that night? Another friend? Maybe someone I know?"

Wally fights her impulse to stroke the woman's hand, to comfort her. Dora's mother turns slowly away from her grief to focus on Wally. Like an eye at a keyhole, peering into some immense space.

"She must have met a friend. I know my daughter."

"Who? Do you know who it was? Did anyone tell you they saw her that night?"

The woman doesn't answer. Her eyes trace the geometrically patterned cloth on the table, as if trying to decipher some message in its bright angles.

"No."

"Did Dora keep a journal?"

She whispers. "I can't bear to look through her papers. I've locked her room."

They sit in silence. Frustrated, Wally doesn't know what to ask her next. Nothing the woman has said is useful. She can't tell what's wrong. Their conversation seems to be ajar.

Dora's mother covers her face with her hands, then pulls her fingers down her cheeks. Her eyes look wildly around the room.

"Gypsies. My husband thinks Gypsies took her. They have charms. They can creep in while you sleep, and you never hear them. They can walk right by your bed. But you're English, you don't know."

"I believe in such things."

"How old did you say you are?"

"Eighteen."

"You speak well for a foreigner. Did Dora ever say anything about her family, about me?"

"She said you were a comfort to her."

Her face sags with relief and sorrow. Wally wishes she had turned her eyes away. They stare at each other. Then she crushes Wally in an embrace, and they're both sobbing.

Later, they walk to the door, their arms around each

other. Their tears have made them more tender with each other. Wally is surprised that she welcomed the woman's soothing words, even her display of emotion. But she also wants to pull away, as if the connection of their hands will betray her.

"You'll come back and visit? I want to give you something of Dora's."

Wally nods, afraid she'll start crying again if she speaks.

After Wally slips out the door she walks for a distance, her knees and feet moving automatically, her vision thickened by tears. She remembers a story the church guide told her. Empress Maria Theresa ordered her daughter Josepha to the Kapuzinerkirche, to pray in the crypt where her relatives who died of smallpox were entombed. Josepha refused. They argued. The empress insisted. Josepha obeyed her mother, and while praying she was infected with smallpox. She died quickly, shortly before she was to have married.

On a street corner near the Judengasse, the Inspector stops at the sight of an extraordinary figure, a woman sponge seller. The thick sponges are threaded on strings wound around her body, so she's completely covered with the weightless, shaggy brown shapes, like an ancient statue pulled from water, overgrown with sealife. She moves with slow and halting steps, as if obeying a different pull of gravity. As she turns to talk to a customer, the wind picks up the second woman's thin silk skirt and smoothes it over the rough sponges. He wonders if he should take this strange vision as a sign. He knows his wife would.

As soon as he arrives at the police station on the Schottenring, the Inspector sends a letter to Herr Zellenka requesting an appointment The messenger has orders to wait for an immediate reply.

When the boy returns to the station, he describes Herr Zellenka's reaction to the letter. He heard Zellenka raise his voice in the next room. He was angry. No, he couldn't make out his words or see his face. Then the secretary came back and said the Inspector could call on Herr Zellenka in his office this afternoon.

It is now three o'clock, and Herr Zellenka welcomes the Inspector, apparently untroubled by his visit. They perform the ritual of shaking hands and he solemnly takes the Inspector's hat and walking stick.

In his office, they light cigars and he graciously indicates the Inspector should sit in front of his desk, looking into the window. This must be deliberate, for the Inspector has to squint to make out his host's face against the light. The stand-up collar of Zellenka's white shirt is a sharp white triangle in the dim room, underneath a jacket he recognizes as the exacting handiwork of Knize, the finest tailor in Vienna. Zellenka is a successful commercial agent and frequently travels out of town on business. He has a handsome man's confidence.

"What can I do for you, Inspector?"

"I'm exploring the facts about Dora's death," the *outrage,* as he occasionally calls it in polite society. He notes Zellenka's meticulousness, his polished fingernails. A small pair of scissors for clipping cigars, a gold pen, and a letter opener are set precisely parallel to each other on his desk.

"I'm certain you can understand this is difficult for me. I don't believe I've ever had occasion to speak to a policeman before." His broad, imperturbable face is creased with a temporary wrinkle of worry.

The Inspector checks his impatience. To let Zellenka know he's ignoring his comment, he searches busily through two pockets before taking out his notebook. He has the impression the man is well rehearsed and feigns an emotionalism he doesn't possess. He puts this thought aside to analyze later.

He asks him to describe his relationship with Dora and her family.

"First let me say what a terrible tragedy this is. I'm very affected by it. I've been close to Dora and her family for over six years. Our families always vacation together."

"Can you be more specific?"

"Every year, our families visit a resort in Merano. My

wife and our children, Dora, her brother, Otto, and their parents. Of course we stay at the Bristol. Have you been there?"

The Inspector makes an entry in his notebook: *Herr K. boastful. Confident chatter.*

"Never. Both families stay at the Bristol?"

"Yes. Dora and my wife were inseparable. They shared a room."

Asked to describe Dora, he shakes his head. "She was a lovely girl, although very headstrong. She had modern ideas, which made things difficult for her at home. She and her mother constantly disagreed. She wasn't fair to Dora, but she's just a backward woman from Königinhof. Dora's health was fragile, and the constant bickering didn't help."

"What did Dora suffer from?"

"Migraines. Women's ills. I don't know, a nervous cough. Inspector, I'm no expert on young women. Ask her mother."

"And her father, what was their relationship like?"

"Ah, now you've touched on something." He rocks back in his chair, obviously relishing what he's about to say. "I'm telling you this in confidence, you understand. Her mother was jealous of the girl's relationship with her father. She could do no wrong in his eyes. He always took her side against the mother, and believe me, I would have done the same."

He leans over his desk, propelling his watch chain to swing from his jacket pocket, heavy, dull gold. The Inspector understands he wants him to pay close attention to his next words. In the same way, a pretty woman driving a fiaker will sometimes tie a bunch of violets to her whip with ribbon, just for show.

"Dora and her father were unusually close. In fact, she and my wife took turns caring for him when he was ill. Dora once told my wife that sometimes her father walked into her bedroom while she was undressing."

The Inspector senses the man is holding his breath. He angles his face toward his notebook, dodging Zellenka's eager eyes, which crowd him, watching for his reaction. His acceptance. He looks up and smiles, his expression guileless, flat as a piece of paper.

"Perhaps Dora's father opened the wrong door by mistake?"

Zellenka makes his mouth into a bitter line. "Doubtful. He's a very deliberate man."

"He also claims you know something of interest about the crime."

He shakes his head. "Because of my peculiar relationship with Philipp, I hope you won't take his statements too seriously. He's told you about our understanding?"

"Yes. I'd like to hear your version."

"When a man has friends he has no secrets, isn't that true, Inspector?" He grants him a joyless smile. "Since you already know our intimate little secret, I don't want to waste your time or mine. But I'd like you to confirm no one else will be questioned about this private matter."

"It's impossible for me to make such a promise. As unpleasant as it might be, it's in your best interest to tell me your side of the story."

Zellenka restraightens the scissors and the letter opener. He doesn't look up. "Philipp has been having an affair with my wife for several years. You'll be surprised, but I have no animosity. He is — or was — my dearest friend. He was stricken with tuberculosis, and she brought him back to health. He believes she saved his life. So do I. He's alive, but my wife's affection was the price."

"He said your friendship had suffered."

"I'm surprised he would say such a thing. I have no ill will toward him. None. It is all very tidy. Everyone knows the circumstances — except for his wife. You must think this is an extraordinary arrangement for two men to make. My motto is *Biegen, nicht brechen."* Bend, but do not break. Although he smiles broadly, his charming show is hardly spontaneous.

The Inspector has never heard a more casual acceptance of adultery. Before he can stop himself, his face becomes a mask, rejecting the other man's assumption of a shared sensibility. He struggles to keep his mind blank, trying not to get caught on Zellenka's words. As if he were being swept downstream and must resist the urge to grab at a branch. He permits himself no safety. He scrawls a few lines in his notebook to calm himself before continuing.

"Was your wife jealous of Dora's relationship with her father?"

"Hardly. She made certain Dora was on her side. She won the girl over. In fact, I suspect Dora had a schoolgirl crush on her. No, my wife is only jealous of Philipp's wife, pathetic as she is."

Zellenka is preoccupied, focused on some impression from the past.

The Inspector quickly speaks, hoping to catch him off guard. "Why did you quarrel with Dora?"

The man's slow reaction signals his discomfort.

"Quarrel? Ah, I see her father must have misinterpreted something. We didn't quarrel. I'll tell you the truth about her. Dora was subject to nervous attacks. She'd take offense and cry at nothing. If someone angered her, she wouldn't speak to them for days. Did her father tell you she'd lose her voice? She'd actually become dumb."

The Inspector continues writing without looking down at the book in his hand. "So there was no specific disagreement. You say the girl was nervous. Just for my records, sir, can you tell me your whereabouts the evening of Dora's murder?"

His face registers no trace of uneasiness. "Certainly. I spent the evening with Fräulein Rosza, Dora's former *promeneuse.*"

"What was the reason for this social occasion?"

"We were discussing my boy. We recently lost our only daughter. She died of tuberculosis in August."

The Inspector nods briefly to express sympathy, then asks for the specific time and place where he met Fräulein Rosza.

Zellenka stares down at his desk. "We met at the Grand Café. Then we drove through the Prater. I wasn't home until after midnight."

"You're certain of the hour?"

His eyes meet the Inspector's. "I remember it was very hot, even that late at night."

The Inspector asks for Rosza's address.

"I don't have her address. I believe she's gone to a new position."

"And you haven't seen her since that evening?"

He emphatically shakes his head, and then readily agrees the Inspector should talk to his wife. He'll arrange a time with her soon — yes, tomorrow. "May I ask you a question about Dora?"

"What is it?"

"Did she suffer much?"

"I have reason to believe death was swift."

"That's a mercy."

Zellenka coaxes the letter opener a fraction of an inch across his desk, a ploy the Inspector recognizes as *stalling*.

"Was Dora disfigured when you found her? How did she look?" He doesn't raise his head.

"Why would this information interest you?" He tries to decipher the intention behind the man's soft words.

"I knew Dora for years. Since she was a girl. I don't like to think . . . you know, you're haunted by thoughts."

The wistful look he gives the Inspector is the first genuine expression Zellenka has made.

They walk through the hall to the front door. The sound of their footsteps reminds the Inspector he'd like to scrape the bottom of Zellenka's boots, see if anything matches the dirt in the Volksgarten.

When they stand at the door, the Inspector notices the heightened color in his face, a faint pink discoloration, a sign the interview has rattled him.

To clear his head, he walks back to the police station. The late October light dulls even the hard color of the buildings painted the same shade as the Schönbrunn Palace, "Maria Theresa yellow."

Recently, the Inspector has observed Erszébet's aura of preoccupation. Something clings to her. Several times he found her most elaborate hat on the small table in the entrance hall, where she'd taken it off in front of the mirror. A sign she'd been out of the house. Where were you this afternoon? I was just shopping, she said, barely answering his question and walked away from him into the kitchen. After that incident, he never found her hat on the table again.

A few weeks ago, he was certain he'd glimpsed Erszébet in front of the Malteserkirche at midday, talking to an unfamiliar young woman in a scarlet cloak. He noticed his wife first, her shoulders wrapped in the long black fox boa he'd given her. By the time the driver had stopped and he had run back along the street, both women had vanished into the heavy traffic on the Kärntner Strasse. He was strangely relieved to find they were gone.

He wonders if his solicitude for his wife is connected to the girl's murder. Two uncertainties. As often as he and Franz have plotted theories, there are no obvious suspects in the crime. Murder is usually committed by someone who knew the victim. He's diagnosed Dora's mother as a hysteric, a woman with an abnormal state of mind, prone to strange behavior. Hysterics have been known to injure themselves or do violence to others. A famous psychoanalytic doctor in Vienna has even written about a hysterical woman with a severe case of *zoöpsia,* animal hallucinations.

But it seems unlikely that Dora's mother would be able to drag her daughter's body to the Volksgarten. Unless she had help. Her husband? Son? An unknown party? Both Dora's parents appear to have sound alibis, although confirmed only by each other.

The excrement found next to Dora's body puzzles him. It doesn't fit the crime. Perhaps that was the killer's intention, since the murder itself is straightforward. *The error in the situation.* The perversity of the murderer's act disconcerts him. He wonders why the girl's body wasn't defiled. For once, he is at a loss as to how to proceed with a piece of evidence.

Sometimes he believes the pure state of a corpse is contaminated by the mechanics of investigation. Debris scattered on the path of a labyrinth.

The physical remains of the crime, its hypothetical reconstruction, his scribbled impressions of witnesses and suspects, can mysteriously become opaque, unfamiliar. Like souvenir postcards of a journey, which gradually replace the true visual memory of the experience.

Possessed by this state of doubt, he will reexamine everything taken from the corpse and the crime scene. He needs to handle *things,* as if touching wood for luck. Once, while he was studying the objects retrieved from Dora's body on a table, Erszébet had quietly slipped into the room unnoticed. When he looked up and met her eyes, he was swept with a peculiar shame.

Wally returns to visit Dora's mother. She immediately embraces Wally at the door. Caught by surprise, Wally can't help stiffening at the woman's touch.

"It's good of you to come."

"Thank you. It is my great pleasure to see you again."

Wally speaks with a formality, a politeness she doesn't have in English.

"I thought we could sit outside for a moment, while it's still warm."

She follows Dora's mother through the house and out the door in the back.

There's a high wall around the garden, obscured by thick trees. It hasn't been cold enough for frost, but the leaves have lost the clear brilliance of their summer color. They're a shade less than green, pivoting to yellow.

They settle themselves on an ornate bench and sit with their shoulders touching, the afternoon sun striping their bodies and the ground in front of them. Dora's mother unfurls a parasol to keep the light off her face.

"You must be lonely here, so far from England."

This is the first personal comment she's made about Wally, and it startles her. She shuts down the fraction of memory and homesickness that emerges.

"No. I have a dear friend here. A woman from Hungary."

"Yes? Who is she? You must bring her here to have *Jause* one afternoon. The days are so long for me now."

Wally changes the subject. "I work as a governess. The family I live with went to the spa at Bad Ischl. The mother and children have an infection of the lungs. Tuberculosis, I think, although they were afraid to say so."

The older woman leans forward. "My husband thinks our son, Otto, has tuberculosis, but I don't believe it. Otto never complained about being ill, not like Dora. My husband insisted on sending him away after Dora died."

"Where is Otto?"

"He's at the Kinderklinik, a hospital for tubercular children. I hope they'll allow him to come home soon."

Now she's content to sit for a while, unmindful of Wally's fidgeting inattention. When she occasionally wipes her eyes or falls into a staring silence, Wally glances furtively around the garden, looking for the fig tree.

After a time, Wally suggests they walk around the grounds. She waves Wally off the bench. You're young, you go have a look around, she says. My old bones only want to carry me to the grave. I don't walk anymore.

Wally pulls her hand out of her muff and presses it into the woman's hands as if it were a bouquet. She walks toward the foliage she glimpsed in the back of the garden; perhaps there are fruit trees. Her eyes also caught the precise glint of glass, a greenhouse.

Five steps inside the greenhouse, Wally unbuttons her cloak; the air is hot and intimate, the sky blinding gray above the roof. The intense light shrinks her pupils to pinpoints, and it takes a moment for the layout of the greenhouse to register. There are three glass walls and a fourth side of whitewashed brick. Dwarf citron, pear, and plum trees are trained against the wall in a straight line, their branches spread flat against the wall, like a mural. There is no fig tree here.

A smell of rotted manure and earth. And something else. A rose climbs up a metal column in the center of the greenhouse, its spiked branches artificially arched, its buds forced into flower.

She pushes her way through leaves so thick the stone walkway is barely visible below them. This is like a labyrinth, she thinks. She's claustrophobic, manipulated by this place. Nothing moves. Even time and light seem suspended here.

Up close, the roses are silver pink. She tries to pick one, but the stem is green and stubborn, its thorns pull against her sleeve, there's a tearing sound in her ears until she rips the rose free. Other thorns catch the edge of her cloak. She feels panic threaded into her body. Her breath comes in stitches.

She tears petals off the rose until her body stops shaking.

Dora's mother is still waiting for her on the bench. She must have read something on Wally's face, for she grasps the girl's hands as soon as she sits down. She strokes her arm.

"I don't like the greenhouse, either. I prefer to be outside. My daughter would sit here sometimes. You remind me of her."

It's colder now; the bench is in shadow. Accustomed to the older woman's silences, Wally waits.

"Dora didn't want to celebrate her last birthday. I imagine she told you? She refused a *Schmuckkästchen,* an expensive jewel case, from a man, a close friend of the family. He'd already given her several pieces of jewelry. Then she stopped wearing jewelry altogether."

Wally slides her arm away. Dora's mother keeps talking.

"My daughter had the same dream several times. Our house was on fire, and I wanted to save my jewel case, but my husband wouldn't let me. He said he'd rather save our children."

"Was that when she stopped wearing jewelry?"

"No. It was earlier." Dora's mother stares straight ahead into the garden. "It was when she threatened to kill herself. Of course she didn't mean it. Thank God my husband found her letter. I only tell you this because she's dead. She never shamed our family. She was a good girl."

"But why would Dora wish to die? It seems extraordinary."

"She was always sick. Headaches, the female troubles we all suffer from. But she could bear those ailments, as I do. No, she wrote the suicide letter to frighten her father. She didn't wish to die. She was angry with him. If only he'd been more attentive. I always told him to listen to her, but when he's in a mood it does no good to talk. Eh, he must live with himself. And Dora was as stubborn as he is."

Wanting her daughter to be remembered, she makes a scrapbook from her words. She shakes her head and gropes for a handkerchief in her bodice.

Wally wishes she could share or soothe her grief, but she feels only impatience. Still needing information, she tries to reenter the conversation.

"But who was Dora going to meet that night in the Volksgarten? You must know."

The older woman looks up, confused, her wet eyes trying to focus, as if she'd been asleep. She wipes her cheeks and clutches Wally's hand. She can't speak.

Wally promised herself she'd leave the minute Dora's mother started crying, since she'll learn nothing else from her. She can't bear to be touched like this. She pulls her hand away and abruptly stands up. Yes, yes, maybe tomorrow, she promises to come back.

Busy with her handkerchief, Dora's mother barely waves farewell as Wally leaves her.

Inside, the house is quiet. Wally considers searching through Dora's possessions, walking into her room's terrible stillness before she remembers the girl's mother has locked the door. Down a hallway she finds the kitchen, where a woman is bent over a table, her arms covered with flour, a white kerchief over her head. She doesn't look up but continues vigorously kneading something in a large bowl. There are smells of cinnamon, of cardamom. The room is very hot, heated by the Dortenpfanne stove against one wall.

"Excuse me."

The woman's big hands meet in the bottom of the bowl. She turns the dough over once, then expertly flips it onto the table. She picks up the soft mass, slaps and punches it between her hands into a shape. Wally pinches a piece of dough and sets it on her tongue. It's cold and salty sweet. She smiles at the cook.

"My mother used to bake something like this for me, back in England. Makes me homesick."

"You should taste my *Buchteln*. They're baked with cheese and fruit, some almonds. Light as a cloud. You're too thin. You could do with one of my desserts."

"I can imagine how good they must be. Have you worked here long?"

The woman explains she's a *Mehlspeisköchin,* a baker specializing in desserts. She moves from house to house, preparing her specialties. She's worked here for over two years, maybe three. Wally persuades her to meet later at a *Kaffeehaus*. Yes, she'd love to know more about *Buchteln*.

As part of his training, Franz has examined weapons and their effects. In *Kriminalistik,* he discovered, *"In wounds caused by cutting instruments, the form of the wound rarely corresponds to the true form of the weapon."*

He also made a study of a bullet's impact in various surfaces and learned that gunshot through glass produces the most interesting results. A high-velocity bullet leaves a clean, perfectly round opening in a pane of glass. A bullet fired from close range and a poor shot from a bad weapon both create a mushy, splintered hole. When fired into glass at medium velocity, a gunshot creates an intricate web of cracks radiating out from a central point. Franz has carefully drawn and labeled each of these examples on paper.

The Inspector has promised to take him to Graz to see a special display of windows. In the criminal museum, rows of windows are hung as if they were fine paintings, and each one has a bullet hole through its center. A card affixed to the frame describes the type of bullet that pierced the glass, the name of the weapon, the distance from which it was fired, the angle, and the weather conditions.

Franz knows that if menaced by a gun, he must cover his heart with one arm.

The Inspector stoops over the desk in his office. The blinds are rolled up to the top of the windows, so light floods the paper directly in front of him. He leans closer, and without lifting his eyes, lays his hand on a pair of tweezers and then plucks nearly invisible particles off the paper and places them in a watch glass.

From across the room, Franz can tell by the way the Inspector's shoulders are positioned that he's holding his breath. He watches him work in silence, afraid if he unleashes any words he'll disturb him.

The Inspector has taken Franz under his wing. He tutors him, carefully asking his opinion before giving his own to help him hone his skills. He encourages him to be more "womanish," to observe relationships between people, to offer neutral comfort, to read silence and gesture, to ask questions in such a way that the person who answers will reveal information beyond words. "Let each witness tell you what they want to say. The more they protest and claim something is an unimportant matter, the closer you must watch and listen."

The Inspector believes listening is one of the most important abilities an Investigating Officer can possess. He frequently quotes the philosopher Plutarch, who instructed men to listen in silence, without asking questions, and thoughtfully consider what they'd heard afterward. This will develop an internal voice of reason.

Franz finds the Inspector's remarks perfectly clear and completely mysterious.

They make a habit of walking the few streets from the police station to the Maria-Theresien Brücke where it spans the Donaukanal. The Inspector will demand that Franz make the wildest speculations, share his most fanciful theories about a case. Just say whatever comes into your mind. Don't think about it, he tells him. At first, Franz could only blush and shake

his head when the Inspector tried to coax some silly theory out
of him. Franz didn't understand what he wanted. Tell me what
to say, he'd plead, confused.

All I can tell you, the Inspector would say, is that ran-
domness and listening will reveal the truth.

Franz admires the Inspector and he's relieved these exer-
cises are private between the two of them. Gradually, this type
of conversation during their walks together acquires the easy
camaraderie of a game. However, Franz is still so young that he
wants to be correct. He can't leap into the uncertainty of guesswork.

Moving slowly, as if in a dream, a group of gardeners pushes a
spindly metal tower on wheels down an avenue of lime trees,
the Park Allee. The tower is constructed of thin bars bolted
into ladderlike steps, a bizarre ziggurat twenty feet tall that
would seem to be made for an electrical purpose or a telegraph
station. The tower sways slightly as its wheels move soundlessly over the grass, which is cut to the evenness of velvet.

The trees facing each other along the avenue are clipped
into a single, perfectly flat surface, uniform as books on a shelf.
The backside of the trees is untrimmed, the branches wild and
unkempt.

The tower comes to a trembling halt in front of a tree, and
two men clamber up its steps. When they reach the top, they
shout and wave their arms, motioning to be moved closer to
the tree. From where she stands across the fountain in Schönbrunn Park, Erszébet is unable to distinguish their words. The
tower is gently pushed forward, and the weight of the men
makes it rock back and forth, as slowly as if it were underwater.
The men unhook shears from their belts and begin to trim the
trees. On the ground, the gardeners leisurely gather the fallen
leaves and branches, correcting the great untidiness dropped
on the smooth grass.

The Palmenhaus is a squat glass building surrounded
by sharply pointed topiaries, diagonally across from the Park

Allee. It's silent inside, a tropical landscape that lacks birdsong. The quiet and the extravagant greenery make Erszébet uneasy. When she first walked in, she'd noticed other strange signs, too. On one of the palms, *Stenia pallida,* tiny wooden splints like matchsticks are tied alongside each fragile waxy flower to keep it from breaking, the handiwork of the meticulous Palmenhaus gardeners.

She locates two fig trees near the center of the greenhouse. Has she found the fig Dora ate, *Col di Signora Nigra?* She angles her head back, squinting up at the tree. Its leaves are small, with three lobes, deeply curved at the edges, and button-shaped buds at the base. She's irritated her opera glasses have been left at home. She remembers figs can take many sizes and shapes, an elongated gourd or a thick pear, a short turbinate cone like a child's top. This fruit is a bright greenish yellow, round, with a short stalk. Disappointed, she now recognizes the fig as *Blanche Hâtive d'Argenteuil.* She finds a sign near the base of one of the trees identifying it as one of the oldest known figs, planted in a garden near Paris during the time of the Roman emperor Julianus Apostata.

She prepares to paint the fig, setting up her easel in front of the nearest tree. There's a match for the fruit's color on her palette, *Indischgelb,* a bright transparent yellow. She treasures this rare and peculiar paint, its faint odor and curious history. She was told *Indischgelb* was made from the urine of certain serpents. Later, she learned it was filtered from the urine of Indian cattle fed on mango leaves. Erszébet sucks on her brush, shaping its point with her tongue, then strokes it over the square pan of *Indischgelb.*

The sunlight stirs up the invisible vapors of the plants, as if the greenhouse were a huge bowl. It is very hot, and her wool dress itches and feels unfamiliar on her body. She hasn't before experienced this kind of heat.

Slow footsteps crunch on the gravel path behind her, the sound magnified by the glass walls. Her knees are suddenly molten. She's vulnerable, the trees around her flimsy and useless, thin, bare trunks that can't hide her. The frame of the greenhouse arches over her like a cage.

She turns to face the man as he steps around the palms. A workman dressed in a stained brown suit, a dull leaf color. Her eyes are filled with the sun behind the man, so his silhouette is dark, his face a featureless shadow. She nervously points her paintbrush toward the trees. She wants him to see her wedding ring.

"I was just admiring your tree."

"A good one. Figured to be forty years old."

He hasn't stepped any closer. She keeps talking, careful not to move suddenly, as if she were a juggler.

"Do you know what kind of fig it is?"

"No, but the fruit's green. Grows two crops a year."

"Can you please get me one?"

He nods and steps into the tall foliage, moving slowly, respectful of the thick leaves.

She prepares a quantity of red paint on her palette, pure scarlet made with iodide of mercury. She charges her largest brush with the color and waits. It shakes in her hand.

In a few minutes, she hears the halting rustle of the shrubbery, then the green leaves swing like tassels as he pushes his way out. She can't read the expression on his brown face. He stops on the other side of her easel, and she keeps it between them, holding her brush with its wet red tip like a spear.

He holds out his hat to her. Nestled inside the dim nest of wool are two yellow figs, perfect as birds' eggs.

Outside, the metal tower sails majestically along between the lime trees in Schönbrunn Park, leaving broken branches and men scrambling after it, as if they were awash in the wake of a passing boat.

That night, Erszébet dreams she is sleeping under a fig tree. A menacing figure, a woman in a black robe, leans over her. She senses the woman is about to speak, her lips part, but then Erszébet suddenly wakes up terrified, her breath coming in gasps. Fear opens new routes for her blood to take; the throbbing of her heart is mapped out over her whole body. After a moment, she strains to remember the face of the figure in her dream. Was it Dora?

Her husband is awake beside her. He silently waits for her breathing to slow, then she turns over and abandons him again for sleep.

The Inspector has just angled his hat on the stand by the door when Franz tells him that they're to go immediately to the Zentralfriedhof. An outrage has been committed on one of the graves.

As the Inspector's fiaker speeds down Rennweg, he recollects Erszébet had told him the Magyar believe that the spirit of the most recent person to die stands at the gates of the cemetery until relieved by the next arrival. A chain, endlessly transformed. Surely the horses would sense such an apparition first, he thinks. Although he chides himself for this fancy, his eyes check both sides of the Zentralfriedhof gates as his carriage quickly passes through. He proceeds along a semicircular arcade, a wall studded with memorials to the eminent dead. Franz and the rest of the men follow directly behind him.

He passes the monuments of Brahms and Beethoven in the musicians' corner, landscaped with the design of a colossal harp in low shrubbery. With the approach of winter, the gravestones mirror the clouds — the same gray opacity — as if they too were temporary, but set in the ground's embrace. Anticipating the disturbed grave, what will probably be a gruesome scene, he feels a claustrophobic weight settle over him. At the end of a long avenue of bare locust trees, a group of men mill around a grave, the only movement in this still place.

Two grave diggers and the cemetery superintendent silently step back as Franz and the Inspector approach. Small clods of dirt are scattered over the site, although the grass looks undisturbed. The Inspector is startled to read Dora's name on the gravestone. No one relayed that piece of information.

The superintendent, a grizzled older man, hesitantly removes his hat and steps forward. "I sent my men for you right after they'd told me the grave was disturbed. First thing I did, sir."

The Inspector thanks him for his trouble. However, he's arrived too late, and the men have already trampled around the grave, confusing their footprints with those of the intruder. He smothers his vexation.

"I'll need all your boots later, to make casts of their prints," he says evenly. "Please, all of you move back so I can examine the area around the grave."

One of the men discovers footprints in the soft earth near the road. There's one clear impression of an entire boot, and the Inspector decides to copy it. He tells Móricz to gather some twigs. Franz runs to the fiaker and returns with his kit. Someone else brings a bucket of water, and a handful of twigs and a short length of string are tossed in to soak.

With tweezers, the Inspector carefully removes large pebbles from the bottom of the footprint. Then he steps aside and motions to Franz. He wants him to take over. To steady his nerves, Franz squats over the print, studying it for a moment before he delicately blots it with thin paper. Mimicking the Inspector, he holds out his hand without looking up, and a pump bottle is placed in his palm. He sprays the footprint with a thin layer of shellac, gentle as a woman applying perfume. He waits a few minutes for it to dry, standing around the print, joking with the Inspector. It's cold enough now that their breath also turns to smoke after they've finished their cigarettes.

Handfuls of plaster are stirred into the bucket of water until the mixture is as thick as cream. Franz spoons it over the footprint, carefully lays in the wet string and twigs, and covers them with a second layer of plaster. In fifteen minutes, he digs around the plaster to loosen it, then grasps the protruding string and pulls up the stiff white footprint. He scratches his name, the date, and the location on the top. A fossilized record of where a man with a size-ten boot had recently passed.

Franz remembers the Inspector told him casts could be taken from footprints in snow. It seemed so miraculous, like walking on water, that Franz hadn't pressed him for details at the time. Now he knows snow is added to the plaster instead of water, so the liquid will be the same temperature as the footprint. Franz also learned that paste, suet, wet breadcrumbs, and porridge can be used to copy footprints in an emergency, when plaster isn't available. Using some secret technique, a legendary investigator in Bavaria even managed to take excellent impressions of footprints left in sand on a beach covered by water.

Acting on a sudden hunch, the Inspector digs a gloved finger into the grass over the grave where a few strands are slightly yellow at the root. The earth underneath is soft, crumbly. He tugs at a clump of grass, and it comes up neatly in his hand. His eyes follow a faint line, a rectangle where the grass has been cut, rolled up off the grave, and replaced so recently it hasn't yet turned brown. Maybe yesterday or last night. He stands up and quietly tells the men to dig up Dora's coffin.

Moving quickly, they spread out a canvas tarpaulin for the dirt and set to work. He shakes his head at the grave diggers' eager shoveling. Slowly, he says. Be careful. If you see any object in the dirt, no matter how small, let me know. Save everything.

While they dig, he sends Franz to check the graves nearby, to see if they've also been disturbed. He shouts after him, "Remember don't walk on the graves. Get on your knees and look at the ground first." Franz doesn't turn around, and the Inspector can tell by the set of his head that his words have annoyed him.

Although he's growing steadily more apprehensive, he resists the temptation to pace while they work. He smokes another cigarette, squinting into the distance, counting gravestones to distract himself. His wife would say this is an unlucky time to dig up a coffin. It's twelve o'clock, and *pripolniza* — the evil spirit of noon — rules.

The men have now removed a mound of earth, and the entire coffin is visible at the bottom of the hole, still intact after nine weeks underground. They continue to dig, uncovering its four sides, the carved details packed with dirt. The coffin had been painted to look like tortoiseshell, and when the Inspector peers down at it in the grave, it appears to be the richly colored carcass of some creature or giant insect. Without a

word, one of the grave diggers swings his legs over the edge of
the hole and jumps in, landing with a thud on the head of the
coffin.

The Inspector winces. He assumes the girl's body has recently been disturbed. His first impulse is to blame some supernatural force. A murder victim has been known to return as
one of the living dead, a revenant. No, the logical explanation is
that it has something to do with her murder. He tries to strip
the event of his reaction, see if a structure is revealed.

The grave digger is still crouched on the coffin, scraping
dirt from around its sides with his hands. Franz tosses him
something, a long canvas belt. Then a second belt. The grave
digger wedges the belts under the head and foot of the coffin.
The superintendent and Móricz help him clamber out of the
hole, their dirty fingers leaving brown stripes on his bare arms
as they pull him up.

The grave digger and the two cemetery workers grab the
belt and hoist the coffin until it's clear, free of the earth. As if
bringing a huge and awkward fish into shore, they drag it over
to the tarpaulin. The coffin's latches are open, perhaps from
scraping against the sides of the hole. The Inspector realizes he
should have checked them while the coffin was still in the
ground. He kneels and examines the latches, crusted with dirt
but unbroken. The grave diggers watch him uneasily, conscious
they're about to do something shameful. They're *Sardeckel-
aufmacher,* men who open coffin lids.

"Shall we unseal the coffin here, sir?"

The Inspector nods. "Don't touch the latches or handles.
There may be fingerprints."

The grave diggers wrap a cloth over the edge of the coffin
lid and hook their fingers around it. With an effort, they pull
up, and the lid opens an inch. They turn to the Inspector and
wait, wanting him to instruct them again. He avoids looking at
Franz and resolutely fixes his eyes on the coffin.

"Go ahead, open it slowly."

The smell reaches them first. Franz covers his nose.

When the coffin lid is thrown back, the Inspector sees
only the pale lining, intricately pleated around the dark shape

of Dora's body. He refuses to look at her swollen face, although he senses her perfectly arranged hair has come loose from her scalp, like a torn pocket. What catches his eye is a soft mass of flesh that is recognizable as her hand, wrenched into an odd position. It's bent back, and her thumb has been cut off. There's a round circle of black where her thumb was, and a white spear of bone sticks up out of its center.

CHAPTER 5

T'S AFTER MIDNIGHT WHEN Erszébet finishes the last page in her husband's notebook, which she'd slipped out of his jacket. He's asleep upstairs. She's at the kitchen table with the notebook, a pen, and her watercolors, copying his words into her book. His orderly writing has revealed the facts and progress of his investigation of Dora.

The murder exists in this disjointed state, his impressions, words spread over paper. Reading his notes, she can decipher his attitude toward certain individuals, even though it isn't explicitly stated. Perhaps his judgment isn't obvious to him. He can't see it. She's familiar with the way this obliviousness works visually, how the eye can uncover a hidden image. The painter Thomas Gainsborough would dip a sponge tied to a stick in watery color and then swab it over paper, not consciously painting any particular subject. Later, he'd transform these amorphous clouds of color into something recognizable — rocks, mountains, sunsets. He'd tease landscapes from blobs. Gainsborough called these pictures his "moppings."

A door opens. Sudden light on the stairs transforms them into a jagged silhouette. She quickly slides a sheet of paper over the notebooks. Erszébet, are you coming to bed? her husband asks. Yes, in one minute. My paper is wet. He makes a suggestive joke about what she's just said. She turns and smiles over her shoulder at him, even though he can't see her from where he stands on the stairs.

"I'm coming right up," she says. "Just wait."

She doesn't make a sound when her hand accidentally strikes the jar in front of her, sending violet-colored water across the table into her lap.

She slips both notebooks into the dry pocket of her damp robe.

The two women are in *das Gewölbe,* the front room at Demel Konditorei. At Erszébet's recommendation, Wally had ordered a *Sicilienne,* raspberry and vanilla ice cream with raisins soaked in Malaga wine. When Wally lifts her spoon, it registers as a blink of silver in the mirrors behind her chair and across the room from their table. I have news, she announces. Dora tried to kill herself. Her mother told me. She said a man gave Dora jewelry, but she didn't tell me his name. But she doesn't know who Dora would have met in the Volksgarten.

Erszébet is quiet, her expression doesn't betray any emotion, even curiosity. Although she's disappointed at her reaction, Wally waits. She holds the spoonful of ice cream unswallowed on her tongue until Erszébet chooses to speak. A cold test.

"And what did she say about Dora's brother?"

"He was sent away after she died. To the Kinderklinik. She said it was her husband's idea. Otto may have tuberculosis."

The boy is suddenly gone from the house. Perhaps someone wanted to stop him from talking, Erszébet suggests. My husband hasn't mentioned him. I'm not a woman who makes wagers, but I could wager Otto's disappearance is what he calls *the error in the situation.* Erszébet's eyes drift from Wally's face as she calculates.

"What about the man who gave Dora jewelry? How can we find him?"

They agree that next time Wally will persuade Dora's mother to reveal who gave her daughter gifts.

Then Erszébet explains how she copied information from her husband's notebook while he was sleeping. He nearly caught me, she laughs. But I've discovered new evidence. A man named Herr K. and his wife both befriended Dora. Frau K. and Dora's father are having an affair. The K.s' real names are unknown; they were written in code. I don't know why. No one has been able to contact Rosza, Dora's *promeneuse*. Dora and her father were strangely intimate. She was suspected of being a hypochondriac. No witnesses to the crime have been found yet.

The women plan to unmask Herr and Frau K., and find Otto and Rosza, the *promeneuse*.

Erszébet doesn't tell the girl that when she finished with her husband's notebook that evening, she went upstairs and got into bed with him, her heart still racing from his interruption while she stole his words. In the bedroom she translated her nervousness into abandon, concentrating on one small area of his body.

Dora's missing thumb wasn't found in her coffin or in the dirt around it. The Inspector and his men also searched above ground, sifting through the loose earth around her grave, parting the intricate webs of grass with careful fingers.

Because of the condition of the grave site, the Inspector believes Dora's coffin was probably exhumed during the previous day or two. The graves nearby were undisturbed.

When questioned, the Zentralfriedhof watchman said no, nothing unusual had happened, I'd notice if someone came in here after dark, I'd see their lanterns. The Inspector doesn't argue, even though it seems unlikely he'd see anything, since the cemetery is vast, holding over half a million graves. None of the other grave diggers or groundsmen recalled anything out of the ordinary. What these men witnessed every day was a procession of black-clad mourners moving slowly across the cemetery, transient figures less permanent than the landscape of gravestones, which they'd memorized.

Franz looked through the cemetery register and established
that neither Dora's family nor the Zellenkas had visited her
grave during the last seven days. He carefully copied down the
names of mourners who had paid respects to loved ones near
Dora's grave, and the Inspector allowed him to conduct the interviews alone. Franz wondered if he knew how difficult these
interrogations would be, since the mourners were immediately
suspicious of his motives, even when he asked the vaguest
questions about the appearance of the grave and other visitors
they may have noticed in the cemetery. The Viennese have a
fetishistic regard for a beautiful corpse, *schöne Leiche,* and an
elaborate funeral.

Wally's glass of coffee slips out of her hand and thunks onto
the metal café table. Someone had stroked her shoulder. She
looks up to see the *Mehlspeisköchin* from Dora's house looming
over her.

"You're here."

When the pastry cook drops down into her chair across
from Wally, the great circle of the *Riesenrad,* the Ferris wheel, is
positioned just behind her head like an iron nimbus. Wally is
touched by what must be the woman's best clothes, a clean
apron tied over a thick, full skirt, an embroidered kerchief over
her head. She is unable to associate her clothing with any particular country.

"This is my first visit to the Volksprater," Wally says.

"Yes? Then you must let me show you around after our
coffee." The woman's loud voice puts Wally on edge. "I know
where to find the Cartesian Diver who tells fortunes. Although
I'm certain I can do just as well. Over at Calafatti's there's a
great Chinaman. Taller than Chang the giant."

Wally's father had told her about a giant and showed her
a grainy picture in a magazine. After she pleaded, he took her
to the fair and balanced her on his shoulders so she could see
the freak on the stage. Wally watched the giant stand and
stretch, his head and hands disappointingly tiny above the
crowd. The noise here in the Volksprater is the same noise she

remembers from the fair in London. It makes her unsettled. She brings her attention back to the cook.

"You make desserts for Dora's family?"

The *Mehlspeiskōchin* nods. "Only desserts. They've kept me on so long because of my torten and *Strudel mit Röster*. I don't share these recipes with others. I know how to keep secrets. My ladies tell me sugar and butter embrace in the bowl when I mix them."

She proudly hands Wally a small square package covered with oiled paper. Wally solemnly unwraps it. Cake. She thanks her, and the woman seems disappointed Wally doesn't devour it in front of her.

"In Bohemia, before I came to Vienna, I cooked for an important family. The father was a colonel in the army. The horse he bought for his wife was an angel to ride but an evil-tempered beast who bit anyone who came near him. He nearly took the arm off the stable boy. One day, the colonel came into the kitchen just as I took a roast leg of lamb out of the oven. Without even asking, he picked up the meat in his gloved hands, marched out of the room with it. I followed him, and what do you think he did?"

She stares at Wally, folding her muscled arms across her chest. Her skin has the opaque whiteness possessed by some blondes, blue veins turning to green, wired near the surface of her thick flesh. Wally shakes her head, puzzled.

She continues. "In the stable, the colonel stood in front of the horse, waving the hot leg of lamb. The horse attacks, sinks its teeth into the meat, burns its mouth." She closes her eyes and throws her head back to laugh. "He broke the horse of its bad habit. He was as gentle as a lamb after that. But I never cooked meat again."

Her story has made Wally shy. She busies herself with her coffee. "You know I was a friend of Dora's. That's why I was visiting the house."

"Terrible what happened to her. God rest her soul."

"Yes. Did you know Dora very well?"

The woman shakes her head, no. Wally gently touches her on the wrist to gain her confidence, keep her talking.

"Dora kept out of the kitchen. She couldn't cook, not at

all. She and her mother argued about it. Dora said she'd rather play the piano and she did. Then her brother complained it was too loud, he couldn't study. So her father took the piano away. Didn't tell her, just had it moved out one day."

"What did Dora do?"

"Don't know. I wasn't in their kitchen for two weeks. But when I went back to the house, everything seemed the same. Her mother was cleaning like she always did, all day, every day. She could never leave anything alone. She'd lock her husband's study and the dining room after dinner, so no one could enter after she'd cleaned. She locked the boy into his room at night. She kept all the keys."

"What about the gentleman who spent a lot of time with Dora? She was always talking about him." Wally holds her breath, hoping the woman will recognize her description of the mysterious Herr K.

The *Mehlspeisköchin* stops turning her spoon in her coffee. It's a meditation for her, a reflex, like stirring cake batter. Her hands are always moving. "A gentleman friend of Dora's? I don't know who that could be."

"He's married. His wife was also a friend of Dora's. I forget their name."

"Must be Herr Zellenka and his wife. Now, they're quite a couple."

"Yes, that's what Dora said. She seemed fond of them. Don't they live in Währing?" She doesn't look up, knowing the woman will read the uncertainty in her eyes.

"No. They have a house in Döbling. They have money. I baked for them once, although they argued about my fee. They took Dora on vacations. Went to spas for their health. But I'm not surprised calamity fell on her family."

"Why?"

"You were friends with Dora, but she didn't tell you much, did she?"

The woman's shrewdness shocks Wally like a slap.

Smiling hugely, the *Mehlspeisköchin* leans back in her chair, her heavy body nearly tipping it over. She lifts up her arms and slowly takes off her kerchief, revealing braids of white blond hair coiled around her head. She spreads the kerchief on the table and forces Wally's hand down on top of it. She lays her hands over Wally's.

Startled, Wally can't speak for a moment, her language scattered, lost. "There are things I could tell you. Dora's father has a curse on him. He has syphilis and he gave it to his wife. Dora thought she had it, too, passed along in the blood, father to daughter. All of them saw doctors, all the time. And the trouble I'd take to please those invalids with my baking. One doctor told them to purge and eat no sweets. I thought it was the end of my time in their house."

The *Mehlspeisköchin* has the physical confidence of a masseuse. She twists Wally's hand around. "Let me read your palm."

Wally's hand is roughly kneaded and stroked. She watches the *Riesenrad* turn, trying to distract herself from the woman's aggressive fingers. The sharp point of a fingernail is drawn across her palm.

"The lines here, furrows at the joint of the thumb, could mean an unhappy marriage, illness, or premature death."

"I didn't ask you to do this."

"I saw something else in your hand that could help us understand each other."

Wally jerks her hand away.

The canvas awning flaps over their heads. Faint music shivers across the park from a small group of string players and a cimbalom on the bandstand. The crowd watching a marionette show roars with laughter.

Wally stands up and drops coins on the table, trying to calm herself. The *Mehlspeisköchin* squints up at her.

"Think over what I've said, Fräulein."

Wally walks away. Later, she remembered she'd forgotten to ask the woman about Rosza and whether there is a fig tree in Dora's garden.

It grows dark as Wally wanders aimlessly through the park. She watches several young men test their strength against a machine that jolts them with electric shocks when it

is touched. One of the men falls and doesn't stand up for a moment. Suddenly, thousands of tiny lights blink on all across the
fairgrounds, an uncanny illumination that mimics daylight but
produces shadows the sun could never cast.

The Volksprater stays open until the early hours of the
morning, and she takes the last ride on the Ferris wheel, imagining she'll see the sun rising before the rest of the city from its
great height.

Dora's mutilated corpse was taken from the cemetery and laid
on a table in the morgue. The Inspector can hardly bear to uncover her neck or the rest of her body, afraid of what he might
find there. The smell is terrible, as intense and choking as a
hand pressed on his throat. Franz is also affected, and avoids
looking at the dead girl. He stares at the Inspector, for his
hands are shaking as he pulls the dirty cloth off her bloated
corpse. Under the harsh lights over the table, they find no suspicious marks or outrages on her body, nothing but the damage
that decomposition has accomplished. The veins near the surface of her skin are clearly visible, an intricately forked brown
network that the pathologist identifies as an arborescent pattern, a natural sign of putrefaction.

After finishing the examination, the Inspector wishes
that closing the door of the morgue would erase what his eyes
have seen. The image of the body's spoiling, swollen flesh, the
dark colors that appear to have been pressed out of its skin —
blue red green and dark brown — have been seeded into his
mind. Sometime in the future, a smell, a glimpse of a certain
color or shape, will bring Dora's corpse back to him, blooming
unbidden in his memory.

Egon is in the morgue to photograph Dora's violated corpse.
Her body is completely covered by a thick cloth, which doesn't
disguise its altered shape, the enlarged abdomen and limbs.

The coldness of the room and the intense, unpleasant odor make him work quickly.

He drops a handkerchief on top of the body, then ducks behind the camera to focus the lens on it. In a muffled voice, he calls Franz to hurry and help him. He caps the lens and waits impatiently, covering his nose with his hand.

In the corner, Franz hastily puts on a white jacket and rolls rubber gloves up over his arms. As he crosses the room, he vows to immediately forget whatever he'll see when the cloth is lifted off the body. He will have a stare of blankness, nothing will register, there will be a wall of white when he tries to rec-ollect it. Before touching the corpse, he disassociates his hands from their movements. He gropes underneath the cloth and pulls out an arm, its skin colder than the air in the room. The limb twists easily in his trembling fingers, and he maneuvers it so the black hole on the swollen hand points up, right into the hard eye of the camera. The instant he releases the arm, he struggles to forget the way the flesh felt under his fingers.

"Now I need you to light the powders. You'll find the al-lumettes in my satchel."

Franz positions the dish of lightning powder on the stand parallel to the camera. He ignites an allumette, touches it to the powder, and it explodes into flame so terrifyingly fast that he jumps back, knocking the fire over onto Dora's body. Panicked, he swats at the burning cloth, feeling the corpse soft under his hands, the smell of the gases from the body indescribable.

Egon had served as an apprentice to Monsieur Bellieni, an eld-erly French photographer who had been exiled by the Com-mune. He taught Egon an old-fashioned system of lighting. To illuminate a room for a photograph, several small gas lamps were burned, and the exposure would last for several hours. For portraits and darker interiors, volatile lightning powders were used. It took one pound of magnesium powder to create enough light to photograph a ballroom, and buckets of water were placed around the floor in case of fire.

It was Egon's task to measure and sift the lightning powders — chlorate of potash, sulphurate antimony, gunpowder, pyroxylin, and magnesium. Sometimes crushed white sugar was burned with potash, or magnesium powder was sprinkled on guncotton. The powders were ill smelling, poisonous, and their transformation into heat and scorching light was fierce and unpredictable. Although he worked for Monsieur Bellieni for several years, he was always terrified of the explosive powders.

Monsieur would wave his hand to indicate when Egon should light the powders. He watched closely for the photographer's slightest gesture, his hands poised over the powder, every muscle tense, ready to strike fire. It was a dangerous, split-second maneuver.

Once Monsieur was engaged to do a portrait by a beautiful woman. She wasn't an actress or an opera singer, just a woman who wanted a picture of herself, perhaps a gift to a lover.

She undressed in front of the camera, her back modestly turned. Egon watched. He didn't move to prepare the lightning powders, even when Monsieur was already crouched behind the camera. Then the woman pulled the pins from her hair, and it fell over her bare shoulders down to her waist, breaking the spell.

Monsieur's head surfaced from under the cloth. *Allez,* get the materials ready, what's the matter, he shouted. Shamed, Egon quickly brought the powders, careful not to look at the woman.

Prepare yourself, boy. *Mademoiselle,* are you comfortable?

Monsieur raised his hand, and Egon struck the allumette. At that instant, he dared to glance up at the woman. Perhaps the flame in his hand had given him courage. She smiled directly at him, stood up, and swept her hair off her naked body. Paralyzed at this vision, Egon didn't pull his hand away as the powder ignited, and the greenish light and simultaneous explosion took away his fingers.

Years later, a man at a dinner noticed Egon's mutilated hand and asked him if he knew the Greek legend of Creüsa, a

princess of Corinth. It's about a body burning, he said. When
Egon shook his head, no, he'd never heard the story, the man
told him vengeful Medea had sent her rival, the innocent
Creüsa, a gift of a beautiful robe. Flattered, Creüsa put on the
robe, and it instantly burst into flames, burning her alive.

Egon began to collect these stories.

He learned Charles VI of France was nearly annihilated
in the same way at a fancy dress ball. The king and four of
his equerries were identically dressed as *hommes sauvages* in
shaggy costumes made of grass. While the king and his equerries danced, the duc d'Orléans accidentally touched one of
them with a torch, and the flames leaped from one man to another. The duchesse du Berry somehow recognized the king
and threw her mantle over him, saving his life. The rest of the
men all burned to death.

The Inspector decides to rebury Dora in the same grave. The
night before she is reinterred in the Zentralfriedhof, he takes
certain precautions so her body won't be disturbed a second
time.

He slips into the morgue and locks the door behind him.
Dora's coffin rests on a table, a dull and solid box. He's still
wet from the rain outside, and as he walks across the room,
the air chills his damp skin, making him suddenly conscious
of his bare hands, as if they had become luminous, swollen,
hugely conspicuous in guilty anticipation of their grim task.
He quickly opens the lid of the coffin, and a stench envelops him as he pulls at the shroud covering Dora's corpse.
He roughly jams a small tin plate under the fabric and works
it down her body until it rests over her swollen stomach.
He takes a long steel needle from his pocket and forces it
into the place he thinks is above her heart. These two precautions — the needle and the plate — will keep Dora quiet in her
grave.

He learned these apotropaic methods from his wife, although he doesn't plan to tell her what he's done. He also

hasn't told her about the discovery of Dora's mutilated corpse. He's puzzled about why he keeps these secrets. Perhaps because Erszébet will always turn to an otherworldly cause to explain an inexplicable event. At this time, his mind can't hold such a speculation.

Later he slips the grave diggers and a priest money to recite prayers over Dora's fresh grave. And a little extra to buy their silence.

A thumb is cut off the hand of a corpse. What is the significance of this act? There is a superstition that revenants can be identified by something extraordinary about their appearance; their middle fingers are missing, or they have the hands and feet of an animal. Was this an attempt at a metamorphosis of the girl's body? What else could provoke such a hostile act? A ritual? Revenge? Revenge for an unknown wrong by an unknown party. Someone in Dora's family, or a friend? A lover? Is it a crime a woman would commit? Could someone acting alone open a grave and disturb a corpse?

He tries to hold the facts about the murder in an order, with no judgment attached to them. In his investigative work, there is always the temptation to organize, to rush to a decision, to collapse the wait. Not to listen.

When Franz first came to work as his assistant, the Inspector knew he believed crimes were solved by a mysterious process, almost a divination. No, he told him, it's methodical, like putting together a jigsaw puzzle. You see a color or a pattern on one piece that matches something else you have seen. Or you notice a blank shape on the puzzle board and it's vaguely familiar, then you suddenly recognize its match. Listening and observation. It's not a mystical operation like falling in love, he said, smiling at Franz's embarrassment.

He asks Franz to read a certain page aloud from the *Kriminalistik* book, where the dangers of the investigative process are presented.

When he starts work, the most important thing for the Investigating Officer is to discover the exact moment when he
can form a definite opinion. The importance of this cannot
be too much insisted upon, for upon it success or failure often depends. If he should come to a definite conclusion too
soon, a preconceived opinion may be formed, to which he
will always be attached with more or less tenacity till he is
forced to abandon it entirely: by then his most precious moments will have passed away, the best clues will have been
lost — often beyond the possibility of recovery. If on the
other hand he misses the true moment for forming an opinion, the inquiry becomes a purposeless groping in the dark
and a search devoid of aim. When will the Investigating Officer find this true moment, this psychological instant, of
which we speak?

It is nearly dark when Wally finds Herr Zellenka's house in
Döbling and walks around to the walled garden in back. She
wears men's clothing, gloves, and a flat cap, borrowed from her
employer. She rummaged through his wardrobe, taking what
suited her. She's a hunter and gatherer. She has an electric
torch, scissors, and pockets emptied to hold leaves from the fig
tree.

Slowed by the man's unfamiliar boots, she clumsily
wedges her feet against the thick vines woven over the wall and
pulls herself up. The cold air is sharp, she feels it tunneling into
her nostrils and flattening her cheeks. There is faint moonlight,
not enough to make deep shadow. On top of the wall, she
crouches and peers down, checking for obstacles below. The
garden is a flat silver dimness, punctuated by the feathery gray
outlines of the shrubbery and the darker mute shapes of the
trees. She jumps, and the plummet lasts for a long count, as if
there is a greater distance to the ground on the other side of
the wall. She lands on her feet, then the palms of her hands are
forced into the dirt as she falls forward.

For a moment, she waits without moving to gauge direction, squinting at the foliage. But the bare branches are too black to read, an army of thick spears against the sky. She's afraid to use the torch in this place. She proceeds cautiously into the garden, an arm outstretched in front of her like a blind man's stick.

She stops, snaps on her torch and spirals its beam up through branches, transforming a tree with this sudden light, giving it the silhouette of a candelabrum. Then she directs the light to the trunks of other trees, hoping to identify the fig by its rough bark, which she's memorized like a pattern of embroidery. The darkness is even more oppressive when she turns off the torch.

There's no wind, no sound but her footsteps as she moves through tall dry grasses and drier leaves, stepping as cautiously as if she maneuvered a long skirt. She finds a tree that seems to have the fig's curious knobbed growth. She rummages on the ground below it and finds a leaf. When she holds it up between her face and the sky, the leaf is pointed where it should be rounded and it is as gray as her hand. She lets it fall. This seems hopeless, she thinks. She wishes the fig tree had an odor that would pull her to it, an invisible trail for her nose. She imagines its scent would be as intensely sweet as honeysuckle or *Viburnum carlesi,* with its clovelike perfume and clusters of tiny flowers, dense and white as salt.

She looked over the wall into the garden a few days earlier, so she guesses she's now closer to the house. A parterre is before her, smooth areas of grass boxed in by broken lines of shrubbery, and in this light they appear to be a series of bare rooms, the roofless ruins of a building.

She skirts around the parterre, nervous about being so exposed, staying under the trees at its edge. She comes to a thick hedge, an *arborvitae* taller than her head, and pulls her hand over the clipped ends of its surface as she walks along it, imagining it's a labyrinth. When the hedge ends, she heads into a knoll of trees.

Less cautious now, she sweeps torchlight over the area, searching for the fig or perhaps the dark mound that indicates where it is buried in the earth. She remembers that the Egyp-

tians made sarcophagi from fig wood, gilding the blind eyes
carved on the lids.

Her light unveils an upraised white arm, stone drapery,
and then the rest of a statue against a wall. A nymph, Syrinx.
There's an urn trailing ivy. Rosebushes are carved out of the
dark by her torch, still holding a clutch of startled white petals.
She uncovers a pattern of leaves, their surface replaced by
deeper shadows as the wind stirs them. Then the wind stops,
and there's a strange waiting silence. She moves forward cautiously. Her light trolls across a row of trees, and there's a
minute flash, a point of silver, which instantly vanishes.

A noise from the place where her light was.

She clicks off the torch. She waits. Something or someone in the garden is focused on her, trying to pick up the thread
of her passage. The sound of slow footsteps opens a place of
dry fear. She's suspended between listening and obeying an interior crimson signal that commands her to flee.

Her back pushes into the *arborvitae,* sharp points against
her skin, but there's no pain. She swings the torch in front of
her, its light finds a man, his strange face as sharp as a painted
image. He flinches. His reaction gives her a moment to run.
Her sense of time is detached, and she thinks she's moving in
slow motion, passing straight along the hedge and around it.
He's at the end of the hedge, running after her. She ducks behind a tree and waits. She's aware of the tree's rough bark
against her shoulder as the pounding of her heart shakes her
body. The garden is silent.

A long stretch of time passes, or perhaps only seconds.
She moves around the tree, her footsteps imperceptible as she
creeps forward, stops, and suddenly hurls the torch. It crashes
behind a bench, the noise amplified by the dark. Everything is
suddenly in motion as the man runs to the bench, believing
she's there. It takes him a moment to go back around it, and by
then she has raced ahead.

She swerves around a tree, some low shrubs, blindly will-
ing her body forward. Panic has erased her sense of direction.
Trees move in front of her; she can hardly dodge around them
and then she vaguely realizes the trees are stationary and she's

running at them. She's conscious of passing through the parterre only by the absence of shadow, a different quality of darkness. The wall is suddenly in front of her. She slams into it, claws at the vines, hauling her body up. She thinks of the man in the garden. Now she understands the gleam of silver her torch picked out. His nose is a cone of metal strapped around his head.

She jumps off the wall, possessed by his image.

CHAPTER 6

RAU ZELLENKA OPENS THE
door and introduces herself to the Inspector.
The pattern of her dress strikes him first, a
brilliant print of huge, unrecognizable flowers. A necklace of heavy amber beads rests
precisely around her neck. She doesn't
smile, but studies him as gravely as if he knelt at her feet, then
silently takes his hat and walking stick. He wonders about the
absence of a maid.

He follows her down the hallway, slowing his steps over
the patterned Turkey carpets on the floor, his admiring eyes
tripped by the maze of lines. I see you enjoy my carpets, she
says without turning around. She raises her voice to an unseen
maid, Fräulein Yella, requesting her to bring them coffee.

The Biedermeier furniture in the drawing room is uphol-
stered in striped fabric, so when she positions herself on the
sofa, its stark geometry is a startling background for her flow-
ered dress. She makes herself part of the composition.

He'd sent a boy with the letter arranging their meeting,
since few homes are equipped with telephones. However, there
is a telephone here, and now he is surprised by its strange, unfamiliar ring. Footsteps and a quiet voice silence it. He wonders if his office has called him here, and it seems miraculous
to be invisibly tracked and found across the space of the city.

Egon had told him how messages were sent in Paris during the war in 1871, when the Germans occupied the city. He

once worked with the photographer who engineered the airborne postal system. Anyone who had a letter to post brought it to the photographer's studio. There, the letters — secret, urgent, and even ordinary — were glued end to end into a single huge sheet, which was then photographed. In the darkroom, the image was reduced to a print of several square centimeters, rolled up inside a quill, and attached to a homing pigeon.

After the bird delivered the miniature photograph, it was inserted in a magic lantern machine and projected on a white wall. At dusk, a crowd gathered in front of the luminous square to read the letters.

In those days, the photographer had explained to Egon, the skies were full of secrets.

Frau Zellenka begins the interview. "You're here to talk about Dora."

"Yes. You've no need to feel concerned. Everyone has been asked the same questions."

"I'm neither frightened nor offended. Do you smoke?"

The lighting of cigarettes takes some minutes. There is a beautiful glass dish on the table for the ashes. As the maid sets out coffee from a tray, Frau Zellenka languidly leans back to inhale her cigarette, tucking her legs up under her. She's bored, and this irritates him. He reminds himself that she's reacting to his mode of investigation, not to him personally. *The Investigating Officer must compel himself to be sincere even to the limit of pedantry, impenetrable by any shock.*

He launches his first question, unconsciously hoping to unsettle her.

"Where were you when Dora was murdered?"

"If she was killed in the evening, I was at home. I imagine my husband told you he was out."

The Inspector doesn't answer, but keeps his unblinking eyes on her as he fishes for his notebook in his jacket pocket. I understand you were very close friends with Dora, he says.

She nods, continues smoking.

Most people's comments about the deceased tend to be embroidered. As he waits for the inevitable recital of praise, his shoulders sag with expectation. She coughs sharply, her cigarette leaving a sketch of smoke around her hand. He understands this is her answer. She waits him out.

Very well. He tries again. "I'm curious about whether you'd noticed anything unusual about Dora's behavior right before she died?"

"It's hard to pinpoint what I truly remember after all this time. In retrospect, everything about Dora seems significant. But I'm certain you find this every day in your work?"

He ignores her question. He'll circle around the information in another way. This is fair.

"Did Dora have any suitors?"

"No. I'm certain of that. She confessed everything to me."

"When did you see her for the last time?"

"A week before she died. We were shopping on the Graben. She was looking for a particular book. I don't remember what it was."

"Nothing struck you about her mood?"

"Dora was always in a mood. She didn't enjoy good health and she wasn't patient about it. When she hadn't lost her voice, she complained constantly."

Frau Zellenka surprises him. He expected her to be more emotional, marooned in shock at her friend's death. Perhaps even tearful. She's very matter-of-fact.

"How did you spend your time together?"

"We'd often play with my children. When Dora couldn't speak, she made it into a game, a pantomime. Sometimes she'd fix my hair, or try on my clothes. I don't know if this is any help to you."

"I really can't say."

He looks down at his notebook, trying to graft the dead girl onto this picture that she has just presented to him. No one has given him an image of Dora experiencing pleasure. The woman sitting across from him is silent too.

There's a moment of almost solemn tenderness as they look at each other. The smoke from their cigarettes lazily changes direction when she abruptly bends forward, recrossing her legs. This time, she couldn't bear the silence.

When he queries her about Rosza, her voice becomes curt.

"She's a troubled woman. I was glad when they got rid of her. She wasn't a good influence on Dora."

"Why, exactly? What did she do?"

"Rosza did certain things I didn't approve of. She allowed Dora to read *The Physiology of Love*. Mantegazza described gross indecencies about the body. I couldn't tell her mother she was reading about such things, it would have betrayed Dora's trust in me. But I know Dora told her mother about Mantegazza's book when it suited her."

She's angry now. Careful not to break the mood, the Inspector mumbles an acknowledgment and keeps writing.

"Yes, go ahead. You can put all this down. Dora wanted to get rid of Rosza. She was jealous of her. Dora finally realized the stupid woman had befriended her just to get closer to her father. Rosza was in love with Philipp. But the woman got what she deserved." Agitated, she toys with her necklace. The heavy beads slide together with a dull click. "I don't know exactly why Rosza was dismissed. I can't tell you anything more about that woman."

He's one step behind, describing Frau Zellenka's angry words, her shift of mood in his notebook. I have you here, *Madame,* he thinks, and wrenches his eyes back to her.

"So, who murdered Dora?"

She thinks for a moment.

"Dora had a strange knack for getting under your skin. She irritated people, but enough to be killed? No, it's too peculiar. It could only have been a stranger who murdered her."

"I see. Tell me who works in your house."

"A woman comes to clean and cook. She's been with us for years. My boy is away at school. As you've probably learned, my daughter died this summer."

"Yes, I was told."

She shrugs and puts out her cigarette. Her other hand idly plays with her earring.

His pen waits.

"This is a large house. No one else works here?"

"My husband has a driver. He helps around the house, does odd jobs, some gardening. His name is Jószef, a Gypsy."

She's thinking of something else. He tries to follow into

her labyrinth of thought. Pick up the string, he thinks, *help me*.
He summons a terrible energy, directs it at her. Waits. Lets it go.

She smiles and shrugs. The moment has passed.

"This is a busy time for me. If you don't mind?"

She takes him to the door, still friendly, but he knows she
ended the interview some time earlier. She takes his hat from
the maid, and the sleeve of her dress slides back, revealing the
Cartier watch on her wrist. The instant he sees it, he has a cold
sense of recognition, although it takes a further effort, a shiver
of memory, to bring the image into mind. A pale, bare arm bent
over a motionless face. Dora. Frau Zellenka's watch is identical
to the watch he cut off Dora's wrist. A pretty thing.

He makes a comment about the watch; she thanks him
for the compliment. He hesitates, uncertain about whether to
question her further, but she anticipates him, drawing him into
a parody of normal conversation. Yes, my watch was a gift.
From my husband. I asked him to purchase one for Dora too,
in honor of our friendship. Her expression is mocking.

After she closes the door, he walks around the house to
look for Jószef. The garden in back is laid out as precisely as the
interior of the house. From the terrace, he has a view of a series
of formal bosquets outlined by low shrubs. There are a few
statues, ornamental columns, and dwarf fruit trees, a monkey
puzzle, exotic palms. At night, without the sun to strike it into
color, he imagines it must appear to be an artificial replica of a
garden, fashioned from stone.

He walks along a hedge trimmed to a shape taller than
his head. He drags the palm of his outstretched hand against
the clipped ends of the branches. The sharp scratches revive
him.

Turning the corner of the hedge, he casually glances back
at the house, where Frau Zellenka stands watching at the window, her loose dress draped like a shroud around her.

Several yards away, there's an opening cut into the hedge.
He goes through it into a long narrow room, four green walls
around a rose bed. He recognizes *R. hugonis,* the Golden Rose
of China, tall stems with withered bronze orange leaves and
discolored buds caught by frost.

The odor of broken earth reaches him before he hears the

thick stab of a shovel. He follows the sound, quietly tracing his footsteps back out of the hedge.

In the orchard at the end of the garden, a man stands next to a hole, waiting for him. Like a priest at a burial.

"You're Jószef?"

The man nods.

The garden, the smell, the man's body angled over the empty plot in the earth, all vanish. The Inspector sees only Jószef's face. There's a piece of silver bent over his nose, held in place with a strap around his head.

The Inspector chose not to confront Frau Zellenka about her relationship with Philipp. He had intended to, but once he was face-to-face with the woman, he decided against it. He'd taken her measure. Her affair with Dora's father is valuable coin to spend at a later date. He'll see her again. He anticipates the pleasure of setting a trap for her, then watching her cold struggle not to react. *You were intimate friends with the daughter of your lover?*

He wonders why Frau Zellenka wasn't murdered instead of Dora. How did Philipp hold all these women together? Daughter, lover, wife. He stages an imaginary scene of the three women standing together, still as statues, while he walks around them, trying to decipher their relationship. Could Frau Zellenka have encouraged the girl as a way to strike at her mother? Was Dora's intimacy with her a revenge against her mother? Or a perverse identification with her father? And did Dora's mother recognize her isolation in this family triangle and blame her daughter? Was any of this reason enough that either woman would want to murder Dora?

The Inspector tells Franz about Jószef, the man with the silver nose. Franz's astonished grin fades when he sees the grim expression on his face.

"But why would the man wear such a thing?"

He shrugs. "Maybe syphilis ate his nose. Archduke Otto was disfigured in the same way. He wore a leather nose that was painted skin color for the last ten years of his life."

"Sometimes syphilis affects the brain, doesn't it?"

"Yes, it can."

"Maybe Jószef is deranged from syphilis? Maybe he killed Dora?"

But the Inspector has his own reasons to retreat from the conversation and doesn't pick up his suggestion.

"So Jószef did know Dora?"

"Apparently, since she was frequently a guest at the Zellenkas' home."

The Inspector turns back to his papers. Franz is dismissed.

That night, the Inspector thinks about dirt. The loose dirt scattered over Dora's grave. The dirt turned over in Frau Zellenka's garden by Jószef. Uneasy, he goes to bed late and sleeps heavily.

In the morning, he remembers a dream that was an image of flatness, heaviness, a dark, unplowed field cleared of plants. All that day, the image of the dream haunts him.

Later, it is replaced by a sensation that seems to be part of his body's sightless memory, for it has no image. He remembers his mouth and body were filled with earth, and it was a comforting, familiar feeling, like sinking into the embrace of thick water.

Walking along the Ringstrasse a few days earlier, their hands secretly touching, Erszébet had explained that perfume and some wines are like an incantation, a magical phrase, an *olvasás*. You can sense an intent, a calculation behind them. Do you understand what I mean? she asked him. No, he didn't understand her at the time. But now he believes he does. His dream had that same quality. He received it with a jolt of recognition — as if someone had sent it to him.

Now when he thinks of his dream he finds his eyes are wet.

Wally's eyes fill with a line of burning light. Everything else is dark. There is a smell of damp dirt, of something sweet, fruitish. She's confined in a narrow place. Sensing something above her, she reaches up to touch leaves. It takes a moment before memory returns. She fled from the man with the silver nose into a neighboring garden. She now reclines in a makeshift shed built around a fruit tree, its winter protection. Her back is against the tree, and when she shifts her weight, its branches scrape against the walls. She freezes, afraid the man will hear her. Nothing moves, no sound from outside. The light in front of her shapes itself into a thin rectangle. A door. She kicks it, and the door swings open on the garden and sunlight, a safe and bright radiance, dazzling after the dark.

She makes her way back into the city, walking confidently as part of her male impersonation. She kicks at something on the cobblestones, just to experience the swinging movement of her legs. She's free, reincarnated as a boy on the street. As if she'd suddenly stepped into a parallel existence.

When a woman selling flowers from a basket calls to her, *Hey boy,* she fiercely shakes her head, leveling her exhilaration. Just to see what will happen, she runs blindly across the Naschmarkt into the dense traffic of horses and carts. A wagon swerves aside, just missing her. The driver shouts at her in anger, not recognition.

She undresses back in her room. The man's rough wool pants leave a blur of red skin on the insides of her legs.

Erszébet ordered a *vadliba,* a wild goose, from a woman at a stall in the Hoher Markt and had it killed exactly two days later. At home in the kitchen, she nervously unwrapped the plucked, cut-up goose and examined its breast meat, which was light in color. She interpreted this to mean snow would soon fall, ending their search for the fig tree. There is a precise beauty about this method of divination, signs read in the flesh.

She cooks the goose and serves it, the dinner a vehicle for this prophecy.

Her husband enjoyed the roast goose, the thin *rétes* filled with cabbage sauteed with pepper and caramelized sugar. She saved the breast bone of the goose for use in later divinations. She knows the time between Christmas and New Year is dangerous, a string of days and hours with significant prohibitions.

That night, before going to bed, she scans the sky outside the window, expecting the first flakes of snow. She can abandon the fig tree to its white cover, since she has confidence in the other facts she knows about Dora's murder, the secret advance of her search.

As if cued by her thoughts, her husband speaks from the bed.

"You've been very secretive. Are you making progress?"

Fear pushes her head around to look at him.

"How are your watercolors?"

She laughs with relief. "What put you in mind of my painting?"

"The way you're watching the landscape."

I see, she says. *My observations are as keen as yours, only different,* she thinks.

Wally sits with Dora's mother in her drawing room. This time when she entered the house, she'd noticed how immaculate it was. The furniture stands like an intrusion on the shining waxed floors. The lamps, draperies, and Oriental carpets are insignificant things against the order this woman has imposed on her house. Wally senses there is an uncompromising system of rules — almost a haunting — that permeates all the rooms stacked above her.

Dora's mother is crying noisily into a handkerchief. Her clothing creaks slightly as she leans forward, her stiff silk dress rubbing against her corset. They're side by side on the sofa, so close the folds of their skirts crease over each other. She has just given Wally a pair of earrings, tiny pearl drops, which belonged to Dora. A memento of what she fondly believes was her daughter's intimate friendship with Wally.

Wally is thrilled and dismayed by the gift. She stares at the earrings in the palm of her hand, fighting the impulse to give them back or toss them away, the confused reverberations of her guilt. The pearls should burn her fingers, reveal her imposture.

While crossing Währinger Strasse near the Votivkirche, Erszébet told her how a witch, a *boszorkány,* is discovered. The first egg of a black hen is dyed, hidden in a pocket, and carried to church on Easter Sunday. Sensing the terrible invisible pressure of this magical object, a witch is unable to enter the holy church.

Wally slips the earrings into her pocket. Nothing happens. The objects are mute.

She puts her hand on the woman's arm, whispers her gratitude. After a short time, Dora's mother is composed enough to speak.

"I still blame myself for what happened to Dora. I shouldn't have let her go out alone."

"You didn't know what would happen."

She continues as if she hadn't heard Wally. "Dora would plead with me to let her leave the house. She'd say, I'm old enough, I'm a grown woman. If I'd say no to her, she'd get her father's permission. Or she would just leave without asking."

Wally patiently tries again. "So Dora did go out alone. She'd done it before that last night?"

"Yes. It's true she had," she whispers.

"Did Dora usually go to any particular place, a café?"

The question makes the woman angry. Wally feels her body tense, and she withdraws her hand.

"I don't know. Ask Rosza, the governess. My husband paid her to work here, but Dora thought she was her friend. They'd go to the cafés and parks together. I don't know which ones."

"Rosza didn't act like a governess?"

"No. They'd be in Dora's room, laughing and talking, and I could hear them. If I knocked on the door, they'd stop.

They pretended I didn't know they were there. That calculating woman. I'm sure it was her doing. Rosza knew I didn't like her."

Even before her next sentence, Wally anticipates her words, their dark weight.

"We went on a vacation with the Zellenkas. To a lake in the Alps. And Rosza came with us as company for Dora and her brother. I remember Frau Zellenka and I had walked to a fountain where you could drink the sulphur water. I came back to the hotel early with my boy and I heard her, she was in her room with Herr Zellenka."

"Dora was?"

"Dora? No, no, Rosza was in the room with Herr Zellenka. What I heard was . . . I heard vulgar, intimate noises."

Wally imagines the woman's bulky silhouette crouched outside a door in a hotel corridor, listening. She falls so completely into this vivid picture she's surprised when her angry voice pulls her back into the room.

"I'm not well. You should go now."

"Where can I find Rosza? I need to speak with her."

But Dora's mother has finished their conversation. Wally reluctantly stands to leave. Her eyes follow the row of tiny silk buttons on the woman's dress that dully reflect light, black-on-black points outlining her body. Her hand is a plump fist over her handkerchief.

"I'll see myself out." She waits, but Dora's mother is too distracted to answer before she leaves the room.

Wally peers into the kitchen. The *Mehlspeisköchin* turns from the stove, motions to the table set with two plates and cups. The woman is dressed for working in this hot room, her big body streamlined by a kerchief over her head and a white apron. She regally moves inside this zone of heat as if it were her tropical kingdom, an island with a different climate and atmosphere than the rest of the house. She lays out a plate of chocolate-covered *Indianer* cakes filled with whipped cream. Wally slips into a chair, glad of the offer of coffee. They eat in silence for a moment.

"What kind of dessert did Dora like? Did you ever bake anything with figs for her?"

The pastry cook dabs cream from her lips with a corner of her apron.

"Never. No figs, no fruit, no chocolate. Dora and Fräulein Rosza both scorned my baking. Wouldn't touch my desserts. They were too common for them."

Wally shakes her head sympathetically and waits through the cook's anger. She watches her lift a large forkful of cake to her mouth. "What else did Rosza do?"

"I don't know if I should tell you about Rosza. Your delicate ears."

"Don't be concerned about me. I haven't lived with my parents since I was twelve. I'm eighteen years old."

"You're eighteen? You don't look it."

Wally still wears her long hair down in the English style instead of pinning it up like the Viennese women. "It must have been difficult for you to work here with that woman. I'm so curious about her. One of the governesses in the Volksgarten told me Rosza had trouble with men. You don't have to protect her. And Dora is dead. She wasn't *schöne Leiche.*"

As if she had received Wally's vision of Dora — a lone figure, a mocking offering sprawled before the statue of the Empress Elizabeth, who was reviled for rejecting her husband's love — the cook relents.

"I'll tell you Rosza was never kind to me. She was wicked. A wicked woman. She wasn't fit company for a young lady. I'd told Dora's mother about her, but she ignored me, fine lady that she is. But she found I was right. She sent Rosza away."

"Why?"

The cook's eyes are naked with grief. "Rosza is an angel maker, an *angyalcsináló.*"

Wally's silence is genuine.

"She could fix you if you were going to have a baby."

The Inspector has become busy with a strange case that hinges on the identification of a few stray hairs. It is a peculiar and unsavory story. A very blond servant girl was accused of an illegal act with a dog. The hysterical girl claimed the straight black hairs found on her pubic area were fibers from her skirt, which was heavy dark cotton.

He suspects the servant girl's employer is somehow connected with the incident. The case has no merit; there is no victim. He refuses to send any men to search for the accused dog.

After a protracted exchange of letters with an *Untersuchungsrichter,* an examining judge, he reluctantly sends the black hairs removed from the girl out for evaluation. To the naked eye, silk, wool, cotton, hemp, and linen threads, certain grasses, and the legs of insects appear identical. Human hair can usually be distinguished from that of animals under a microscope or by certain tests.

He's confident the investigation will be prolonged indefinitely. Hapsburg bureaucracy is notoriously slow and complicated. It is considered unremarkable that a single tax payment passes through the hands of twenty-seven officials. *Fortwursteln* — the process of muddling through — can be useful at times.

Other cases also divert his attention. Two prominent men, related by marriage, had a financial dispute that escalated into blackmail. His initial interview with their sister-in-law, Elisabeth von R., was unsuccessful. She has all the tiresome symptoms of a hysteric, and he isn't looking forward to a second meeting. Franz has put aside his search for Rosza to pursue a pair of horse thieves.

The Inspector is under pressure from another examining judge to arrest one of the Gypsies he interrogated and charge him with Dora's murder. He answers the judge's request with a flood of documents to buy himself time. His lack of progress with Dora's case is frustrating. When he was an assistant, he learned how to photograph shiny objects at a crime scene. To neutralize their reflection, mirrors, polished silver, and glass objects were painted with plumbago or with Russian talcum mixed with essence of turpentine.

Now he turns to this visual image for reassurance. I only need to observe what is in front of me, he thinks. All the facts are here, thinly disguised.

❀

Wally pushes the bicycle to the Volksgarten, where she props it against the bench next to her. Soon, a few children wander over and shyly examine the bicycle. She permits three of them to take turns riding it. The next day, she again waits in the park with the bicycle. When one of the boys she questions says yes, he knows Otto, she lets him go around the fountain and as far as the Grillparzer monument.

Then she asks him if he knows Otto's governess, Rosza. Preoccupied, the boy fiddles with the bicycle's pedals, turns the front wheel from side to side in the gravel. Rosza isn't with Otto's family, he says. But I know where she lives. Wally trades him the bicycle for his information.

She finds the house where Rosza lives with a family. She loiters across the street and watches for the governess, who now takes care of two little boys. After a time, Wally memorizes Rosza's routine, her comings and goings.

She doesn't dare make any advance to the woman yet.

By mid-November, the military band in the Volksgarten has moved inside the restaurant for its afternoon concerts. It is four-thirty P.M., and their music, *Morgenblätter,* is faintly audible. It is almost too cold to stand outside. Wally taps her feet to keep warm. Over the past few days, she's followed Rosza, accompanied by the children of the family that now employs her, to this area of the park. Now she waits for her.

Frost has burned the tender leaves off the plants, leaving only the bare, blackened stalks upright in the ground. It looks as if fire has swept through the landscape, leaving ruins.

She remembers her mother loved to garden, even planting the empty space between pear trees in the orchard with hyacinths and shrub roses. Her father ignored the garden unless there was a crisis, then he'd frantically hoe weeds, pluck caterpillars, or fumigate the plants with tobacco smoke from a bellows.

When she was very young, one of the small grafted fruit trees didn't take; clearly it was dying. Her father jerked the sapling out of the ground while she watched, horrified. Daughter, let me recite what Virgil wrote, he said, holding the sapling up in front of her as a lesson. *"An awful portent, wonderful to tell. For from the first tree, which is torn from the ground with broken roots, drops of black blood trickle and stain the earth with gore."*

And it did seem as if black drops fell from the sapling's twisted web of roots, writhing in protest. She ran screaming for her mother, her father's shouted apologies faint behind her. To this day, the acts of uprooting, digging, turning over the earth make her uneasy.

Egon has been watching Wally from the other side of the Kaiserin Elizabeth monument, wondering if she'll remember him. In her red cloak, she is a solitary, fiery figure against the whitened grass.

"Excuse me, Fräulein?"

Wally whirls around, the gravel grating under her feet. He frightened her, but when he approaches she smiles and extends her hand.

"I'm the photographer, do you remember?"

"Yes, yes, I do remember you, Egon." She asks about his camera.

"No pictures today. I've been so busy, I needed a rest." After an uncomfortable pause, he says, "Maybe I shouldn't tell you this, but I photographed your friend again, the dead girl that was found here."

"You photographed her? How could you? She was buried."

Wally is uneasy. Not wanting to hear his answer, she nestles her chin deeper into her collar.

He bends his head toward her, eager to talk. "Someone dug up Dora and cut off her thumb. The police put her back in the ground. They told me another blessing was said over her grave, but I think they should have taken other precautions. What happened is unnatural. There could be a curse of some kind on the body. Perhaps she's a revenant."

Wally suddenly needs to sit down, so they perch on the

stone edge of the monument. She doesn't speak, just hunches over with her elbows on her knees, a posture no Viennese girl would ever allow herself in public.

He thinks he's made a mistake. Uncertain about how to comfort her, he hesitates, stowing his hands in his pockets. He's accustomed to having a piece of equipment, his camera, as a foil for his awkwardness, his loose hands.

At the sound of footsteps, she raises her head. A woman sweeps around the corner, chased by two small boys. Now they race ahead of her into the park. She claps her hands and shouts at them. Her voice sounds clipped, faintly foreign. She doesn't speak the resonant upper-middle-class German. It's Rosza, and Wally is afraid of the place where her greeting will take her. She has no idea how to approach her.

The woman stands close to them, on the place where Dora's body was found. She silently returns their scrutiny.

"Can you light this for me?" she calls, waving an unlit cigarette in her gloved hand.

Egon walks over and introduces himself.

She gives him her name, nervously shifting her feet and pulling her scarf up around her face. Fräulein Rosza.

Wally joins them. Even with half her face and her hair muffled by scarf and hat, she can see Rosza is beautiful. Her narrow eyes are watchful and thinly lashed, which accentuates their shape.

Egon offers her a light, and her puff of smoke obscures the red dot of fire cupped in his hand. She stares at him for a minute, boldly searching his face until he's puzzled and uncomfortable, before nodding her thanks. She turns to watch the boys playing in the distance.

Then Egon makes jokes until they all laugh, circled around the smoke from their cigarettes. The women hug their coats closer; it really is freezing. Wally is wild with impatience, wanting to ask her about Dora, but she holds her questions like the smoke in her lungs. The statue of Kaiserin Elizabeth towers above them, her face and figure cold blue stone in this light.

Suddenly Rosza says *Excuse me* and marches away, her narrow skirt giving her a jerky gait, her feet crunching bitterly

on the frozen gravel. The boys stop tussling when they see her
approach. She talks loudly to one of them, then transfers her
cigarette and slaps him, hard, with her free right hand.

"They're little devils," she says when she rejoins them.
"They're really unbearable. There are too many children in this
world. I thank God I have none of my own."

"I take care of children too. But they're away right now,"
Wally volunteers.

"Aren't you lucky. Paid for nothing. No wonder you have
time to stand around in the park on a cold day." Smoke streams
out of Rosza's pink nose. Then she drops her cigarette and
neatly crushes it with the pointed toe of her boot.

Egon hesitantly suggests they meet in a warmer place.
Does she play cards?

"I have trouble sitting down for very long games, but I do
love to play tarok."

They agree to meet at Café Landtmann for a game later
in the week.

The Inspector takes his wife to the Burgtheater. It begins
to snow lightly while they are inside. After the performance,
the audience gathers at the door, opening umbrellas against
the frozen shower descending from the sky before stepping
under it.

Erszébet and the Inspector make the first dark footprints
in the snow on the narrow street behind the theater. He holds
an umbrella over her head and follows her directions to the
Minoritenkirche. She's drawn to this Gothic church, always
approaching it a certain way in order to view its strange asym-
metry, an alien shape set in a greensward.

She touches his arm and they stop across from the Minoritenkirche. Her eyes scale the untapered octagonal tower,
two of its sides dimly visible through the falling snow. Preoccupied, he ignores the church.

Some evenings when they walk together side by side, not
looking at each other, Erszébet will talk about the Gypsies she

encountered as a child. Her Magyar accent becomes stronger, the words emphasized on the first syllable. Her musical voice soothes him.

Tonight she tells him about a vacation she took with her family when she was a child. They'd traveled by train to Hatvan to stay with a couple at their country estate, Ecsed. Their host took them through the house, the orchards, and the extensive kitchen garden. As they toured the barns, he complained that his hens and geese had been disappearing. He suspected the Gypsies camped at the edge of his land were the thieves.

Later, Erszébet and his two little boys hid themselves near the barn to wait. They all fell asleep in the sun, and woke up to find a Gypsy woman pitching bread from her apron at the geese. The birds hissed and fought. After the largest goose swallowed a hunk of bread and began to waddle away, the woman gripped her hands together and crouched down. The bird swung violently around toward her. Magically, as if the struggling bird were connected by an invisible string, it was pulled closer and closer to the woman. The goose was unable to escape or resist. Was it under a spell? Erszébet clapped her hand over her mouth to keep from crying out. Suddenly the woman leaped forward, grabbed the goose, and wrung its neck.

Later, the adults told Erszébet that the Gypsy woman had hidden a fishhook on fine wire in the bread. The herb asafoetida had been rubbed on the bread, which made it irresistible to geese.

"Can you tell me something else about the Gypsies," her husband asks after a moment of silence. "What do they do with their dead?"

"Why, they put their dead in the ground, like everyone else." She addresses her words to the Minoritenkirche, not to him. "But the Gypsies' act of dying is truly remarkable. They are moved outside so they can die in a field, in open air. This is their family's responsibility. They also have particular burial rites. Some Gypsies bury a corpse wearing its clothes inside out. They believe this will keep the body in the grave, I don't know how. Other tribes burn everything that belonged to the deceased."

"For what purpose?"

"The dead haunt whatever they've left on earth. They have no peace until their possessions are destroyed, or put in a place where the living can no longer touch them."

He sees Dora's body in its coffin, the terrible round cut on her hand.

"Would Gypsies ever mutilate a body?"

She steps away from him, away from the umbrella, and tilts her head back so the falling snow spangles the veil over her face.

"I'm not certain. I've heard some Gypsy mothers will cut off their boy's finger or a thumb so he can't serve in the military. Who could blame them, when the country treats them so poorly."

"But would they cut fingers off the dead, is there some superstition about mutilation?"

"Would they dig up a body?" She shrugs. "Yes, if the corpse is a revenant, a living dead. Gypsies know a revenant can be dissolved by stabbing it with a steel needle. I remember what the peasants in our village believed. If the illegitimate child of two illegitimate parents killed someone, that corpse would become a revenant. To kill it, the peasants disinter the corpse and cut out its heart. Then it is burned."

He watches Erszébet's profile.

She's silent as wind stirs thick snow around them. The shifting white pattern transforms her, makes her silhouette as indistinct and mysterious as the dark church in front of them. She turns toward him, half her face hardened by shadow, her hat a blur against the tower. The snow has destroyed his sense of perspective. Erszébet seems to be simultaneously close and distant, as if she stood on a ship that was rapidly moving away, but his eyes were filled with her familiar face, so he didn't notice the space between them until she suddenly became a blur.

He feels helpless, incapable of understanding what she's just told him. Before he met Erszébet, he would have dismissed such talk as primitive superstition, childish ghost stories. Even a hysterical female fantasy. But now he has a tug of fear in his muscles. He struggles to find the reason her words have released this feeling. Perhaps the stories he's woven about Dora alive and Dora dead are just as tenuous.

He is trained to look for the error in the situation, but all the errors he's identified could be his own. Everything could slip through his fingers. He stamps his feet to distract himself, then reaches for her hand.

"Did you ever see such a thing, a revenant?"

The pleading tone of his voice surprises him. He's relieved when she shakes her head, *no*. But when I was younger, a strange thing happened, she says. I was about twelve years old. On a hill near our house, a French botanist collected plants, bending and stooping over the ground in his cloak. The peasants saw him crouched there and thought he was a *csordásfarkas*, a wolfman. When he stood up, it seemed as if he'd changed shape again, transformed himself back into a man. The peasants rushed over the hill toward the botanist, ready to kill him and burn his heart, when a wagon drove by. The terrified botanist ran after it and leaped inside.

I know. I saw him. I was in the wagon.

CHAPTER 7

ALLY WATCHES ERSZÉBET
enter the Café de l'Europe. She wears a vel-
vet hat and an immense black fox boa, which
obscures her neck, shoulders, and half her
face. There is pale embroidery around the
bottom of her coat, so her ankles appear to
be hobbled by a chain of intricate circles. Wally takes pleasure
in the dramatic silhouette she makes. She covets her furs.

Later, after Erszébet leaves their table to talk to an ac-
quaintance, Wally quickly slips the furs off her chair and loops
them around her bare neck. The black hairs are finer than eye-
lashes, and the heads and paws of the animals are dry and surprisingly weightless. She detects Erszébet's scent spread along
the inside of the furs, the skin part, where they touched her
body.

Erszébet returns to the table. Wally watches apprehen-
sively as Erszébet strokes the furs and settles them back
around her shoulders, afraid the warmth from her own skin
still clings to them and will betray her trespass.

Wally rehearsed the announcement of her story so she
could recite it without a false step or slipping accent. "I have the
most terrible news" is the dramatic way she introduces Dora's
corpse. "Someone dug up Dora and cut off her thumb. Egon
photographed her body for the police and told me about it."

Although Erszébet listens with a calm face, she's instantly suspicious. There was no mention of the mutilation of
the corpse in her husband's notebook.

"Why would someone cut off Dora's thumb?" Wally

whispers. Now that she is with Erszébet, she can become more emotional about this gruesome act. She wonders what kind of knife was used.

"I'm certain the thumb was stolen to use as a talisman. We must consider who would have use for such a thing."

"Maybe the police took the thumb?"

But Erszébet barely hears her question. She calculates, *Was it a deliberate or a random theft? Or did the corpse — a revenant — make its own way out of the brown earth?* Some Gypsies believe anyone who dies alone will became a revenant. She recollects a gravestone in Veszprém. Two holes had been bored in it, the sign it was the grave of a vampire, a revenant. She'd watched while two men poured boiling water from iron kettles into cracks over the grave to kill the unholy occupant. She'd enjoyed the heavy, comforting smell of the hot mud. Revenants also fear rosaries, certain types of wood, crosses, and steel needles. The Moslem Gypsies carefully watch pumpkins, since they can become a type of revenant, moving and making noises. This story once gave ten-year-old Erszébet and her brother a nervous walk across a field that was strewn with the haunted, unharvested golden yellow globes.

But Dora. Erszébet sees the scrabble through hard earth to her coffin, a mute box at the bottom of a hole in the ground. She can't quite distinguish the figure standing next to Dora's open grave. This vision takes place in silence, in the same way that she dreams of the familiar dead, who never speak directly to her but pantomime their unspoken wishes, which are clearer than language.

Erszébet leans over the table, the furs forgotten, sliding off her shoulders. There's something else, isn't there? she asks.

Wally tells her about the man she saw in Herr Zellenka's garden, the silver glint that was his nose. How he pursued her. How frightened she was. How nothing else existed during those moments. She is surprised by the details she remembers.

A man in a garden. Erszébet is certain Dora was killed by a man. He wasn't a stranger. She has no other sense of him. Not now.

Wally interrupts her thought. "There was no fig tree in

Herr Zellenka's garden. Not that I could find. There were fruit trees in the garden of the house next door. And I dressed like a man to climb over the wall."

"You wore men's clothes on the street?"

"No one looked at me. I could have been a stable boy. Even the horses on the street were fooled. Anything in trousers must look the same to an animal."

They both laugh.

"I walked back into town in only thirty minutes. In my dress it takes over an hour."

Erszébet wonders about the strange weightlessness of trousers instead of a skirt. Two legs instead of fabric ballooning out with every step.

The waiter brushes against their table. They order two slices of *Esterházytorte* and coffee with brandy to celebrate.

After they've raised their cups in honor of her accomplishments, Wally reveals she's found Rosza and will interview her alone.

Erszébet hesitates. Her voice nervous, Wally says the plans are made, and that it will upset the balance of the conversation if Erszébet is with her.

Erszébet tightens her smile, and they pass on to other matters. Wally is relieved.

Rosza is disliked by Dora's mother, Wally says. She suspects Rosza had been intimate with Herr Zellenka. She didn't see anything suspicious, but she eavesdropped on them in a hotel room. I can only bear one more visit to that woman. Last time she cried so much I couldn't ask her about Dora's jewelry. Perhaps if I take her to a café she won't cry, won't cling to me.

They agree that Wally will go back to Dora's house, to more thoroughly search the garden for the fig.

"You must do it soon," Erszébet says. "A heavy snow is coming."

Wally quickly agrees and then changes the subject. "What does your husband think about the crime?"

"He tries to keep from making up his mind, to consider everything. If you met him, you'd notice even his conversation is calculated. I can't ask too many questions or he'll become suspicious."

Without its being discussed, Wally understands that Erszébet keeps their friendship a secret from her husband. This suits Wally. Perhaps it confirms what she believes, that the place she's mapped out for herself in Vienna is temporary, artificial. As if her presence could be easily erased. But she's committed Erszébet to memory, all the details of her face. And when Wally occasionally asks about her husband, it's as if he were a distant relative or a guest. She can't consider him as someone who studies Erszébet in the same way she does.

Erszébet continues. "When my husband first told me about Dora's murder, he said that strangers, Gypsies, might be responsible. Dora had blond hair. You know Gypsies consider blonds and redheads good luck, *Bolo hameshro.*"

"Dora was hardly lucky."

"I know. Something went wrong."

The waiter brings them more coffee. Erszébet arranges her furs and says she has more information from her research. She's discovered the fig was sacred to the god Priapus. And that *fig* — *fica* — was the word for a woman's quaint.

Wally says she has some evidence, too. She places a knotted handkerchief on the table.

"What do you have here?"

Erszébet feels two small hard objects inside the cloth. She unties the fabric and smooths it flat on the table.

Pearl earrings.

They were Dora's earrings, Wally whispers. They were given to me, and now they're yours.

But Erszébet is silent. She has a strange vision of another small object wrapped in a cloth.

In that part of his mind he identifies as the hysterical element, the Inspector wonders if Dora's corpse was violated by some animal. Perhaps a dog. Or a *csordásfarkas,* the wolf who is sent, a shape-shifter. In Latin the creature is *Versi pellis,* "turn pelt." Erszébet told him about these legendary wolfmen, who gather once a year. When they remove their wolf skins and hang them up in a tree, they are temporarily transformed back into men. However, if a wolf skin is stolen and burned, its owner can remain in his human body. It is said the *csordásfarkas* are grateful for their violent rescue.

He quiets himself, dismisses the tale as superstition. His wife's story. But if Franz had made the same suggestion, he would have encouraged his speculation, treated it with serious consideration, teased it along. Why not? Every speculation has some value or use, even a dream. Somewhere he read a phrase that stayed with him, *Man muss ein Stück Unsicherheit ertragen können,* "One must learn to put up with some measure of uncertainty." He believes this.

He remembers that Professor Gross frequently invoked Leonardo da Vinci during his lectures. His favorite quotation was *"The organ of perception acts more rapidly than the judgment."*

Gross told his class, "Once you understand and can truly conduct yourself according to da Vinci's observations, you will be a superb Investigating Officer. You must possess the restraint and discipline of a great artist."

The Inspector turns to the page he'd marked in *Kriminalistik* that complements da Vinci's words.

> In carefully examining our own minds (we can scarcely observe phenomena of a purely psychical character in others), we shall have many opportunities of studying how preconceived theories take root: we shall often be astonished to see how accidental statements of almost no significance and often purely hypothetical have often been able to give birth to a theory of which we can no longer rid ourselves without difficulty, although we have for a long time recognised the rottenness of its foundation.

The history of the cards called by the French *tarot,* the Italians *tarocco,* and the Germans *Tarok,* is all speculation. For centuries, experts have argued about these mysterious cards, some becoming fanatical in their convictions. At various times the

Gypsies, Egyptians, Italians, Indians, Chinese, Portugese, French, and the Spanish have been credited with or claimed the invention of tarot cards. The eighteenth-century French scholar, pastor, and Freemason Antoine Court de Gébelin erroneously claimed *TARO* was derived from the Egyptian words *tar,* meaning "way" or "road," and *Ros,* "king" or "kingly." He interpreted the cards as the royal road, an allegory for life. The designs published in 1780 in de Gébelin's book, *Monde primitif,* are the basis for all tarot cards since that date.

Tarot cards are used to predict fortunes or played as a game. In Austria, the card game tarok can be played with up to fifty-four cards.

Egon has always been fascinated by one particular tarot card, which depicts the figure of a man — the Fool — carrying a bag over his shoulder, symbolizing the faults he doesn't wish to see. However, there is a tiger biting at his leg, which represents remorse. In games of cards, the Fool is called *l'Excuse* or *Sküs,* since it is a wild card, worthless in itself, giving value only to the other cards.

Egon sits in a high-backed booth next to Wally in the Landtmann *Kaffeehaus.* Tarot cards are stacked between their cups of *Einspänner* and glasses of water. Rosza is across the table by the window.

Even though the room is warm, the women keep their hats on. The beads hidden in the elaborate folds of Rosza's hat reveal their presence with erratic glints, the movements of her head striking them into black sparks. A veil shadows half her face as she bends over the cards. Egon's memory fastens on something familiar about her. Then he suddenly realizes he associates her veil with his camera, the black cloth that hides his head when he takes pictures.

As if on cue, she raises her eyes straight to his. Embarrassed, he looks away, caught staring.

"Let me see what your fortune is." She hands him the cards and instructs him to shuffle them three times. "Now pick the top card."

The card he draws is the Tower. It has the image of a man and a woman plunging from a tall building, their figures sprawled in midair, as stiffly geometric as if they were depicted on a stained-glass window. Behind them, a lightning bolt violently splits the tower.

When he sees the card, Egon's dismay grows until it becomes a knot of fear in his stomach.

Wally asks if he's feeling ill.

"No. But I have this extraordinary card. It isn't a good symbol."

Rosza takes it from him. "The Tower card symbolizes an end, perhaps a catastrophe. Disruptions, relationships abandoned," she says without embarrassment or sympathy. Her breath moves the veil over her face as she speaks. "Impulsiveness brings failure. I see violence. This card is called the House of the Devil."

She leans back to study his face, calm, as if she'd just finished reading a story to a child.

"It's just a game. You're not a Gypsy fortune-teller. It's only fair you pick a card."

Bored, Rosza lifts a card from the stack, glances at it, tosses it down. "So?"

Egon smiles. "I know your card."

La Papesse. A seated woman with a crown on her head, an open book on her lap.

"The wisdom of women. She is Juno as well as the goddess Diana. A perplexing card. You communicate silence and secrecy. You have a secret, Fräulein?"

He studies her face and waits for her answer.

Without lifting her eyes from *la Papesse,* Rosza gropes around the table for cigarettes. Wally notices the strong aura of the woman's perfume, a darkly pungent scent, perhaps musk.

"A girl in the family I lived with was murdered in August."

"The girl that was found in the Volksgarten?"

Rosza nods, lighting a cigarette without looking at them.

"We were the dearest of friends, like sisters. Her name was Dora. She went out alone one night."

"How terrible for you," Wally murmurs. "Did you sense something was going to happen to her?"

"Yes. It was strange. I was working for another family at

the time. But I remember it was a stifling hot evening. Something wasn't right."

"Where were you that night?"

Wally instantly regrets her question. She's forgotten to be hidden, to be slow. Rosza looks at her sharply. To soothe her, to go backwards, Wally makes sympathetic noises.

"I was with Herr Zellenka, a friend of mine. I'm surprised the police haven't talked to me. It makes me nervous. I keep expecting them." Rosza laughs uneasily. "Fortunately, I have no information to give them. I'm perfectly innocent."

Wally examines her cards, pretending to be preoccupied. "But Dora wouldn't go to the Volksgarten alone. She must have met someone there?"

"I can't imagine who it might have been. She would have told me if it was important." Rosza's face is impassive. She doesn't look up from her cards.

Egon suggests Dora might have had a secret rendezvous with a handsome Hungarian officer. An elopement. Rosza shakes her head.

Across the room, a ragged boy shuffles from table to table, pulling aside his coat to display the photographs in the waistband of his trousers. Some of the men dismiss him without looking up from their newspapers. Others casually leaf through the pictures of nude and partially nude women while the waiting boy fidgets.

Egon begins to deal the cards for tarok, going clockwise.

They proceed with their game. Six cards are turned face down on the table, a stack called the widow or *le chien*. They play without further conversation. Wally notices that Egon furtively studies Rosza's face, as if he were puzzled. He seems to have dismissed the negative fortune she predicted for him.

Rosza coolly ignores him. She is a surprisingly aggressive player, and her strategy is impossible to anticipate. She wins with her last trick, *Pagat,* the lowest trump. On the earliest tarot decks, *Pagat,* the juggler, was the arbiter of fortune. Over time, he was transformed into a Mountebank.

Rosza smiles at them for the first time. "Do you know there's an expression about tarok? *Riuscir come il Fante ô Matto de tarrocchi.* It means to be the knave of tarok, good for nothing."

She settles her shawl around her shoulders and stands up slowly; perhaps her skirt is caught on something. Egon eagerly offers to see her home, but she insists on leaving alone, hurrying to catch the last tram, the car marked by a blue light.

After she's gone, Egon gathers up the cards. "Perhaps you should have drawn the same card as Rosza."

"What do you mean?"

"You have a secret, too. You knew Dora but didn't choose to mention it to her."

Wally says nothing.

"Do as you like," he says. "You can trust me not to tell her."

Wally is so anxious to see Erszébet that she arrives early at the Café Schrangl, a low building on the Graben near the Dreifaltigkeitssäule, a monument commemorating the cessation of the plague.

Since a woman without an escort isn't welcome at Café Schrangl, Wally walks up and down the Graben, looking in shop windows. She stops in front of number thirteen, the Knize men's store. The windows are filled with expensive neckties laid out in circles, flat as playing cards.

She follows the street until it turns and meets the Stephansdom. She admires the *Bischofstor* on the north side of the building, an elaborate Gothic portal that is the entrance for women.

When Erszébet arrives at the door of the café, breathlessly late, they go straight to a table inside. Wally waits impatiently for the waiter to take their order and leave.

"Rosza has confirmed Herr K.'s — or Herr Zellenka's — alibi for the night of the murder. They were together. Of course, she didn't really understand the significance of what she'd said. I didn't let her know I wanted the information. I was very *roundabout,* that's the English word for it."

"They were together the entire evening? You're certain she was telling the truth?"

"That's what she said. Why would she lie to me? There's no reason."

Erszébet heard what Wally said, but she wonders how carefully the girl listened to Rosza. It isn't a young person's skill. "But how did Rosza *seem* when she told you her alibi?" Wally shrugs. Seem? Does that mean she wasn't telling the truth? Rosza did have a wariness about her. Her impression of the woman was set by their first encounters, as she followed her, watched her in the Volksgarten. Rosza as quarry. She remembers her inscrutable face as she read Egon's character with the tarot cards. Wally sensed her hidden pleasure in revealing his misfortune, like the sharp glint of a gold thread in a piece of embroidery.

And what about Otto, Erszébet asks. Did Rosza have any useful information about him? Why he was sent away so quickly?

"I didn't ask her about Otto," Wally says stiffly. "She would have been suspicious. How would I have known Dora had a brother when Rosza didn't mention him?"

Though Erszébet nods reassuringly, Wally feels as if she's failed her somehow.

The waiter brings more coffee, a second *Kapuziner* for Erszébet, and a *Böhmische dalken* pastry with plum jam.

Erszébet proposes they immediately proceed to the Kinderklinik, where Otto is being treated. The tubercular children under Professor Piquet's care live on top of the building, even sleeping outdoors with only a canvas roof overhead and a single extra blanket on their beds. Piquet believes exposure to the cold builds the body's resistance to tuberculosis. He prescribes no medicines.

They get off the tram at Währinger Strasse and walk through an undistinguished neighborhood. The Kinderklinik is an imposing building, eight stories high, and Wally and Erszébet can just see the tips of the trees on the roof from where they stand on the sidewalk.

They had previously rehearsed their imposture. Erszébet snugs her furs up around her neck and face, so she'll be unrecognizable. Wally copies her, wrapping her thin scarf over her chin.

Inside the Kinderklinik, Erszébet introduces herself as Otto's mother to the receptionist, a harried woman with thick round glasses. She is clearly irritated at the urgency of Erszébet's concern for her sick son. Without glancing up or stopping her pencil, she says they must wait to speak with a doctor before seeing Otto. This is an infectious place, she mutters. I have a cough myself. You can't just walk in.

Erszébet motions Wally over to a chair, and when a nurse and a mother with a crying baby crowd around the desk, they quickly slip out of the room.

In the hallway, Erszébet produces a handkerchief and sets her face with a grief-stricken expression as protection against anyone's asking why she's in the building. Wally nervously tries a door, and it opens on a white room furnished with a bed and a table. The next two rooms are identical, a strange contrast to the luxurious carpet and ornate wallpaper in the hallway. Wally is puzzled. She'd pictured rows of cots filled with coughing children. The Kinderklinik seems deserted, a castle of empty boxes.

Erszébet walks briskly ahead. "Let's find the roof. The children must be there."

They pass through double doors into a dark staircase. Cold air envelops them as they climb the stairs.

As they step out onto the roof, a huge gust lifts their skirts and Wally's hat, sending it rolling across the floor, a round black shape. She runs after it. When she stands up, triumphantly holding the recaptured hat, she stares straight at a group of trees, their bare branches hung with silver stars and half-moons twisting crazily in the wind, strangely festive. The children are here.

Behind the trees, a wall of white canvas strains against the wind. They approach it cautiously, a huge blank shape that is eerily out of place, like a section of a drawing left unfinished. There's a door in the center of the canvas, knotted with rope at two corners. Wally unfastens the ties and steps into a maze of white tunnels.

Erszébet follows Wally into a corridor. They move slowly, arms outstretched, protecting themselves from walls that might suddenly become animated shrouds, wrapping them in a suffocating embrace.

The first corridor leads them into a large space crowded with rows of children's beds, an identical blanket folded over each mattress. As if sleepwalking, they make their way between the beds.

"What is this place?"

Erszébet shakes her head and keeps walking.

They stop at the entrance of a large dining room filled with small tables and chairs. As Wally moves closer, she sees that leaves and powdery crumbs of snow cover the empty plates, an abandoned banquet, a fairy feast. Wally imagines she's been transported like Alice in Wonderland. *I'm through the looking glass,* she thinks. She says nothing to Erszébet, since Alice isn't a character familiar to her. Erszébet has her own goblins, the *táltos,* cunning folk, and the *szépasszony,* the fair ladies, demonical female spirits whose very name is taboo.

They move silently through other corridors, passing empty rooms.

The wind is continuous, moving the walls, pressing the canvas against their faces and their long skirts, as if to tangle them into a waltz. Wally flails against the fabric, against its claustrophobic blankness.

She remembers being similarly unnerved by a yew maze at Somerleyton as a child. The same heavy silence, a strange quality of waiting, of blank suspense. Her mother and father had walked ahead of her into the maze and vanished around a corner. Lost, she began to cry. *Where are you?* they called, their laughing voices floating over the hedge. Then there was no noise but her sobbing. I'll tell you how to get out, her father shouted. Stop crying and listen. Put your right hand on the hedge. Now walk forward. Never take your hand off the hedge and you'll find your way through.

Remembering his instructions, Wally touches the canvas with her right hand.

Erszébet is a black shape in front of her.

Faint voices come from somewhere in the distance. Children singing.

A small child runs around the corner headlong into Erszébet's skirt, then falls backward, landing hard on the ground. He starts to cough violently.

Suddenly a woman in a white uniform appears and picks up the gasping boy. She hoists him over her shoulder and glares at them.

"No one is allowed on the roof."

"But my son is here."

Erszébet passionately argues with the woman while Wally sidles around them. The boy gravely watches her over the woman's shoulder. He coughs up a splot of blood and it runs down the back of her blouse, but by then Wally is already past them, running, losing all sense of direction. She turns a corner. What she sees makes her stop moving.

Under the open sky, rows of silent children sit at school desks, their backs to her. At the front of the room, a thin man gestures at a blackboard, his breath hanging white in the air. Snow shows where it's blown across the children's dark coats.

She senses Erszébet is now standing behind her. The man waves his hand at them, not unfriendly. The children obediently bend their heads to their books as he walks across the room.

"Good afternoon, ladies, I'm Professor Piquet. How can I help you?" His expression is guarded, his cold voice at odds with his friendly greeting. His lips purse above his neatly pointed beard. He stands very close to them, his body blocking them from the room.

Erszébet says she must speak with one of the children about an urgent family matter. In private.

Wally steps to the side, frantically scanning the children's heads, searching for the boy. "Otto, are you there?" she shouts.

A piece of paper spirals to the floor beneath a boy's desk. Wally takes it as a signal.

The man moves in front of Erszébet.

"The children may not be interrupted, even for a moment. This is part of their treatment. You must leave now."

When Erszébet lowers her head, his hand clutches her arm. She pulls away, her eyes locked on his face. Perhaps it's a trick of the light in this shadowless space, but it seems Erszébet's silhouette grows blacker, her movements deft and quick. *You have my boy here.* Her voice loud and shrill.

He hesitates, then grabs her wrist.

Erszébet shoves him hard against the wall.

He grunts, then soundlessly falls backward onto the canvas, which tears loose from its scaffolding and folds over on top of him, gentle as a wing.

A week later, the Inspector comes home unexpectedly early for lunch. He opens the door of the study and finds Erszébet sitting at the desk. Startled, she looks up, and her hand strikes a glass vial that rolls off the desk and shatters on the floor. As if an enchantment is suddenly broken, the fig from Dora's stomach is transformed into a brown lump, glittering with glass. The sickly odor of formalin fills the room, and they wait without moving, like actors in a play standing in terrible silence onstage, expecting news of a catastrophe.

CHAPTER 8

HE INSPECTOR SENDS FRANZ, two assistants, and four boys from the office to search the grounds of the Volksgarten again. The leaves on the trees have fallen, so the branches are sharply outlined in black, like ironwork keeping the sky back. The dense underbrush around the site where Dora's body was found has thinned out. The atmosphere in the park is tense, a landscape waiting for snow.

They divide the site into squares and mark it off with stakes and ropes. Franz asks the searchers to remove their gloves and work bare-handed in the cold, so their examination will be absolutely precise. Without complaint, they pick through the leaves and part the grasses in each square, their fingers quickly cooling, thin flesh taking on the temperature of the air.

They work their way across the area near the Kaiserin Elizabeth statue and discover nothing of significance. Then one of the boys notices a bundle stuck in the cleft of a huge tree, a dark shape like a strange nest. He climbs the tree and carefully retrieves the thing.

When the bundle of fabric is unwrapped and unrolled on a table at the police station, it is recognizable as a woman's cloak, its geometric pattern recast into pale, indistinct shapes by its exposure to the weather. The lining is unscathed.

The Inspector oversees the process of turning the garment into evidence. Under his watchful eyes, Franz carefully examines the cloak, his face crimson. He slowly dips his fingers into the pockets, afraid something terrible — Dora's missing thumb — might be inside. Both pockets are empty. He's relieved, but he feels guilty, as if his search was somehow a trespass.

The Inspector makes a note to contact Dora's mother, anticipating the cloak had belonged to her daughter. Poor girl, her clothing stuffed in a tree. At least the garment was better preserved in the air than under the ground, where it would have rotted.

Franz found no bloodstains on the cloak, just a few small tears. There are blond hairs caught inside the collar, and a label embroidered with a stylized rose and the words *Paul Poiret, rue Pasquier 37, Paris.* He removes the label with a razor and places it in an envelope. The hairs are folded into a sheet of paper. They will be examined by a microscopist for a match with Dora's hair and scalp. While someone measures the cloak, Franz writes an account of the garment. He has trouble describing its appearance, the geometric pattern melted into stains.

When the Inspector isn't watching, he leans close to the garment, hoping to sense a clue, the smell of a woman or her perfume, or a dent left by her neck in the velvet, like a ghostly handprint.

The Inspector paces when he reads aloud or tells a longer-than-usual story. Without looking down, he always steps precisely over the same procession of geometric flowers on the carpet. He reads well, a sonorous voice proceeding back and forth. Franz always associates these extemporaneous lectures with movement. He is accustomed to his supervisor's habits and is familiar with his path. He cherishes these periods of instruction.

An impartial observer does not exist, the Inspector reminds Franz. Witnesses are devious. Not from any evil intention, but emotions will always distort a witness's impression.

You'll find the best discussion of witnesses in here, he continues, taking *Kriminalistik* from its special place in the drawer of his desk. He paces in front of the window, reading aloud from the chapter on "Examination of Witnesses and Accused."

> It must not be forgotten that a witness, at the moment of being an actual spectator of the occurrence, or at the time of reporting it, is frequently in a state of agitation and over-excitement which leads him to slide easily from one conclusion to another. Once these inductions are in full swing, it is difficult to say where they will stop; and if this is the case with impressions arising under normal conditions, the reality is enormously accentuated when things have strongly struck the sensation and especially that of sight.

He stops pacing and closes the book. "So you see how a witness can cause confusion? A witness can tell his account in good faith and not realize he's lying. Better to always have two witnesses, so you can compare their stories. Sometimes even two witnesses aren't enough. I have a true story to illustrate my point."

The coffin of Mary, Queen of Scots was opened in 1830. They found two ax marks on her body, one on the nape of her neck and a second stroke that removed her head. The queen was executed before a crowd of people, and there were numerous eyewitness accounts. Here is the mystery. Every witness claimed they saw her head fall with a single stroke of the ax. Isn't that strange? The first blow was erased from their memory as fast as the ax fell. The witnesses were all in a state of shock.

So every witness lied, marvels Franz. A killing took place, visible but invisible to hundreds of eyes. At this moment he rejoices in the Inspector's learning. He doesn't write down his words, but commands them to heart.

"But sir, how could that happen? How could so many people forget the ax blow? It seems uncanny. Maybe they were hypnotized."

"The question is, did the witnesses actually *not remember* what they'd seen? I'm not certain there's a word for something which is clearly seen but not remembered. It's not a memory."

The Inspector believes the ax stroke was blocked by an

impulse of the witness's eyes or brains before it reached the
state of memory. Hid it from whatever root in the mind that
stored such an image. Just as he fears his memory of Dora's
corpse will come back to him, unbidden. The incident was *ver-
drängt,* repressed.

But Franz knows something else. The witnesses were be-
set by abjection. What they rejected was the wait — the infinite
suspended space — between the first and final strokes of the
ax. How time hurtled then stood still for Queen Mary, waiting
for death on her knees.

Franz takes the queen of Scots as his patron saint of witnesses. Later, he will sense her presence hovering invisibly behind every witness he interrogates, eternally patient.

Franz and the Inspector walk down the hallway of the
Naturhistorisches Museum. They've just had lunch together,
and Franz is light-headed from the attention.

"What did he smell like, the Gypsy at Herr Zellenka's?
My mother said Gypsies smell like rancid fat and mice. Is that
true?"

"Gypsies smell like mice? Franz, the man isn't a character from a folktale." The Inspector is exasperated.

"Yes, sir."

Nervous, Franz stumbles as they continue to walk in silence. He counts the lamps in the hallway, to distance himself
from the Inspector's rebuke.

"I'm not angry at you. Try to avoid patterns, Franz. An
Investigating Officer never accepts another person's conclu-
sions or prejudice. You must prove every fact for yourself. This
is the best advice I can give you."

Franz nods mournfully, his face flushed.

The Inspector has always prided himself on his ability to
listen, as a good *Bürger* is confident of his business acumen.
During interrogations, he can distinguish the different qualities of the witnesses' silence, as if it were a tone of voice.

He's admonished Franz more than once for interrupting him. Don't be so hasty. Slow down and listen. In the Pythagorean system, disciples would spend five years listening before they were allowed to ask a single question. This was in the fourth century B.C. Another philosopher, Philo of Alexandria, wrote about Banquets of Silence, where even the correct posture for listening was determined.

In *Kriminalistik* there is a text on the subject. He orders Franz to read it as part of his lesson. *"To observe how the person questioned listens is a rule of primary importance, and if the officer observes it he will arrive at his goal more quickly than by hours of examination."*

The city is totally silent as its streets are gradually buried by flying dull white powder, as thick and purposeful as Pompeian ash. This is the first heavy snowfall.

Wally knows Erszébet mirrors her movements and stands at her own window, also watching the snow. She's never seen Erszébet's home, but she has a clear vision of her now, holding a blue curtain back with one hand, peering out at the snow's impenetrable whiteness, imposing its transformation over the landscape, radical as fire. She's certain their thoughts are the same; snow has buried the fig tree. That part of their investigation has ended. Wally consoles herself with the idea that perhaps the fig was symbolic. Perhaps Dora's last meal was the murderer's private joke, which they accidentally intercepted. Perhaps she's just trying to fit her own story onto Dora's murder, something she made up.

Now she worries about telling Erszébet the evidence is entirely lost to them. If there is a fig tree behind Dora's house, Wally failed to find it. She twice stopped to visit Dora's mother, but no one opened the door at her knocking. The thick curtains were pulled tight against any escaping light from inside. The garden gate was locked.

As uncomfortable as it is to anticipate this rebuke, she would gladly endure more severe punishments to keep Erszé-

bet's esteem. When someone crosses Erszébet, Wally has seen
her turn unexpectedly icy, as if some opaque transformation
had taken place. A few days have passed without conversation between them, which makes Wally alternately fearful
and sad.

When Erszébet learns all her research on figs has come to
nothing, she frowns and makes a brief entry in the notebook
about Dora's case. From this point, she will exclude Wally from
the progress chronicled in the notebook.

The day after the snowfall, the front door of the house is
wedged shut with ice, but Wally shoves it open, then half
slides, half falls down the steps. Vienna has been altered into an
unfamiliar place. There are no visible landmarks. Snow covers
the street — up to her waist in some places — and thickly dis-
guises windows and doorways. The ground floors of the buildings are unrecognizable. It is strangely soothing after the
isolation of the last few days.

At first she enjoys making her way through the snow, for
there are no pedestrians and no traffic. At the end of one street,
two figures slip and fall on the ice, moving in irresistible slow
motion, the woman's full skirt flying up just as she falls, transforming her into a dark swinging shape, a bell.

Tired by the effort of walking, the thick one-two stab of
her boots into the snow, Wally begins to stagger. She is standing just off the curb when she hears the crack of a whip, and a
huge dragon hurtles around the corner, soundlessly moving
straight toward her. She's immobile, her legs encased in snow,
and in the next moment she realizes the dragon is a carved
sleigh drawn by black horses.

How can she place what she just witnessed? The snow's
radiant blankness, its soundlessness, the freezing air — seem
to be details torn from a dream. As if she'd fallen asleep and
dreamed of being pursued by a fierce animal, then woken to
find black hairs curled between her fingers.

Erszébet began to spend a great deal of time away from the house. The household continued to be immaculately kept, and the meals ordered from the cook still revolved around her husband's favorite Hungarian dishes. She frequently served *tokány*, a stew made with veal, sour cream, mushrooms, peas, parsley root, and goose livers. Another stew was prepared with the famous sausage from Debrecen. Shakers of sweet paprika, *különleges*, and hot, *erös*, were always in their customary places on the table next to the salt and pepper. She brought home fondant from Lehmann's and petits fours from Scheidl's.

Bouquets of hothouse carnations and roses no longer decorated the parlor table and Erszébet's vanity table, since she didn't shop for flowers and didn't trust the maid to select them. She was oblivious to the cigars and cigarettes that perfumed her clothing, a souvenir of the hours spent with Wally in the various *Kaffeehäuser.* Her knitting had been abandoned.

Erszébet continued her watercolors. Some mornings, her husband found damp brushes on the table, but he never saw her at her easel. He considered it indelicate to ask to see a finished painting. He knew this from his work. She left bowls of dried figs sitting out until they were inedible. Just leave them alone, she said when he asked about them, they're a *nature morte* for artistic observation. I'm painting them. He noticed the pack of tarot cards was missing from its usual place in the drawer. He later discovered the deck in her satchel. She constantly consulted her book about dream interpretation.

He added up all these small changes and deviations from their routine domestic life. *The error in the situation.* He wondered if Erszébet could be in poor health or was secretly troubled by something. He didn't consider the idea she might be having an affair. Had he offended her? Perhaps he'd been too preoccupied with his work. Another case had come in, a forgery, and he'd spent most of the week searching out a penmaker familiar with the characteristics of various antique inks. He was also looking for another expert who could duplicate sealing wax.

He doesn't discuss the fig and the broken glass vial with
her. It was just an accident. She discovered the vial in his
satchel and was curious about it. That's what she told him. He
identified his uneasiness but kept it to himself.

Franz is handling the identification of the cloak found in the
Volksgarten. In preparation for Dora's mother, he displayed
the cloak on the desk in his office rather than in the grim
morgue room. The Inspector was pleased by his choice. It
demonstrated a sensitivity that he didn't think his assistant
had yet developed.

When Franz ushered the woman into his office, she took
two steps and refused to move any closer to the garment. She
said she could see the thing well enough and it did not belong
to her daughter. She took out a handkerchief and, between
sobs, asked if they'd made a mistake, perhaps it wasn't really
Dora in the Volksgarten? Perhaps it was another girl?

Franz was taken aback at her reaction. The Inspector re-
assured him that hysterical women were always surprising.

Erszébet's whispers echo up the elaborate staircase in the Historisches Museum der Stadt Wien. She encourages Wally to
return to Herr Zellenka's.

"Jószef is a Gypsy, so if he stole the thumb, it will be hidden in his room. There might be other charms, a jar of ashes or
an amulet, some strange object. Or a paper with pictures on it,
since no Gypsy can read or write. I promise you, there won't be
much to see."

Wally is reluctant. The Zellenkas' house is an unpredictable place. "I don't know how to find anything."

"My husband said Jószef lives in the stable. He drives the
fiaker, so if the horses have been taken out, you'll be perfectly
safe."

Wally is silent. They proceed to the exhibition hall at the
top of the stairs.

"I'll wait outside their house in the fiaker. You can search his room in the afternoon, so there will still be light. Nothing can happen to you."

When she still doesn't answer, Erszébet abruptly leaves her, passing into the next room, the angry tap of her umbrella escorting her across the marble floor.

Wally follows her into a place filled with the somber presence of metal, battle trophies captured from the Turks. It's as if she's walked into a huge and silent engine. A machine of war. On the walls are curved scimitars, Kurd lances, *hanjars,* shields, swords, daggers, wheel locks, and flintlocks for muskets. Suits of armor are ranged against both sides of the door, none of them taller than she is. As she moves around the room, the light wavers and changes shape, as if the objects it strikes were submerged in water, touching a knifepoint, the cheek of a shield, the curve of scales on armor, the dull nest of mesh under a helmet. On the ceiling, an ancient banner of crimson silk bearing the hand of Muhammad is a relief in its simplicity.

One case is filled with dark lengths of what looks like rope, and when Wally gets closer, she discovers rows of neatly braided horse tails, jeweled at the ends where they were cut from the animals' bodies.

Inside another glass case there's a skull balanced on a peg, its rough surface the color of tobacco. A folded shirt and a cord are displayed next to it.

Her face floats above the skull, a pale moon reflected in the glass. Erszébet's head suddenly appears behind Wally's shoulder, her eyes sunken into black half circles below the brim of her hat. She translates the card in the case.

In 1683, when the Turkish general Kara-Mustapha was defeated in battle outside Vienna, the Sultan sent him the silk cord. Mustapha hung himself with this cord, wearing this shirt. A suicide on a point of honor. The skin was stripped from his face as proof of his death.

Wally squints at the skull, looking for marks made by the flaying knives. Erszébet's voice is close to her ear.

"When Kara-Mustapha was defeated, he destroyed his

two most precious possessions to keep them from the infidels. His beautiful wife and his ostrich."

"You would never find a skull displayed like this in the British Museum," mutters Wally, moving away.

After the dark rooms of the Historisches Museum, the intensity of the winter light outside narrows their eyes. It is an afternoon of burning sky. Wind rolls a man's hat over the thin snow in front of the Rathaus Park. No one runs after it. Erszébet tightens her hat veil under her chin and takes Wally's arm as they descend the steps.

"Gypsies hate the wind. They'll do anything to avoid it. They also believe certain days of the week are unlucky, but time can hardly be avoided like the wind."

Sometimes Wally can recognize the distance between them, the boundaries on the map of their ages and characters, nationalities and languages. Once Erszébet smiled when Wally, not understanding something, asked her to explain herself. A characteristic of Magyar, my first language, is its inexactness, she said by way of explanation. My husband comments on it all the time. He wonders if I listen in the same way. I tell him everything is in the interpretation. He calls it *the error in the situation.*

Erszébet has it in her character to punish, to pay back for infractions, disagreements, trespassing. In this way, she is as straightforward as a superstition. What will happen as a result of an action can be predicted. A magpie indicates a guest will arrive. A bat is a sign of misfortune. It is bad luck to start a journey on Friday. A dog's howl signifies an approaching death.

She is as secure in her beliefs as if a vision had authenticated their correctness. Wally imagines Erszébet underwater and then resurfacing, transformed but unable to describe what it was she encountered in that dim place without breath.

Without being aware of it, she has started to consider Erszébet a seer.

Others might believe Wally has been bewitched, judging by her nervous wait for Erszébet's approval, the way she studies the woman's face and gestures, her smile.

However, at this moment, when Erszébet urges Wally to

search Jószef's room, *will you do it?* Wally doesn't answer. Her hesitation, like a pause in music, forces Erszébet to fuse all her attention on Wally.

Erszébet doesn't look away.

"Yes, I'll go to his room," Wally finally answers.

"Good. Tomorrow, *csütörtök,* will be fortunate for us."

Wally rolls her head back against the padded red leather upholstery, which relieves the ache in her neck. She's waiting in a fiaker outside Erszébet's house. Time passes slowly until Erszébet gets back into the carriage with a large flat parcel. This is your disguise, she says. Go ahead, unwrap it. Inside there's a thick pad of paper and colored pencils, which will be Wally's excuse in case she's caught trespassing. She's an artist, sketching the fine homes in the neighborhood. Today the *Föhn* wind is a presence in Vienna, turning the temperature freakishly warm. A day for an artist to work outdoors.

The driver whistles the horses over to the side of a street near the Zellenkas' house. Erszébet squeezes Wally's hand encouragingly. I'll be waiting nearby. Remember, even a pebble in a Gypsy's room can be significant. Sharpen your eyes.

The outside gate is unlocked. Without looking back, Wally pushes it open and walks confidently past the Zellenkas' house. She enters the garden and finds it altered from her night memory into a place where trees are fixed in their leaflessness and color fills in shapes — a parterre, a row of dwarf conifers — she'd only guessed at before. She recognizes the white statue of a nymph and an urn.

The stable is a large stone building on her left, empty of both horses and carriages. There is straw on the paving stones by the door, a haphazard spill of stiff, pale gold threads.

A dog begins to howl.

She stops. Fear makes her body suddenly hollow, threaded by the pulse of her heart. She waits. Erszébet told her that when Gypsies break into a house, they'll rub their shoes and trousers against the sexual parts of a bitch in heat, to pacify the watchdog.

She pieces the sensations of her body back together. She slowly walks around to the stable. She guesses the outside door must lead to Jószef's room. Before touching the doorknob, she looks at it closely, to see if it was sprinkled with powder. Erszébet told her to check for this. She also examines the threshold for dust or broom straws that her feet would disturb, another trap set for unobservant intruders. Her investigation has the charm of a fairy tale, the clues as cryptic as crumbs on a path, a broken chair and a bowl of cold porridge, a boy with a bone for a finger.

No response to her knock on the door.

Inside the room, she's aware of a curious, intimate smell, although it's as bare as a prison. No one could hide here. She expected to find strange stones and roots arranged on a table, sinister dried objects nailed to the wall, a cabinet of curiosities. Relieved, she sets her pencils and paper on the table.

The blanket on the bed is rough wool; she can't bear to handle it. She pulls it off and tosses it in the corner. The mattress is surprisingly awkward, stuffed with straw, and she struggles to hold an end up, exposing the bare slats of the bed underneath. Nothing to discover. Under the bed there's a moldy-looking bloom of dust she won't disturb.

She's reluctant to handle the bright jacket hanging on a peg. Even wearing gloves, the contact seems too intimate. She recalls the man who wore it as a frightening figure, his metal nose like a toy on his face. It takes her a few minutes to examine the entire garment, turning the sleeves inside out, pressing her fingers into the pockets and all along the lengths of the hems, feeling for a lump or a slip of paper. It would be easier to just take the jacket with me, she thinks.

While searching the room, she listens for noise on the paving stones outside, so she doesn't notice when a shadow breaks the light through the open door. She looks up when heavy boots scrape the step, the sound filling the room so the man in the doorway seems immense, a dark shape. She drops the jacket and grabs the edge of the table, upsetting it with a crash.

He moves his head, and there's a glint of silver as the metal triangle over his nose draws all the light in the room.

CHAPTER 9

NEW THEORY MUST BE CRE-ated from the facts of Dora's murder. A girl discovered dead in a park. After several months, the Inspector had anticipated there would be enough evidence to identify the murderer. But now the careful measure of his investigation seems to mock him. This isn't a fault of his character, he reminds himself. It's just his strategy. He goes over the case, wondering what he's left undone. Has logic not taken him far enough? What are his shortcomings? He needs to find the false step, the unforeseen error, the loose end that the murderer has left for him to unravel.

He focuses on Dora's family. Philipp claimed he was at home the night of the murder. His wife confirmed his statement. But Philipp and his wife could both be lying. He's certain that if confronted, the hysterical woman will only weep her way through a falsehood to help her husband. More probably, her statement is true to what she knows. But the boy. He's let the boy slip. Otto might be pressured into giving a different account of the evening of Dora's death. *The error in the situation.*

But here is not a task in which one can advance little by little, along a natural and clearly demarcated route, terminating when one has completed a certain amount of work mapped out in advance; there is always a new problem to unravel; the investigator whose work is half done has accom-

plished nothing. Either he has solved the problem and quite
finished the work: that means success; or he has done nothing, absolutely nothing.

With threats, official documents, and patience, the Inspector
has forced his way into the Kinderklinik.

Firmly clutching Otto's hand, a nurse bustles him into
the bare white room where the Inspector waits. Although she
instructs the boy to answer the policeman's questions and not
be frightened, the tight grip of her fingers tells him otherwise.
She leads him to a stool across the room.

The Inspector gently suggests Otto be moved closer, so
they can talk. She grimly shakes her head.

"He must stay at a distance from you. It's for your own
good. The boy is infectious. He's under quarantine."

Otto is skinny and hollow-eyed in his thin pajamas. He
gives the Inspector an embarrassed grin.

"Now Fräulein, I'd like you to leave us alone." She begins
to protest, and he continues speaking without raising his voice.
"I want the boy to concentrate on my questions. I need his assistance. Please. May I remind you I'm investigating a criminal
case?"

The nurse sighs heavily and pinches Otto's cheek —
hard — before she leaves. The Inspector is certain she'll wait
outside the door. The boy is visibly relieved and waits for the
Inspector to speak first.

"Otto, let us stand here by the window." He knows another focus makes it easier for children to talk. "I'm sorry
about your sister. I'm trying to discover what happened to her.
Can you help me?"

Without taking his eyes off the street below the window,
Otto nods solemnly.

"I know this might be difficult for you, but I just have a
few questions. Did Dora have any suitors?"

"No."

"There was no one — a man — she was fond of?"

"No one."

"Did she get along well with your father?"

The boy begins to rub his finger against the window. "I don't understand."

"Did they have arguments?"

"Yes," he whispers. "Papa took her piano away because I asked him to." He turns to the Inspector, his eyes shining with tears.

The Inspector briefly touches the boy's shoulder. "I'm certain your papa had a good reason for what he did. Don't let it disturb you."

Otto stares out the window and says nothing. He smears his hand across the moisture condensed on the glass.

"This was a long time ago, but can you remember what happened the last night Dora was at home? Your family ate dinner together. Then how did everyone spend the evening?"

After some hesitation, Otto says his mother was home all night. She went to bed early. Right after dinner, he was sent to his room to study. He remembers his father came home very late. He knew he'd been out since he was wearing a jacket.

"Why do you remember that night? Did something happen when your father returned?" The Inspector submerges his excitement. He must test the boy's story as if it were a coin, see if it's real gold.

Very matter-of-fact, Otto explains that his bedroom adjoins the dining room, so he woke up when his father came in and then watched him through a crack in the door. His father went to the cabinet where the brandy was locked up. His mother always kept the key with her. His father pounded on the glass door of the cabinet until it broke open and cut his hand. He stood there for a long time without touching the brandy. Blood covered his hand. He believes it was three days later when his father told him that Dora had died. That's all I have to say, he adds, nimbly stepping away from the Inspector. He begins to cough violently, his body shaking.

The Inspector watches him helplessly. When the boy is quiet again, he motions for the Inspector to come closer, he's having trouble speaking.

"Will you ask Mama when I can come home?" he rasps.

He gravely makes a promise and then thanks Otto for sharing his information. The interview is over.

Afterward, the Inspector is surprised by the vehemence of his pleasure. Otto has destroyed his father's alibi. Philipp has been caught in a lie. However, his pleasure in the confirmation of his suspicions is precarious, since another piece of information may overturn it. His accomplishment is flawed with the fear of loss. A vessel with a hidden crack.

Occasionally, a suspect's or a witness's words or facial expression will instantly become a point of connection to other circumstances previously established in a crime. This magically alters its structure. The facts fall into a new order, becoming as clear, dry, and final as a game of cards. This never happens chronologically. It can never be anticipated. He can never force the process.

He finds himself going directly to a familiar street and entering Philipp's building. A shy secretary scurries from her desk to announce him, then stares at the floor as he enters Philipp's office.

This time there is no offer of a cigar. Sending a silent message, the Inspector aggressively angles his chair in a different direction before he sits down in it. He makes a leisurely search of all his pockets for his notebook, never taking his eyes off Philipp's expressionless face.

"What time did you return to the house the night of your daughter's murder?"

Philipp turns and looks out the window, but not before the Inspector notices his eyes rapidly blink.

"As I certainly told you, I was at home for the entire evening." His voice is weary and patient.

"Your son has a different story."

"Ah, yes? His mind must be sharper than mine."

"The boy had no doubt about the date and remembered you'd injured your hand."

Philipp touches his lips, then rests his hand on the desk. The room is silent.

"Perhaps my memory is at fault. To be honest, I'd been drinking. I do believe that I spent some time with my physician, Dr. Steinach. Maybe we ran into each other that evening in Café Pucher." He folds his arms across his chest and leans back in his chair.

The Inspector quickly jots down a half sentence describing the man's change of posture. *Defiant. Uneasy about his alibi.* Their conversation has speeded up. Dora's father is rattled, and he intends to keep him off balance.

"Do you recollect what time you met Dr. Steinach?"

Dora's father regretfully shakes his head.

"How late was it when you returned to the house that night?"

"Unfortunately, that I don't remember." After a moment he adds, "It was a while ago. It's difficult to be exact about such matters."

"Never mind. I will contact the doctor. Perhaps he'll remember the time."

The Inspector suddenly stands up and permits himself a stiff smile.

"I'll be back in touch with you very soon."

Philipp hesitates, and his hands fumble with some papers. "My son isn't well. As you know, he's hospitalized for a lung ailment. I wouldn't rely on his memory if I were you. I doubt anyone else would take his statements seriously. No one would believe a sick child." He looks as if he's about to say something else, and then the moment slips away.

"I'll need to see your appointment book to verify your activities on the day of the murder."

Philipp frowns. "I'll consult the book when I have a moment."

"I have time now. I'd like to wait."

"Very well." His voice is loud and insistent. "Fräulein Fürj?"

The door opens, and the young secretary soundlessly enters the room. She's uneasy, and stands with her eyes fixed on the carpet.

"Would you bring my appointment book? You may have trouble finding it."

Without raising her head, she nods and leaves.

The Inspector noticed the indirect instruction and the change in Philipp's voice when he asked her to get his book. He's certain she won't be able to locate it. The men make stiff small talk about *Bürgermeister* Dr. Lueger's attempt to organize a servant's registry until Fräulein Fürj reappears, embarrassed and empty-handed.

Philipp shakes his head. "What a shame. No luck. When my appointment book turns up, I'll let you know." His voice barely apologetic.

The Inspector suddenly stands up. "Fine. I'll be expecting to hear from you soon. Fräulein, a few words alone with you?"

Now she raises her eyes in alarm, glancing wildly at her employer. He shrugs, and his gesture looks like a warning.

"Come with me, please?"

The Inspector quickly ushers her out the door and closes it behind them. To make himself less threatening, for he is a tall man, he leans against the edge of her desk. She stands in front of him, waiting, poised as a shamed schoolgirl. He notices her scuffed shoes and the soiled cuffs on her blouse. She's a plump blonde, and he suspects her ill-fitting skirt is held at the waist with a pin. She can't afford to help me, he thinks. He struggles to find a place between kindly concern and authority before slipping into the routine of an interview. He gently tells her it is absolutely necessary to find the missing appointment book. It may have crucial information to help solve Dora's death. He's careful not to associate her employer with the murder. The deceased girl was about your age, Fräulein, perhaps you knew her?

She fidgets, looking frightened. He smiles reassuringly. Her nervousness reminds him of a small animal. If she were a rabbit, he'd slowly, slowly reach out his hand and cup her pale head right behind her ears before lifting up the rest of her body. Alarmed, as if reading his mind, she stammers she didn't know Dora, she met her once, and she'll search for the appointment book. She can't imagine how it disappeared. Truly.

When he asks her to describe it, she tells him it's a fancy
leather book from Pachhofer with gold-edged paper. One page
for each day. Yes, she writes down all of her employer's appointments. He once had a smaller duplicate book to take on
his travels.

"Fräulein Fürj, I trust you'll keep your eyes open for me?"

Her nod of agreement is tremulous, and when she looks
up, her eyes are magnified by tears. He solemnly kisses her
hand.

The Inspector makes an official appointment to meet with en-
docrinologist Eugen Steinach to discuss his patient Philipp.
The Inspector is familiar with the renowned doctor's research.
Neue Freie Presse has often published reports of Steinach's terrible method of forcing oxen to give milk and shriveling the
breasts of female guinea pigs, turning them into hermaphro-
dites. By altering the hormones of his human patients, the doctor claims, he can grant them perpetual youth. The office of
Steinach and his partner, Dr. Last, is located near the Institute
for the Investigation of Radium, on Waisenhausgasse in the
Ninth District. Steinach's experiments on animals are conducted in a laboratory attached to the medical office.

The Inspector joins a group of men and women, most of
them elderly foreigners, in Steinach's overheated laboratory.
They make a strange procession, filing between the towering
stacks of wire cages — a city of ziggurats — filled with small
animals. The ladies pinch their nostrils or hold handkerchiefs
against the smell and pull their wraps close around their
shoulders to keep them away from the cages.

Steinach motions for everyone to gather around a cage.
Smiling, he instructs them to breathe deeply, inhale the unfamiliar animal odor as the first step of their treatment. Look
here, he says. This rat is ten years old but has the energy and
appearance of a young animal.

The women giggle nervously and hesitantly move closer.

My rejuvenation process will restore your youth, he tells
them. You'll have joy again. Under the intense overhead lights,

the bars of a cage are reflected on his spectacles, dark lines that waver as he speaks, striping his eyes. When a frail-looking man asks how the process works, Steinach's face floods with color, and he twists around in the small space. He gazes at them with the fervor of a man dispensing salvation.

The reproduction channel in the male generative gland will be sutured, he explains, to increase the production of a second liquid, which enters the bloodstream and preserves vigor. This halts the aging process. There is no danger or pain from the surgery.

The elderly man nods. Several of the women are bothered by this discussion and two of them quietly leave the room. The Inspector watches their hats bob away between the cages.

An hour later, the Inspector sits in Steinach's office. The file on Dora's father tilts on top of the other papers shipwrecked on the desk. The doctor opens the file and leisurely glances through it before handing it over.

"Here's the file you requested. I've had a copy made, so you can keep the original."

The Inspector leafs through the papers, pages of elaborate, scrolling handwriting. He stops at a photograph. It's difficult to make out. He frowns at the black-and-white splotches, whorls of dark lines, before he recognizes it as a man's genitals.

"This is a photograph of Philipp?"

"Yes. He has syphilis. I'm treating him with mercury. The *Krankengeschichte* photographs chart the course of the disease. Unfortunately, syphilis has more visible effects than what you see in the photographs of his male organ."

"His face?"

"You must have met him, yes? His nose is caving in. There's only a slight change in the cartilage now. Later on, I'll have to insert wax or an ivory plate to fill in where the bridge will sink. Otherwise, he'll have a hole in his face."

The Inspector involuntarily touches his own nose. "How long has he been under your care?"

"Three years. Does your visit have anything to do with his daughter's death?"

He nods.

Steinach leans forward, lowers his voice. "Terrible, terrible shame. The girl was so young. Puzzling case. Any idea who is responsible?"

"I couldn't really say."

"I'm certain it must have been a foreigner. Or Gypsies. Remember that young seamstress who was murdered in Polna a few years ago? A ritual murder, wasn't it?"

"It seems highly unlikely."

The doctor asks if he's seen the crowd of men in the Volksprater, all unemployed criminal types.

The Inspector says nothing. He opens his notebook. "Let me ask you to bring your attention back to your patient Philipp. He claims you were together on the evening his daughter died." He's gratified to see Steinach blink and frown.

"We occasionally meet at a café in the evening. It's possible we met that night, yes." Steinach's face folds into a helpless, worried expression.

The Inspector studies him, directing all the energy of his skepticism into this silent exchange. In that instant, he recognizes his own pleasure in the process of calculation. Even the silences and the waiting. There's a word for it, *Schwebezustand,* suspended in time and space.

"Perhaps I met Philipp that night, but at the moment I simply don't remember. Where did he say we were?"

The Inspector raises his eyebrows in answer to this question.

"Yes, of course." Steinach throws up his hands. Since there's nothing more to harvest from the man's expression, the Inspector resumes his questions.

"Have you noticed any changes in Philipp's behavior since his daughter's death?"

Steinach shrugs. "He's lost weight. He's missed some appointments. He's not a man who shows his cards, if you understand what I mean."

"But what is his mental state?"

"Mental state? Grief has strained his health. His lungs are infected. He's a man in mourning. That's all I can tell you."

"And his wife?"

Steinach is restless from the questioning. "Regrettably, Philipp contracted syphilis before he was married and passed it on to her. She goes to spas for treatment. I know she's obsessed with her illness. The whole family is sickly."

Steinach abruptly asks if he'd like a private tour of the laboratory. Yes, the Inspector says, I'd like another tour, and puts away his notebook.

The laboratory is a nervous hive of activity, the jerky movements of small animals. The doctor sweeps his arms over the cages. My kingdom, he says. My assistants call them my subjects. Guinea pigs. Rats. Rabbits.

The Inspector walks ahead. He sticks his finger into a cage, and it's nuzzled by a lively rat with a red scar zigzagged across the shaved skin on its back. My most celebrated patient, Steinach announces. I turned this male rate into a female rat. The nipples were transplanted in pairs. Amazing how you can toss a creature from one sex to the other, isn't it?

The Inspector finds his way out of Steinach's laboratory. He recollects a passage from *Kriminalistik*. *"The Investigating Officer must always make himself form an idea as to whether the person has spoken the truth and the whole truth, or whether he has lied or passed over something in silence."*

Both Philipp and his doctor may have very different reasons for not telling the truth. Then again, perhaps there is some other link between them that he's not aware of. Not yet.

The Inspector closes Steinach's file on Dora's father and flops it on the desk toward Franz. A boat launched on the water. Here's our case, he says. Have a look at these photographs. He begins to pace the room.

"Philipp has syphilis, has had it for decades, and he's being treated with mercury. Probably infected by a *süsses Mädel.*"

Franz leafs through the file. Without looking, the Inspector senses he's staring at the photograph of Philipp's genitals.

Franz whistles. "This is certainly a lesson, sir."

His face flushed, Franz goes quickly through the rest of the file, his fingers skipping over the photographs, uneasy about touching or studying them too closely. As if they were contagious.

The Inspector leaves Philipp's file on the table in the hallway while he reads in his study. Erszébet goes through it, stopping at the photographs. She can duplicate the papers, carry them sentence by sentence into her notebook. But the photographs must be copied with brush and paints.

Late that night, alone in the kitchen, she studies the details of Philipp's photographs, his snarled pubic hair, the dark, starry patches of infection and lesions like thumbprints on his pale skin, the flaccid gray penis. Then she begins to paint.

She copies one of the black-and-white images in colors of her own imagination. The blotches on his genitals become a livid rainbow of green tints and yellows tinged with red tones, luteous colors. The penis is transformed into the tense hanging shape of a ripe fig, a rich violet red darkened with imperial purple, a paint made from acid extracted from the excrement of Peruvian gulls.

Uninterrupted, she finishes her watercolor of the photograph. Afterward, she tapes the damp paper on the underside of the kitchen table to dry. Her secret.

Her husband is asleep when she comes up to bed, holding a rim of violet red paint under her fingernails, a color she transfers to his body.

Wally, Otto, and Dora's mother take a closed fiaker to Stadtpark. They get out at the north end. Wally notices that the landscape of the park has changed since she was here a month ago, before the tender trees and ornamental shrubs in pots were wheeled into the greenhouses for the winter. Now the ground is completely white, and the artificial lake is frozen, ready for ice skating. Otto pays the attendant six kreuzers so they can sit on the benches along the side.

Across the lake, a line of workmen join hands and slowly slide forward, testing the ice. Two of the men at the end slip and stagger forward, arms windmilling until they fall. The others break the line to help them to their feet, and then the procession moves again.

Wally helps Dora's mother settle herself on the bench, tucking a fur lap robe around her legs. This should keep her in place. Otto has just been released from the Kinderklinik, and she plans to talk to him alone.

"Has Otto ever skated here before?"

"We came last year with Dora. I remember it was a very cold day. A band played Strauss waltzes. You could hear the music across the ice." Dora's mother falls silent and stares at the lake.

Wally wonders if she anticipates her dead daughter will materialize from the ice.

Eyes still focused in the distance, the older woman begins to speak, but it's as if she's talking to herself. "I skated here when I was younger. After Tegetthof's expedition to the Arctic, ice-skating was very fashionable. We called ourselves *Esquimaux*. Some daring women had costumes made. I had a cap, a coat, breeches, and leggings all made of black fur, and I carried a muff. I remember I made a pirouette and my cap came off. I had very long hair then, down to my waist, and it flew all around my head."

Wally gazes over the lake, a dark white oval, picturing a young woman spinning on the ice, her long pale hair a blur, a horizontal halo around her head.

"Maybe you'd like to look at the ice, the bandstand? We can go closer."

"No, no. My legs are too frail. You go ahead, take Otto with you. Be careful. Promise me you won't step on the ice."

She seems older, the sad bulk of her body immobilized by the lap robe. Glad to leave her, Wally guides Otto over to the lake, their feet crunching on snow. She can tell he is eager to run, to throw sticks on the ice, which would provoke a call to come back from his mother.

"If you walk carefully, we can go around the lake where she can't see us."

He glances back and then takes Wally's outstretched hand. They edge around the lake until the woman huddled on the bench becomes a diminutive brown shape. He drops Wally's hand.

"Cold out today."

"Doesn't bother me."

"No? You're a brave boy."

"Mama opened all the windows to air the house before we left. I'd rather be out here than freezing in my bedroom."

"What did your sister do when your mother opened all the windows like that?"

"She hated it. They argued. Dora would start coughing and wouldn't speak."

They're a quarter of the way around the lake. From the corner of her eye, she sees his mother stand up and wave in their direction. Wally quickly looks away, looks out over the ice. Soothed by its dull, blank surface, she continues her interrogation. Did your sister have a sweetheart? she asks.

"A sweetheart? Dora? No."

"No one?"

The boy shakes his head.

"What about Rosza, Dora's *promeneuse?* Did Rosza like your father? Did they ever talk together?"

"They talked together sometimes."

"But did they go anywhere alone, did you see them?"

He's silent. Wally taps a stone with her foot until he talks.

"Rosza made me promise not to tell anyone, but I guess I can tell you. Sometimes she made me stay in the kitchen because she'd go upstairs with him. I went up there once, and the door to her room was closed."

"How many times did that happen?"

"I don't remember."

The boy picks up a rock and politely shows it to her. See, it's not so big, he says. Can I throw it? She shrugs, and he steps back and pitches it over the ice. There's a faint cry behind him. They disregard it and she urges him to walk faster, away from his mother's voice. Stumbling on patches of frozen snow, they hurry to the far end of the lake.

"I need to know something about your father and Frau Zellenka."

"I don't want to talk about them. Can I toss another stone?"

Answer my question, she says, or I'll take you back to your mother. He searches the ground for a stone while he talks about his father and Frau Zellenka. Their walks together while Mama cleaned or napped. At Franzenbad, the two of them would often go back through the pines to the cottage while everyone else stayed by the lake. He tried to follow them. Once he saw his father push Frau Zellenka in the hammock. Once he heard Dora angrily tell her she'd seen them together in a café, and Frau Zellenka closed her eyes and turned away, her face suddenly pale. He recites his story with a remorseless happiness, settling a score with his father, Rosza, and Frau Zellenka. When he's finished talking, he stares at her, the stones clenched in his hands forgotten.

But Wally doesn't notice him. She's furiously considering a new hypothesis. *Was Dora's father intimate with Rosza and Frau Zellenka?*

Suddenly, a handful of stones rattles on the ice, and the men shout; Otto's missiles went too close. They both laugh and run away onto the lake ice, sliding, their balance suddenly transformed by its slippery surface. Otto turns around and furiously lobs another rock in their direction.

Wally barely hears the men's angry cries. She believes the stones that struck the ice have cracked it into a web of silver slivers, a flat explosion that moves faster and faster across the lake. She runs, imagining the ice silently shattering into lace behind her. It will break beneath her feet, and she will plunge into the bitter water.

Erszébet persuaded her husband to come to bed early. She waits for him there. As he enters the bedroom, he senses her perfume unfolding around him, a narcotic atmosphere of musk, ambergris, vanilla, iris, rose. She prepared this invisible landscape for him to cross.

As Erszébet planned, he is compelled to reenter a memory, their intimate encounter in the woods near Csurgó, when she'd worn the same fragrance. Even as he steps forward, shadowless, he marvels at his wife's deliberation, how she's doubly invoked her presence.

The curtains are pulled back from the window, and the moonlight illuminates her reclining figure. She is polished stone, she doesn't move. He crosses the space between them like a dancer, oblivious to the scenery, the audience, everything in him wholly focused on his next cue, his next step, his arousal.

As she rises over him in bed, he glimpses a trembling, teardrop-shaped swell of light at one of her ears, the unaccustomed gleam of a pearl earring. He reaches up to touch it, but she slips away from his hands.

In the next moment, before he passes into the state toward which Erszébet drives him, he recognizes the earring. He believes they are identical to Dora's.

In the morning, remembering what he saw, he sweeps her hair back on the pillow, checking for the earrings. Her ears are bare. When she turns her face to him, he reads a calculation in her eyes that he is unable to decipher.

Then he does something surprising. Instead of asking her about the earrings, which her expression seems to demand, he watches as she obligingly narrows her eyes and transforms her face into its familiar mask of pleasure, following the urging of his fingertips.

Later, he tells himself that what he saw — Dora's earrings — was a trick of the light.

There's a Hungarian word for his state of mind, *lidércnyomás,* meaning dread, depression, nightmare.

Seated in the library, the Inspector listens to Dora's father confidently explain his wife's disappearance. She suddenly left Vienna for Franzenbad, a sanatorium in western Bohemia. She needed rest. Grief caused her nerves to fail. She may return in a few weeks. No, he had no idea he should notify the police before she left. None at all. Why did they need to talk to his wife again? Are there any new developments in his daughter's investigation?

Philipp seems anxious to help, deferentially inclining his neat head toward him. The Inspector lets a moment of silence pass before he answers, struggling to rid himself of a fuzz of impatience. His voice is almost lazy.

"There are some developments which I am not at liberty to disclose to you. However, I want your wife's address in case I need to reach her. Is there a telephone at the sanatorium? No? I didn't imagine there would be."

The Inspector had come to the house to talk with Dora's parents about another matter. Now he regrets that his treasured information will only be displayed in front of this man. He considers whether this is a conceit or a strategic error, and takes out his notebook, stalling for time.

"Sir, I have interviewed Dr. Steinach. He has no memory of meeting you at a café the evening of your daughter's death."

Philipp raises his eyebrows. He meets the Inspector's eyes.

"He doesn't? Now that is very strange indeed. I even remember the meal we were served. *Szegedi gulyás.* Pity I didn't leave my hat or walking stick there. At least I'd have some proof to offer you besides my good word."

"Yes. Have you managed to locate your missing appointment book?"

Philipp strokes his nose. He has a patient and regretful expression on his face.

"Unfortunately, the book has failed to turn up. I'll ask the girl to search the office a second time, just to be certain."

"Thank you. I appreciate your help." The Inspector nods and makes a note to discreetly contact Fräulein Fürj again. *"But it is necessary to face in advance the possible falsehood of every statement of witnesses. To do so is not to display exaggerated mistrust, but is only a proof of prudence and experience; for one has often found that false depositions slip into an inquiry in the most innocent and least suspected form."*

While Philipp is relaxed, confident the issue of the missing appointment book has been resolved, the Inspector quickly continues his questioning.

"I understand you've had a relationship with Frau Zellenka for several years. She had no expectation you would marry her?"

"We never discussed it. The arrangement suited everyone as it was. My wife has a blind eye about my relationship with Frau Zellenka." His attitude is that it is too complicated to explain.

The Inspector is silent. Sometimes this can be interpreted as a judgment.

"If my wife wanted a divorce, the *Landesgericht* would investigate her. All her faults would be made public."

"Surely your wife has conducted herself in a blameless fashion."

"Certainly. But she could never face such scrutiny. She isn't well, inspector. And why should my wife put herself in such an unpleasant situation? It's an ugly process. Even if a woman has good reason to file for divorce, the *Landesgericht* usually dismisses her claims. That is the procedure unless both parties agree to a divorce. But I'm certain you're familiar with all this."

Philipp offers a Regalitas, and the Inspector understands he wishes to end this topic of conversation. He thanks him for the cigar and ignores Philipp's last comment.

"The situation couldn't have been pleasant for your children. Dora knew about your relationship with Frau Zellenka. She must have been extremely jealous."

Perhaps his comment about the man's children was a mistake. Never show judgment. And Philipp doesn't answer his question but shifts the objects around on his desk.

"If Dora was jealous, I wasn't aware of it. In fact, she and Frau Zellenka were very good friends. When we were on vacation, they were constantly together."

"I believe Frau Zellenka is much younger than your wife? In fact, she's closer to Dora's age?"

"Yes, Frau Zellenka is younger than my wife, but you could have answered that question yourself, since you've spoken with her."

Now the man sitting across from him is flustered. His fingers touch his nose and lips.

The Inspector feels his words contract and narrow around him. He raises his voice and is dismayed at how bitter it sounds.

"Did Dora sense it was unnatural to be friends with her father's lover?"

Philipp stands up behind his desk. "Since you came here without an appointment, I must ask you to leave. I have an evening engagement."

He walks to the door and waits for the Inspector. He doesn't acknowledge his farewell or shake his hand.

The Inspector is certain Philipp has lied to him about his whereabouts on the night of the murder. And possibly his wife's disappearance. He prides himself on his ability to pick out the thread of a lie and follow it through the events of a case. Sometimes he can even decipher the structure of the falsehood before the confession, as some men can recognize a certain tailor's hand by the set of the shoulder on a jacket.

Without any advance notice, a fiaker was dispatched to bring Frau Zellenka to the police station.

The Inspector ushers her into the bare room next to the morgue and then brings her a chair. She sits down without even glancing at the tattered cloak spread out on the table. She's obviously not pleased to be here. It's an ugly place, and the lighting is harsh. She takes out a cigarette and lights it.

"Do you mind if I smoke?"

He says no but doesn't offer a container for her ashes. She crosses her legs and elaborately flicks her cigarette onto the floor.

He makes her wait a moment.

"Frau Zellenka, thank you for coming here on such short notice."

"My pleasure, although I'm not very presentable at this hour of the morning. I hope your assistant didn't mind waiting for me."

Sarcasm is one of the most difficult obstacles in an interview. Even silence offers more nuances of interpretation.

"That's his job. Now I'd like you to examine the cloak on the table."

She pivots around in her chair, the cigarette between her lips. Grudgingly, she gets up and walks to the table.

"May I touch it?"

He nods. She gingerly opens the dirty cloak at the top, checking the inside of the neck.

"The label is missing."

"You'll find it inside the envelope on the table."

She opens the envelope, reads the label without removing it. She stares at him, her expression confused.

"I believe this is my *kazabaika,* the cloak Dora borrowed from me. Of course, it's hard to recognize, the color is quite faded. The lining held up remarkably well."

"Any idea where Dora might have worn it?"

"You mean a special evening?" She laughs. "Dora had no special evenings. Maybe she wore it to one of her lectures."

There's silence between them. He senses she's waiting for something.

"Strange thing to borrow in the summer, a cloak."

"It was." She shrugs. "Dora paraded around the bedroom with the *kazabaika* wrapped around her, laughing. It pleased her. She never returned it to me. Where did you find the cloak?"

"In the Volksgarten."

Stalling, he thinks. He takes out his notebook. They face each other across the bare room, awkward and oddly formal, like actors rehearsing without the benefits of props or scenery. His voice is gentle.

"Frau Zellenka, anything you can do to help me. Is there anything you remember about Dora that might be significant? Did anyone bear her a grudge?"

After a moment she looks up at him. Her mouth has relaxed.

"It's nothing, really. Last summer, Dora left her new reticule on the bench in my garden. Jószef found it and buried it. I guess he was teaching her a lesson, although he claimed it was a joke. Of course she told her mother. I had to reprimand him and he returned it. He hadn't stolen anything, all the coins were still inside. But Dora was hysterical when she saw her reticule, all dirty."

Now he can tell she believes she's said too much. She falls into smiles, pretends confusion, but her eyes are wary.

"I have things to do, will you excuse me?"

No. He's tired of her self-righteous dodging.

"Frau Zellenka, you've been having an affair with Dora's father for some time now. Isn't that correct?"

"May I ask why this intrusive question is necessary?"

"I'm investigating a murder."

"And?"

"You had an illicit relationship with Philipp. Does it not seem remarkable that you were also an intimate friend of his daughter's?"

"We never discussed her father. I assure you, I was very discreet. The adults all consented to the situation, except for his ignorant wife. Although I suspect she knew about our relationship."

He can't believe their intimacy was a secret from Dora. Is this his key to the crime? He's conscious of his hostility toward Frau Zellenka. And a strange protectiveness toward the dead girl.

She hasn't removed her cloak, and now she hugs it around her body as she paces around the table, not looking at him.

"I will tell you Dora was jealous of me. She admired me. That's why she borrowed my clothes. No one else paid her any attention, poor girl, except when she was ill. She was hardly my rival. Objectively, I'd say she conspired with me. She took care of the children so I could spend time with her father. Can you really imagine she didn't know what was going on between us?"

She looks down at the cloak on the table with a tender expression.

"If I had wanted to obliterate Dora, there are other ways I could have accomplished it. But it was unnecessary. I'm the one who should have been killed, for stealing her father. Maybe it was a mistaken identity? Dora was wearing my cloak."

He feels himself turning to stone, his jaw stiffening with anger.

"You might be more careful about the statements you make to the police, Frau Zellenka. Jokes are suspect here."

Her astonished expression is a satisfactory answer.

The manner in which an individual presents himself, looks around, allows himself to be questioned, replies, asks questions in return, in a word the way in which he behaves, ought never, even in the most insignificant affair, be a matter of indifference to the conscientious Investigating Officer.

After Frau Zellenka leaves, he walks to his favorite *Tabak-Trafiken* and purchases an entire box of Britannicas cigars. He retraces his interview with Frau Zellenka. His permanent self-scrutiny. During their conversation, he twice became emotional. Once when he felt protective of Dora. The second time, curiously, was when Frau Zellenka joked about being the intended murder victim.

Kriminalistik has no strategy for an Inspecting Officer's passion for a victim.

The Inspector dreamed about Dora in the Volksgarten. Although the face and figure of the murderer weren't revealed to him, a feeling of dread still remained the next morning, like a scent with a faint, half-recognized memory attached to it.

He adds this dream to the observations in his notebook about the girl's murder. His dreams, hunches, and impressions are his version of the crime, just as his wife's *nature morte* is an arrangement that satisfies some unconscious theory of hers.

Waiting on the Franz-Josefs-Kai, Wally can't distinguish Erszébet from the other women in the crowd, all of them dressed in broad hats and furs. Their figures blur into a black pattern moving over the cobblestones. There is even less to distinguish the men from each other, since identical bowler hats top each head, and walking sticks extend their arms. Above them, the suspended cables of the tramway are woven into a tense and asymmetrical web.

Erszébet appears and they barely have time to exchange a greeting before the tram arrives. As Wally hoists herself up behind Erszébet into the car, the edge of her fur wrap brushes her mouth.

They sit silently next to each other until the tram reaches the Stubenring, and Erszébet points out the Museum für Kunst Industrie. When they pass Stadtpark, she directs Wally's eyes to the Kursalon, where military concerts are held on Sundays. On Kolowratring, there's the Adelige Casino Club, which only noblemen can join.

Wally is drowsy, her mind slipping into English, relaxing into the security of Erszébet's presence. Even when she was searching Jószef's room, Wally believed she was safe, moving under Erszébet's guardianship. She wishes Erszébet gave her the same attention at other times. But it had been gratifying when she saw Erszébet by the fiaker, peering at the Zellenkas' house, waiting for her. The worried expression on her face vanished when Wally ran through the gate. Erszébet actually embraced Wally until she stopped crying. Jószef had badly frightened her, and she discovered nothing in his room.

As she waited outside Herr Zellenka's house that day, Erszébet was entirely focused on Wally in a way that is impossible for her when they are together. She was relieved to see Wally after she'd escaped Jószef, but she also resented her anxiety. She had kept a distance in her friendships since she nursed the young woman stricken with cholera. Now she understands that her investigation of Dora — its ruthlessness, hidden rules, unfathomable denouement — has replaced that intimacy. She remembers wandering to the window in the white room while the sick woman slept to watch for harbingers of death. She listened for a dog's howl. She heard nothing, saw nothing. Her tarot cards — all the signs she relied on — were useless. Prophecy had failed. She was merely a witness as the woman died.

Wally watches their reflections, strangely distorted in the tram window, until the elderly woman sitting behind them leaves. Now they can whisper their theories. Otto's new information has confused their calculations. Are the boy's stories about Rosza true? Can they trust him? Was Dora's father simultaneously conducting an affair with both Rosza and Frau Zellenka? Their vision of Dora has changed. She has gradually become an even more fragile apparition, pushed aside by her father, who forced his way into every relationship the girl had.

Erszébet can still visualize Dora's face as her brush touched it, but now she craves another face. She wants to see Dora's father.

They get off the tram near Haarhof. Erszébet wants to try the Hungarian wine at the Esterházy Keller.

In the restaurant, Erszébet shakes her head and turns down the *Speiseträger*'s offer of a sunny window table, so he scornfully ushers them to a secluded place in the back. After the waiter vanishes with their orders, Erszébet takes a book from her satchel.

"Now I'm going to show you my evidence," she announces. She removes the paper wrapper from the book, turns it inside out, and lays it open on the table.

Puzzled, Wally leans over to examine the bright patchwork of indecipherable shapes painted on the paper. She senses Erszébet's triumph, her hunger for praise, but she doesn't recognize the image. *I'm sorry,* she whispers, *what is it?*

My dear child, Erszébet murmurs. This is a man, Dora's father. I painted a copy of his photograph from the doctor's files. See what syphilis has done to his genitals.

Wally stares at the image, fascinated by the colors, the unfamiliar swollen shape. Erszébet's painted judgment.

❧

Frau Zellenka watches from the doorway as the Inspector, Franz, Móricz, and two assistants search Jószef's room. They don't tell her what they're looking for.

The furniture is examined first. Móricz goes over the chair and table with a magnifying glass, looking for suspicious marks. Then he turns both pieces of furniture over and scrapes the bottom of the legs with a knife, looking for holes that might have been drilled there, a hiding place for a slip of paper or some small object. The others slash open the mattress and dump the straw on canvas tarpaulins spread outside on the thin snow. They pick through the straw, a handful at a time.

Móricz digs his knife into the putty around the small window. Franz pulls apart the steps in front of the door. They rapidly finish their search.

Nothing to report, sir.

Don't dismiss this place so quickly, the Inspector tells them, seeing they're too easily satisfied. "Remember, criminals often keep souvenirs of their misdeeds. When I stripped a suspect after his arrest for housebreaking, I found a newspaper clipping about an unsolved murder hidden in his hat. The man broke down and confessed to the crime." He reminds them of a previous case when Franz discovered a locket and twenty gold coins in a pot of soup boiling on top of a stove. And another time, a search turned up an incriminating letter under the lining of a birdcage.

They turn their attention to Jószef's bare room. They divide the walls into sections, starting at the right of the door and going clockwise. They remove their jackets and brush down the plaster walls, scattering the thick dust that might conceal a daub of fresh plaster or a hole. The room is cold, and they work in silence, settling into a rhythm. No matter what the circumstances there is always a sense of trespassing about a search, as if they were despoilers of the hearth.

The Inspector looks over his shoulder and is surprised to find Frau Zellenka still standing in the doorway, a bored expression on her face.

As Franz carries the chair out the doorway, he intentionally bumps into her. She doesn't look at him, doesn't expect an
apology, she simply pulls her coat tighter around her body.

Móricz slowly sifts the ashes from the stove into a box,
then methodically works the broom across the floor, pushing a
gray tide of dust from corner to corner. He scoops the sweep-
ings into two envelopes and hands them to the Inspector.

"Anything here, Móricz?"

He nods.

Inside the smaller envelope there's a bone button. A clod
of clay. A small silver coin found between stones on the floor.
Two pins.

Almost magically, a maid materializes with coffee, milk
rolls, and *Kipfel*. A faint, cloudy smear of heat drifts up from
the cups when the coffee is poured, it's that cold in the room.
While the others finish their coffee outside, holding the thin
cups in their reddened hands, Frau Zellenka stays next to the
Inspector. Her loose silk coat, printed with a geometric pattern, and the elaborate silver coffee service seem strangely festive in this poor room.

His annoyance with her is distracting. Even without her
words — for she's barely spoken since they started work —
she gives the impression they are laboring in her service. She is
bored and critical at the same time. He remembers a passage
from one of Gross's lectures: *The emotions which are always
produced in an important case interfere with and confuse one's impressions.* That is why it is so necessary to scrupulously describe every object, record every word from a witness, so they
can be dispassionately evaluated later. For now, he's too busy to
do the necessary documentation in his notebook.

His assistants follow his orders, working within the structure of the investigation. Hopefully, they're learning to recognize the disorder that authenticates a piece of evidence. They
should also sense when to trust — and not trust — their own
perceptions to decipher it. Not trusting is key. Not like falling
into faith or love, other revealers.

"Are you nearly finished with your search?" Frau Zellenka asks the Inspector.

"Not yet. We do the floors last. When you've finished with your coffee, my men will need mops, sponges, and several buckets of water."

Puzzled, she gestures to the maid, tells her to help the Inspector with his request.

Now they're ready for the last step of their work. In the far corner of the room, one of the men tips a bucket and slowly pours a thin line of water directly in front of Franz and Móricz. They kneel and peer closely at the wet floor. Additional buckets are passed hand to hand and gently emptied onto the floor, wetting a quarter of the space. The Inspector joins them, squatting on his heels, carefully examining the edges of the stones. In the deliberate posture of a crab, he makes his way across the room. Nothing catches his eye. Everything is equally gray. There's an odor, the cold heart of wet stone.

Later, while the buckets are being refilled, he stands outside with Frau Zellenka. It's in his interest to be patient with her. He's conscious the others are less skillful at hiding their resentment at her presence. He offers her a cigarette and lights another one for himself.

"Tell me what you're doing in this room. What is the water for?"

"The water will give us a sign. It reveals whether any stones have been disturbed. If anything's hidden underneath them."

"So the stones speak."

He doesn't understand her joke and looks at her blankly. She quickly asks him to show her what he means.

Back in the room, she bunches her coat around her waist and crouches next to him. Móricz pours water on the floor near them, careful as a servant, mindful of her fine shoes.

The Inspector points to the crusted edge of cement around a stone. "The water should be equally absorbed by the dirt and mortar here, between the stones. If the water bubbles and sinks quickly, it means the area has been tampered with."

She nods and stays where she is, watching. Franz joins them, and she reluctantly moves aside for him.

Móricz and the other assistants take turns slowly lapping

down more water, trying to distribute it evenly. Each time the
Inspector and Franz finish their examination of the floor and
move back, the next full bucket is ready. They've finished half
of the room.

There's noise outside, the metal jangle of equipment that
announces Egon's arrival with the camera. The Inspector intends to document Jószef's room as if it had been the scene of
a crime. Tell him to wait, the Inspector says without raising his
eyes. Finally, he stands up to stretch.

"Here, sir." Móricz bends over a spot on the floor.

A row of small bubbles — the frailest of beads — slowly
rises and breaks in the dirt rimmed around a large stone.

The Inspector takes a magnifying glass from the sabre-
tache looped to his belt and crouches down for a closer look.
Then he stands and motions for help. The men move quickly,
trying to contain their excitement. Hands set down tools and a
pick on the floor. Resentful of Móricz's discovery, Franz sul-
lenly unwinds a bulky leather roll and unpacks a lancet and
pliers.

Picks are inserted at opposite ends of the stone. Móricz
forces his tool down and then up, loosening it enough for
Franz to wedge a hand under it. They pry the stone from the
floor, and a heavy odor of mildew rises behind it. There is black
dirt underneath, the texture of velvet.

The Inspector gently loosens the dirt with a trowel, then
combs through it with his bare fingers. A box is set down next
to him, and he crumbles the dirt into it. He digs deeper. Móricz
delicately searches through the dirt in the box. Nothing. He
looks at the Inspector, disappointment on his face. The hole is
as deep as the Inspector's elbow. He throws down the trowel.

The stone is laid back into the floor and the Inspector
chalks an *X* on it.

They move over the floor again, leaking fresh waves of
water over the stones. The afternoon light is fading. Small electric torches are unpacked from kits and handed around.

Something here.

Franz trains his torch on a spot near the center of the
room, parallel to the window. A stone circled with bubbles.

"Look, I've found something." His voice loud, triumphant.

Shrugging off their exasperation and fatigue, they gather around him, bleaching the stone with light from their torches. Frau Zellenka pushes her way between them. The Inspector had forgotten her until he notices her perfume drift over the odor of the wet stone and the men's bodies.

Again they put their picks into the floor. Franz and the Inspector wrap kerchiefs over their fingers and wedge their hands under the stone. Without a word, they turn it in the same direction, loosening it from the floor's grip, and pull it up. The smell forces everyone's head back. After a moment, they spike torchlight into the hole, illuminating a crumpled wad of cloth at the bottom.

The Inspector gestures frantically for them to move away. "Don't touch it," he shouts. "Get back. Where is the photographer?"

His voice breaks their concentration. He lights a cigarette.

Trailed by his assistant, Egon hurries in with his equipment. He works as swiftly as a waiter setting a table, shaking out his black camera cloth while his assistant wipes a glass plate and drops it into the back of the camera. He unscrews the tripod legs and they grow — magically as a bean stalk — until the camera is four feet in the air, its lens pointing down at a precarious angle. The assistant carefully sets a metal ruler next to the object in the hole. Someone brings a ladder, and Egon clambers up to focus the lens.

After a moment, he wriggles his hand out from under the cloth. His assistant strikes an allumette and touches it to a strip of cloth, which instantly erupts into a thin column of flame. There's an intense chemical smell and a light so bright it obliterates the white object in the hole and turns the rest of the room into a deeply shadowed cave. The camera shutter clicks, slow and deliberate as a book closing.

Egon takes three more photographs and then pulls the cloth off his head. He seems angry his work is finished. When Móricz goes to help him unscrew the tripod, he roughly pulls it away from him. He jerks the camera down to the ground, slamming the legs one at a time into their slots. Everyone watches silently, waiting for this hostile ceremony to finish.

Now their torchlight crosses over the hole on the floor. The Inspector crouches down, scoops the wrapped thing out of the dirt with a gloved hand, and places it on a clean sheet of paper.

The mysterious object is unexpectedly light. Perhaps there's nothing inside the cloth. He handles it as if it were breakable, gently unwinding the fabric until the edge of something pale gray is visible, then the thing tumbles free. A severed thumb falls on the paper.

CHAPTER 10

ÓSZEF WAS ARRESTED AND taken to the police station. Franz stands quietly outside his cell, squinting into the peephole set in the door. Hearing the Inspector's footsteps behind him, he waves his hand, cautioning him to approach more quietly.

The Inspector leans over his shoulder to peer into the dim cell.

As they watch, Jószef stands up and digs his hand through his pockets. He pulls out a tiny bottle, shakes it into the palm of his hand, and swiftly pops something into his mouth. Franz is roughly shoved aside as the Inspector flings open the door and charges into the room. Jószef is frozen in a crouch; he doesn't move until the Inspector hits the side of his head and he collapses onto the floor.

Franz winces, afraid the blow has knocked off Jószef's silver nose. He doesn't want to see the black hole in the man's face, the ruins of his nose.

The Inspector stoops and picks up something with his handkerchief. He holds it out to Franz as if it were something precious, a bird's nest, a jewel. Franz is puzzled by the small white square on the cloth and the sharp odor in the room.

"What is it?"

"It's a sugar cube. He's an ether addict."

Now Franz can see a wet spot spreading around the square of sugar in the handkerchief.

Jószef is curled up on the stone floor, his hands pressed dumbly against his head, the ether already leaked into his body.

He's locked up under observation.

In Jószef's pockets, Franz finds small bronze coins and a piece of ribbon tied in a single knot. His shirt, jacket, and pants are ripped apart and searched.

Nothing is found sewn into the seams.

A day later, deprived of his drug, Jószef is even more sullen than when he was first arrested. He stares at the floor in answer to their questions about the thumb found in his room. The Inspector is uneasy, certain the man's silence is filled with a stream of foul incantations directed at him. *Armaya* is the word Erszébet gives these curses when they're spoken out loud.

Two days later, Jószef talks, no longer defiant, apparently worn out by his confinement in a windowless room, the worst punishment for a Gypsy. Timid, cringing, he tells them what they already know: the number of years he's worked for Herr Zellenka and his wife, his fine opinion of them, his duties, his lack of an alibi. Yes, he knew Dora. For years. He loudly claims he had nothing to do with her murder. He closes his eyes when speaking about her. The death of a young person is a cursed event, he says. May my blood spill — *Te shordjol muro rat* — if I brought harm to the girl, he swears.

He has no idea the severed thumb was hidden in his room. Anyone could have put it there. The room has no lock.

What he says is true, but the Inspector knows this circumstantial evidence is probably enough to convince most examining judges the man is guilty of grave robbery, mutilation, and Dora's murder. *Bürger* regard Gypsies as less than dogs. His investigation of Dora could end here, with Jószef.

Perhaps the man senses the Inspector's hesitation.

"I caught a girl in my room," he says eagerly. "A trespasser, a thief. She put the thumb there. May I be buried next to Dora — *Te prakhon man pasha o Dora* — if I lie."

The Inspector is suddenly tired. A girl, a thief in a Gypsy's room? No. He tries to rein in his exasperation. All his skills of patience, his set of practices, are useless with this man. Is there a better strategy he could take?

Jószef will say nothing further. Franz returns him to his cell. His shouted words echo down the hall, *Si khohaimo may patshivalo sar o tshatshimo.* There are lies more believable than truth.

That afternoon, Jószef is escorted to a room and ordered to stand in a line with other ragged men. He asks to remove his *diklo,* a bright silk kerchief that clearly marks him as a Gypsy.

Franz frowns and shakes his head, relishing his power to say no, but the Inspector gently puts his hand on his shoulder. It's fine, Franz. Let him stand without his kerchief. There is nothing Jószef can do about his feet, which are sockless according to Gypsy code.

Franz brings an elderly governess and a shoe-shine man into the room. He discovered these two witnesses, who swore they recognized Dora's photograph, and were in the Volksgarten the day of the murder. They exchange formal greetings with the Inspector, who thanks them for their time and asks them to carefully study the individuals standing in front of them.

"Did you see any of these men in the Volksgarten?"

The Inspector's voice is gentle, but it pulls like a string, and the men shift their feet, change the position of their hands, and either glance away or stare at him defiantly. One man coughs nervously, as if the ill feeling in the room were contagious.

The shoe-shine man is just as uneasy, aware that he's just one step away from joining the shabby group in front of him. He nervously searches their faces.

"No. I don't recognize anyone. Nobody here I've seen before. I'm sure of it."

The governess is even more uncomfortable. She glances quickly at the men, then squeezes her handkerchief and bows her head, too shy to speak. The Inspector takes her aside, hoping her reluctance indicates she recognizes Jószef.

"Please, Fräulein, you must study the suspects. There is no need to feel embarrassed. You may speak to me later in private."

She stares at the floor.

"No," she says. "I can't help you. It's beneath me to look at these men. I'm a lady."

The Inspector and Franz exchange a pained glance and dismiss the men.

Protesting loudly, the Gypsy is returned to his cell.

Franz compares Jószef's boot to the plaster footprint from the Zentralfriedhof. Although they look about the same size to his eye, he knows a plaster copy is always slightly larger than the sole of the original boot or shoe, the difference calculated at about 2.5 millimeters. Jószef's boot is measured and is calculated to be the same size as the boot that left the print in the cemetery.

However, the plaster model doesn't show any wear and patching, details that would unmistakeably match it to Jószef's well-worn boot. The soil in the cemetery was too dry to pick up these details. A dead end.

A large cabinet in the Inspector's office is filled with skulls of both criminals and victims. The collection was assembled by his predecessor following the methodology of Caesar Lombroso, a professor of psychology in Milan. Lombroso supported his claim that physiology could identify a criminal by measuring the skulls of countless murderers, rapists, thieves, petty criminals, and unfaithful wives, both dead and alive, and comparing the statistics. The meticulous measurements of the skulls in the cabinet are recorded in several thick volumes on the shelves.

One of the skulls in the case — that of a murder victim — was used as evidence in a trial by Professor Hans Gross and was later presented to the Inspector as a curiosity. During the trial, Gross carefully showed the skull to each man in the jury, then set it on a table. After a dramatic pause, he placed his hand on the skull and gently pressed down, shattering it into a thousand pieces. Gentlemen of the jury, this was the victim's head as the murderer's hatchet left it, he announced. They swiftly convicted the murderer.

To prepare this evidence, Gross had boiled the skin off

the crushed skull and reassembled the bones, gluing them together invisibly with cigarette papers.

The Inspector imagines the gratifying effect Dora's severed thumb will produce when it is shown to a jury.

A pathologist stewed the severed thumb in formic aldehyde to preserve it. Before the jar was permanently sealed with wax, the thumb was fished out, dried, inked, and a print was taken. It was compared with the prints taken from Dora's hands. The severed thumb print was identical.

Unnerved by the eerie reuniting of the thumb with its identification, Franz refused to have anything to do with this process. He is surprised that the whorls and ridges on Dora's thumb remained completely unchanged during its time underground.

"Fingerprints only vanish with the destruction of the skin," the Inspector patiently explains. "It's impossible to alter fingerprints on the living. In Lyons, Locard and Witkowski tried a series of mutilating experiments, pouring hot oil and boiling water on their fingertips, even burning themselves with heated metals. After their skin healed, their fingerprints were still intact and identical."

Franz stares at the palms of his hands.

The Inspector continues. "Fingerprints are like a piece of lace. No matter how it is twisted, it returns to its original pattern."

The Inspector isn't completely convinced Jószef murdered Dora or even severed her thumb, although this is a straightforward conclusion supported by the evidence. The idea that Dora's parents or friends would mutilate her body is terrible. And he believes unlikely. Or was this hideous dismemberment meant to falsely transform the crime, making it only explicable by superstition or the actions of a madman? Was it designed to

draw him away from the truth, a distraction while the suspect
slipped away? He must step back, be careful not to read himself into the crime.

He sends a second letter to his colleagues with a knowledge of Gypsy lore, asking for information about human talis-
mans. None of the men have responded to his first inquiry
about excrement left at the scene of a crime.

From time to time, the Inspector has experiences of déjà
vu, prompted by certain odors, colors, slants of light, and shadows. Even a stranger's gesture or manner of walking can sometimes seem uncannily familiar. He's convinced these sensations
are proof of his prowess as an investigator, his skill of observation. He values these signs for their usefulness rather than as
connections to his own most intimate memories.

He wasn't surprised when the thumb was discovered in
Jószef's room. It was as if he'd been waiting, expecting something to darken his foreboding. He considers the excrement
found by the girl's body. The fig in the vial. The thumb in the
floor. Dora's reticule, buried in the garden. He recognizes the
same mocking attitude. The Gypsy was correct. *Si khohaimo
may patshivalo sar o tshatshimo.*

A woman on the street bumps into him, a red-faced flower
seller he's never seen before. The heavy liquid weight of the jar
containing the thumb shifts in his satchel, weighing down his
arm. Agitated, he tosses the woman a few coins. *"Küss die
Hand,"* she thanks him.

He stares at the bunch of pale hothouse roses she's forced
into his hand, closed petals with the greenish tint of dead skin.
For a moment, he's convinced the piece of flesh — the thumb
in his satchel — has some weird power. No, it's nonsense. He
dismisses the notion. He's taken other objects connected with
crimes from his office, certain that their meaning can more
easily be deciphered by isolating them. At various times, he's
carried around a button from a missing child's jacket, a thin
blade pulled from a murdered man's chest, a cheap bracelet

from a suicide's wrist, a lock of hair from an adultress. Once he had a cane that concealed a dagger the width of a pencil. He kept a whip that was found near the tracks just outside of the city, apparently thrown from the train. His collection of fetishes.

He tells himself he took the objects for study.

Erszébet puts her husband's roses in a vase taken from the *credenza* in the dining room. After he walks upstairs, she opens his satchel. She does this as a matter of routine. Pandora's privilege. In the bottom of the satchel she discovers a heavy jar, a clumsy shape wrapped in paper. She takes it into the hallway, hoping he won't hear her footsteps.

She holds the jar in one hand, the glass gradually growing colder against her palm as she unwinds the paper from it. When she sees what's inside, she nearly drops the jar. In the dim light, the thumb moves like a strange fish in the thick liquid. The thumb itself is intact, attached to a chunk of exposed muscle and ragged, mottled skin where it was roughly cut away from the hand. Dora's name and a date are written on the tag affixed to the jar.

She wonders what chain of events created this hideous souvenir.

Very late that night, falling snow covers the house like a bell jar. Under that perfect silence, Erszébet sets out her supplies in the kitchen. She paints a replica of the thumb, touching a brush to paint, to water, and then to paper. The captive thumb in the jar is the mirror image of her own hand holding a brush in front of it. She works very carefully, since the least motion of the table makes the thumb spin lazily in the jar.

She imagines if the thumb were set free in water, it would swim away.

Erszébet had no concept of the way her husband searched a room. She worked backward, hiding objects. She taped some of her watercolors flat to the underside of the kitchen table. Smaller papers were curled into the linings of her hats. She folded the veils and tissue paper over the hats in a particular way before the lid of the box was closed. A secret trap set for intruders.

During the search of Jószef's room, the Inspector had been too distracted to pay close attention to Frau Zellenka.

"Franz, did you watch her reaction when the thumb was discovered?"

Embarrassed, his assistant blinks and shakes his head. He'd been too caught up in the excitement, his eyes fixed on the floor.

The Inspector doesn't feel a second reprimand is necessary. He had noticed the woman's remarkable coolness, her self-composure. She was invisible during the discovery of the evidence. A curious woman. He schedules an interview with the Zellenkas at their home.

Fräulein Yella opens the door, takes his hat and walking stick. They're expecting you in the drawing room, she says, giving him a stare he describes later as *insolent*.

Herr Zellenka greets him like an old friend, urging him to take coffee or a glass of *Slivovitz*. His wife says nothing, just briefly nods and continues smoking, a sullen figure in a loose silk dress brilliantly patterned in yellows and reds.

"Inspector, we are very distraught about this terrible discovery. My wife hasn't been able to sleep from worry. A finger hidden in the floor? How could such a thing happen?"

"That's what I'm going to discover." He produces his notebook.

"My wife described the thing to me, of course. But whose finger is it? And where is the rest of the body?"

"I'm afraid that is a police matter."

His cold reply ignites Zellenka's temper. The man isn't accustomed to rebuffs.

"But exactly how was it removed from the body? Was it cut off? I don't know why you can't tell me anything. After all, the evidence was found on my property."

"I'm here to discuss how the evidence came to be placed on your property." The man's curiosity irritates him. He's encountered the type before, morbid seekers of information who eagerly quiz him for gruesome details when they learn his profession. He had to dismiss the last police photographer, who was caught peddling pictures of crime scenes to wealthy collectors.

"No fingers are missing from anyone in our household."

Frau Zellenka's voice surprises him; he'd forgotten her during the conversation. She kept herself distant, just listening, a calculation he recognizes.

"That makes my job easier."

"Excuse my wife, Inspector. She sometimes speaks out of turn."

He studies — or feels — the tension between them. Lets this silence hang in the air.

"What my husband means is that we all know Jószef is guilty. He clearly mutilated someone, hopefully a corpse."

Her fingers toy with a cigarette, and he realizes even this gesture is a challenge to him. A quick, unconsidered response would put him onto the game board she's set up for him. He steps back.

"Jószef hasn't been formally charged with any crime yet. It isn't the way the system works," he says, his voice mild.

"But is the finger related to Dora's murder? It seems so extraordinary, there must be a connection."

The Inspector rewards Herr Zellenka with a tiny smile. A straight stretch of his lips. That's his only acknowledgment of his question. The rest of the interview also doesn't go well. The couple claim to know nothing that could help his investigation. They protest their involvement in this scandal. Herr Zellenka hopes the police won't be coming back to dig up the garden.

As anticipated, the Inspector learned nothing new about the evidence, but he knows more about Herr and Frau Zellenka. He's angry. She's in control.

While he interviewed the Zellenkas, the maid slipped out before he could talk to her.

The next morning, Franz and three assistant officers dig

up the floor of Jószef's room and the entire stable. They find
nothing.

Erszébet gives Wally her watercolor of the fragment of the human hand in the jar. Dora's thumb. Wally pushes her *Kapuziner*
away, sets down the picture, and closes her eyes. They're at a
table in the automatic restaurant at 59 Kärntner Strasse.

When she first saw the unholy contents of the jar, Erszébet had immediately understood the stolen thumb was to be
used as some kind of talisman. That made the Gypsy the suspect. But why Dora? Perhaps the thumb had to be stolen from
a dead virgin. Or an interred hysteric. Or the daughter of a
man and a woman who had fallen out of love. Perhaps any dry
human bone would do.

Later, she began to believe Herr Zellenka mutilated
Dora's body. His motive is more difficult for her to read. Was it
done to punish or blackmail Dora's father? Is it a secret souvenir of his first crime, the girl's murder? Did he have the assistance of Jószef — or was it done to implicate him? What
happened during Dora's life that led to this grotesque mutilation after her death? The fig, the thumb. *Something added to the
girl's body, something taken away.*

"Why did Herr Zellenka hide the thumb in Jószef's
room?" Wally asks.

"To put the blame elsewhere. Of course he couldn't keep
the evidence in his house, it might be discovered."

"Maybe he couldn't sleep with such a vile thing under his
own roof?"

But how can they pursue Herr Zellenka? He's inac-
cessible.

I'll ask the tarot what's going to happen, Erszébet says,
and draws the top card, number fifteen, *le Diable.* She frowns.

The card has a grotesque devil with bat wings, antlers,
and sharp claws standing on an altar. At his right and left sides
a smaller demon is tethered to him with ropes around their
necks.

"This isn't a positive sign. The card means the devil never lets go of those who belong to him. It reminds me of a Polish proverb: *When the devil grabs you by a hair, he grabs you completely.*"

Erszébet knows Dora is joined to her murderer as if bound by an invisible rope. She visualizes the scene that brought them together as clearly as if she had been a witness. There are two struggling figures, but only the girl's face is revealed. There is the smell of earth and grass, then dark trees against the sky, their branches suddenly red, bursting as a brilliant web across Dora's eyes, locked there as her breath stops.

The red image vanishes.

Wally stares at her. A wave of unease circles the two women, isolating them from the noise and confusion in the restaurant.

Erszébet is conscious of a wave of longing for her husband and a sudden loneliness. How does he stay in this wavering place between suspicion and confirmation? *What are we doing?* she wonders, looking at Wally and hardly recognizing her.

This is how it is when you discover something, she thinks. She had believed an answer would be a fulfillment, a thing that was smooth and useful, not this blurring, not this fall into strangeness. A suspension. There's a word, *Erlebnis,* that means knowledge that comes in a flash, and she shrinks from it, although she knows she's already caught. It's too late to stop this process. She's been grabbed by the devil.

Jószef is still being held under suspicion of murder, although not formally charged with the crime. There is pressure to charge him with grave robbery, even though officials admit the evidence against him isn't conclusive. No witnesses saw him in the Zentralfriedhof or the Volksgarten. No one needs to point out that Gypsies are blamed for crimes on flimsier — and sometimes even nonexistent — evidence.

Perhaps Dora made an impulsive late-night visit to Frau

Zellenka, she encountered Jószef by chance, and he abducted her. This is Franz's hypothesis.

But consider the other suspects, the Inspector muses out loud to Franz, who doesn't look up from his paperwork. Herr Zellenka and his wife had access to Jószef's room in the stable. Remember her crouched next to me when the thumb was found under the stone? She didn't behave like a woman, didn't cry out or scream. Think of the victim's father. Philipp could easily have planted the thumb there, since he was familiar with the Zellenkas' property. Perhaps Philipp killed his daughter, deranged from the effects of syphilis. He has an image of the *csordásfarkas*. Men bewitched into a ravening state.

As he paces, he reminds Franz to approach a conclusion cautiously, always think of it sideways, if you understand my meaning. But Franz has his own theories that he doesn't wish to share right now. He's growing more independent, becoming less of a sounding board. The Inspector recollects that Seneca believed a disciple served only until he reached a point of autonomy through the teachings of his master. Then the disciple must leave. Uncomfortable with this possibility, the Inspector doesn't finish his train of thought.

He turns to the pages of *Kriminalistik*.

> A scheme of inquiry is drawn up in view of circumstances which alter of themselves, which are often unknown, and which do not depend on the person applying the scheme. It resembles, not the design of a house to be built, but a plan of campaign.

Franz renewed his efforts to find Rosza. His pursuit of her has extended over the city to the pages of the official servants registry, a famously incomplete index that does not include her name. Franz has little aptitude for paperwork, but he has honed his interview skills, copying the Inspector's mannerisms. His words are more carefully considered, and his speech is slower.

However, even after two patient and lengthy interviews, neither Dora's mother nor her father can recollect exactly where Rosza lived before she came to Vienna. Franzensfeste, or a village near the Caverns of St. Canzian? Do you know where Rosza passed her free time in Vienna? he asked, and they looked at him blankly. A servant's leisure activities were never considered.

On a whim, he stopped by Kment, a glove store on Gold-schmiedgasse, and described Rosza to the proprietor. He went into a few toy shops, figuring Otto might have cajoled Rosza into a visit. He also tried an umbrella store on Brandstätte. No luck.

Without a photograph of Rosza, there is no way to identify her, even with the assistance of the governesses he recruited. Two of the younger women promised to contact him immediately if they spotted her. Rosza hasn't been forgotten, even though she was disliked. An uppity woman.

Even if he had the woman's picture, she could easily pass by unrecognized at a glance. Young women wear their hats poised fashionably low over their foreheads, and sometimes a veil is pulled entirely across their faces, further obscuring their features. Only chance will bring Rosza to him.

His failure to find Rosza is a difficult point with the Inspector. Although Franz optimistically keeps him posted on new developments, he's stopped suggesting plans for his assistant to follow. The Inspector notes his dull lack of progress in a report.

The Inspector has been distracted and irritable lately, and frequently pulls out his copy of *Kriminalistik* when frustrated with Franz or other bureaucratic matters. Once he wheeled around, furious at being interrupted, even though Franz had seen he was just sitting at his desk, staring into space.

The nurse says Dr. Steinach is busy with another patient, so his partner, Dr. Last, will see Wally now. Alarmed, Wally turns to exchange whispers with Erszébet. Fine, says Wally after a moment. I'll follow you. She glances back over her shoulder to see Erszébet already confidently eyeing the wall of dark wood cabinets where the files on Dora and her father might be found.

The nurse ushers her into a plush room entirely furnished in red. There's a painted screen, a sofa, and elaborate curtains, sashed back for the benefit of the potted ferns. The effect is intense and claustrophobic, as if a much larger room had been condensed into this space. She notices the collection of objects arranged on the desk. A metal pole with a sponge on one end, rollers, blunt rubber tubes, leather straps, a magnetic coil, a metal box, various wires and cords. A machine with knobs and a coil is set up at one end of a bare metal table.

Wally sits down and the nurse squeezes her wrist, counting out her pulse. She can't read the woman's expression; her face is as flat and blank as a doll's. Perhaps she's from some exotic, unfamiliar place — Herzegovina, Istria.

Dr. Last slips into the room and takes his place behind the desk. He's younger than she imagined, although his pale hair is fading over his scalp. He takes out a gold pen and begins to write without looking at Wally or the nurse.

"You've been married how long?"

"Just six months."

Wally wears a wedding ring borrowed from Erszébet. She explains her husband is a kind man, much older than she is. They met when he was traveling in England. She is surprised to find herself describing Erszébet's husband, or her husband as she imagines he is. A tall, handsome man. The lies are easy; she could be telling a story to the children.

He writes down her words without comment, hardly glancing up, even when she occasionally stumbles and breaks into English.

"Very well. And what exactly are your medical troubles?"

"Headaches. Nerves."

He suggests his special operation for female glands. A small cut in a delicate place.

"Nothing painful, just a little discomfort. It will increase your pleasure later, when you're older." He's reassuring and looks straight at her for the first time.

She's too embarrassed and confused to ask him to explain clearly what he meant.

Did she ever touch herself down there? he asked, and she shook her head. She could tell by the tone of his voice what her answer should be.

The nurse begins to place objects on top of the table. At the sound of a dropped instrument, a sharp metallic clang, Wally jumps, her nervousness exposed. Jolted out of her story, she wonders if Erszébet has finished searching the files outside.

He frowns. "And how much pain does your sexual connection with your husband cause?"

The nurse suddenly opens the door, and when Wally cries *Don't leave,* the woman turns around. Through the door, Wally sees a dark shape move as Erszébet steps away from the cabinets in the reception room.

"I want the nurse to stay here."

"Certainly. She'll help with your examination."

Wally panics. Her body can't lie the way her mouth can. She senses her legs weaken into a tremble before she even stands up.

She undresses behind the screen, removing her clothing with heavy fingers, counting to ten before freeing each button. She keeps her chemise and stockings on and puts on the robe hanging behind her, tightly knotting the belt. In the thin garment she feels lost, shadowy.

While she was undressing, a chair and a large basin of water were moved to the middle of the room. Now the doctor tells her to put her feet in the basin. He watches as she clumsily removes her stockings, too intimidated to protest. She sits and slides her feet into the water.

He moves toward her holding the end of a long metal coil that trails back to the machine. Now he's so close she can see a glaze of perspiration over his face and smell the bitter wool odor of his suit.

"This is a Vibragenitant. It will affect the rhythm of your nerve vibrations. It won't hurt. You'll just feel a slight tingling."

He shows her the dull black object in the palm of his hand. He turns it over, and the other side is covered with raised knobs. She's afraid, hypnotized, her feet are frozen in place. She's pinned in a box of color, the deep fringed curtains at the windows, the carpet, the brocade on the walls, everything thickly red. Even the light in the room seems soaked with scarlet.

"The nurse. I want the nurse." She whispers the words in English.

He switches on the machine. It crackles, and electricity alters the air.

"Now I'll guide this over your body. The electric current will flow deep into your muscles. Stay very still." The doctor holds up the black object. Electricity will be applied to certain parts of the body, he says, indicating where the device is connected to the machine.

A loud buzzing. She feels a strange, damp tickle, the pressure of a shadow between her closed eyes, as if she's being blessed by something otherworldly. Then his moist fingers move across her forehead. A warm hum of noise and a slight pain, a sting too fine to identify, is traced over her face and neck.

She can't anticipate the slow movements of his hand. Later, when she is more knowledgeable, she'll recognize this pattern of suspense and wait as the blueprint of desire.

Hearing Wally's scream, Erszébet and the nurse jerk their heads toward the doctor's door just as it crashes open.

Fräulein Yella had avoided the Inspector when he interviewed her employers after the severed thumb was discovered. Two nights later, he stops by the Zellenkas' house without notice, intending to talk with her. He doesn't object to Herr Zellenka's presence during their interview, since he's interested in observing their relationship.

Fräulein Yella is twenty-five, was born in Cetinje, and has worked for the Zellenkas for several years without any problems. She's a good girl, Herr Zellenka says, and extravagantly compliments her. Flustered by his comments, Yella begins to giggle and toy with her braids.

The Inspector quizzes her about Jószef, and she promptly moves behind Herr Zellenka's chair, clutching the back of the cushion. No, she's never seen any strangers near the house or stables. No, she's never been in Jószef's rooms or even ridden in the fiaker, she adds, giving Herr Zellenka a sly look.

The idea that someone put a cut-up finger in the stable room gives her a terrible feeling. She melodramatically rolls her eyes, and Herr Zellenka pats her hand. He seems somehow pleased by the maid's nervous testimony, only betraying himself by the sudden relaxed slump of his shoulders.

The Inspector imagines Herr Zellenka's hands elsewhere on Fräulein Yella. He dismisses her as another hysterical woman.

"Syphilis, wasn't it?" murmurs Steinach, in answer to the Inspector's question. "I can't really remember how far Philipp's disease has progressed."

The doctor's vagueness does little to lighten the Inspector's mood. He arrived here in a state of irritation, since someone had misplaced Philipp's file at the police station.

"Would syphilis make Philipp mad? Would he harm someone?" The image of the man's genitals, mottled with specks, flashes into the Inspector's mind.

"Harm someone?" Steinach looks skeptical. "I have no interest in how disease alters a subject's behavior. I'm more concerned with physical changes. I'd have to look at the man's case file again, but illogical behavior is the only indication of an abnormal state. Believe me, the best way to analyze a brain is to take it out of the skull."

"I imagine our Vienna Psychoanalytic Society would argue your point."

The Inspector has seen brains removed from their bony oval cases in postmortems. After the top of the skull is sawed off, the coiled-looking mass will pop out if the pathologist is skillful.

"I'd hate to have to define sanity," says Steinach. "It's not my specialty."

The Inspector returns his grin. "I've encountered men who have given perfectly rational reasons for murdering someone. Krafft-Ebing said that even in madness there is method and logic."

"Yes, I guess even Bluebeard had his valid points."

Steinach edges past the Inspector to peer at a guinea pig in a cage. A row of red nipples ornaments the animal's shaved belly, the stitches deep in its skin like a brand.

"Inspector, have you encountered many crimes committed by someone who had been hypnotized?"

"No, but I'm familiar with such things. I've heard of victims who were hypnotized. Baroness Rothschild was hypnotized and robbed in her railway carriage."

"Ah, yes? Let me tell you a strange story. When I was younger, I was a doctor's assistant. I went with him one night to help a man with a toothache. We found the man lying on the floor in terrible agony, and we decided to pull his tooth. He absolutely refused to take morphine, even though we urged it on him. I had the man's arms pinned down, and the doctor was straddling him, breaking the tooth in his jaw. Blood was everywhere. And then a woman — his wife — came into the room, wearing a fur coat. She didn't say a word, just stood there. She opened her coat a little. She was naked underneath. The man was writhing and moaning, but he never took his eyes off her while the doctor hammered his jaw. Strange thing was, the man seemed to enjoy the experience, even the pain. He watched her until the tooth was out."

Steinach faces the Inspector.

"Did the woman hypnotize him? Was the man sane? Later, I discovered he was a famous author. Herr Sacher-Masoch. He wrote *Venus im Pelz.* His wife's name was Wanda."

Afterward, the Inspector lunches alone at Bellaria, near the Naturhistorisches Museum. It's a gray November day, and he orders *fácán vincellérne módra,* pheasant cooked with brandy, grapes, liver purée, red wine, and bacon. He reviews his conversation. Steinach doesn't believe Philipp has symptoms of insanity. But there is madness that only shows itself once, or intermittently. A perfectly normal woman can act abnormally during her menstrual period. In *Kriminalistik,* Professor Gross clearly stated his position on the subject. *"Premeditation, cunning, and prudent calculation are not incompatible with insanity."*

He finds fault with his impatience during the interview,

his failure to follow the doctor's statements with neutral questions. He was too personal, he put too much of himself into the
dialogue.

He's afraid he isn't subtle enough.

The Inspector tells Erszébet about Jószef's ether addiction
and hands her the knotted ribbon found in his pocket to identify. She studies it.

"It's a charm to protect the person who carries it against
the police. There are words that work with it. *Sweet dead one, let
the noose about to be tied around my neck be undone.*"

He asks where the ribbon comes from.

"After someone dies, Gypsies measure the length of the
coffin with a piece of cloth. Then they tear it into these ribbons."

"But whose coffin? Someone in the family? Another
Gypsy, a stranger?"

She doesn't know the answer.

During one long night, he wills his wife awake in bed. *"I don't
know what is happening,"* he whispers. Then instantly hopes she
hadn't heard him.

Erszébet is awake, but silent, unreadable. He knows she
won't fall asleep again.

"Your investigation is like the telling of a dream," she
says, her voice thick with sleep. "Each time you discuss it, you
add other facts, even change their order. You remember the way
you told it, not the way the events happened. You can't help it."

What she also wants to tell him is *You're afraid.* You observe a crime, its sequence of facts. In order to understand the
terrible images you've witnessed, you make them into a story
so you can carry it. Or it will carry you.

If he'd asked her, Erszébet would have told him that his
wish for a conclusion is *délibáb.* Magical thinking. A mirage.

❧

Later, the Inspector is more strongly conscious of his uneasy feeling, even though he's walking in the Haupt Allee in the Prater on a surprisingly mild day, at a fashionable hour, surrounded by people, horses and carriages. At his left is the Casino, a rounded, cream-colored building partially obscured by bare horse chestnut trees. In the spring, these trees drop thousands and thousands of thick petals, and the sound is a soft, constant thrumming, like insects flying against a screen. After crossing the grounds, he would find the brim of his hat filled with fallen petals, quickly browning souvenirs of the trees' radiance.

Erszébet consults a tarot card reader and asks about her husband. The card the woman draws for him is *le Bateleur,* the Mountebank, a figure standing behind a table set with conjuring items and dice, a game of chance. Among other things, he represents the mind, which is both instinctive and profound.

Tell him to take contemplation over action, the tarot reader counsels.

Wally has demanded that the nurse stay in the room with her. She grips the woman's wrist. Erszébet is outside in the reception room, searching for the files a second time.

As Wally lies uneasily on the examining table, she intercepts a silent exchange between the nurse and Dr. Last: *Hysterical girl.* The nurse frees herself from Wally's hand. The doctor readies the equipment, untangling the limber silver coils. With the smallest movement of his finger against the machine, electricity suddenly becomes a presence, its aura blossoming into the room like the sharp smell of a flower. He picks up the small black device at the end of the coil. She remembers it from her first treatment. The nurse smoothes Wally's hair back from her forehead. She closes her eyes, pretending the woman wishes her well.

The doctor's jacket brushes the side of the table, and then his damp hand, radiating pinpricks of electricity, hovers over her face. The warmth moves down her neck and past her shoulders. She frowns and puts her hands over her breasts. He mutters something to the nurse. She takes Wally's arm and gently lays it alongside her body, palm side up. Suddenly, there's intense pressure on the inside of her elbow; Wally opens her eyes as her arm magically jerks up, jackknifes, and falls down across her chest, as if it were no longer attached. For a moment she can't move, shocked by her body's betrayal.

"Now I will use just my hand because I can control the current better. Don't think of it as my hand. It's simply a tool."

Something warm is laid on her bare stomach, and then electricity contracts her skin, her flesh suddenly light and flexible as cloth. Her intestines churn and gurgle in waves. There is no pain. When her breath comes back and her eyes open, she struggles to remember Erszébet. Her stomach is wobbly, as if she's been sick.

Towering over her in his white jacket, the doctor looks as solid as a pillar. He asks how she feels. As if from a distance, she hears his words, but to answer him the space is much greater. She feels her mouth open.

A cloth is laid over Wally's face, and there's a bittersweet smell. After a moment, it is removed and she's dimly aware of their faces above her, watching. The nurse leans over and holds Wally's wrists down on the table.

"I have one more contact point for the electricity. This will finish the treatment. It will be better if you close your eyes. Nurse?"

Wally tries to twist away, but the odor has slowed her movement. Once when she fainted, it was preceded by burning white circles at the outer corner of each eye, which grew larger and larger until they passed out of her conscious observation. Now the red color of the room is fading to white as she watches the doctor lift her robe. Her abdomen jumps at the touch of his hand, and then she feels another slow movement she doesn't recognize. Then her head jerks back, her mouth shapes itself into strange convulsions. She rides her body, then she's strangely thrown free, lost.

There's moaning, and she dully realizes it is her own voice that she hears.

CHAPTER 11

HE INSPECTOR HAS BEEN OVER-
whelmed by work. For days at a time, he's
only spoken to Franz in passing. A forgery
remains stubbornly unprovable. Horse
thieves have struck several stables, daringly
even those of the Princess of Auersperg, fa-
mous for her four handsome horses and postilions. And Dora's
case lingers. He knows his wife attributes his ill luck to *mana*,
an impersonal supernatural power.

To clear his head, some afternoons he vanishes without
leaving his itinerary with his assistant. He can be found walking
purposefully along Wipplinger Strasse, through the Hoher
Markt and into the Stephansdom, where he climbs the tower.
He's a familiar visitor, and the sacristan admits him without
charging the forty-heller entrance fee. The Inspector incor-
rectly assumes that his clandestine practice is unknown to his
office. However, Franz once tailed him to the Stephansdom
door, his face a blushing red beacon.

When he was courting Erszébet, she brought him here to
see the remarkable pulpit of pale carved sandstone. The deco-
ration is a display of the artist's dreams, she told him, pointing
out the salamanders and toads chasing each other along the
handrail, symbolizing the pursuit of good and evil. Sharp sta-
lactites, flames, and writhing foliage ornament the pulpit. He
remarked that the artist had carved away almost everything
that would physically support the pulpit. It looked like a filigree of bones.

Because the church nave has no upper lights, it is a perpetual twilight inside. Even on the sunniest days, the fractured
shapes of color cast by the stained-glass windows next to the
high altar don't dispel the somber dimness. Franz, he thinks,
would be unnerved by the silence here.

He walks into the sexton's lodge and looks straight up
into the immense height of the tower. The light through the
narrow windows transforms the space into an illuminated column, so that the tower glows like a candle in a stone case. The
staircase is widest here on the ground floor, spiraling upward to
the left and growing steadily narrower for five hundred and
thirty-three steps. As he climbs, he brushes his hand against
the wall, a habit for luck.

He's breathing heavily and his coat is unbuttoned by the
time he reaches a tiny balcony, level with the rooftops of the
neighboring buildings. Below him, the irregular lines of the
streets are laid out for his surveillance, square cobblestones
imposed over ancient cart tracks.

Here the steps end and a ladder leads to the next level. He
climbs until his head rises out of the floor into the belfry, a
small space made even smaller by the oppressive bronze bells
hanging in bunches from the beams. They appear frozen, incapable of movement, their huge clappers thicker than his arm.
The walls and ceilings are crisscrossed with massive beams,
slabs so rough and rocklike they give the impression of having
been thrust into place by some ancient geological shifting of
the earth. The beams are bolted with ornamental serpents'
heads. He likes to imagine he is the only one to notice this
strange, hidden detail.

He clambers up the primitive ladder in the corner —
going slowly, for the thing is shaky — counting fifty steps before emerging into a dazzling square room filled with light and
air. Two uniformed men nod at him without interrupting their
pacing in front of the windows. They're fire-watchers, stationed in the spire, the highest point of the city.

It's his habit to check the view from the northeast windows first, where the plains of Hungary and Galicia are backed
by the darker blur of the Carpathian Mountains. The next

window shows the Danube, marked with a long white streak, the airy scar of a steamboat's passage. When he looks straight down, his forehead against the window, the cathedral's roof is visible, with its thousands of polychrome tiles, a dizzy geometric pattern. The frail, displaced noise of voices and carriages floats up from the street.

He admires the huge telescope set up in the center of the space, a device invented by a professor of astronomy specifically for the fire-watchers. Once he was in the spire when a fire was spotted in the city below. Shouts and frantic activity filled the small room, and he retreated to a corner, fearful the spire would capsize, like a boat on stormy water. The fire-watchers focused the telescope on the building below the rising thread of smoke, which locked a dial on a number corresponding to a house and street registry of Vienna. The number was telegraphed to the *Feuerwehrzentrale,* the cavernous central fire station, and a procession of uniformed men raced to the fire.

One of the fire-watchers told him that before the telescope was installed, they would shout the approximate location of the fire into a huge speaking trumpet, startling anyone standing below. Then a boy would run — or a fiaker gallop — to the *Feuerwehrzentrale.*

He admires the telescope's precision, the certainty of the city as a procession of numbers, the streets and buildings flattened into a graph, the location of a fire passing invisibly through the air.

He asks permission to use the telescope. They've indulged him before when things were quiet, and now he fiddles with the elaborate mechanism, sharpening the focus. The glass eye flies across the city, swifter than a bird, finding a toy-sized boy pulling a cart on a street, the head of Hercules on the Michaelertor, the flash of wheels — perhaps a motor cab — on the Seilerstätte.

Doodling, dancing in the air, an acrobat, he idly trains the telescope on the area where Herr Zellenka's house is located. He skims the lens to Dora's rooftop, a route that might reveal a telltale clue, like smoke from a fire. Even here he brings his work with him.

❋

Since her last visit to the doctor, Wally has been uncomfortable under Erszébet's eyes. She never told her exactly what happened, feeling strangely shamed by the experience. She's unwilling to ask for comfort.

Erszébet recognizes the girl's retreat. She isn't unsympathetic, but she knows Wally will speak to her when she's ready. They have evidence now. Better to get on with their work. She senses there is little time left.

A frazzled waiter brings their *Kapuziner* and plates of caramel-glazed *Doboschnitten*. As he sets a glass of water on the table, some of it spills. The women are silently patient while he dabs a cloth around their cups.

Erszébet holds the thick file stolen from Dr. Last on her lap. She discovered it under Philipp's name, and has waited to open it in front of Wally. She takes out a photograph of a young nude woman seated in a chair, her face obliterated with lines of black ink, as if it had been slashed. It's a *Krankengeschichte,* a photograph taken as a record of medical treatment.

She puts the photograph facedown on the table. Her eyes meet Wally's.

Dora.

"Are you certain you want to continue?"

Wally nods. The next photograph shows the woman's buttocks. The photographer knew exactly where to place his light, because the sinister pattern of puckers and scars over her skin is perfectly visible. They study the pictures in silence.

Erszébet slides another photograph from the file. It shows the tender area from the woman's waist to the cleft between her legs; the skin is a hideous mass of dark patches and welts, like marks made by an angry animal. It takes them a moment to realize what's missing. The woman has no pubic hair. Her face is blanked out in all the photographs.

There are several other pictures of the same woman, taken from different angles. At the top of one photograph, several lines of handwriting have been blackened with the same heavy pen strokes that cover her face. Erszébet turns it over. *Fräulein X* is written on the back.

After the pictures have been put away, Wally begins to cry.

"Why would the doctor have those pictures of Dora? Did he do this to her?"

For a moment, Erszébet stares at Wally's flushed face without reacting. Her mind is filled with the photographs. She tries to expand what she sees, to visualize the entire room where the woman stood before a camera and a powerful explosion of light.

"The pictures were filed under Philipp's name," she says slowly. "He must have had something to do with them."

"Did he kill Dora because of the pictures? So she wouldn't tell anyone?"

Erszébet puts her hand on the girl's arm and closes her eyes. Why was Dora disfigured? How did it happen? She's suddenly fatigued, wondering why she brought this girl with her. What is the periphery she inches toward?

"What do we do now? Tell me. Who do we talk to?"

Erszébet brings herself back into their conversation. Listen carefully, she says. "You may not understand everything I tell you. This story of Dora's begins to remind me of something. There's an apparition Gypsies call the *mullo,* the living dead who come back to haunt this world. The Magyar have another name for them. Sometimes a *mullo* will have intercourse with a woman, and she is the only one able to see him. If she talks about the *mullo,* or describes him to anyone, she and her family will die. No matter how repulsed or frightened the woman is, she can only scream during her intimate encounters with the *mullo.* That is the only time it is safe. The scream is the only thing that makes the *mullo* exist for her. Do you see?"

Wally is conscious of some half-buried memory. She ignores it and stares at the cup in her hands while the older woman continues to talk.

We must be careful. We are becoming like the woman who can only react in the presence of the enemy, the *mullo.*

Erszébet passes into some knot within herself, hoping to bind her rage. She thinks of Dora, haunted by her constant illnesses, her craving for attention. Her suicide attempt. Her frequent attacks of laryngitis and the loss of her voice. A woman who can't scream, can't tell. The father as *mullo.*

Erszébet has never discussed her deepest fear with Wally. *What if you keep evil at arm's length not because you're afraid of being harmed, but from fear it may provoke recognition, some answering tug, a welcome?*

When she leaves the restaurant, Wally takes the photographs of *Fräulein X* with her. There's no reason for Erszébet to paint copies of the stolen pictures because they won't be returned.

Wally hides the photographs in the back of her armoire. She doesn't look at them again, but she is aware of their malefic presence, which works on her like an unpleasant memory.

Erszébet tells the driver to stop the fiaker. He remains in the front of the carriage, lazily smoking a cigar, until she orders him to go and see if the snow on the walk in front of a certain house has been disturbed. It's very early in the morning, a weekday.

The driver clambers back into his seat. No, the snow is just as the clouds left it last night.

Good. She doesn't take her eyes away from the house, her fingers blindly busy with needlepoint.

After a time, when the door opens and a man steps out, she's disappointed. Bowler hat, walking stick, loose dark coat, the uniform of a successful Viennese, *ein angesehener Mann.* Dora's father. Her needle is forgotten in her hand.

She felt nothing. She'd hoped for a vision, a man with something alien in his appearance. A physical sign of his monstrous character. Like the *csordásfarkas,* a man changed into a beast. Like the French botanist pursued by the peasants, who were convinced he was a wolfman, a shape-shifter.

Now she's no longer convinced the botanist was as innocent as his terrified face made her believe when she was a child. Now she wouldn't believe a face.

Erszébet and her husband have dinner in the fine restaurant at
the Sacher, in celebration of an intimate anniversary recognized only by themselves. She wears her mother's diamond
necklace and a new dress made at Drecoll for the occasion. Diamond earrings — her husband's gift — glitter at her ears. She
touches his leg under the table. Both of them are slightly drunk.

When he looks across the room, who or what he sees there
makes him slowly set down his glass. All the expression leaves
his face.

"What's the matter?" she asks, nervously steadying his
arm with her hand.

He doesn't answer, so she turns around, to see a tall man
stand up behind a table. As Erszébet watches, he makes a
barely perceptible gesture, just slightly inclines his head, his
eyes never leaving her face. She reads a significance there she is
unable to understand. The man quickly exits the room.

"Who is he?"

"Someone I worked with once on a case," he says. His
voice is thoughtful.

She knows her husband well enough that his reply
doesn't ring true.

"Did he help solve a crime? What did he do?"

He comes back to himself and folds her hands in his. "He
proved to be of very little use. It was a case of murder."

Guntramsdorfer is a coffee-and-milk room on Weihburggasse.
Late every afternoon, the marble tables are crowded with children and their caretakers, impatiently waiting for their sweets,
hot chocolate and *Schlagobers*.

Wally and Erszébet sit in the back, away from the clamor.

The photographs of Dora are still hidden behind Wally's
armoire. Erszébet is uneasy about the presence of these talis-
mans and watches for signs the photographs might be working
some misfortune on the girl.

"I'm not certain you should keep the photographs in
your room. It's not safe."

Wally shakes her head. Everything is fine, she says, crumbling a *Kaiserschmarren* on her plate.

"Dora's photographs have affected you, I'm sure of it. I have a sense of these things. You dream about the pictures."

Wally smiles. "If that's my only misfortune, I can bear it."

"Wait and see what happens next."

"I'm English. I don't really believe pictures can harm me."

Erszébet's wisdom about these matters is instinctive. She's glimpsed a veil of stubbornness in Wally and puts aside her questions. She proposes they confront Dora's father with his daughter's photographs.

"Why, do you think he'll blurt out the truth when he sees the pictures?"

"It's possible. Truth is spoken when the mind is occupied with something else."

Erzsébet believes words can break a disguise. Her grandmother told her how a *váltott gyermek,* a changeling child, was tricked into assuming his true shape. A woman carefully poured milk into an eggshell and put it to heat on the stove while the ugly *váltott gyermek* watched. The changeling was so astonished by his mother's nonsense that he forgot himself and impetuous words flew from his mouth. He instantly reassumed his human body. Words transformed him.

"Isn't there someone else who can tell us about Dora's photographs?"

Erszébet suggests they find the photographer who took the *Krankengeschichte* pictures. "Perhaps there's a way to ask Dr. Last who takes pictures of his patients without arousing his suspicion?"

No. I won't go there again. Wally feels stained by what happened in the doctor's office, as if something had seeped into her body along with the electricity. She looks away, wanting to be disassociated from her refusal. She's afraid of Erszébet's reaction and waits for her to loose her temper, to spill the coffee.

But Erszébet says nothing. She simply moves her spoon in a slow circle inside her cup.

There is something I don't understand, Wally says hesitantly, her mind still on her visit to the doctor. How do you get rid of a baby?

Erszébet gives Wally a sharp glance.

"There are ways. I know women who secretly consult Gypsies for an abortificant. They prepare a bitter herbal brew from ground ginger, nutmeg, mint, cloves, sage, borrage, rue, wood aloes, and goosegrass. It is boiled for three hours while the Lord's Prayer is recited. White wine is added, and then the liquid is strained for three days through an apron that the pregnant woman has worn."

"How does it taste?"

"Like death."

Erszébet tells her there is a place you can go if you are a man to see women's bodies, then smiles at Wally's expression. No, no, she says. Only men are allowed to visit the Josephinum. Wally isn't familiar with the place. It's a museum with wax figures of men and women, the *anatomica plastica,* Erszébet says. One thousand models were created in the eighteenth century by a Florentine, Paolo Mascagni, for the pleasure of Emperor Joseph II. Enough figures to make an army.

Without resolving their strategy for Dora's photographs, they leave each other outside the café. Erszébet walks home, following a meandering route along the Hofgarten. It's snowing steadily. The snowflakes' determined acrobatics become visible as they spin into the gauzy aura of light around the street lamps.

A rabbit darts across the road in front of her, an unlucky sign. May the *mar sara,* the spirit of Tuesday evening, carry you off, Erszébet mutters. It is November thirtieth, the feast day of Saint Andrew, the patron saint of wolves. It is believed that on this day the just can see heaven and animals can speak. At this time of year, witches and the spirits of the dead reach the height of their powers.

Wally pulls Dora's photographs from their hiding place behind the armoire. On each picture, the embossed name of the photographer's studio has been scraped out with a sharp instrument. She tilts the photographs toward the lamp, hoping the letters will be legible, pulled from oblivion by the light. She wets a finger and rubs it over the cardboard. Nothing. All she can make out is *Strasse,* or perhaps her eyes have just read what she expected to see.

The Inspector is sidetracked by an unhappy development. If it weren't such a pointless and unpleasant exercise, he'd almost welcome the distraction from his other investigations. It had been weeks since he'd sent the medical examiner the unidentified black hairs found on the servant girl accused of an illicit sexual act with a dog. He never recontacted the office for the results of the tests on the hairs. When the report finally arrived, it sat untouched on his desk. He caught Franz staring at it several times, wondering why he hadn't read it immediately. It wasn't like him.

One afternoon, he reluctantly reads the report. The black hairs discovered on her genitals had been boiled in a 5 percent solution of sodium hydroxide. After ten minutes, the hairs dissolved, which proved they were from an animal — a black dog — not from her skirt, as the girl had claimed.

It is his unfortunate job to show the girl the vial, which contains only a clear liquid, and explain the terrible consequences of her unnatural act. Protesting her innocence, she bursts into tears and throws herself on the floor. Franz and Móricz gently pick her up and carry her out of the room.

The Inspector realizes he delayed the examiner's report because he hoped the girl would leave Vienna. Now he wishes he'd made that suggestion more strongly to her.

The Josephinum is an immense dark stone building on Währingerstrasse, modeled after the Hôtel-Dieu in Paris. It houses the Anatomical and Pathological Museum, and only men are admitted. Soldiers from the nearby barracks and the

Military Infirmary at the Allgemeines Krankenhaus occasionally visit, the slam of their polished boots echoing in the hallways.

The uniformed *Herrenportier* at the door of the Josephinum is dwarfed by the carved stone gateposts that stand twenty feet high, each topped with an urn.

Wally passes the guard's scrutiny and proceeds through the gates, feeling safe in her men's clothing. She tries to widen her steps — to walk like a man — since her narrow skirts have given her the habit of a short stride. Inside the building, she gives a few bronze coins to the ticket taker, but doesn't ask for directions since her voice will give her away. Upstairs, a sign indicates the *anatomica plastica* are available for viewing from eleven A.M. to one P.M.

When she wanders into the room, the first thing she notices is the strange effect of the light on the figures, life-size models of nude men and women upright on stands. Although muted by its passage through the tall curtained windows, the sun warms the figures' wax limbs, turning the thinnest parts of their bodies translucent, as if they burned from inside. Wally cautiously approaches a female figure, half expecting the woman to break her enchantment and suddenly yawn and blink. She touches her finger to the wax fingertips; the color and texture are identical. Only the temperature of the spellbound hand is inaccurate.

She peers into a cabinet against the wall. Inside, mounted on elaborate gold stands, is a wax ear, half a face with grimacing lips, a single glazed eye wide open in astonishment. The surrounding skin is gracefully peeled back, curled like paper. Larger cabinets hold legs, arms, heads, and torsos.

The next room is filled with *écorché* figures standing in heroic poses or reclining on yellowed cushions, their bodies stripped of skin as if they'd been flayed. Their exposed sinews are eerie orange and red, twined with darker tentacles of blood vessels. One skinless male lies on his back, his muscles bound with a tracery of blue veins so fine it seems that the surface of his body is cracked. His inner organs glow through his wax muscles like a cupped hand held to a candle.

A wax woman, a nude Venus, is ecstatically sprawled on a
fringed cushion. Her head is tilted back, eyes half closed in
permanent rapture, as withdrawn as Saint Theresa. Wally
touches the cushion. It's silk. The Venus has a string of pearls
around her neck, and her long pale hair is arranged over her
shoulders. A deep line is cut around the top of her body, cir-
cling from the base of her throat down to her pubes. Wally suddenly realizes the figure's breasts, stomach, and abdomen can
be lifted up in one piece. The body of this Venus is a casket.

In the glass cases behind the Venus there are partial sections of pregnant women's bodies. Their wax legs are spread
apart and cut off at midthigh so neat circles of bone are visible
in the center of the red muscles, like a beautiful ham. Single
hairs, short and curly, are punched into the pubic areas. Cloth
is draped over the women's huge stomachs, a peculiar modesty
since their genitals are completely exposed. The creases and
folds of flesh in the slit between their legs are unfamiliar. She
recognizes the texture and the color, a wrinkled brown violet,
like a fig. There's a secret knowledge here, some skin memory
she turns away from.

If Wally had Erszébet's skill, she'd sit in front of the wax
bodies and copy them with paints in order to possess their images. Her father once explained that after you trace a pencil
through the map of a maze, you can never become lost walking
through it again.

She isn't conscious of anyone else in the room until she
hears a man laugh. He's near the door, a soldier in a green
jacket and tight white breeches looking up at a male nude on a
pedestal. He stares at the thighs wrapped with veins, the yellow
orange genitals with the weight and tenderness of an egg yolk.
The soldier laughs again. He's uneasy; she recognizes the
sound.

She blushes and moves away from the glass case, swept
by a feeling of shame.

The soldier sees a tall young man in a suit and cap turn
and walk out of the room.

Snow continues to descend on Vienna, a white shadow spread over the streets and roofs, remaining a presence even through the warm afternoon.

Erszébet stands inside the four glass walls of the Palmenhaus watching as the topiaries — elements of the Hofgarten's formal design — are slowly changed into softer white shapes, equally artificial. A few men, and women accompanied by men, carefully move between the topiaries, dark umbrellas open over their heads.

Inside the Palmenhaus, the air is swollen with the scent of lilies of the valley. In a few weeks, the greenhouse will be completely stripped of flowers, which will reappear the same evening as bouquets on five hundred tables at the elegant Hof Ball.

On the way back through the city streets, Erszébet's fiaker passes laughing *Schusterbuben,* cobbler's apprentices, tossing snowballs at each other, still wearing their work aprons.

The driver waits on Rotgasse near the synagogue while she shops in the Hoher Markt. The square is almost empty of customers because of the poor weather. Canvas has been secured over the makeshift wooden stalls, and snow has resurfaced the rough, uncovered pyramids of root vegetables and firewood.

Erszébet decides to prepare *felvidéki finom nyárileves* for dinner, and hurries to a table heaped with dead game. An immense woman, a kerchief over her head, fans the display with a whisk as if brushing off flies, not snowflakes. Can you show me a nice hare? Erszébet asks. The woman seizes a skinned hare by its ears, the fur still attached to its hind legs, and proudly revolves the red thing before Erszébet's critical eyes. Although the snow is coming down fiercely, Erszébet doesn't have the heart to bargain down the price. She turns to search in her satchel for coins, and the woman, misunderstanding her gesture, tosses the hare down and begins to praise it. Killed this morning, she says. Fresh as fresh. The dog will eat it if you don't. See him? She jerks her head over one shoulder, where a large muzzled dog is tied to a cart.

Erszébet catches something in the woman's voice. She smiles in recognition and shifts into the same dialect, a cross-

hatch of words emphasized on the first syllable. The game
seller chatters back, energetically offering her half a dozen
hares, partridge, even tiny *császármadár,* grouse. She purses
her lips when Erszébet presses money into her hand.

"*Kérem.* I beg you."

The woman reluctantly drops the coins in her apron
pocket, then produces a small heavy sack.

"The finest Hungarian flour. The famous double zero.
Made for the monarchy. Here, it is yours."

She scoops some fine white powder out of the sack, holds
it out in her cupped hand.

Erszébet is startled when the woman's hand — disembodied by the thickly falling snow — comes toward her. Time
falls away, and she again witnesses the mummified hand of
Saint Stephen, glimpsed years ago in a ceremony in Buda Pest.
Her vision is obscured with tears.

Wally makes her way along the Tiefer Graben to stand on the
Hoher Brücke, a metal bridge built over the street. Darkness
falls at such an early hour now that street lamps are lit just
after midday.

She leans over to watch a pair of Hussars strut past, identically uniformed in pale blue jackets and pink trousers. The
limp black lines leading from their eyes to their jacket pockets
are the only visible evidence of their monocles. Behind them, a
woman in a thick fur coat and felt boots drags a struggling
child by one hand.

Wally has decided not to tell Erszébet what she saw at the
Josephinum. She hides her information like a coin. The dark
slit of flesh between the wax women's legs is her secret, concealed like Dora's blacked-out face in the photographs. She remembers the dim room in the museum as if it were a dream
and she'd walked among standing figures of the dead, waiting
for resurrection to reclothe them with flesh.

Erszébet told her about the *lidérc,* an unclean spirit, the
devil's familiar, which can assume human shape and pass
among men. The *lidérc* is simultaneously man, animal, and

light. Erszébet heard of a woman whose husband left town, and she allowed herself to be comforted by this spirit, disguised as a handsome soldier. The neighbors became suspicious and convinced the woman to set a trap for her lover. She spread ashes on the floor, and the next morning, in the powdery grayness, she saw the *lidérc's* misshapen footprint. He had a single webbed foot that he'd kept hidden from her.

Wally wondered what unimaginable pleasures the *lidérc* had given this woman. A demon lover. Was she reluctant to uncover his true identity and give him up? Was she afraid, even while she embraced him? Had she been suspicious? How is this possible?

She is unable to ask Erszébet these questions. And Erszébet would have been unable to explain it in a way Wally would understand. She is too young to imagine how it is possible to live with duplicity. How it might also have pleasure attached to it.

Erszébet waves from the other end of the Hoher Brücke. Wally carelessly stubs out her cigarette and drops it to the street below. She picks up the portfolio leaning against the wall.

"My husband said Dora's mother has left the sanatorium. She's returned to Vienna. You should go and see her."

What was a familiar landscape has suddenly changed.

They continue talking over cups of *Türkischer* and rich *Powidltascherin* in the Central Café. Wally feels secure here; the ceiling of the *Kaffeehaus* is arched into accommodating parabolas above their heads. She's glad of the crowd, the thick, soothing pattern of voices.

Erszébet encourages Wally to give Dora's mother the *Krankengeschichte* pictures. "Perhaps she can identify the photographer. And explain Dora's accident."

Her face anxious, Wally leans toward Erszébet. "I'm not certain she should see them. She's in frail health. It might affect her badly."

"If showing her the photographs might reveal who killed Dora, why spare her feelings? You don't make sense. Don't you want to find out what happened?"

"Why is everything done according to your plans? I went into the garden. I had to see the doctor." Wally begins to cry.

Erszébet decides the *Krankengeschichte* pictures must be having a malign influence on the girl. It would be better if they were stored in a neutral place. When there's time, she'll consult someone about Wally's distress. She grew up with wise women who placed peas, stones, and nose dirt on the road to cast a spell.

Erszébet gently touches Wally's shoulder.

The girl won't look at her. "I haven't seen you in a week. Why are you avoiding me?"

Erszébet is shocked to realize she is the source of Wally's unhappiness. As if she owed the girl something. Now her head is clear. She takes off her coral necklace and loops it around Wally's wrist. This will keep you safe, she says. *But not from me or what I bring,* is her silent thought.

Wally hopes Erszébet will be distracted and forget her angry outburst. She is ashamed of her tears, but her behavior won an acknowledgment. Erszébet was forced to give way. She gave Wally a charm.

Suddenly Egon appears next to their table, and she's jealous, wondering if Erszébet told him to meet her here. Why would she need to talk to him? Wally tries to catch her eye, but Erszébet is rummaging in her satchel. Without glancing up, she asks Egon to join them in a game of tarok.

Erszébet deals, sending cards around the table with deft movements. Wally imagines her in a kitchen, preparing food with the same motions. They each have sixteen cards; six cards go to the *chien.*

"The Magyar have a variation of this game called *paskiewitsch.* In Vienna, it is *königsrufen,* 'call the king.' A trick-taking game. Wally might recognize it as similar to the English game of whist."

More coffee is brought to the table. Wally goes into the game, relieved they won't be able to discuss the photographs with Egon present. He doesn't seem to notice the tension between them and sets down his cards with confidence. He's winning.

During a quiet period between hands, he points at the
package on the empty chair. "A portfolio of your work? May I
see it?"

Distracted by the sight of his hands——she had forgotten
his mutilated fingers — Wally quickly looks back at her cards.
"No. There's nothing I want you to see. Just some photographs
that have been ruined by water."

"Perhaps I could help repair them. I sometimes retouch
photographs. My clients tell me I have some skill."

"I'm afraid Wally's pictures are beyond help."

Though she smiles at him, Erszébet spoke very sharply.
Wally doesn't say anything, not wanting to embarrass him.
However, when she checks his face, he is studying his cards as
if nothing has happened. She notices he's holding them at a
slant, so his missing fingers are less visible. A courtesy, she
supposes.

Erszébet wins the game. Wally says she's going to leave
instead of staying for another round. When Erszébet doesn't
protest, Wally gives her a cursory farewell. As she hurries across
the *Kaffeehaus,* she has a pang of pleasure, a transcript of the
hurt that she's certain her rudeness has caused Erszébet.

The café is crowded, and she edges past a newspaper seller
with damp, freshly printed sheets folded over his arm. Behind
her, a man takes an envelope over to Erszébet and Egon. He
asks if they're interested in photographs, and before they can
answer, he quickly produces pictures of actresses.

One slow morning the Inspector leaves the office alone and
finds his way to the Zellenkas' house. Without disturbing the
occupants, he slips around to the back. Everything is quiet.
He's prepared for this furtive excursion by wearing a fur coat
and his warmest boots. They're thick and embroidered, fashioned from several layers of pressed-fur felt.

He's returned to the stable on a hunch, remembering
there was snow outside when Jószef's room had originally been
searched. There have been a few sunny days since then. The

grounds should be thoroughly checked again. Something might have been overlooked. An error in the landscape.

> Thus the zealous Inspecting Officer will note on his walks the footprints found on the dust of the highway; he will observe the tracks of animals, of the wheels of carriages, the marks of pressure on the grass where someone has sat or lain down, or perhaps deposited a burden. He will examine little pieces of paper that have been thrown away, marks or injuries on trees, displaced stones, broken glass or pottery, doors and windows open or shut in an unusual manner. Everything will afford an opportunity for drawing conclusions and explaining what must have previously taken place.

No footprints disturb the snow around the stable. Jószef's door has a new lock. Interesting. He takes the magnifying glass and a stiff broom-straw brush from his satchel. The fine webs of snow in the corners of the steps, which have the delicate appearance of something produced by a spider, are easily dusted away. He searches the area next to the stable, a tangle of frozen grasses. He works his way around the side of the building. His knees begin to ache from the cold and the crouching. He finds nothing.

A bit of red, half buried by snow, catches his eye. The color is so strange and out of place against the whiteness that for a moment he mistakes it for a lost jewel. No. A red pencil.

He automatically picks it up and reads the gold script stamped on its side. *Cumberland* and *Rose Carthame*. He has an image of a shop and the smell of oil paint. Erszébet's pencils. He bought a set of Cumberland pencils for her at an art store in Paris.

Dora's mother looks better. She was lulled into regular sleep at the sanatorium with doses of valerian and morphine. The sharp edge of her grief is gone.

She's glad to see Wally, embracing her even before she can

take off her coat or set down her portfolio. Wally notices she still wears the same black dress; it seems as if no time has passed since their last visit.

"Here, please sit down. Let me move the cushions for you. Are you comfortable? Would you like coffee?"

Her fussiness irritates Wally, but she finds herself unbending to it. Erszébet has been so distant with her lately.

Dora's mother talks about the sun in the south. She walked every day. And the water. As part of her treatment, she sat in a tub of dark water that had bits of decomposed roots and grasses floating in it. And it stank of putrid sulphur.

A maid brings coffee and a layer cake, *Pischinger Torte*.

She continues to chatter. She enjoyed the whey milk sweetened with sugar at the sanatorium. Yes, she feels better, thank you. She's decided to wear mourning dress for the rest of her life, just like the Kaiserin Elizabeth. Did Wally know that even the empress's pearls were black, her grief was so great after the suicide of her son, Prince Rudolf.

After the torte is served, she takes Wally's hand.

"I'd like to make you a gift of one of Dora's books."

Wally isn't paying attention. She fumbles with the portfolio, her fingers too nervous to undo its wrapper. With her hasty effort, she tears it.

Alarmed at her nervousness, Dora's mother watches her without speaking. She takes the photograph Wally hands her.

"What is this?" she asks, her voice fearful.

Wally stares at the picture as if she's never seen it before. In this light, the nude girl is a harsh, ugly sculpture, her flesh carved up by scars.

She barely hears Dora's mother gasp and move away, doesn't notice the sofa cushions sink as she stands up and walks stiffly out of the room.

Wally doesn't look after her.

Snow has left white hats on the statues and thick, mushy lines across balconies, windowsills, gateposts. Even though she

counts the snow-covered and receding lampposts, trees —
anything passing outside the windows — nothing distracts
Wally from her feeling of deceit. Remembering the expression
on Dora's mother's face, she's tender with regret. She watches
the spire of the Stephansdom approach, a fixed point above the
rooftops, which are silver white or black, depending on the
passage of sunlight during the day. Someone — a bearded doctor — told her a fable about Vienna: the skyline was created
when a tea tray was tipped over the city, scattering its contents,
which became the curiously shaped chimneys. However, the
image of Dora's mother, hands trembling as she held the ugly
photograph, is stronger than anything else she sees.

She loudly asks the driver to go faster. He snugs his
muskrat coat closer and urges the horses along Weihburggasse,
the Parkring, and into Stadtpark. In the park, snow and the
fading light have conspired to obliterate the head and breasts
of the nymph of the Danube statue and double the size of the
turret on the Moorish Pavilion.

She tells him to go past the lake, since it is sometimes illuminated with torches for skating in the evening. And now
faint dots of light are visible behind the black woods.

The fiaker turns, and the lake is suddenly revealed, a great
flat oval that appears to radiate a cold heat off its surface, transforming the surrounding icy trees into weightless, glittering
lines. The torches at its edge are reflected on the ice, two broken white lines like a double strand of pearls.

Daredevil skating instructors in otter-skin caps and
braided jackets boldly speed over the ice alone. Others move
more slowly, coaxing their halting pupils. When the women on
skates spin and turn, their long black veils float around their
bodies, as if animated by some power of enchantment.

She gets out of the fiaker and watches until her feet are
cold. Then Wally leaves Stadtpark for another destination.

The fiaker waits as she takes small, cautious steps along
the icy walk in front of a large house. There's a suggestion of
light behind the curtains in the windows, perhaps a single
lamp or candle burns in the room. She pounds on the door. After a few minutes, a tired-looking maid opens it and crossly

tells her no one is at home. Wally shoves the portfolio of photographs at the woman and instructs her that no one but Erszébet is to open it. She tells her a second time. Yes, yes, the woman nods angrily, I understood you.

The driver is surprised when Wally runs back to the fiaker.

She's giddy with relief. As the fiaker jerks forward, she falls back against the seat and doesn't sit up again, just lets her body rock with its movement. Everything seems to be happening very fast. Go back through Stadtpark, she shouts at the driver, remembering the skaters executing circles and thinking she'd like to see them again.

Erszébet and her husband go away for the weekend, to stay with friends east of the Danube. It is a four-hour train ride, and the snow is much heavier outside Vienna. The train stops at the station late at night. They're transported by sleigh to an immense house in the country, and their arrival is greeted by fires burning in the two fireplaces downstairs and glasses of strong *Vilmoskörte,* pear brandy.

His suspicions about the evidence — the rose-colored pencil — that may belong to Erszébet are unspoken between them, like cards that have been dealt but remain facedown, unplayed. There's nothing he can do but cultivate an active patience. The bitter feeling around his heart surprises him.

If Erszébet notices he's less withdrawn when they are in company, she gives no sign of it.

The next morning, a group of boar hunters gathers below Erszébet's window. The men are identically dressed in jackets, huge caps, and gaunlet gloves, all of white fur. Heavy white felt boots cover their legs and thighs. She doesn't recognize her husband until he waves at her.

As the hunters turn and walk across the white field, they suddenly vanish as completely as if they'd stepped into a black night without a moon, their clothing making them invisible against the snow. She can only follow their movements by the minute glints of light on the silver knives at their belts. They are like ghosts that move in sunlight.

Egon works just off the Graben on a street lined with photography studios and engraving firms. Wally finds him identified as *Portrait Photographer* on a plaque next to the door. A dark silhouette of steps leads up to his studio on the top floor.

Answering her knock, Egon opens the door himself and shows his surprise to see her. She's breathless from the climb, stamping the snow from her boots in the hallway.

"I hope you don't mind I came to visit."

He reassures her it is his pleasure to see her.

Behind him, she can see a space filled with light. She walks into a room that seems unfinished, temporary, leaving a transparent trail of droplets from her wet boots. There's little furniture, and the floor is bare wood. The light from a bank of slanted skylights is the heaviest presence in the studio.

She stares up at the ceiling.

"The skylights face north. They give the most perfect light," he explains, eager to impress her.

"I have a friend who paints pictures. She said Leonardo da Vinci did his portraits in bad weather or at twilight because that was the most perfect light."

"I don't need to wait for the weather or the sun. The camera operates with a different type of light. See what I can do?"

He hooks a pole into a thick black curtain at one side of the skylight and expertly jiggles it across the glass, plunging the room into artificial darkness. Another shade of stiff black fabric unrolls up from the bottom of the skylight with ropes and pulleys. It's as flexible as a kite. By manipulating the curtains, he can make the light in the room grow brighter or dimmer, as if the entire daily procession of the sun were at his command.

"I can put shadows on the left or right side of someone's face. Or I can move a light in front of them, so it appears they're standing outdoors. Someone told me this light is as strong as the sun in the desert. I call it Egyptian illumination. I can only create it in the winter, since I need snow on the roof for reflection."

Standing in this open space makes Wally uneasy. She's been in few places that were this empty and she's at a loss about where to position herself without the guidance of chairs, tables, rugs. Like familiar conversation. She notices painted lines radiating out from a point in the center of the room to the walls. Each line is marked at the baseboard with a number at fifteen-inch intervals.

He notices her staring. The lines are to calculate perspective, he says.

He hovers close behind her, and she walks away to examine the camera, a square wooden box as big as a trunk set on a wheeled table.

"See the bars set into the floor?" He points to a thick metal track embedded in the boards. "They're for the camera. Let me show you how it works. Stand back."

At the push of his hand, the camera hurtles straight toward her, like a blind thing, its transparent glass eye shuttered. She jumps back just before it hits her. The machine abruptly stops at the end of the track.

"Could you make me some tea?" she gasps, trying to smile.

"Of course. I'm sorry I didn't ask you before. Excuse me a moment."

He leaves to heat water on a ring behind a screen. She makes her way across the room to examine the photographs tacked up on the wall, which appear as indistinct gray images from a distance.

When she looks at the pictures, it's as if she's suddenly stepped into a void. They're the same photographs Erszébet stole from the doctor. In one picture, the nude woman is seated, her hands at her sides. In the next three pictures, she faces the camera, cut off just below her knees. Her bald genitals are clearly visible, the center point of the photographs, the skin puckered and fiercely blotched. In all the images, her body would appear headless except for the thin outline of a hat, which completely shadows her face.

Wally is startled by footsteps, then Egon is standing behind her. She's too shocked to be frightened.

"You took these pictures?"

"Yes. Some time ago."

"Who is she?"

"No idea. She came here with a man. He asked me to take
photographs of her as a medical record. Maybe he was a doctor. He said the woman had just finished surgery and was healing. She never spoke, never said a word, but I could tell she was
unhappy. I take enough pictures to read bodies like a face."

Her eyes are fixed on the photographs, but she's only conscious of his presence. She moves back, but he's behind her
and she panics at his closeness. She's suddenly claustrophobic;
her breath comes from a tightness deep in her chest. She
doesn't turn around but focuses her eyes on one of Dora's photographs until her breathing is easy again. Now she can ask a
question.

"Who was the man with her? Do you know his name?"

"No. He didn't make an appointment. He just walked in
with her. He paid in cash, no argument about my price."

"How old was he?"

"In his forties, I guess."

"You'd recognize him if you saw him again?"

"Probably. He wasn't unusual, a businessman. Very
proper, a good *Bürger*. Why?"

"I'm just curious. These pictures are so strange."

Her father had taken pictures too. She remembers her
surprise when he solemnly handed her a photograph, and there
were the familiar trees in the orchard, robbed of color and converted into black and white, strangely flat. She thought the
trees were dead and she started to cry.

Egon brings her a cup of tea and a stool, and she sits next
to him with her back to the photographs. His props and other
paraphernalia are stacked against the wall in front of them;
large wooden frames covered with white muslin, which he says
are light reflectors; painted backdrops of pastoral landscapes
and ruined castles; a stack of balustrades. He twists his legs
around the rungs of his stool.

"After I photographed the woman, I heard the man ask her how many pictures I'd taken. She was too distraught to remember. He made me give him all the photographs. Even the glass-plate negatives. I secretly kept the four photographs that I printed, the ones on the wall."

Wally fixes her eyes on his mutilated hand in order to concentrate on her questions.

"Did he seem friendly with her, the woman? They knew each other well?"

"Yes, I had the impression they knew each other, although they were a little uncomfortable. It was a strange situation. We were all a little uneasy."

"How old was she?"

"I'm not sure. She seemed young. Twenty? She didn't really want me to see her. That's why her face is covered in the photographs. She wore a hat with a veil. She always looked at the floor. He did all the talking. Look, why are you so interested in her? I have better pictures."

He plucks the cup from her hand and vanishes behind the screen, his footsteps dramatically loud on the bare floor.

When he returns, she makes her voice enthusiastic, to pull back the thread of their conversation.

"Your photographs are so wonderfully artistic."

He grins, makes a mock bow, and presents her with another cup of tea. He tells her about an apparatus for picture taking he's created, a system with a dynamo light and reflectors. He rummages in a box, then brings over a silver metal cone connected to a wire that will be synchronized to the camera's shutter. Somehow it will direct light onto an object, correcting the exposure for the camera's eye.

"Since I lost my fingers, I've been trying to make a safer light for the camera. The metal cone will contain the explosion."

To gain his confidence, she fusses over the gadget. Eventually, she brings him around to discussing the mysterious woman's visit to his studio again.

"She didn't want the man to watch her being photographed," Egon says, still patient. "He left the room while she undressed. I had the black cloth over my head, I was in back of the camera, so I guess she could pretend I wasn't there. She came out from behind the screen with just a shawl around her. She stood where you're sitting, right in front of the backdrop."

Egon shifts his feet on the stool, straightening his lanky body out of its slouch. She waits, afraid to breathe, her balance on the stool slipping. She looks at him.

Frowning, he nervously revolves the silver cone in his hands. "I don't know if I should tell you this. I haven't told anyone. The man who wanted the photographs must have had a great deal of money. He came to the studio alone the day before he brought the woman here. He paid me to put a hole in the wall so he could watch her. I could see his eye, just there, when I took her picture."

He points to a dark spot on the wall.

"I thought it wouldn't matter, since she didn't know he was watching. She'd been burned all below her waist. You can see it in the pictures. Her skin is ruined. I used his money to make this light for my camera."

CHAPTER 12

HE COLORED PENCIL IS TAGGED and stored in a drawer in the police station, along with the rest of Jószef's meager possessions. A description of the pencil is entered in the logbook. The Inspector leaves it in storage, having convinced himself it is official property and cannot be removed.

When he discovered the pencil outside Jószef's stable, the Inspector automatically classified it as evidence. A key and an enigma. In the next moment, when he recognized the pencil as *perhaps identical* to one he had given Erszébet, he felt the thing would burn his fingers, it was a red-hot wand. It was only with a great effort he slipped the pencil into his pocket, his hand trembling.

His discovery of this evidence has somehow marked him, made him a coconspirator without knowing the plot.

Had the pencil been planted near the stable? Clearly it didn't belong to Jószef. And Erszébet? It is inconceivable that the pencil belongs to his wife. Could this unlikely evidence be connected to the mutilation of Dora's corpse — or did a careless hand simply drop the pencil in the grass? Perhaps it has no significance.

He aches to forget it entirely. Why has he saved the memory of this object to resurrect it now? One thought chases another. He tries to calm himself. Seneca reasoned it was easier to prevent the inception of the emotions than to subdue them.

The solution is simple and secret. He can search through Erszébet's art materials. He knows exactly where the box is kept. He could even dust it for fingerprints; there is charcoal powder in his satchel.

No, he refuses to tie Erszébet to his string of suspicions. He will not look through her belongings. He believes this is the correct decision. But in the back of his mind, he's afraid of what he might *not* find in her box of art supplies. A certain pencil, rose carthame. At the same time, he longs for the relief of her denial — or confirmation.

He recollects a passage from *Kriminalistik* that details an officer's approach to a problem: *"When he starts work, the most important thing for the Investigating Officer is to discover the exact moment when he can form a definite opinion."*

This sentence will now haunt him like an accusation.

In the evenings, when Erszébet brings her husband a glass of sweet wine from Badacsony in the library, her presence — the momentary grace of her hand on his cheek and shoulder — soothes his unease. After she leaves, his sense of restless waiting returns, as if the trace of her perfume in the air reignited his fears.

He watches her movements around the house more assiduously. He finds himself in the kitchen, studying the leftover lime-blossom tea in her cup as if the fragrant liquid holds a secret message for him.

Lately, he's noticed she's been acting strangely. A fiaker edged too close to the curb, splashing her coat with gray water from a puddle. A gentleman jumped from his carriage and profusely apologized. The Inspector assumed she would graciously accept the man's regrets. Instead, she turned her back on both of them and walked away.

She moves in the presence of her husband's distress. She is aware of it. In her language it is *lidércnyomás,* a state of fright and intense depression. Their nightly ritual — when she serves him a glass of wine — serves to keep her connected to him.

She does this as much for herself as for him, since it is her habit to ignore any unpleasant situation between them.

She believes she has the tools to reveal the murderer. Once she knows the name, it will relieve her husband's pain, which is now directed at her.

Wally has been waiting in the Volksgarten for one cold hour, hoping to find Rosza. It's just past three o'clock, but twilight has already worked a transformation on the park, soaking the snow in its solemn, violet gray tint.

Since her visit to the photographer's studio, Wally has been afraid. There's a waiting connected with this fear, and it seems as if it never leaves her. It occupies the same space as a depression. It's a presence, like her fear of digging, of uprooting, which she can't free herself of or embrace.

She walks to shake off her mood. Near the Temple of Theseus, two small figures scuffle silently on the walkway. She recognizes the boys she's seen with Rosza.

And Rosza stands in the distance, a diminutive figure in a dark coat. Wally watches the woman shift the fur muff in her hand and lift her veil to puff on a cigarette. She's startled when she hears her name called.

They tour the Volksgarten together, talking about the freezing weather, their thin boots, the care of children. Wally barely hears what the woman is saying; she's focused on when to slip Dora into the conversation. They turn to watch the boys. Rosza shifts her feet from side to side to keep warm, forcing the fringe on her coat into shivering motion.

Wally glances back over her shoulder, and the impression of their footprints reminds her of the photographer's glass plates, the positive and negative images. Now is the moment.

"Do you remember if Dora ever posed for a photographer?"

"No. I don't think she did. Not while I was at her house."

"But I discovered a strange picture of Dora. Maybe she was photographed when you were away."

"Possibly. Or perhaps she went with her mother or father to have it taken. Her parents should know."

"Her mother doesn't remember the photograph. I showed it to her."

Rosza shrugs impatiently. "I really have no idea. Why are you asking me about this?"

"Please, don't be angry. It's a serious matter. I believe the person who arranged for Dora's photograph was blackmailing her. Or perhaps the photographer is the blackmailer. She threatened to expose one of them, so she was killed."

"Blackmail Dora? That's ridiculous."

"Dora's mother said she'd stopped wearing her jewelry, and I think it was because she'd given it to the blackmailer."

"Why are you concerned? You didn't even know Dora. Let the police take care of it."

Angered by her questions, Rosza pivots and strides away, kicking her skirt out in front of her. Wally hurries to catch up with her. The path is banked with snow; it's only wide enough for one person. She won't let Rosza escape. She clambers over the drift and blocks her way. They face each other, their breath a cloud between them.

Wally senses that pleading won't persuade her to reveal anything. Rosza is beyond her youthful skills of negotiation. She is slipping away, taking Dora and Erszébet with her. Rosza tries to get around her, but Wally grabs her arm.

"Please, just answer one question. Did Dora have an injury? You must know, since you helped her dress. Was she hurt somehow below the waist?"

Rosza squints at the boys. They're off in the distance. She slides her hand into the crook of Wally's elbow.

"Very well. Tell me about the photograph of Dora." Her voice is calm, confident.

"I saw a *Krankengeschichte,* a medical photograph of her from a doctor's office. Dora was naked, and her face was blacked out. Her skin was dark all around here. As if she was burned." Wally points to her abdomen. "Other parts of her body looked injured too."

Rosza holds up her fur muff and buries her chin in it.

Wally knows she's considering something. In the next moment, the suspense her information created is gone. Rosza lowers the muff, and her frosty breath scatters around her face.

"I never saw Dora without her nightdress. She was modest. A prude. She didn't mind if I changed my clothes in front of her, though. She'd watch. Maybe there was something wrong with her, but she never told me. Where did you find this picture?"

"I saw it in a photographer's studio."

"Whose studio?"

"Egon. You met him. We've played tarok."

"Egon? What did he tell you about the picture?"

Rosza's eyes are fixed on her, following her expression as closely as her words. Now Wally feels as if she's the one being examined. She hesitates.

"He said a man paid him so he could spy on Dora through a hole in the wall while he photographed her. He doesn't know his name. I think it was Dora's father."

"He told you this?" Rosza is incredulous.

"Yes. I didn't even have to persuade him. He seemed happy to tell me. But who took Dora to the photographer? Do you think it was her father?"

Suddenly Rosza turns sharply on her heel and calls the boys.

Wally clutches at her sleeve. "Tell me who took Dora to the photographer."

"I can't help you. But I'm certain the picture has nothing to do with the murder. Just forget it."

"Don't leave."

But Rosza has already moved away from her.

Standing in the empty park, Wally can hear horses stamp and the cold click of their harnesses out on the Ringstrasse.

Erszébet comes home late one afternoon with a headache and goes straight up to the bedroom to nap. Her husband waits until she sprinkles eau de cologne on a handkerchief to put on her forehead and the familiar scent drifts down to him before opening her satchel. Nothing but small change inside the coin purse. He examines her cigarettes and a sketching pencil. A silver vanity case holds a mirror, powder, and a pressed leaf, a souvenir from their tryst near Balatonföldvár. He finds a piece of paper tucked in the inside compartment and takes it to the window. Unfolded, it's a map of Vienna with crosses darkened over a few parks: the Botanischer Garten on Rennweg, the Palmenhaus at the Hofgarten, the Augarten, the Volksgarten, the Belvedere Garten, and Esterházypark.

He figures it's some botanical pursuit of hers, or locations for watercoloring. He replaces the items exactly as he found them.

Afterward, he can't dismiss the idea that everything in the satchel was there by deliberate design. She prepared it for him to find. In the same way she arranges objects for a still life, which only look haphazard to his eye.

In the morning, she can tell he's searched through her satchel. She understands this comes from his possessiveness of her.

Her discovery of his trespass makes it easier to examine his notebook. She reads through the most recent entries about Dora's investigation. When she finds the list of Jószef's possessions, she closes her eyes. She visualizes a rough stone building, and then a bright line of color against white snow. A coral pink colored pencil, rose carthame. A gift from her husband. Did he recognize it? She wants to tear the page from his notebook, although she knows it is already too late.

Her husband is vague when she quizzes him later about Dora's case.

"But what about Frau Zellenka?" she asks, careful not to say more than she is supposed to know. "Surely she has something to do with the crime. I feel there's something suspicious. The woman resented Dora. Dora was jealous of her. And Rosza, has she been found?"

"No, no. Franz is still looking for her. She seems to have disappeared without a trace."

"You have such patience with him." They're in the library and she's holding his evening glass of wine.

He shakes his head. "It's not simple to find a servant who's disappeared. After Rosza moved in with another family there was no way to trace her. The whole case is complicated. With all the time that's passed, I have to depend on something unexpected. A mysterious friend of Dora's. Or perhaps the mad stranger who accosted the girl will confess."

She holds the smile on her face while frantically reviewing what she and Wally have discovered. She can't separate what she has learned from his information. Did she overlook something? Has he found Wally? She silently watches his face.

The wineglass slips from her hand and shatters on the floor. It reminds him of another shattering glass. The broken vial containing the fig. Does she think of it too?

Only her eyes make it clear she had the same thought. Strange. He puts her reaction out of his mind. He'll think about it later.

Erszébet is an impatient figure, pacing by the Kaiserin Elizabeth statue in the Volksgarten. She stabs her umbrella into the snowdrift near the statue and leaves it there. It's midmorning, the time when nursery maids and governesses escort children here to play. Today there are few children, since the snow is inches deep, covering the ground with a dry white blankness, as if clearing space for another scene to replace it. Even the kaiserin's statue is thickly swaddled in white from her throat to her lap, a change of dress. The image reminds her that the kaiserin was reportedly sewn into her clothing every morning, beginning with a skintight chemise of kidskin.

A sudden movement between the tall junipers catches her eye, then a man with a shovel stands up. She'd missed him, motionless against the dark trees.

Now she recognizes Wally's figure at the gate in the distance. They took a chance, meeting here at their usual place, their usual time. Perhaps the police have followed the girl here. Perhaps they're both being observed. Before Wally is halfway across the park, Erszébet circles the boarded-up fountain to intercept her. She hurries her down another path cleared through the snow and into a waiting fiaker. The driver's formidable whistling urges the horses down the Burgring, past the Naturhistoriches Museum. Erszébet collapses against the seat in relief.

"We must be very careful from now on." She lifts her veil, lights a cigarette, and offers one to Wally. "I was afraid my husband had discovered you."

The idea that her presence might be tracked is peculiar. Wally still gets lost; the narrow and illogical streets in the inner city are as twisted as the *calli* in Venice. "I have information about Dora's photographs," she announces.

But Erszébet is distant, thinking of something else. Wally is afraid to interrupt, but she's eager for Erszébet's attention, for her praise. Perhaps Erszébet intends to stop their investigation.

"I've seen Egon," she repeats, more anxiously.

"Egon? What did he tell you?"

Wally describes the photographs of Dora she'd seen in his studio.

"So he photographed her?"

"Yes. It was all very secret. A man came with Dora to the studio, but Egon doesn't know his name. He described him as ordinary looking. But the man did something strange. He spied on her when she was naked. Egon let him do it."

"He watched while she was being photographed? It must have been Philipp. What about Dora's mother? Did she explain the photographs?"

Wally turns aside the memory of her encounter with Dora's mother, wanting to forget the woman's shocked eyes, how she walked blindly out of the room. This feeling of selfish deceit is new to her.

No, she says. She didn't recognize the pictures. She cried. Wally looks at Erszébet, hoping to replace the vision of the woman's teary face. Perhaps Erszébet already knows what happened. Wally sometimes thinks she could never say anything that would astonish her.

The fiaker suddenly runs over a line of train tracks, jolting them into momentary silence.

"Rosza doesn't know anything about Dora's photographs." Wally's voice is sullen. "I saw her in the Volksgarten. She wasn't helpful. She ran away from me."

"I see."

Erszébet sets a thin parcel in Wally's lap.

"What's in here?"

She picks it up. The parcel isn't heavy.

"The photographs, my colored pencils, and Dora's earrings. I can't keep them any longer. It's too dangerous. It was very foolish of you to leave them at my house. What if my husband had answered the door, or found the parcel?"

Wally doesn't answer. Nothing has taught her how to hold through the anger that shakes her. It feels permanently pressed into her body, as if there's no space now for her feelings for Erszébet.

"But they're Dora's earrings. I want you to keep them."

"I'm sorry. Look, I have new earrings. They're from my husband."

She shakes her head, provoking points of light to appear in the shadowed space between her hair and her shoulder. Diamond earrings.

"You can look at them."

Wally puts a tentative fingertip under one earring, balances it tenderly as a butterfly. She touches Erszébet's neck.

"They're beautiful. Like stars."

"Yes."

Erszébet pulls her collar up, as if to erase the touch of Wally's fingers on her skin.

Erszébet realizes that her investigation has reached an impasse. Her surreptitious reading of her husband's notebook has revealed nothing new. Neither Dora's mother nor Rosza can identify who took the girl to Egon's studio. Unless her

husband discovers fresh evidence, there is nothing for her
to do.

At that moment, she decides to begin a *ráböjtölés,* a black
fast. She believes there isn't much time left to her.

For nine weeks, she will abstain from food and water
every Friday, and pray three times a day. All the energy of her
black fast will be directed at Dora's murderer. When this magical process is finished, the identity of the murderer will be discovered — or the guilty person will become ill or die. Some
believe if the subject of a *ráböjtölés* dies, that person will then
haunt the living as a revenant. If ten years were abbreviated
from the revenant's mortal life, he or she will return ten times.

The person conducting the black fast is in peril too. If the
ráböjtölés is stopped before nine weeks, or if the fast is broken
by a meal, a crumb, or even a sip of water, everything is reversed and the spell-caster will die. The same thing will happen if the fast is against an innocent person.

Erszébet tells no one of her plan. She is alone with her
practice.

During the period of *ráböjtölés,* Erszébet's artistry in the
kitchen is unsurpassed. She prepares *gánica,* corn-and-wheat
dumplings that are first boiled, then fried in bacon fat, bread
crumbs, and paprika. She grinds sausage, roasts a suckling pig.
She searches for the finest ingredients, even cajoling some of
the merchants from the Hoher Markt and the Naschmarkt and
the fruit sellers from the Stefanie Brücke to bring their specialties to the house. One day, a man knocked at the back door
with a precious handful of truffles wrapped in a cloth. An old
woman delivered live *szalonka,* snipe that had been captured
in a net. The maid swiftly dispatched the tiny birds while
Erszébet watched. Another time, two shy girls brought a fat
goose that had been force-fed corn and white clay dissolved in
a special mineral water to enlarge its liver. When the bird was
butchered, its blood ran yellow, discolored by its own fat.

On Fridays, Erszébet watches her husband enjoy these

spectacular meals while she drinks and eats nothing. Late every evening, she continues to serve him sweet wine.

He eats heartily, has nothing but praise for her efforts. Joking about these endless rich feasts, he accuses her of tightening the waists of his trousers while he sleeps. The first Friday of her fast Erszébet complained of a stomach ailment as the reason for her lack of appetite. By the second Friday, he would begin to feel like a condemned man enjoying a meal before his captors.

The morning after one of her elaborate dinners, Erszébet told him she'd lost her Cumberland colored pencils, the set he'd brought her from Paris.

"I must have packed up my supplies and left the pencils next to my chair. I think I was sketching in the Volksgarten, that last warm day we had. I didn't want to tell you since they were your gift. I'm sorry."

If his relief and gratitude surprised her, she didn't show it. He promised to buy another set of pencils. Maybe they would travel to Paris together this spring. A second honeymoon.

A week later, he announces he has a surprise. Mystified, Erszébet dresses quickly, scenting her skin and clothing with the perfume he pleaded with her to wear. They leave the house directly after dinner.

A fiaker takes them along the Ringstrasse, past trams and the Palais of the Prince Coburg-Gotha. They stop at the Gartenbau, an ornate building where flower shows are held at other times of the year. The cavalry officers waiting in front of the building are more splendidly dressed than the ladies they accompany. It is still a source of pride that the Austrian Artillery was awarded first prize for its elegant uniform at the Paris World's Fair in 1900. Erszébet picks out the Hungarian Guard lancers, in blue uniforms with bordeaux red trim and gold embroidery.

She hears the Gypsy orchestra as they walk in. Following the music, she races ahead of him, laughing. When he enters the ballroom, the place is dense with smoke and people. It takes him a moment to find her, standing at one side of the orchestra, raptly watching the musicians. The *primás,* a dark young man in a jacket, solemnly motions for the orchestra's attention. The room falls silent. The *primás* drops his arm, and the crashing strains of a *csárdás* begin.

In one motion, the audience stands and pushes its way into a clear space between the tables. The Inspector watches as his wife is swept along by the crowd. Strangers, both men and women, grab partners. Erszébet rests her hands on a man's shoulders. He nods, and without speaking, puts his thumbs alongside her neck. They begin to dance, stamping their feet, working their way into the music, their bodies pivoting.

The orchestra is inexhaustible, pitiless. A violinist with a scarlet *diklo* around his neck fiddles as if possessed, his eyes never leaving the face of a woman at a table. Other musicians sway, ecstatic, gripping their instruments as if barely able to restrain them. The arms of the cimbalom player blur into furious white motion, his expression vacant. Their music is devilish, rapid, it impetuously swoops and changes following the direction of the inscrutable *primás.*

Men raise their arms and shout *Éljen!* The women wail, a wild noise that speeds the dancing. The music is as calculated as a perfume, invisibly spiraling back on itself, its previous state, then carrying everything forward, past and present. Erszébet has no sense of time passing.

The music abruptly halts.

For a moment, the dancers keep moving. Then the men bend over and weep. The women stay numbly in place, as if turned to statues.

The Inspector finds his wife standing dazed and alone. He's almost afraid to approach her, but he takes her arm and gently ushers her to a chair. She gulps the water from the glass he hands her. Some of it falls onto her dress.

She doesn't remember the dancing. Later she says, I was in the realm of *mulatni,* when the world vanishes.

She secretly wonders if her husband watched her with the stranger.

🥀

Wally has seen Erszébet only once in the last two weeks. They'd attended an afternoon concert at the Kursalon in Stadtpark. At that time, Wally had found Erszébet changed, but it was too nebulous to pinpoint. She had an aura of slowness, as if looking up moments too late to witness a plate's fall or a bird's flight. On the way home from the concert, Erszébet wasn't quick enough to avoid a beggar pushing a cart. He brushed against her coat and then walked over her shadow. She swore something under her breath and then refused to translate her angry words for Wally. It's just bad luck, she finally explained. Step on a shadow.

The weather has turned very bitter — five degrees Reaumur — and Erszébet stands by a shivering chestnut seller in the Hoher Markt. She's swathed in fur, a density of black fringe, finer than needles. She deliberately chose this location to meet Wally. The crowd suits her purpose.

Wally arrives in her red cloak, glad of Erszébet's company. Without waiting, Erszébet abruptly turns and walks through the market, talking to her over her shoulder.

"You know, there's a legend about Emperor Franz Josef visiting here? He toured the markt and deliberately turned over a basket of eggs, just so the egg seller would scream at him. She was so furious, she forgot he was his Apostolic Majesty. He paid for the eggs and believed it was worth the experience of being treated like a commoner."

Even in the cold, the market is very busy, and Wally dodges around shoppers to keep up with Erszébet. She loses sight of her when a man with a bushel of firewood blocks her way, and a second time when the canvas awnings over a stall flap down in her way. She finds Erszébet at a vegetable stand, calmly balancing a cauliflower in each hand. Serenely ignoring Wally, she makes her way to another stall, where a woman is curtained by strings of dried peppers. They have an animated conversation about different *paprikás*. After Erszébet makes her purchase of *félédes,* semisweet paprika, she seems surprised to find Wally still waiting for her.

Wally grabs her arm. "What is the matter?" she says wildly. "Listen to me."

Erszébet shifts her basket to her other hand, forcing Wally to drop her arm.

"I'm listening."

"Why are you ignoring me?"

Erszébet shakes her head. "I can't talk to you just now. I'm waiting."

Wally loses her language. Her words come out in English. "Waiting for what?"

Erszébet moves over to the next stall to carefully examine a stack of bread and rolls. When she turns around, Wally has knocked over a sack of potatoes and vanished into the crowd.

If Erszébet could study her own face at this moment, she'd recognize her expression as identical to that of the *látó,* the wise women who could make contact with the dead. An internal gaze.

Erszébet stays home, telling herself the snow keeps her inside. She cooks feverishly, stewing dried figs and prunes, marinating game birds, filling dumplings by hand. During this period, the house is fragrant with the smell of roast pork and *paprikás.* She spends afternoons preparing her husband's favorite desserts, an elaborate *Mehlspeise,* rice pudding soaked in red wine, and *csöröge fánk,* sweet fritters, which he'd enjoyed on their honeymoon in Buda Pest.

Wally follows Egon into the Zentralfriedhof, its vastness transformed into a pale desert of snow. It's early morning, but the sky is stubbornly gray. There is no noise but their footsteps on the brittle surface of the snow. Egon is a dark shape in front of her. As they make their way up a hill, he sends a great cloudy breath over his shoulder.

They find Dora's monument and quickly set up their candles on a nearby grave. It is the three-month anniversary of Dora's burial. Wally has persuaded Egon to visit the Zentralfriedhof on this particular day, hoping the dead girl's family will pay their respects. Perhaps Egon will be able to identify Philipp as the man who came to his studio. They wait, pacing around the plot, trying to keep warm.

Wind steals the veil of her hat and it streams around her head. She tucks a corner of it under her hat, leaving just enough of the fine black silk to hide her face. She is startled by Egon's hand on her arm.

"Are you frightened?"

"No. Not a bit." She refuses to share her fear with him.

"That's good. I'm going to tell you about a corpse I once photographed."

He stands so he can watch her face while he talks. She doesn't blink, doesn't look away.

"The police found the corpse of a man in the woods outside the city, in Heiligenstadt. He was hunched over, frozen stiff. It was the middle of winter. We dragged the body into a house and left it in a chair in the kitchen. Then we went out to search the area. Guess what happened?"

Wally raises her eyebrows.

"It was extraordinary. The heat from the stove thawed out the corpse so it changed position. When we came back, the body was sprawled in the chair, its arms thrown back. When I looked through my camera, I could see his foot actually move, like this."

He slides his foot toward her. She slowly gets up and backs away from him.

A group of dark figures, darker than the trees behind them, laboriously make their way up the hill to Dora's grave. When their candles are lit and set around the grave, the flames make a strange, artificial light against the snow, as if they were only imitating fire. A woman and a smaller figure, a boy, set wreaths against the monument.

Wally bends toward Egon and whispers, "Can you see her father?"

Egon stiffly turns to face Dora's family, his face concealed by his bowler and the high collar of his coat.

Suddenly, the woman wails loudly and drops to her knees, her coat pillowing around her. Then she falls forward into the snow. Otto begins to cry. Philipp stoops over his wife and takes her arm. As if he can feel the intensity of their watching eyes, Philipp suddenly raises his head and stares straight at Wally.

Startled, she jerks back, and her veil floats across the flame of a candle. She hears screams, the thin, hungry whoosh of fire eating silk a second before the color around her head is transformed from black into yellow and light envelops her.

The Inspector is surprised when Franz pushes the door open and breathlessly announces that Fräulein Fürj is waiting for him in the outer office.

"Temper yourself," he says, for Franz is clearly over-excited.

Blushing, Franz nods and straightens his shoulders.

After he leaves, the Inspector tries to quiet his own nerves. The girl would only come here if she had something of significance to tell him. He'd slipped her his card at Philipp's office for just this reason. Thoughtful as a suitor, he covers the top of his desk with clean white paper and moves two chairs into a corner of the room for their interview.

Fräulein Fürj enters his office, visibly ill at ease. She awkwardly shifts a large bag from hand to hand. The Inspector suggests Franz wait outside.

"Please have a seat, Fräulein. I'm glad to see you."

She indicates no, she doesn't want to remove her coat. She sits down and gingerly holds the bag on her lap.

He leans forward, careful not to make any sudden motions that might startle her, remembering her skittishness.

"You seem troubled about something. Is that why you've come to see me?"

She silently begins to cry, the tears a shiny parade down her cheeks. She takes the handkerchief he offers, keeping her other hand on the bag.

"Now then. Tell me what you've brought me." He keeps his voice low.

As if she hadn't heard him, she begins to talk, her voice rushed, high-pitched.

"I thought about what you said about Fräulein Dora when you came to the office. After you left I heard terrible stories about how her grave was disturbed. Everyone at the office was talking about it when her father wasn't listening. Someone said wolves dug up her body?"

The Inspector doesn't dare nod or even make a move for his notebook. Everything in him is focused on the girl, trying to keep her calm.

"I found this in the stove at work."

She reaches into the bag, and he suddenly jumps up.

"Don't touch it!"

She freezes.

He stands over her, peering down at something loosely wrapped in the bottom of her bag.

"It's burnt, isn't it?"

She blinks up at him, terrified.

He puts his hand on top of her head. Under her thin blond hair, her scalp is hot.

"You did well to bring it here. Tell me what happened."

"I looked for his engagement book as you asked. I never found it, which was strange, since it was always kept on my desk." Her voice trails off as she follows her chain of calculation.

He waits.

She shifts the bag on her lap, won't look at him.

"One day when I worked late, I noticed something was still burning in the stove. There was smoke. So I opened it and found this."

He lifts the bag off her lap and carries it to his desk. He takes a knife from his pocket and swiftly slashes through one side of the bag, then folds it down around the object inside. A bitter smell fills the room.

"It's his diary."

"Fräulein, I'm not going to open the parcel here, since it's very fragile. I'd like to know exactly why you stole this from your employer."

Her pink mouth drops open, and she stares at him, so astonished she has forgotten to avert her eyes.

"He said I was going to lose my job," she blurts.

"Unless?"

"He said other things to me. He tried to kiss me."

Now she stares at the floor, and he strains to hear her.

"I need to work."

"Please look at me."

Their eyes meet. The girl has more backbone than he thought. A budding blackmailer and an accomplished thief.

"So you were going to threaten him with the diary you saved from the fire?"

She nods, pressing her lips together until her mouth disappears, a fine white line.

"Fräulein, I won't reveal what you've done. You should try to find another job. You may use me as a reference."

At first she politely refuses the money he hands her, but then thinks better of it after he hands it to her a second time. Then he asks her to bring him a sample of Philipp's handwriting. She tearfully agrees.

That night he goes over his interview with Fräulein Fürj. It's a pity women aren't allowed to work for the police, he thinks. Erszébet told him that fortune-tellers are often unable to distinguish between policemen and thieves. All the signs are the same.

The Inspector is anxious to begin work on Philipp's diary. If just one sentence or a phrase can be deciphered, he imagines he can pull the meaning out of the burned book, as if the script were a long black thread connected over all its pages. He's certain the evidence they need to convict Dora's father is in these black pages.

Earlier, Móricz had numbered seventy sheets of tracing paper and pinned them to thin boards. Then he painted each paper with transparent gum arabic, a rectangle about the size of the diary pages.

Franz and the Inspector join him in the laboratory.

To eliminate dust, they wear gloves and jackets of white cotton, and as they move between the long worktables set with the treated papers, they appear to be waiters at some strange banquet.

Under their curious eyes, the Inspector gently unwraps Fräulein Fürj's bundle over a table. It's a slim diary, badly burned. The front of the book, where it rested on the fire, is completely ruined. A thick section of the back is also blackened and buckled.

The Inspector cuts open the binding of the diary and removes the cover.

"I'm going to try and save the first pages, since the author's name may appear there. Look carefully. Fire produces different effects on ink and paper. See, the writing is visible if the light falls in a certain way."

Under the lamplight, a few black words eerily stand out on the warped black paper, as if the letters were written fire on fire. Only the disciplined spikes and loops of the letters seem to be holding the fragile page together.

He slides a clean paper under the burned page, jiggles it loose and deftly maneuvers it onto the sticky tracing paper. It is more fragile than a butterfly's wing. Franz fights the urge to sneeze.

"We'll try to relax the warped paper. Franz, move very slowly. Any motion will make the paper fly."

Frowning in concentration, Franz sets small stones down on the tracing paper, all around the edges of the burned page. It looks like a child has built a fortress. When he's finished, the Inspector lays a fine damp cloth over the stones, pulling it tight across so it won't touch the black paper underneath.

"If we're lucky, the moistness of the fabric will gradually soften the page. Sometimes paper isn't hygroscopic and it just crumbles."

They repeat the process with the next few pages from the diary, filling the entire table with stones and black squares. It's a painstaking process and it takes the better part of a day.

Once Franz slipped and they all watched helplessly as a page wafted out of his hand, moving in lazy motion to the floor, where it silently shattered into black shards. The Inspector held his tongue. It's useless to reprimand someone for an accidental mishap.

When Egon walks into the laboratory, none of the men bent over the table looks up. Móricz wiggles a warning finger, and he slows his steps. Franz and the Inspector hold the sides of a small black square with tweezers. Moving together, they lay the square gently on a paper. It instantly crumbles into ash. Franz squints in exasperation.

The Inspector wordlessly motions Egon to follow him outside.

"I see you're working with black powder."

"It's burned paper. A diary."

"I just had a strange experience with fire."

The Inspector looks at him quizzically.

"I respect fire. When I work with explosive powder, I can never predict what it'll do. Sometimes even a footstep can make it go off. Look at the powder the wrong way and it'll spontaneously combust. I'm convinced a mental state can cause an explosion. Perhaps that's what happened when I had the accident with my hand. Did I wish for it?"

The Inspector shakes his head. "That's like saying a knife jumped off the table and cut you."

But his answer to Egon was a reassuring lie. He knows objects have a life of their own. Erszébet has influenced him. Sharp steel — a needle — can turn away evil. A sprig of vervain will open a locked door. The corpse of a woman who died in childbirth is to be feared.

He is astonished to find himself thinking, *The victim loves the gun; the victim loves the knife.*

An army of fir trees suddenly occupies the Hoher Markt. At night, under the light from the streetlamps, the ornamental paper streamers and ribbons twisted through the branches are the only color in the black and silent mass of trees.

A few streets away, Am Hof Square has been transformed into the Christkindlmarkt, a shantytown of wooden stalls filled with Christmas toys and sweets, a children's paradise. It is the holiday season.

The Inspector struggles behind his wife through the children clamoring around the displays of rocking horses, miniature trains, marionettes, dolls, Noah's arks, wooden swords, gilded bugles and drums, and unhappy caged parrots. Other stalls beckon with dried fruits, oranges threaded on string, candies, fruitcakes, gingerbread, and *Bischofsbrot*. A *Krampus*, a miniature figure of the devil, is attached to every box of chocolate.

Erszébet becomes lost in the chaos. When he catches sight of her again, she seems momentarily unfamiliar, a mysterious figure returned to him. He wonders if his perceptions are playing tricks on him again, like the shape-shifters, the *csordásfarkas*.

He squeezes her arm, then secretly touches her body under her coat, his gesture unnoticed by the children intent on their toys. Over their heads, her smile dazzles him.

His Christmas gift to Erszébet this year is a fur-lined velvet cloak, a *fourrure de ville*, elaborately embroidered and made in Paris. She wraps it around herself, twirling in front of him in the bedroom. Why, it weighs nothing, she exclaims. Imagine the fur against bare skin, she teases, and he spontaneously embraces her.

She loves the cloak and wears it constantly, sometimes leaving it unbuttoned, so it hangs off her shoulders like two heavy wings. His pleasure in it is secretly enhanced by his memory of Frau Zellenka in a similar garment, and lessened by the image of the dirty cloak abandoned in the Volksgarten.

During the Christian holidays, Erszébet practices sexual abstinence. A child conceived on Christmas Eve is considered unlucky and will later resent his parents for their unholy transgression, their wild lack of control and piety. The child may be deformed with a harelip or be cursed with the ears and head of a wolf. Or the infant may be born a werewolf, a *csordásfarkas*.

When Egon opens the door, he's so surprised to see her that he stands there without saying a word. She interrupted him in the darkroom, and a chemical smell clings to his bare hands and his leather apron. The woman asks if she can enter.

Certainly. I won't be a moment, he says and disappears into the darkroom to fix a print. Inside the studio, wan sun leaks in from the skylight, patchily blocked by the black curtains. Nervously pulling at her gloves, she walks over to study the photographs on the wall, portraits of actresses and an opera singer, a street scene and a landscape, a view of the Volksgarten near the statue of Kaiserin Elizabeth.

When he comes back in the room, Rosza is removing her veil and hat.

"I want you to take my picture." She's abrupt, as if she's in a hurry.

"I usually ask people to make an appointment, but since you're here, I'll make an exception," he says, trying to joke with her. "May I take your coat?"

"Thank you."

"Have you played tarok recently?"

She shakes her head, doesn't look at him. No connection. She's cold, acting as if they've never met. He's used to dealing with difficult women. Children are easier subjects for a portrait. She's made him self-conscious, and he shoves his hands under his apron to hide the odor of the photographic chemicals.

"I see. So you want a straightforward photograph? A portrait?"

He mentions a price for his work. She agrees. He again retreats into the darkroom. By the red light of a lantern, he uncaps jars of chemicals and measures the lightning powders.

When he emerges from the darkroom, she's already changing behind a screen. He adjusts the camera, cranking the tripod higher, readying the plate holder. From the sharp crease in a folded paper, he sprinkles a line of magnesium powder onto a metal trough. He checks that the string with the loop for his finger — the remote trigger — is tightly wound. Although this is all routine work, his hands are jittery.

"Which background would you like for your photograph? I have a pretty one with a ruined temple."

"I don't want any backdrop. Just make it black behind me."

He shrugs his shoulders in exasperation, then tacks a length of dark-colored muslin up on the wall. To direct the artificial light, he maneuvers a thin white canvas panel — like a blank painting, about five feet high — at an angle to the camera.

He ducks behind the camera, pulling the black cloth over his head. Seemingly blindly, his hands adjust the instrument.

"Fräulein? I'm ready now."

"Close your eyes."

"But I won't be able to work the camera," he says patiently.

"Just do as I say. I will pay you."

He's intrigued, wondering what is her strange game. Obedient, he closes his eyes. Soft footsteps cross the floor and stop in front of him.

"Are you near the camera?"

"Yes."

"May I open my eyes?"

His blinking eye fills the camera lens, one curve fitted to another. First he notices her shawl has fallen around her feet, a bright pool of color. Then he sees the outline of her nude body, and his eye goes up to the black veil over her face, the smooth, bald place between her legs, the discolored scars over her abdomen. He's shocked, as if the camera created this image without his participation, stealing it unerringly from his memory and making it flesh. His finger automatically pulls the trigger, and there's an explosion of light. His eye is white-blind from the flash. He claws the cloth off his head while she's still screaming.

She's kneeling on the floor, sobbing. He watches her for a moment, the black cloth dangling helplessly in his hands. Then he gently drapes it over her shoulders. He lifts the veil from her face.

When she's quiet, he helps her into a chair. Without the artificial light, the studio is almost dark.

There's no noise but her ragged breath.

He finds his voice.

"You've been here before. You're the woman in the photographs."

She's still in shock, her body shaking.

"It's the fire you're afraid of, isn't it?"

"I thought . . . I thought I could make you sorry."

The room goes dark around them.

CHAPTER 13

HE INSPECTOR HAS CATALOGED Erszébet's emotional state, her anger and unexplained brooding silences, lack of appetite, the stormy expression on her face, which darkens when she catches him watching. He's the audience when she loses her temper. More than once, he's found her staring down the maid. No loud words, just Erszébet's thick silence and an angry gesture as she grabs the mending or the half-scrubbed pot away from the startled woman's hands.

Erszébet avoids activities that require thoughtful attention, painting and needlepoint. Instead, she continues to physically tire herself in the kitchen.

She's lost in cooking. He counts the various paprika dishes she serves. *Gulyás,* an intensely onion-flavored *pörkölt* with thick gravy, *paprikás,* and *tokány,* made with veal and parsley roots. She prepares *sült libamáj,* roast goose liver. An entire wild goose is cut up and simmered with onions, peppers, and bacon. Everything is cooked with fresh pork fat. Desserts are heavy, cradled with cream: *vargabéles* of curd cheese and raisins, and strudels, including *Mohn* and *Nussboutizze.*

She feeds him lavishly but gives him only a thread of her affection. Why is he compelled to do this, make these observations? Does this mean she will leave him, these are his last memories of her?

Erszébet is wholly directed by the spell of her magical purpose. She senses her husband is unhappy, but she can only react to him distantly, as if he wobbles outside her orbit. She moves in a different climate, the *ráböjtölés*. It will soon be over. She can only swim if she forgets how to float.

On New Year's Eve, "Sylvester evening," Erszébet sticks an evergreen sprig in a shallow bowl of water on the kitchen table. Left there overnight, the needles will remain green, or turn spotted, or black, which indicates health, sickness, or death in the coming year.

She doesn't sleep well that night. In the dark hour before sunrise, she creeps downstairs and stands outside the kitchen, hugging herself to stay warm. The stove has gone out. She waits there, afraid to come closer, afraid to see the color of the evergreen sprig. After a time she enters the room, keeping the bowl on the periphery of her vision as she begins her morning routine, preparing *kávé,* slicing bread, lighting the *sparherd*.

Later, when her husband looked around the kitchen, he couldn't find the bit of evergreen or the bowl that held it. I threw it away, she told him, smiling. But the sprig was a deep green, thank God. It means luck. We'll have good fortune this year, that's certain.

He was surprised by his sense of relief. It only momentarily lightens his mood.

Fasching begins late in December and continues until Ash Wednesday. Balls are held all over Vienna during the pre-Lenten season, sometimes fifty in a single night. The city is in a state of exhilarated obliviousness at this time, intractable as insomnia. During the war of 1866, the Viennese danced at their balls even though the advancing Prussians were only a two-hour march away.

Last year, Wally was startled by party-goers stumbling into the cafés for coffee in the early hours of the morning. As she walked the children to school, two bedraggled women in masks and costumes, strangely tall in their powdered wigs, staggered in the snow on the pavement in front of them. The children were enchanted.

The Inspector usually dreads *Fasching* and its frenetic social activities, since the seasonal merriment is accompanied by an increase in reports of robberies, assaults, and public drunkeness. Some nights, he has raced to the scene of a crime from a ball, still wearing his top hat and tailcoat. Once, to soothe a crying child, he gave her his carnation boutonniere. Often he's found the hysterical behavior of the victims similar to that of the guests at the party he just left. He relishes his ability to slip between these two worlds.

Erszébet is still remote, possessed by an eerie confidence. He's afraid she will refuse to accompany him to the round of parties he is officially expected to attend. Traditionally, they are honored guests at the Concordia ball at the Sophien-Saal, given by the Press Club. He hasn't discussed the event with her. Two nights before the ball, he notices she's laid her costume out on the bed, a low-cut blouse and a lampshade-shaped skirt over pantaloons. And a black mask for her eyes.

On the way to the Sophien-Saal, the traffic is backed up, and it takes them longer than usual to cross the city. As far as they can see, *Einspänners,* fiakers, and motor cabs block the street. They're directly behind a stalled omnibus. The driver shrugs when the Inspector politely asks how much longer they'll be waiting. It will be a while.

The Inspector removes his top hat and sets it on the seat. The light from the streetlamp paints a wavering line on the hat's silk surface, so it looks as if it were made of metal.

"We're going to miss the performance," he says.

She puts on her mask. In the shadowy carriage, her eyes are inscrutable, liquid dots behind a black band. Her mouth appears larger.

"There are other ways to pass the time." She folds his gloved hand in hers.

It is close to midnight when they finally arrive at the ball. The music of the orchestra ushers them out of the fiaker. A crowd of revelers in costumes or evening dress — like the entire cast and audience of an opera — moves slowly up the stairs into the building. Erszébet picks out fancy shepherdesses modeled after Marie Antoinette, caped knights bearing swords and their kingly attendants, men in white wigs and breeches, women in tiaras and plumed crowns, their arms daringly bare. The throng parts for an astonishing young woman — who must be an actress — hair down to her waist and a jeweled asp coiled around her torso. A few boisterous couples — men with men and women with women — waltz drunkenly on the pavement.

The Inspector whispers his name to a uniformed man at the door. He escorts the Inspector and his wife down the room between a double row of members of the press. The line of faces, the noise and the heat are overwhelming. Erszébet slips away. Her husband's name and title are announced; he mounts a platform and bows to the audience and then to the Altar of Fame behind him. Cheers shake the room.

Erszébet finds him afterward, and they lift their glasses to his Apostolic Majesty, to each other and their mutual happiness.

The orchestra surprises them with a fast ragtime tune, something from Chicago. As they dance, he closes his eyes. Erszébet's back is so warm he imagines she is naked beneath his hands. The odor of her body reaches him, a familiar perfume of ripe peaches and tobacco.

They are separated by other unrecognizable partners, who lead them into a frantic *Ländler.* They dance with several strangers before they join each other again. His shirt is damp, and her hair has floated loose from its pins. She puts it up again, unself-conscious about this intimate gesture and the dark ovals of perspiration under her arms.

While her arms are still raised to her head, a man grabs her around the waist and waltzes her away. The Inspector watches her face, unfamiliar behind its mask, as she whirls across the room.

The man she's dancing with is also masked, dressed in a green military uniform with scarlet trim, tight white breeches, and high boots. She guesses he may be a gentleman. His eyes are fixed on her face, but she won't look at him or speak, not wanting to be distracted from her body's response to the music. The band begins a fast *csardás*. Voices whoop around them; the floor shakes with the pattern of footsteps. Although his hands press down on her shoulders, he is lost to her. He is something to use, a bridge to an intimate place. She's dimly conscious of his frustration.

When the music stops, she moves back from him, gasping for breath, laughing up at his face. He grasps her arm, and his lips touch her ear. Would she care to step outside with him? She shakes her head, still smiling. He doesn't release her, but unbuttons his collar and thrusts her hand inside his jacket, against his bare neck. She can't move, too many people are wedged around her. When she finally pulls away, her fingers shine with his sweat.

She waits until they're inside the fiaker to tell her husband about the incident. He's sleepy and nestles his head deeper into the fur cloak over her lap. She doesn't believe he understood what she said. She strokes his hair. Did you hear me?

"Once I arrested a man who had a strange compulsion," he mumbles, his voice muffled by the cloak. "A saliromaniac. He threw ink on women's dresses. On the street, right in front of everyone."

Two days later, Franz has worked his way through another seven pages of the burned diary without success. The brittle pages crumble when pressed to the gummed paper. None of the writing is legible. He resents this tedious work, since it takes him away from his pursuit of Rosza.

One of the governesses he'd contacted in the Volksgarten came to see him at the police station. The woman, a ruddy

blonde from Silesia, was enormously pleased to tell him she'd
seen Rosza the day before at Wiener Molkerei, on the Schottenring. She draws out the sketchy details. Rosza was accompanied by two little boys and carried an umbrella, a description
that fits nearly every fräulein of a certain age.

Franz drops his pen. "Doesn't she have any distinguishing features? No limp? No crippled hand?" He couldn't stop
himself.

The governess is offended by his sarcasm. Rosza is very
pretty, she says stiffly. I have heard certain rumors about her
that are unflattering.

Franz recovers. "You've been very helpful. I can't express
my gratitude, *gnädige Frau."* He kisses her hand. Most people,
he's beginning to realize, are afflicted with a visual illiteracy.

The governess gave him one interesting lead. You should
visit the Queen Victoria Jubilee Home for British Governesses, she told him. You might find someone there who
knows Rosza.

Franz asks the Inspector for advice on methods of recognition.

"All the women in the street are beginning to look alike to
me," he mutters. "I'm losing my skill."

"Seems you've lost your sense of humor, too." The Inspector grins. "Focus on a specific portion of the face. A person
is usually recognizable by the space between the lower half of
the forehead and the bridge of the nose. You've noticed this is
the part of the face covered by a domino. When a mask is worn
and the hair on the head is covered, identification is nearly impossible."

Franz looks up "Recognition of Criminals from their
Photographs" in *Kriminalistik* and finds that identification in
broad daylight can be exactly measured.

> a) Persons whom one knows very well can be recognized at
>   a distance of 45 to 80 meters; in exceptional cases up to
>   150 meters.

b) Persons one does not know well and has not often seen
are recognizable from 25 to 30 meters.

c) People one has only seen once can be identified at 14
meters.

As soon as he can excuse himself from the laboratory,
Franz makes his way to the Queen Victoria Jubilee Home for
British Governesses, impressively situated on the Graben.

From outside, the home is dimly lit. Inside, the rooms
visible from where he stands in the foyer are in deep shadow,
tunnels into the building's deeper gloom. There is a faint stale
smell of dust, permanently colonized in the upholstery and
carpeting. An unseen clock ticks dryly.

Slow footsteps announce the appearance of a prim elderly woman. Her hair and long gray dress are of the style of
twenty years ago, reminding Franz of the implacable governess
who ruled his childhood nursery. She inserts the black circle of
her monocle into one eye and regards him sternly. His confidence evaporates.

I'm here on police business, he sputters, producing his
official letter. Without taking her eyes off him, she extends her
hand for it. Franz tries not to fidget while she reads. He looks
around, growing accustomed to the dimness, and notices a
group of old women in armchairs in the side room, silently
watching him.

"I'm Miss Revelstok. This way please."

He follows her into the room where the ladies are seated,
and his letter flits from hand to hand as they excitedly chatter
in English. He explains he is looking for Rosza, who worked as
a governess for a Viennese family. She left her employers last
winter or early in the spring. This was her address. Franz is
thankful the light in the room is subdued, for he can feel the
red heat of embarrassment flame up over his face. He can't
catch the women's words, their sharp language is too quick for
him, but he can read their reactions. None of them is acquainted with Rosza.

Frowns and puzzled looks. The matron touches his arm.

"Let me ask upstairs."

She vanishes, leaving him to stand awkwardly in the circle of women. He smiles uncertainly, trying to revive the few words of English he knows, something about the weather, about rain. Yes, he'd like tea, he says in answer to one of the ladies' invitation.

He helps her from the chair. She grandly waves him away and proceeds alone across the room, infinitely slowly, the shuffle of her slippers preceded by the delicate thump of her cane.

He studies an unsympathetic portrait of Queen Victoria while the elderly women weave whispers behind him. It suddenly occurs to him that they all believe he is an abandoned suitor, trying to find his lost love. He blushes again.

His face is still red when the matron returns. She hands him a card with an address elaborately inscribed on it. I'm sorry this took so long, she says. Our resident with the best memory is dreadfully hard of hearing. She lays a thin hand on top of his. You must be very anxious to find her.

Franz stammers his gratitude in English. He's even more flustered when her eyes are transformed by tears. He awkwardly kisses her dry hand and then departs, forgetting his tea.

It wasn't until that night that he remembered the aged governesses of the Jubilee Home had kept his official letter.

When fire caught the veil of Wally's hat in the Zentralfriedhof, she screamed and fell. Otto had rushed over. Egon was afraid they'd attract the cemetery attendants, and he quickly led her away. She was dazed, her scalp ached, there was a terrible smell of burning in the air.

Only Dora's father didn't move. He stood as if frozen in place, unable to answer when his wife urged him to go and help.

Wally has a memory of her veil burning, its edges unfurling and yellow with flame, a reflection of the candles around her. She didn't see Egon jerk the scarf off her head and the curve of bright color it made as he threw it in the air. Later he told her it was his practice with the cloth over his camera that enabled him to move so quickly.

Wally spent two days in bed. Then she met Egon at Demel Konditorei. "That man in the cemetery, Dora's father, did you recognize him?"

She grabbed his hand.

"No, I didn't. He wasn't the man who came to my studio with the woman."

Without any preliminary explanation, Franz hands the Inspector the card he was given at the Queen Victoria Jubilee Home. Astonished, the Inspector reads the name and address, then congratulates Franz on his work. A genuine accomplishment. This is the first breakthrough they've had in weeks. Even though Franz found the governess, the Inspector will interview her. Franz doesn't protest. The situation is too delicate for an assistant officer. By her long absence, the mysterious governess has grown in importance. She has become the key to Dora's murder. Now they almost have her.

That night at dinner, the Inspector is strangely ebullient, even requesting a second glass of fruit brandy. Erszébet sits on the arm of his chair, watching him drink.

"I've found the missing woman in Dora's case. I believe she may be the last witness. I hope everything will fall into place when I interview her tomorrow."

"Who is she?"

"A young woman. A governess."

He refuses to say anything more. And even though Erszébet teases, he won't reveal the woman's name. Buoyed by his discovery, he shuts her out.

Which governess? Rosza? Wally?

Erszébet's throat begins to ache. She slips into bed, but sleep doesn't arrive that night. She possesses various ways to stop him, but she's already deep in *ráböjtölés,* the black fast. Spells are unpredictable things.

The last thing her husband remembers is her cool hand sliding over his flesh and his turn toward her in the darkness. He's grateful her desire is more calculated, rougher than his. She leads him into the labyrinth.

The Inspector arrives at the house without giving any notice. The *Hausmeister* who admits him takes careful note of his appearance and his business. A policeman. He's certain the woman he's visiting will be reprimanded later for entertaining such an inauspicious guest.

Now he sits across from Rosza, watching an angry line crease her forehead. She has just confirmed she was with Herr Zellenka on the evening Dora died, and she isn't pleased with herself. Or the Inspector. Although it's only midafternoon, the room is a dim, lamp-lit gray cave. A cage with two noisy canaries hovers on a stand next to him.

"Tell me about that evening with Herr Zellenka. What do you remember?"

"We had dinner at the Grand Café in the Alsergrund district. We were there from eight o'clock until past midnight."

"And did Herr Zellenka escort you home?"

"Not right away. We drove through the Prater in a fiaker. As I remember, it was a very hot evening."

He writes down everything she says, making no criticism of her conduct with a married man, even though her irritability tells him she expects it.

"I understand you left Dora's family rather suddenly. Did you and Dora remain friends?"

She doesn't answer. He resists the urge to ask the question again.

"No."

"Why did your friendship change? You were very close at one time."

"Dora resented me. She was a grown woman, and she

didn't want a chaperone. I tried to leave her alone. I spent most of my time with her brother, but she hated having me in the house."

He leans forward over his notebook. "You and Dora had a quarrel. What was it about?" His voice now has an edge.

She assures him it was nothing, really. Just a silly misunderstanding between friends. Dora always exaggerated everything. Then she falls silent. She lets him wait, fidgeting with her hands in her lap.

Do you mind if I open the curtains? he asks, and without waiting for her answer he violently yanks them open. Sometimes questions need sunlight, he says, sitting down in another chair closer to her, away from the birds. Their chirping was affecting his nerves.

"Fräulein, we're alone here. I want you to answer my questions quickly, before the lady of the house returns. I'm certain you'd prefer it that way too. Otherwise, I can make your situation here very uncomfortable. You and Dora argued about her father. Correct?"

He's struck something familiar in her.

"Yes. Although it wasn't until August that I told her everything. We arranged to meet in the Volksgarten. I hadn't seen her for months. I guess she was curious about what I'd hinted at in my letter."

By the tone of her voice and her posture, he can tell she's eager to have him believe her story. Even take her side against Dora.

"I told Dora it was unconscionable to be friends with Frau Zellenka, since she was her father's lover. I explained the situation very clearly, that Dora was just a pawn between them. The woman had no friendship with her. She was just using her."

Now he no longer needs to be careful with his questions. Her character is uncovered; Rosza is scornful and self-righteous. For the moment, she's even forgotten she's a beautiful woman and dropped her flirtatious mannerisms. Although he believes in words as well as observation, it always surprises him when they strip away a defense.

"How did Dora react to your enlightening her?"

"She was hysterical. She wept and said she didn't believe me, but I'm certain I told her exactly what she already knew. She could hardly miss the intimacy between her father and that woman. It was as obvious as the nose on her face."

Rosza wrinkles her own nose in disgust.

"And did Dora confront Frau Zellenka?"

"I'm sure she did. Dora never let anything rest."

She looks at him with a strange grim pride.

"Perhaps I was wrong to tell Dora about her father's shameful behavior, since they'd always been close. Well, it's too late. The truth destroyed our friendship. I hadn't calculated on that. And Dora died about two weeks later. The poor girl had no one she could trust, not her father, her dear friend Frau Zellenka, or even me, her *promeneuse*. But it's always better to know the truth, isn't it?"

He doesn't say anything. His notebook is forgotten in his hands. He wonders if she has any remorse.

"You don't like Frau Zellenka."

"I blame Frau Zellenka for everything. It wasn't enough for her to have a wonderful husband. She had to steal Dora's father too. Dora was calculating in her own way, but she was also an innocent. I tell you, the situation in that house was unbearable. I wasn't at all sorry to leave."

Even though she says she has no regrets, her voice is angry.

Without enthusiasm, he thanks her and wishes her well. As he leaves the room, he looks back and sees her angrily jerk the drapes back over the windows.

If we find that the witness has any sort of connection with the affair, we must, to some extent, accept with mistrust all that he says and verify every one of his statements; we must spare no trouble to ascertain the point of view at which the witness stations himself. This is not so difficult as one would think; the witness almost always betrays himself, if only by a word.

In the laboratory, Franz and Móricz continue to work with the burned diary stolen from Philipp. They experiment with some of the buckled pages, to soften them so they can be flattened onto the gummed paper. One black page is held over boiling water in a sieve, but it breaks apart. They immerse another page in a large basin of water, hoping it will float. The paper contains a high percentage of baryte, so it disintegrates. Móricz fishes it out of the basin as cinders.

Egon agrees to come in and photograph a few sections of the book. Perhaps technology will show what their eyes can't see. Or a hunch may prove more revealing; the Inspector begins to wonder if shy Fräulein Fürj tossed her own diary in the stove.

Discouraged at their slow progress, the Inspector encourages everyone to take frequent breaks. After Franz and Móricz finish their recess, it's his turn to smoke outside. In the hallway, he lights a cigarette, tipping the ashes into a jar. The burned diary refuses to give up its secrets. The words remain stubborn hieroglyphics on fragile black tablets. He has been handed a key but can't find its accomplice, the lock. He's certain the solution to Dora's murder is on the table in the quiet room behind him. The book contains the answer to every puzzle and the motive for every action.

All he must do is take apart the tender leaves of a blackened book, a process he begins to regard as unlikely as uncoiling the shell of a snail.

Because of the inaccessibility of their suspects, Wally and Erszébet have circled back to an object. The fig, a witness to a murder. *Ficus,* a word for a woman's quaint, and the tree of Judas, the betrayer. They decide to search one last location. This is Erszébet's suggestion, and it came to her under the influence of *ráböjtölés.*

Wally slips out of the Arkaden-Café into a waiting fiaker, nervously following the instructions in Erszébet's letter.

Erszébet waits for her on a corner, a solitary figure, her

shoulders enlarged by a huge fur wrap. Wally is ill at ease; she hasn't seen Erszébet for several weeks. Had Erszébet missed her? Wally is too proud to ask. She takes off her hat, hoping Erszébet will notice her singed hair. She doesn't. On the point of tears, Wally describes her fiery accident in the cemetery. Erszébet mutters some unintelligible soothing words and embraces her.

Her embrace doesn't mollify Wally. She pointedly avoids Erszébet's eyes. Friends shouldn't vanish. There is a darker fear in the back of her mind — that Erszébet would walk out of her life — but she dismisses it.

Now the ice on the walk slows their steps, and Wally clutches at Erszébet's arm just as she falls. Erszébet helps her back on her feet and dusts the snow off her coat. This eases the tension between them.

Erszébet pretends not to notice Wally's coolness, knowing she can be charmed back. The girl needs her. She attempts to explain her absence.

"I was unable to see anyone. It had nothing to do with you. But today is an ominous day, so I could finally leave the kitchen."

"The kitchen has an unlucky day?"

"It is considered bad luck to bake on a Friday."

Then Wally relents and tells Erszébet that Dora's father is no longer a suspect. "Egon saw Philipp in the cemetery and didn't recognize him, so he wasn't the man who brought Dora into the studio. It must have been Herr Zellenka."

Erszébet juggles her news. There is only the photographer's word that she came to his studio with a man, she reminds Wally. What if Dora's unknown companion was a woman? Or someone unsuspected, another man?

Erszébet fastens her mind on such an order. Wind strikes the tall row of trees above her head, and their ice-lined branches crack and chime.

They cautiously approach Steinach's clinic from a side street, staying away from the windows. Everything seems quiet. Erszébet motions Wally around to the back of the building, where they find an iron fence burdened with ivy.

"I'll hold your feet and help you over. Then open the gate for me."

A snowbank softens Wally's fall on the other side of the fence. The gate is unlocked, and the heavy door swings open at a tug from her gloved hands. Sketchy snow whitens the ground inside the garden and covers a long, low mound of snow in front of a clump of trees. It could have been made by the wind's caprice, shaped by some invisible geography, like water breaking over a hidden reef. Or perhaps the snow hides something. They make their way across the frozen grass, moving as quickly as they can from tree to tree. Snow works its way into the tops of their boots as their feet punch into the deeper drifts.

Screened by a spiny holly bush, they crouch next to the mound. Erszébet finds a branch and scrapes it into the snow. She looks over her shoulder at Wally.

"Why don't you help me?"

Squatting next to her, Wally digs through the snow until she reaches a layer of dead grass and leaves, a sodden brown mass. Their cold fingers nervously pull apart the rotted vegetation, ruining their thin gloves. Erszébet's hands tremble as she picks up a wet leaf and tenderly unfolds it, frail as seaweed. Spread open, it makes an almost transparent stain on the snow. A familiar shape. A fig leaf.

Our tree is buried here.

His patience is at an end.

A week later, the Inspector strips off his white gloves, stained black to the knuckles with ash, and angrily stalks out of the laboratory. Franz gives a low whistle. He exchanges a look with Móricz and then continues to silently pore over the diary.

The Inspector didn't return to the office for the rest of the day.

The Inspector is increasingly irritable. He blames Dora's unresolved investigation for his uncharacteristic behavior. He refuses to associate it with Erszébet's strange mood. But he's a planet pulled to her gravity. The slightest infraction now

provokes a physical response from her. He watched as she be-
rated one of the laundry maids — the linens weren't white
enough — and then realized with horror that she was slowly
peeling off a glove with the intention of slapping the poor girl.

At first, he pressured her with questions about her state
of mind. Was she angry with him, troubled about something?
She shrugged off his questions. *It's just the time of year,* was the
best answer she gave him.

Then he redoubled his efforts at surveillance. Every day
she's come to expect some part of her closet or bureau or desk
will be subtly rearranged. They never speak of it.

He finds her more beautiful, even though her *voll-
schlank* — full-slim — figure is thinner. In the evening, she
takes the pins from her hair and lets it fall over her shoulders.
It's so heavy it gives me a headache, she complains.

Some evenings she permits him to comb it for her.

For some reason he can't fathom, this intimate act fills
him with despair.

None of this matters. This is what she gives him. He is
still enthralled, entering the bedroom right after Erszébet has
finished dressing, when her scent and the sense of her activity
linger there, a ghostly presence for him to enjoy.

Franz and Móricz have worked through the moat of black
paper surrounding the center of the burned diary. This less-
damaged section is their treasure. Here, the fire transformed
the paper into a rainbow of grays, from dark charcoal to a powdery ash. Like a magic wand, the heat also affected the ink, so
some words have a matte or brilliant surface and the handwriting was reversed from black to white. Here and there, they can
decipher innocuous words: *business, what, him, meeting.* There
is a list of disjointed figures and a mention of Simmerling, an
outer district of Vienna.

On other pages, the handwriting left the ghost of its
image on the facing page, a double reverse. But when Móricz
holds a mirror up to the page — his clever idea — the words
are still mysteriously illegible.

Móricz sets down the mirror and stares at the Inspector and Franz in silence. Their work has come to nothing. There's no legible name. Not even a date. The black pages are scattered in hundreds of pieces on the worktables, like lace that has been picked apart. They are too fragile to even be put away.

A letter arrived from one of the Inspector's former colleagues, a Hungarian named Csoma, who lives near Lake Balaton.

> *I am pleased to respond to your inquiry. As you well know, criminals are slaves to strange superstitions. The severed left thumb of a corpse is a powerful talisman. It is cut from a body that has been buried for nine weeks and disinterred during a new moon. Criminals believe anyone who carries the thumb is charmed and can walk invisibly through a house without waking the occupants. For this reason, the talisman is called the "slumber thumb." French thieves call it a "main de gloire."*
>
> *In answer to your second question, it is common for excrement to be left next to a victim's body to magically prevent the discovery of the crime. As long as it preserves its warmth, the crime will stay hidden. This is the reason the handkerchief was placed over the excrement next to the girl's body.*
>
> *You may also find datura seeds hidden where a crime has been committed. This peculiar habit is exclusively practiced by Gypsies.*

The Inspector is confident this information resolves the mutilation of Dora's body. Jószef is guilty. However, the news isn't enough to break his foul mood.

A few days later, Philipp's new secretary admits the Inspector to his office. She's about the same age as Fräulein Fürj but even plumper, with pale skin under faint freckles. Without hearing her speak, he guesses she's from Bohemia. He drops a business card on her desk blotter, announces he'll let himself in, and strides into Philipp's office. She bustles indignantly after him until Philipp's curt voice from the next room stops her. Her skirt swishes aggressively as she quickly turns and walks out.

Philipp is at his desk in a pose that indicates he's been waiting for the Inspector. His hands are folded in front of him, his pen alertly upright in its metal holder. But the man doesn't look well. Perhaps it's the light in the room, but his face is thinner, his nose appears to have receded slightly. He doesn't say a word in return to the Inspector's brusque greeting.

But the Inspector seems not to notice or be in any particular hurry. Without taking off his gloves, he removes a small parcel covered in black cloth from his satchel and holds it over Philipp's immaculate desk. He slowly unwraps it, showering the desk with bits of burned paper, as deliberate as if he were sweeping leaves.

Philipp doesn't flinch, doesn't move his hands away.

With a flourish, the Inspector holds up a thick black square. There's a strong smell of ash, of something bitter and burned.

"Do you recognize this?"

Mystified, Philipp shakes his head. "It isn't familiar, but I would guess it once was a book."

"It was burnt here in your office."

"May I see it?"

The Inspector extends the black thing, then quickly pulls it back as Philipp reaches for it. "Better not. You'll dirty your hands."

"If you've brought it here to threaten me with, do you really believe I'd be put off by burned paper?"

"Probably not. I have good reason to believe this is your diary."

The Inspector doesn't miss the sliver of recognition in his eyes. He's familiar with the man's decoy tactics and believes all gestures become stage-managed under stress. Even his own face will go suddenly wooden, his expressions close down, when he's self-conscious. Erszébet and Franz have both noticed this habit. She delights in teasing him about it.

But now the Inspector's face is carefully neutral as he waits for Philipp to betray himself with words, something that can be carried to someone else. Proof. The burned book lies between them on the cloth, black on black, a ceremonial offering. Only the Inspector knows the dirtied pages between its black covers are false, a Trojan horse to provoke him into a confession.

"If I admit it is my diary, you understand I'm able to do this because I have nothing to fear from it?" Smiling grimly, Philipp casually brushes the black crumbs of paper from his sleeves. "And I assume your search of the ashes in my office stove is connected to my daughter's murder?"

"That is correct."

"Am I to be formally charged with murder?"

"I am here to discuss that possibility with you."

"Is my arrest predicated on the information in the book?"

"That and other proof that has come to my attention. You remember your son's statement has put your alibi in jeopardy."

Philipp leans back in his chair, coldly confident. "Suppose you tell me what I've allegedly written in the book? Go on, read me an excerpt."

"I'm afraid that is outside my duties. A jury must hear it first."

The Inspector's bluff has been called. There's nothing further he can say to him. He has a sick feeling, as if he's been caught stealing.

Philipp quietly says that he wishes he could condemn the Inspector to the same experience he suffers, to have his mourning marred by suspicion and fear.

Only afterward, as he stares at the freezing Danube below the Franz-Josefs-Kai, does the Inspector marvel at Philipp's performance, his absolute command of himself. How he sat without reacting under the Inspector's deluge of sooty paper, as if he wasn't even present during this indignity. He's a contrast to his daughter, Dora, who made dramatic demonstrations of every disappointment and affront, real and imagined.

Perhaps Philipp is a man who unleashes himself on

women. He thinks of Fräulein Fürj, Frau Zellenka. Perhaps
Dora too.

> The Investigating Officer must . . . reconstruct the occur-
> rence, build up by hard labour a theory fitted in and co-
> ordinated like a living organism; and just as on seeing the
> fruit he will recognise the tree and the country of its growth,
> so from the scrutiny of the deed he can presume how it has
> been brought about, what have been the motives, and what
> kind of persons have been employed in it; the secondary
> characters in the picture will find themselves.

Erszébet paid a Thomas Cook & Son guide to drive a motor
cab to the summit of the Kahlenberg, so Wally could enjoy the
view of Vienna and the Danube Valley, the Lesser Carpathians
and the Styrian Alps. This is Erszébet's conciliatory gesture.
They take the Höhenstrasse toward the northeastern edge of
the Wienerwald.

The snow is heavier here, a few miles outside Vienna. The
guide stops the motor cab, and Wally clambers out. Erszébet
waits inside.

Wally walks on the road, carefully stepping within the
cab's tire tracks to avoid the deep drifts. There are vineyards
here, and the bare grapevines resemble a forest of dead twigs,
as if the earth were covered with salt, not snow. The fog is a
brown gray color, a monotonous fuzz hanging over the distance to the city. Wally thinks it's a dull landscape.

She gets back in the cab, politely thanking Erszébet for
bringing her here. The driver noisily backs the motor cab down
the steep hill.

"So, you've seen Vienna and her famous woods. I'm sorry
I can't show you a view of Buda Pest from its hills," Erszébet
muses. "In Török-utcza, you knock on the gate of a villa for entrance to a sheikh's monument, the Gül-Baba Mecsetje. He
was a Turkish monk known as 'the father of roses,' and the
whole city is visible from his grave. I prefer my landscape
framed by roses rather than grapevines."

They sit close together, their features now masked by the early twilight. Outside, the planet Venus can easily be studied in the January sky, an icy diamond punctillo visible as early as five o'clock in the afternoon. The snow is a ragged sheet over the landscape, an eerie pale blue color, as waxy and unnatural-looking as some early spring flowers.

Wally has grown quieter around her lately, and sensing this, Erszébet touches her frequently, making wordless small gestures of affection, smoothing the girl's hair, resting a kind hand on her shoulder.

All day they've avoided the subject of Dora. The light is too gray for Wally to distinguish Erszébet's face, but she can sense the heaviness that possesses her. And Erszébet doesn't seem to feel the need for conversation. She has her own dialogue.

Wally brings up the fig. The tree they found behind the clinic. Could Steinach be involved in the murder? Did he conspire with Dora's father in some way? Wally speculates. Perhaps his partner, Dr. Last, was the man in the photographer's studio? After all, Philipp is Steinach's patient. Wally's voice trails off.

Yes, it almost makes a circle, Erszébet says softly.

Did Dora carry away proof in her body — the fig — of her visit to Steinach?

But Erszébet is less interested now in theories, in puzzling. She believes what will bring them an answer — the name of the murderer — is working in her own body.

"This is a magical period," Erszébet suddenly announces.

"Magical?"

"It is believed that on the feast day of Saint Peter, January sixteenth, the howling of wolves will be heard. Listen."

Now there is no point of light outside in the landscape. And nothing but silence.

Wally shivers. Then she dismisses Erszébet's information as a childhood story. Animals who talk.

I know something about transformation, Erszébet says, as if she's read her mind. "I heard stories when I was growing up. My governess read me *The Duchess of Malfi*. I still remember it." She closes her eyes and recites the words.

Two nights since
One met the duke 'bout midnight in a lane
Behind Saint Mark's church, with the leg of a man
Upon his shoulder; and he howled fearfully,
Said he was a wolf, only the difference
Was, a wolf's skin was hairy on the outside,
His on the inside.

In the silent cab, the heavy blanket over Wally's legs and the comfortable pressure of Erszébet's body suddenly become weightless, as if the ugly image has numbed her skin.

The Inspector stands before the door of the Zellenkas' house. Fräulein Yella answers his knocking, and he can tell by her sour expression she isn't pleased to see him. The woman isn't prepared to lie, can only confirm that Frau Zellenka is at home. She reluctantly accepts his hat and walking stick and takes her time leaving the room. He could believe she counts *one, two, three* between each of her steps. The women intend to make him wait, and he resists the impulse to pace. Two days earlier there was an assault and a robbery at a *Tabak-Trafiken,* and he spent hours searching the dirty floor for spilled coins and bloodstains. His knees still ache.

The next footsteps are Frau Zellenka's. She's calculated her entrance.

"I'm to have the pleasure of your conversation yet again?"

He ignores her sarcasm.

"As you see. I thought you'd prefer meeting here rather than the morgue."

They move to the next room. She produces cigarettes and they smoke, repeating their last interview, as if he's stepped into a photograph of the scene. However, this time she's dressed in a scarlet robe, which drains her face of its color.

He's conscious of the immense weight of his hope that she may have an answer for him, something to end Dora's story. No debate, no further developments, just the dry precision of a fact, like a sealed envelope. He takes out his notebook.

"Another witness claims you argued violently with Dora."
She considers this for a moment.

"Strange the way events come to light. Yes, Dora and I
had an argument. She displayed the most reprehensible behavior toward me. After all I'd done for her."

He notices her gestures have become more agitated.

"As you know, my only daughter died in August. Tuberculosis. While I was still in mourning, Dora decided to confront me
about my relationship with her father. Can you imagine Dora's
selfish, disrespectful impertinence? She screamed at me, and I
slapped her face. I still don't regret it, may God forgive me."

She glares at him.

"Now if you think this was motive enough for me to
murder Dora two weeks later, you are wrong. No one would
believe a bereaved mother would kill a dear friend. No one.
And now I must ask you to leave. The extent of my courtesy
has reached an end."

He abruptly rises to his feet. She's turned everything
around. He has no words. Not even sympathy.

The traffic was very slow, some accident on Josefstädter Strasse
with a horse and wagon. While Erszébet and her husband sat
inside a dark fiaker stalled on the street, she told him about a
contest some aristocrats had created, purely for their own entertainment. A gold coin was embedded in a lit candle. While
they watched and cheered, a Gypsy attempted to remove the
coin with his teeth without extinguishing the flame, burning
his hair or the skin on his face. If he succeeded, the coin was his
to keep. She reassures him this cruel story was documented by
Prince Constantin Brâncoveanu's secretary some time ago.

She chose this moment to light a cigarette.

He presses his lips to her hand, and as he smells her skin
and sees the dot of fire that is her cigarette, he's conscious that
these two sensations have summoned the genie of memory.
She senses his mood has shifted.

He recognizes nothing yet, although the emotion that pre-
cedes the memory — one of sadness and loss — is completely

present. He waits. As if he looked down from a height, only gradually does the diminutive scene become visible in his mind.

"My father did something to me when I was about six years old," he says, his voice thoughtful. "I held my hand over the top of a lamp; I didn't know any better. I burned the palm of my hand. You'll learn not to do this, my father shouted, angry at my foolishness. He made me sit at the dinner table and use my knife and fork to eat, even though my burned hand bled. I always thought he was secretly proud of me because he couldn't make me cry."

He slowly bends over and buries his face in her lap.

Although it has never occurred to her husband to ask, Erszébet is very familiar with certain love spells. Some are even ironic. She knows of lovers who have become convinced their passion for each other is so great it must be caused by a supernatural force. As if the sunlight they've been sitting in has gradually grown too hot for their comfort. They realize a *rontás,* a spell, has been put on them.

One remedy is to consciously fall out of love. A passionate quarrel.

The other cure is to discover who is responsible for the spell and have it removed.

The consent of only one of the lovers is necessary for this process.

Erszébet no longer approaches her husband in bed. She sleeps unmoving in her voluptuous imperviousness to him. He burrows his head under the sheets, just to be enclosed with her scent, wholly surrounded.

He believes he is lost. For the first time in his life, he wants to howl like a dog.

But he keeps silent, and shivers until he falls asleep.

CHAPTER 14

S HIS FIAKER SPEEDS WEST out of the city, the Inspector notices the dead grasses near the road move by more quickly than the woods in the distance, a slowly unfurling grayness inflicted on the luminous white hills. The snow is steadily growing deeper, as if the ground were sinking, pulling him in. But at least that suffocation would be a relief from the speculations that torment him. He's no closer to a solution to Dora's murder. Correction. Just as he approaches a solution, it proves to be a false image, a mirage that vanishes, a *délibáb*. Perhaps this next interrogation will settle matters. He doesn't have long to wait, as the lunatic asylum is visible through the trees.

The fiaker turns off the main road into the asylum grounds. The snow is in drifts here, a sea of pointed billows, and the horses slow down to wade through it, making their entrance seem irreversible.

From the bottom of the hill, the asylum is an ominous fortress, sixty nearly identical brick structures with unusually small windows. In the center of this drabness, the Kirche am Steinhof, with its glorious gilt dome, stands like an abandoned bride. The church was designed by Otto Wagner, and the Inspector is looking forward to a meditative Sunday service. He asks the driver to let him out.

Under the tolling of great bells, a crowd streams into the *Kirche*. As he walks closer, he sees the worshipers are patients, some coaxed along by nurses, others pushed in wheeled chairs.

The blind and violently disturbed are loosely roped together, hurried along by harrassed orderlies.

Depressed by this clumsy parade, he turns his eyes to the *Kirche*. Marble plates are bolted over the facade of this severe structure, and the figures of four immense, icy angels are balanced over the portal.

Slightly ill at ease, he follows the inmates into the *Kirche*. Inside, it's bare and cold, unfinished looking. The ceiling bristles with rough silver pipes, deliberately left exposed. The altar is situated inside a fantastic structure of scrolled metal, like a giant cage. Gibbering voices, wails, and shouts bounce off the white tile walls.

Struggling with the patients, the orderlies take no notice of him. Two burly uniformed men shove half a dozen unruly worshipers into a pew, then slam the gates at each end, locking them in for the service.

The Inspector steps gingerly into the nave, dodging jostling bodies. The echoing noise, the strange, antiseptic aura of the church, the smell of incense and unwashed bodies, all of it seems artificial yet familiar, as if he has been lured into a terrible purgatory of his own imagination. There must be some mistake, he thinks. How have I found my way here? He tries to stay calm, keep his bearings in the chaos. Then his feet are unsteady, and he looks down to see the floor slope into a drain. Now he understands. The church was designed to be easily cleaned, the black-and-white tiles are hosed down after each service.

Hands suddenly grip his shoulder from behind, then move around his neck. He tries to wrench them away, but his unseen attacker jerks his weight back, transforming everything into noise and blurred motion as he falls.

The man is on top of him now, a grimacing brown face. The Inspector gropes his chin and nose, digs fingers into the stranger's eyes. There's a hard pressure on his throat, and a blurred black shadow moves across the back of his eyes like a cloud eating the light. He feels the weight lift. Two orderlies pull the man off his chest. Other hands grab the Inspector under the arms and heave him to his feet.

He sags against the wall, gasping for breath, trying to

clear the rawness from his throat and chest, the red veil from his eyes. He dimly recognizes the classic symptoms of strangling. Dizzy, he shakes his head, trying to focus on the strange circle of men around him. Some stare at him expressionlessly. Others laugh.

A voice asks how he feels. His eyes blink. Did he bite you? the voice demands, and he realizes it comes from the concerned face next to him. A young man. I don't think so, he rasps.

The deep chords of an organ begin, momentarily overwhelming the indescribable din in the church. As if translated into a physical sensation, the music seems to swell against the bruised places on his neck.

The priest enters, walking easily down the aisle into the noise, serene as a man contemplating a garden.

The Inspector stays where he is, unable to hear a single spoken word of the service. Relieved when it is over, he leaves without waiting for the blessing or holy water from the fountain, rubbing his sore neck.

Two thumbprints, red and blue as jewels, are pressed into the skin over his jugular veins.

The walls in the director of the lunatic asylum's office are lined with papers and charts. Inside a cabinet, the Inspector recognizes familiar round shapes, a collection of skulls. Probably harvested from patients, he calculates.

The director doesn't make him wait, abruptly entering the room while he's still studying the contents of the cabinets. He's a slim man with long and tousled hair, surprising for a doctor. Two pairs of pince-nez swing from a cord around his neck. They exchange courteous greetings.

"Inspector, I deeply regret your encounter with one of our patients. The man had escaped his orderly. Nothing broken, I trust?"

The Inspector shakes his head. His neck throbs inside his collar.

"Good. Then we can move on to business. I think you'll

be very interested in the patient I mentioned in my letter. He fits the description of the man you're looking for."

"I appreciate your help in this case."

"Certainly. It is my duty to assist when I can. During my time here, I've developed a personal interest in the criminally insane. In fact, I have records of my conversations with all the patients, if you'd ever care to read through them. I can recommend some of the more fascinating cases."

He waves his hand at the sleek rows of books lining the walls. Without waiting for the Inspector to reply, he eagerly continues.

"The inmates have told me terrible stories of their childhoods. Sometimes I believe it is a privilege to bear witness. Of course, many days I hear nothing but the nonsensical ravings of madmen. I feel like their confessor."

"How do you know they're telling the truth?"

"Ah, that's the problem. Perhaps their stories are an elaborate game to gain my sympathy. At any rate, it's difficult not to give their ravings some sense. You know, organize their words."

The Inspector says he feels the same way when interviewing a suspect. He's learned you have to let them go. Just wander into their dialogue without a destination. Don't impose a beginning or an end.

The director agrees. "I've found you have to watch your reactions. It's strange, but even a madman can sense when you're skeptical. I've had to discipline myself. I work to keep my face expressionless. My wife hates it. She tells me I bring the job home, I should smile more."

He looks worried. The Inspector smiles back at him.

"I have a similar problem. Eye contact. My wife says it makes people uneasy."

"It does affect your life, doesn't it? You know, I let the inmates do drawings with colored pencils. I save some of the better sketches." He's embarrassed now. "Some people believe I'm too easy on the patients. But it isn't like the days when we locked up the mad in the Narrentum, that circular dungeon."

He's momentarily lost in reflection.

"Although you can't be too sympathetic. The patients are

sly. Once they've found a crack of pity, believe me, they'll stick their fingers into it any way they can. Enough of this. Shall we visit my patient? He was brought in about five months ago. In early September."

The Inspector figures the man would have been free when Dora was murdered in August.

As they step into the dark room, the Inspector senses they're being watched, even though it seems empty, and their footsteps tunnel a hollow noise into the space. There's a slight movement in the corner. As his eyes adjust to the level of light, he makes out a ragged young man hunched on the floor, his hands tied together in front of him. The Inspector walks over to him and then crouches down, bringing their faces level.

The director waits by the door, giving him freedom to work.

"He was found behind a barn, howling at the moon. Blood all over him. Claims he's a *csordásfarkas*. Don't get too close. We sometimes keep him restrained."

The Inspector doesn't move back. His voice is so slow he feels his lips clearly shape each word.

"Tell me your name, sir."

"Karl."

"Tell me, Karl. What strange things have you done?"

Karl shuffles forward; his eyes never leave the Inspector's.

"The moon. The full moon comes, it's like a window opens. Do you understand me? I go through it. I wander. I forget where I am. In the morning, my clothes are torn."

Becoming agitated, Karl spasmodically jerks his head from side to side.

"Karl, did your head become larger, like a wolf's?"

"My lips swell. My mouth is dirty. My hands are dirty."

"Any women? Did you harm any women when you lost yourself?"

"I don't know. I woke up once with blond hair in my mouth. And I found something, a button in my pocket, but it wasn't mine. I took it from someone. Red under my fingernails too."

Eyes closed, Karl rocks back and forth, rhythmically striking his bound hands against his knees.

The Inspector quiets his thoughts. Empties himself. Strangely, it is almost a pleasurable sensation.

Suddenly Karl stops moving.

"I have dreams, but I can't tell if they're dreams or if they're real. I dreamed I was a *csordásfarkas*."

"Yes, yes. I'm here to listen to you. Karl, were you ever in the Volksgarten? The park by the Hofburg. Do you remember?"

"The Volksgarten? I don't know. One tree is like another in the dark, isn't that true?" He can't hold still, he starts rocking again.

"How do you know you're a *csordásfarkas?*"

The sore points on his neck ache. He senses Karl has no orderly retrieval of memories, and whatever he summons has no meaning. An image is just an image. The young man is truly mad.

Karl bites his lip. He pantomimes *Come here*.

The Inspector leans closer, completely focused, feeling his body too clumsy for the fineness of his concentration.

Karl laughs and lifts his hands. His excited words tumble out, he can't get his breath right.

"See my hands? I have long hairs on the palms, that's how I know. That's the sign of a *csordásfarkas*. And my mouth, my mouth is the mouth of a wolf. See? See?"

Karl throws his head back and opens his red mouth wide, his tongue lolling out.

The Inspector slowly stands and puts a kind hand on his head, then leaves the room. Karl's shrill howling laughter follows him out.

For a terrible moment, the Inspector thought he saw hairs on the man's palms, silky dark threads, but he dismisses it as a trick of the light.

Back in his office, the director studies the Inspector's face. "What did you think of Karl? Is he delusional or was he telling the truth?"

The Inspector shrugs. He's still troubled by his vision of the man's hands. Surely *that* was a delusion.

"It would make my job easier if a madman could be attached to every crime. But most madmen don't reveal their true natures as straightforwardly as Karl."

The director nods. "He's really no trouble to anyone here except at certain times of the month. I'm investigating whether his fits are tied into the cycles of the moon."

He hands the Inspector a folder.

"I thought you'd be interested in this account of another wolfman. He lived long ago, and apparently was covered with thick hair. He was found in Compiègne, crouched over the bodies of four animals he'd torn to pieces with his teeth. They brought him to King Charles IX. Right in front of his majesty, the wolfman attacked and bit the king's dog."

"At least there was a reliable witness to the crime."

They bid each other a cordial farewell at the door.

It has been frequently remarked that madmen, especially certain varieties of madmen, are excellent observers; they are not nearly so averse to telling the truth as many people who rejoice in all their faculties, for they do not allow themselves to be guided by considerations of propriety; they have also more opportunities for observation, for things are done and said in the presence of a lunatic which would not be done or said before others.

In the fiaker going back to Vienna, the Inspector can't shake his restlessness, as if he'd caught it from Karl. The creaky rocking of the carriage sickens him. He fixes his eyes on the snow, hoping its whiteness will soothe him, blank out his disappointment and fatigue. He puzzles over the evidence, shifts it around and tries to follow the trajectory made by its new order. Tilt a photographer's glass plate in a certain way, and when the light strikes it, a hidden image will suddenly flash into recognition.

No matter how he sets himself at Dora's case, it defeats him. The asylum was another dead end.

He's gradually lulled by the optical rhythm of the trees passing outside, the hypnotic pattern of dark-light, dark-light. The disorder in the pattern is what catches his eye. The broken whiteness next to the road. *The error in the situation.*

The tracks of a large animal — a wolf — disturb the snow. As if his carriage were following something. He looks into the distance. Something moves in the woods, a blacker shape between bare black trees.

He presses his forehead against the window and shouts to the driver to slow down. The place where he saw something is just ahead of him. Now he can make out dark figures standing in a circle. Their gestures are strangely abrupt; they hunch over and drop to the ground in an unfamiliar way. In the instant his carriage flashes past, he believes he recognizes the figures as *csordásfarkas,* shape-shifters, turning back into wolves.

He slaps his forehead. I'm in the *Gregynia dakuluj,* the devil's garden, he mutters. My wife would tell me so. Lately, he's noticed her superstitions have become increasingly powerful, intruding on his thoughts as imperceptibly as the sky changes color. Only occasionally does he consciously struggle against her.

What is mine? he wonders.

Wally has never studied a face so well as Erszébet's. Today she notices bluish half-circles under her eyes, like swipes made by a painted finger. Her skill at deciphering character is based on physical observation, a function of her youth.

Wally longs to see her own presence reflected in Erszébet's eyes. But Erszébet easily hides from her. She is nearing the end of her period of *ráböjtölés.* The black fast is a heavy presence within her, not the airy dislocation she had anticipated. On this Friday, she sits across from Wally in the Heinrichshof Café. She can neither eat nor drink.

Twenty-two years ago this month, under the arc of the planet Venus, Crown Prince Rudolf committed suicide with his mistress, eighteen-year-old Mary, Baroness Vetsera. To avoid scandal, Mary's stiff body was removed from the hunting lodge where she died by her two uncles, who held her upright and "walked" her out. In the carriage, the men stuck a broom down the back of her dress so she sat straight between them. Mary had been dead for forty hours.

Wally was fascinated by the story. A corpse that walked. Like Dora.

Erszébet wants Wally to make a prediction, and she agrees. Now Erszébet's fist flattens her left hand to the table.

"It won't hurt."

Wally closes her eyes. Erszébet delicately punctures Wally's middle finger with a hat pin, then presses it until blood shows.

"Hold it over your right hand. The drop of blood must fall on your middle fingernail. Now look at the shape it makes. Tell me what you see. It will forecast the future."

First drop. Flustered, Wally squints at the red spot on her fingernail.

"I can't tell. It's blurred."

Erszebet pinches her finger again, harder. A second drop of blood falls.

"A fire? I'm not sure."

She wipes the blood off her finger with her napkin.

Third drop of blood.

"It's a woman's head. A profile. Yes."

Wally sucks her finger. Erszébet frowns and hands her a lace handkerchief.

"The woman must be Dora. Something to do with a fire. You did very well."

Wally is embarrassed about the handkerchief, now blotched with red. She reluctantly hands it back. Erszébet closely examines the bloodstains. With a satisfied smile, she folds the handkerchief and tucks it in her reticule.

"Do you really think a blood reading will work?"

Erszébet nods. "I've found it infallible."

"Why don't you prick your own finger?"

"Your interpretation is better, since you've never done it before. My eyes aren't as fresh as yours."

The waiter brings a single *Kleinen Schwarzen* and a glass of water. Wally doesn't ask any more questions, but the incident has made her uneasy.

"You know, it's strange, but only the Gypsy women tell fortunes, and they never read another Gypsy's fate," says Erszébet, staring over Wally's shoulder into the distance.

Wally stirs cream into her coffee, and it shapes itself into sinister whorls. Erszébet notices.

"There's your fire. Doesn't it look just like smoke?"

Wally set out on a bitter cold day, punctuated by brilliant and sharp snowfall, to run errands. She moves quickly on the streets, afraid she's being followed. Boots and gloves are left to be mended. Books are picked up for the children. Her search for Pears soap at a certain English-style pharmacy is unsuccessful. She's speaks curtly to the clerk behind the counter.

The storm grew while she was in the store. A stinging white cloud transformed the street into a place strangely populated with contorted, staggering figures; the furs and thick scarves bundled around their shoulders give them a hunchback's posture. Only a military man strides through this whiteness still upright and unbending.

Wally welcomes the blizzard's fierce camouflage. She has just looked up to study the shell-pink facade of a Baroque building on Naglergasse, curiously radiant even in the snow, when a hand drops on her shoulder. She pulls away, nearly slipping on the cobblestones. Rosza stands behind her. There's a smile on the woman's lips, but her eyes look pinched and wary. She circles her fingers around Wally's wrist and pulls her along to the corner, where a fat driver waits by his fiaker. He sweeps the door open for them. Wally is surprised by Rosza's abruptness, but glad of the carriage.

They sit side by side while the fiaker proceeds down Naglergasse.

"My God, I've been looking for you everywhere. I didn't know how to reach you. Where have you been?"

Wally is taken aback by Rosza's agitation. "The family I stay with has returned, so I've been busy taking care of the children."

Although Rosza sits stiffly upright, she is betrayed by her hands. Her fingers nervously toy with the reticule in her lap. It is so cold that even inside the leather-upholstered cabin their breath is visible. Rosza's perfume — heady and strange, something with ambergris — mingles with it.

When Wally looks out the window, it seems that the carriage is imprisoned in a kaleidoscope, the snow falling furiously from every direction, as if some mechanism twisted it into patterns around them. The carriage shakes across trolley tracks.

As if the jarring motion reminded her of something, suddenly Rosza turns from the window and grabs Wally's hands.

"Listen, I've decided to help you. Remember you asked about Dora's photographs?"

Puzzled, Wally nods.

"Now I'll tell you about the pictures."

There is a strangely contemptuous expression on her face as she leans back against the seat. Staring at Wally, she pulls up her skirt, transforming it into a dark mass around her waist, and shoves her hips forward. Rosza is naked under her skirt. Light from a streetlamp flashes into the carriage, skewering her legs — two white lines — in its glare. The place between her legs looks as if it has been melted or erased; the skin above it is crossed with a dark patchwork of scars.

Wally tries to speak, but her mouth is a dry cavern. She's struck dumb. Frightened, she peers at Rosza's face, but the woman is bent over, her legs spread apart.

After a moment, she whispers, "You were burned?"

Rosza sits up and smoothes her skirt down. She doesn't look at her.

"I'll tell you the story from the beginning. When I was with Dora, as her *promeneuse,* her father pursued me. He was polite, amorous, gallant. I tried to resist him, believe me. I knew it would bring trouble. Dora found out about us. She wasn't a child. I don't blame her. I didn't blame her then. She was clever. She turned her mother against me, and I had to leave their house. But I continued to see her father. He gave me a little money. We went to the Vienna Skating Club masquerade at Stadtpark. I wore the most beautiful costume, an enormous dress of white silk tulle. I'd spent all the money I had to buy it. I could tell Philipp was in love with me. I began to dream perhaps he'd even marry me."

Rosza's face is fierce. Wally doesn't speak or move.

"We skated over to the side of the lake to smoke. He lit our cigarettes and leaned over to kiss me. I wanted to tease him, not kiss him so easily. You understand? Is that so terrible that I should be punished?"

Rosza closes her eyes for a moment.

"He was impatient and reached for my mask. His cigarette touched my skirt, and it caught fire. Suddenly I was alone, I was a circle of flame. I skated away, burning. I don't remember screaming. Someone in costume, a Pierrot, skated after me and shoved me down on the ice. I lay there, my skirt in black shreds. Even my skates were black with soot, they told me later. I was burned all over below my waist. I'll never forget the smell. Burnt flesh. I can't get rid of the odor, even with perfume."

"Is it painful?"

"Constantly. I can't wear a corset. And what man would want to see this mutilated flesh?"

There's silence between them for a time.

"Philipp left you alone at the lake?"

"Yes. He didn't want a scandal, and I was unconscious. No one knew who I was. The *Rettungsgesellschaft* carriage took me to the hospital. I was there for weeks. Although Philipp had abandoned me, he recommended me to one of his doctors. Dr. Last operated on me several times. Out of pity, Herr Zellenka paid for everything. To be discreet, he let them think I was Philipp's daughter. I thought he was kind. When you said he had watched when my picture was taken, I went mad. I went back to see the photographer, to confront him about his shame. He took money for my pain and my nakedness. It's unforgivable what they did. Both of them."

Rosza won't allow herself to weep. She's beyond any comforting words Wally can offer.

"Since Herr Zellenka paid for my treatment, I agreed to tell the police he was with me when Dora died. He asked me to lie. Now that I have no obligation to him, I will tell you he wasn't with me that night. Maybe he harmed her, I don't know."

Dora's story has fallen into a shocking chain of order. *I am lost,* Wally thinks. This is a place of dread, *Gregynia dakuluj,* the devil's garden.

When she closes her eyes in sleep that night, Wally dreams about Mary, Baroness Vetsera. Three indistinct figures emerge from a rough building, their shadows preceding them. Then she sees that two men are balancing the hunched and motionless figure of a girl between them, her head bent at an odd angle, her unmoving booted feet hovering just above the ground, as if she had another way to move without them, if only they would release her. Their haste, their skulking movements say *deceit*.

The next morning, Wally realizes why the dream seemed familiar. She pictured Dora's killer moving in the same way as he left the Volksgarten after releasing his victim from this earth.

CHAPTER 15

GON PINCHES A LETTER BE-
tween his mutilated fingers, waves it teas-
ingly at Wally and Erszébet. He's sitting
between them at a back table at Gerstner's.
"The letter is for Wally," he announces.
"For me?"

"It's from Rosza. She left it at my studio for you."

Wally reaches for it, but Erszébet stops her hand.

"Wait. Let the tarot predict what it says."

Erszébet quickly scoops the cards up from the table and
shuffles them. Wally rests her hand on top of the deck, then
picks the top card, turns it over.

The card has the image of a woman in an elaborate hat,
prying open the jaws of a lion. She gazes at the beast with an
expressionless face.

"How do you interpret the card?" Wally asks, relieved she
didn't draw *le Diable*.

"The woman represents strength, a cardinal virtue. You
see on the card, she masters the lion, easily opening its mouth.
She's like Diana, goddess of the hunt. Rosza's letter must involve mastery over something, a situation or instinct. Or perhaps passion."

Wally opens the letter.

Rosza destroys Herr Zellenka's alibi. She's written an account of her affair with Dora's father, detailing her accident,
Herr Zellenka's financial support of her medical treatment, her
lie about his whereabouts the night Dora was murdered. No

accusation of his guilt. She confesses she was unable to tell the police about her foolish complicity with Herr Zellenka. She trusts Wally will explain everything to the proper authorities. By the time they read this letter, she will have left Vienna. Rosza's illegible signature is at the bottom of the paper. The envelope has no seal.

Erszébet feels the arc of a black rainbow open. There is something she can't see at its far end. She is filled with utter confidence.

Wally is dismayed at the letter and Erszébet's reaction to it. There's a hollowness to her eyes, as if she's consumed by some internal process. Wally finds her unfathomable, like a lighthouse in daylight, her purpose hidden.

Wally remembers when her mother was dying she had the same detachment. The smallest gesture of emotion — and then even recognition — wearied her. Wally watched and waited as her mother slowly unhooked herself from her surroundings, and finally from Wally and her father.

Now Wally recognizes the same quality in Erszébet, and it frightens her.

Later, Wally and Erszébet puzzle over the letter. Rosza told Wally she had confronted Egon in his studio, but it may have been a righteous lie. If Rosza was unable to forgive him, why did she trust him with the letter? They decide there was no other way for her to reach Wally, since she didn't have her address. This seems to hold true.

Perhaps Rosza's letter is a ruse. Perhaps she didn't write it. Neither of them has ever seen her handwriting. Could Egon have written the letter himself?

And Rosza has mysteriously vanished.

Wally is uncertain about what to do with the information. Maybe Egon intends to double cross them.

"Should we tell the police Rosza's story about Herr Zellenka?"

No. Erszébet slowly shakes her head. She needs time. "Let's keep everything to ourselves for a little longer. Nothing's resolved yet."

Wally readily agrees, reluctant to argue with her.

There is one piece of evidence they are unaware of. Egon didn't mention that he left Rosza's original letter on the Inspector's desk earlier that day. He wanted to show off in front of Wally and Erszébet. Guilt prompted him to give the letter to the police.

A few days later, Wally thinks she catches sight of Rosza in the lobby of the Hotel Imperial. She is on the arm of a distinguished man, but the couple vanishes before Wally makes her way across the crowded room to them.

At the end of the same week, she glimpses Rosza in the window of Wopalensky, a hat shop on Kohlmarkt. Rosza is engrossed in conversation with a second woman. Wally walks to the end of the street, debating about approaching her. When Wally returns and enters the dim shop, the woman turns away and quickly pulls her veil over her face. The shopkeeper looks at Wally strangely, and she apologizes and leaves.

Wally didn't recognize either of them. She continues to watch the shop from across the street. Only the veiled woman walks out.

Wally wonders if the mirrors and the dim light inside the shop caused her to mistake the woman for Rosza. However, she's certain she identified one thing in the shop correctly. The unmistakable odor of Rosza's perfume.

In his investigations, he assigns the blame for a crime to a number of people — the calculating guilty, the provocative innocent, a bystander with bad luck. This allows the Inspector to keep his distance. He is the last witness with the pointing finger.

However, now that his relationship with his wife is strained, he takes the blame for it. His suspicions about her have become manifest in her behavior, like a premonition that has come true.

Their routine intimacy has changed. The familiar is now

strange, in the way a crime can transform a common object —
a drinking glass, a hairbrush — into something suspicious. In
the language of the body, an ill-timed gesture, hands that won't
be still, eyes that look away — also betray guilt.

His observations, words, his affection — all of it is of no
use against Erszébet's silences. Nothing rouses her; she seems
weary of everything. Even her sporadic happier states seem to
have nothing to do with him. Something else occupies her.

Erszébet's state of torpor alternates with eruptions of
anger. She disagreed with him about something while they
were in a fiaker. She angrily shouted to the driver to stop and
then got out and strode away while he sat inside, stunned and
miserable. Once she came into the bedroom and found him examining her toilette items. He held a blue glass jar of her face
cream. She said nothing but swept her arm over the top of the
bureau, and the container of talc opened as it fell, becoming a
weightless white cloud.

One evening, the violent quality of her lovemaking left
him feeling even more isolated.

Did he somehow wish for this unhappiness between
them? What has he done to provoke her? He doesn't believe a
blameless party exists. Dora's case has shown him this. Everyone who knew her is guilty.

He was secure with his concept of Erszébet as his wife,
her days filled with small errands, busywork he couldn't
fathom. He was confident all her efforts were directed at him,
at the temple of their marriage. He is no longer certain of this.

But he won't judge her. He says nothing; his strategy is to
listen and observe. He wills himself into the role of the good
disciple, setting a Banquet of Silence for her. He waits for her
to reveal herself.

He recognizes the atmosphere of *Vormärz,* when something is going to happen.

The next day, Erszébet sends Herr Zellenka an anony-
mous letter by post. *There is something of interest I have to tell you
about Dora. This information is significant only to you.* She will
wait for him at Café Gerstner, and she names a time. He should

carry his hat in his left hand when he enters the café. In two days.

It is the bitter end of January.

Franz and the Inspector are working late in their office. Their investigation of another crime is falling into place. The examiner's report has just confirmed that a woolen thread snagged on a chair at Klinkosch, a jewelry store that had been robbed, matches a minute hole in the suspect's jacket. The Inspector is jubilant, almost like his old self. He jokes with Franz, even urges him to speculate about a vile horse thief they arrested yesterday.

Later, the Inspector turns his attention to the papers on his desk, which he's neglected for some time. He idly flips through the mail, and the hesitant writing on one envelope catches his eye. Perhaps a crank or a suspect, or an anonymous confession. He frequently receives mail like this and can usually pick out the odd ones. He opens the envelope.

He reads Rosza's letter, then — still holding it in his hand — races across the room. He grabs his hat off the stand, shouting instructions to Franz as he bolts through the door and down the hallway.

It takes Franz half a second to find the Luger pistol and follow him.

Something has erupted. Franz ducks through the spray.

Outside, a thick winter fog has descended, and their journey through the streets is a sinister expedition. Pedestrians vanish when they're four steps past each other. On the Ringstrasse, only the crooked tips of the branches are visible, as if the rest of the tree had been swallowed by flood water. Preceded by the sturdy clank of their horses' harnesses and the whistles of their drivers, carriages suddenly materialize out of the fog.

The terrible visibility slows their passage. The Inspector smokes one cigarette after another and cajoles the driver to hurry, hurry. Franz has never seen him so agitated.

As he explains Rosza's letter — talks Franz through it, since it's too dark in the carriage to read — the sense that something is finished is clear to him. It is remorseless and certain. A fissure closed. Herr Zellenka, guilty. The pistol is strange and heavy in its holster. He peers hopelessly at his pocket watch. They can't be far from the Zellenkas' house. He struggles against his feeling of euphoria.

No response to the Inspector's fist on the door, even though light is visible behind the curtains in the windows. Finally the door opens a crack. He urges Fräulein Yella — the stubborn shadow blocking the light from inside — to admit them at once.

Frau Zellenka lazily looks up from her cigarette when they're ushered into the parlor. Franz blinks, dazzled by the brilliant colors after the dim carriage.

My husband is not at home presently, she says. Pity, they've just missed him. And she isn't certain when he'll be back. Or where they can find him. She offers coffee and *slivovitz*. Her vexed expression deepens when she understands Franz and the Inspector are prepared to wait for her husband. She doesn't ask why it is urgent they speak with him, and the Inspector doesn't volunteer any information.

The Inspector begins to wonder if she's stalling them for a reason. Perhaps her husband has fled. His anxiety makes him feel transparent and frail. He calms himself with a deep breath.

Frau Zellenka sits with them for another hour and then excuses herself and proceeds up to bed. It is just before midnight.

After she is safely upstairs, he uses her telephone to call Erszébet. He imagines an invisible impulse traveling to the switchboard and then to his house, where it will end, cradled in his wife's hand.

There is no answer.

Puzzled — and then alarmed — he calls her several times during the long night, while Franz dozes on the settee.

That same evening, Erszébet leaves the house early to avoid telling her husband where she's going. She's afraid he might return early, and she doesn't have the strength to lie to him. Secured in her bodice is a protective charm, *Mandragora officinarum,* a piece of mandrake shaped like a little man.

The fog slows her fiaker and her perception of the time it takes to inch from narrow Schreyvogelgasse to Kärntner Strasse. She believes she's alone on the streets.

She hurries through the Café Gerstner, where Wally waits, slouching over a corner table. Sulking, the girl doesn't look up until Erszébet silently glides out a chair and sits down. A saucer on the table is overflowing with the ends of Russian cigarettes.

Wally leans back in her chair and stares at Erszébet. You're very late, she says in English.

"I'm sorry. The fog is terrible."

Erszébet settles herself, orders a *Schlagobers* and a *Kirschenstrudel* and takes out her tarot cards. She shuffles, places her right hand on the deck, and closes her eyes to concentrate. She tenderly draws the top card, flips it face up on the table. Number fifteen, *le Diable.*

Interested, Wally bends over the card, her sulk forgotten.

"What does it mean tonight, that card?"

"You should ask what my question was, that's the important point."

Seeing Wally's face, she quickly touches her to reassure her, bring her back to attention.

"No, no. Don't act like that. I didn't mean to correct you."

I need her, she reminds herself. She must stay with me. There isn't much time, and I'm very tired. "The card says the devil loves his own," she explains. "You serve him when you serve your lowest instincts. This is temptation."

The waiter brings their order, clatters down the coffee and sweets, slops a little thick cream on the table. Wally draws her finger through it.

The card is as real as the cup in my hand. Unnerved by the card's prediction, Erszébet turns away from it. There is something to fear.

As if the girl has read her mind she says dismissively, it's only a card.

Erszébet leans forward and takes Wally's hand.

"Listen to me. I've done something that may make you angry. I wrote Herr Zellenka a letter. He'll join us here tonight."

Wally is astonished. "He's coming here?"

"I thought it would be best to meet in public. I'm going to tell him everything we know and see how he reacts."

"But why didn't you talk to me about it first?"

Blinking back tears, Wally frowns into her cup, swirls the dark liquid around, edging it close to the rim, almost spilling it.

Erszébet waits until Wally's curiosity overcomes her anger. She takes her time letting the older woman know this. Wally is relieved the intimate conspiracy between them is restored. She eagerly reenters their charmed circle.

"So if he answers our questions, will the investigation be over?"

"Yes."

Erszébet orders an expensive bottle of Tokaji. They drink it slowly; the wine is heavy and sweet. It's made from grapes called *aszú,* she says. They're picked as raisins.

They're becoming intoxicated, drinking the rich wine, eating nothing but cake. An hour goes by. Wally studies the tarot card with the image of the devil. A waiter brings fresh glasses of water and a second bottle of wine. They don't mention Herr Zellenka again, but Wally is distracted, glancing continually at the door. She waits for a sudden tap on her shoulder.

They smoke, play a few hands of tarok. Erszébet calls *Pagat Ultimo,* even though she isn't concentrating on the game. She imagines all the noise in the room will quiet at the entrance of a sinister figure, Herr Zellenka. She strains to detect a change in the tide of conversation.

More time passes. It's very late. Without a word, Erszébet begins to pack up the cards. She is serenely confident that *ráböjtölés,* the black fast, will give her an answer. If not tonight, then surely later. Disappointed, Wally retrieves her red cloak, and unsteadily crosses the room.

During the hours they were inside, the fog thickened. When they step out into it, all the comfort of the café is instantly wiped away. The golden stripe of light on the walk is broken by the bodies moving across the glass door behind them, like moths against a lantern. Wally's shadow shows violet around its edges.

Several fiakers wait on the street, and Erszébet searches for an empty one.

A man in a dark coat suddenly steps in front of them. They didn't hear his footsteps.

He holds his hat in his left hand. The man who received her letter. It takes Erszébet a moment to recognize him. He danced with her in the Sophien-Saal during *Fasching.* He left the mark of his sweat on her skin.

"Ladies, will you join me?"

Erszébet shakes her head and links her arm through Wally's.

"No, you'll follow us."

They sit in heavy silence inside the carriage. Wally hunches down in the seat and looks out the window. The streets are a pale gray blank. Because of the fog, she can't tell if Herr Zellenka is following them. In front of the Reischsrat, she glimpses the colossal figure of Athena, the goddess's stern features unrecognizable, masked with snow. She imagines Dora, her face sliding into shapelessness during all these months underground. She imagines the fig tree, its dark leaves and knobs of budded fruit muffled in darkness. Everything's buried.

Wally is possessed by such lassitude she can barely speak. She feels that the curve of her lips was put there with a chisel. Frozen clods of snow kicked up by the horses thud rhythmically against the carriage. Its drowsy movement rocks her back and forth, and she struggles against its feeling of ease, of well-being. *Where are they going?*

Erszébet hasn't said a word to relieve her apprehension. The quiet between them seems unbridgeable, almost solid. We're frozen in place, Wally thinks. Erszébet sits with her hands inside a fur muff on her lap. When she turns from the

window, her face has a hard expression. Even her eyes seem
dulled, as if she barely recognizes Wally.

"Don't worry. The driver knows where to go."

Wally remembers Erszébet helped her into the fiaker
first. Then she stepped around to give the driver directions.
She didn't hear what was said.

Opposite the opera house on the Kärntner Ring, she sees
an enormous phantom shape that must be the Heinrichshof
apartment house. Then the ornate bulk of two hotels — the
Grand and the Imperial — sail past, blind and solemn as
ships.

The fiaker turns into Stadtpark.

The road twists through thick woods. The fog has lifted
here, leaving a few wispy rags of its passage in the hollows. In
the distance, Wally can see faint dots, as if an enormous chandelier had collapsed among the trees. She guesses it must be
the light from the sulphur torches around the lake. They travel
deep into the park before Erszébet orders the driver to pull
over on an empty road.

When the carriage door is suddenly opened, the bolt of
cold air makes Wally shrink back against the seat. Herr Zellenka stands outside with his hand on the latch. He bows his
head, as if he were a suitor.

"A strange meeting, but I'm here at your request. May I
help you?" His voice is mocking.

Erszébet says she'd prefer to talk with him inside the
fiaker.

He laughs. "Madame, I've followed you into the park. You
can at least oblige me by getting out of the fiaker. You're quite
safe. The driver can wait for you. Here, I've brought an extra
cloak. We can walk together."

Wally is enfolded within Erszébet's hesitation, the driver's puzzlement, Herr Zellenka's measured impatience. Behind
that, she is afraid.

The carriage dips as Erszébet gives him her hand and
steps out.

Wally hesitates. Seeing the two of them standing next to

each other, she senses something, a complicity or physical familiarity between them. Erszébet extends her arm. *Come down.*

Wally gingerly descends from the fiaker. Since Erszébet is warmly dressed in a heavy fur cloak, Herr Zellenka smoothes the one in his arms over Wally's shoulders. He smiles at her. She glances at him, then quickly looks away.

"I suggest we keep moving to stay warm. We could go closer to the lake if you like."

Erszébet tells their driver to wait for them. They won't be long. He nods and takes out a cigar.

Herr Zellenka acts as if he's on a pleasure excursion. He gallantly takes Erszébet's arm, helping her over the frozen ruts left by carriage wheels in the snow. Wally walks behind them, moving automatically. The air is so cold it magnifies the brittle sound of their footsteps. Wally can't think; there's only room in her head for fear. What is her place here?

"Your letter explained you had news that would interest me, although I didn't expect it would be delivered by two charming ladies. What could you possibly have to tell me?"

"We've spoken to Rosza. We'd like to hear your side of the story."

"My story? I don't understand."

"Rosza told us about your relationship."

"I see. No harm in helping the less fortunate, is there?"

He speaks slowly, in no hurry to respond to Erszébet, as if the answer might float from the peace of the winter night around them.

"Rosza was grievously injured. She had no money, nothing. But her employer, a dear friend of mine, couldn't bring himself to help her. I pity his lack of conscience. We argued about the woman."

When he moves his head and shrugs his shoulders, Wally is conscious of his height. He looms above them.

"Ladies, it's a cold evening in the woods. Can you put your mind to the point?"

Resolute, Erszébet doesn't back down from his scorn or his gestures, which are exaggerated enough to be threatening. A man and two women.

"We have another reason to be interested in your relationship with Rosza. We believe it's connected to Dora's murder."

"Clever guesswork, in the way of women." He speaks so softly Wally must keep close in order to hear him. "*You'll* be my jury?"

He turns and grins at Wally, including her in the question. She shapes her dry mouth into a tremulous line. Next to him, Erszébet is a dark triangular shape in her cloak. They both seem foreign to her.

"What can you do? I'd be surprised if you even understood the gossip you heard correctly."

"Let me be the judge of that."

His laughter booms, heightened by the freezing air. Then the three of them are plunged into stony silence.

"You met Dora when she was a girl." Erszébet's words are now carefully neutral. "What was she like?"

He says nothing. They continue walking.

"Dora seemed happier when she was with me," he says finally. "When I was away, she became ill. I was happy to think I could affect someone that deeply."

Wally realizes the man is talking to himself, as if justifying his own behavior.

"Since I was an intimate friend of her father's, our families spent a great deal of time together. My children adored Dora. I was confident she returned my affection. She never discouraged me. She wrote me letters whenever I traveled. I gave her jewelry."

Wally's body is numb, her face solid, cold, masked by winter air.

"This was all done with her father's knowledge and agreement. Of course, we never spoke of it directly, but there were no secrets between us gentlemen, you understand. We were respectful of each other."

"And Dora's father was involved with your wife?"

"That is correct. How could I object to my wife's behavior, when I had romantic feelings for Dora?"

As they approach the top of a steep hill, the airy shape of a waltz coils into their ears. They rest for a moment, their breath clouding around them. The lake is visible in the distance, a frozen and substantial gleam. The torches around its edge banish the shadows of the trees into the woods and illuminate the tiny figures of a few skaters lazily rotating on the ice. The scene looks enchanted, and Wally half expects some shaggy fairy-tale creature to emerge from the trees and carry off one of the skaters.

He continues. "Dora and I had an argument, a misunderstanding. We were walking by a lake. She was so angry she struck me. I was at fault, I admit."

They make their way down the hill, the ice on the road sharp as rocks. Erszébet slips, and he catches her elbow, steadying her. She gently takes her arm away from him.

"Dora wouldn't speak to me for weeks. She returned my letters. I began to think her mother was suspicious of me, I came over for *Jause* so many times. And I tell you, no woman had ever treated me like that. I was sick with love. Even my wife began to feel sorry for me."

He's silent. The women say nothing. He stops walking and reaches into the pocket of his coat for cigarettes. He courteously offers them his cigarette case, a thick square of gold. Remembering Rosza, Wally recoils when he puts the burning allumette near her face. He doesn't notice her reaction and eagerly continues speaking as if they are good, sympathetic friends.

Erszébet knows he's enjoying himself. A confident and boastful man.

"Dora was angry with me. She was proud and very stubborn. Do anything to me, I begged her, but don't leave me. Punish me, do as you like. We were in the Volksgarten that night, the only place where we had privacy. She slapped me. I dared her to slap me again, and she did, even harder. It was part of our little romantic game. It was always exciting."

He looks away from them, presumably descending into some treasure house where the memory of the physical pleasure of Dora's body waits for him. The reflection of the torches on the ice ricochets a faint luminosity onto his face. He sadly shakes his head and travels back to them.

"I ran and hid in the shrubs. She found me. She fell on

me, attacking me with her fists, a stone, whatever she could find. I didn't touch her or try to stop her. You understand, I didn't fight back? That isn't what she wanted of me. I ran; she caught me. She scratched my face, she bit my chin, my ears. She was possessed. I didn't make a sound. She called me the foulest names. She was relentless, her breath was like gunfire in the park. I only wanted to please her. I would have taken a knife for her, anything."

The three of them stand in a loose triangle. He lights another cigarette. A shower of red ash falls down the front of his coat. Wally can't bear to look at him, but she can't look away. She smells his sweat. When he turns toward the lake, one side of his face is striped with weak light.

Erszébet remembers the devil has no backside, only a front side.

"Dora and I rolled over and over on the grass, fighting. Her hands were on my neck. I remember I roughly pushed her away. Then everything was quiet. I sat up and Dora was beside me, not moving."

"So you killed her."

"My memory is that her death was an accident. No one would believe anything else." His cigarette is forgotten in his hand.

After a moment, he drops the cigarette and grinds it out with his boot. Then he's silent, absently patting his pockets for his case when Erszébet moves over to him so they're face-to-face. He looks at her, puzzled.

"Go on. Run ahead of us. We'll give you the count of ten."

He studies her for a moment in surprise, then something in the expression on his face makes Wally take a breath and step back. In the distance, the carriages rumble away down the road.

"So, it's my turn?" His voice is taunting.

He slowly walks away, then he veers off the road, falters through a snowdrift, and disappears into the woods.

Wally watches Erszébet. In front of Wally's eyes, she suddenly appears taller, her cloak loose and swollen around her body. She calmly strips off her gloves and throws them on the

ground. She removes her hat, drops it, and claws her long hair
free. After a moment, Wally does the same. Without a word, Erszébet strides into the trees after him. Wally follows.

At first they move slowly, they can't see his tracks, their
eyes are still fixed to the muted iridescence of the lake. Once
they're in the darker realm of the trees — where the light is
suffocated — their eyes adjust, as if they've adapted to breathing underwater. Their breath hangs in front of them, frailer
than ice. Now the moonlight is brilliant. They begin to run,
branches tearing at their faces and cloaks. Wally has no sensation of pain. They find his path, a violet-colored surface of broken snow churned up by his boots.

Wally is light and nimble, not cold, conscious only of
moving forward. All fear has left her. She hears him laugh.

They see him.

She is ahead of Erszébet, the woods fracturing into black
and white around her. His tracks lead around a tree. She's close
to him, his strained breath in rhythm with her own. She
clutches at his running dark figure, and the heavy weight of his
coat surprises her when she pulls it with her hands.

He crashes to the ground and stays there. Wally wonders
why he's waiting, and then suddenly Erszébet is above him.
She watches in shock as Erszébet's hands scratch at his face,
tear at his eyes. His body jerks and he moans. He pushes himself up, but Erszébet holds him down by his coat. Her mouth
hooks the side of his neck. She can't move fast enough for her
fury. Rage is a chain linking them together.

Let him get up.

The women are hunched over, unsteady, their breath
shaking their bodies in unison. Wally doesn't recognize
Erszébet.

He staggers to his feet, holding his hand to his head. He
runs blindly forward, zigzagging, as if searching for the road.
Once he looks over his shoulder at them, and his white face
seems strangely misshapen, his mouth a hole.

He trips and falls forward, striking his head on something — the black shape of a rock — as he lands heavily in the
snow.

The place where he fell this second time is brighter, a clearing between the trees.

Wally sees everything as if in slow motion. She's petrified, powerless to move, to do anything. The sound of their breathing — automatic, savage — echoes between the trees, fills the space above their heads.

They stand over him. His body is motionless, a bent, strangely postured figure in the snow.

Erszébet throws back her head and her voice is a high shriek that ends in a laugh.

Her blood pounds through her body like a stake, the only thing holding her up.

At dawn, two officers arrive at the Zellenkas' house to relieve Franz and the Inspector. Herr Zellenka never returned. His wife slept through the night.

Numb and exhausted, the Inspector arrives home. He enters the bedroom, Rosza's letter still in his pocket. Erszébet is awake and tenderly helps him undress. He groggily wonders if she's slept at all; she seems completely alert. And somehow her ordinary day face has changed.

He hands her Rosza's letter. Even in his state of fatigue, he doesn't want to watch as she reads it. He's afraid. He feels his perception has been altered. As if he looked through the telescope in the Stephansdom and the landscape was intensely, unnaturally bright, almost real — but *wrong. What is this wide net that he stands on, the edges of it becoming visible as it is hoisted up around him?*

The room is silent as she reads the letter. Then she laughs, and his relief is overwhelming.

So you've found Dora's murderer.

She pulls him into the depth of an embrace.

Franz and the Inspector search Herr Zellenka's bedroom and seal his clothing in paper bags. They take his hairbrush, his collection of walking sticks, his monogrammed personal items. They strip the linens from his bed and carefully roll up the carpet in his dressing room.

The examiner in the laboratory performs tests on Zellenka's clothing and finds a pale silk thread deep in the pocket of a certain summer jacket. The thread appears to match fibers taken from the cloak found in the Volksgarten, which Dora had borrowed from his wife. The identification is as close as their tests can prove.

Wally returns to England. That summer, she visits Brighton. On the beach she sees a woman walking at a distance. She is certain it is Rosza. But as she watches, the woman crouches over on all fours, like a beast — her silhouette grows shaggy, immense — before she stands up again, a woman in a gray dress, her skirt blown by the wind.

ACKNOWLEDGMENTS

This is a work of fiction, although some of the characters were inspired by historical figures. The details about crime investigation and life in Vienna are based on period sources.

I would like to acknowledge the invaluable information on the folklore and customs of Hungary in *A magyar nép hiedelemvilága, Hungarian Folk Beliefs,* by Tekla Dömötör, from the 1981 translation by Christopher M. Hann (Corvina Books and the University of Indiana). The lines in italic on page 17 are from this text. The lines in italic on page 11 are from *Hungarian Peasant Customs,* by Károly Viski (Dr. George Vajna & Co.). I have also quoted extensively from *System der Kriminalistik,* by Hans Gross, published in 1904. Information about Dora and her family was drawn from *Dora: An Analysis of a Case of Hysteria,* by Sigmund Freud (Collier Books), and *Freud, Dora, and Vienna 1900,* by Hannah S. Decker (The Free Press, a division of Macmillan, Inc.).

A number of people have contributed to this book. At Little, Brown, a particular thank-you to Judy Clain. My appreciation also goes to Betsy Uhrig and Sandy Bontemps.

I'm also thankful for the help of Simon Taylor and Jo Goldsworthy at Transworld Publishers in London.

A special acknowledgment to Susan Bachelder.

I should also like to thank the following for their kind support: Karen Blessen, Marilyn Cooperman, Grazia D'Arnunzio, John Dugdale, Mark Epstein, Patricia Halterman, Trevor King, Allison Leopold, Nancy Manter, Lee Mindel, James Perry, Ana Roth, Ann Shakeshaft, Edna and Leo Shields, Lori Shields, Valerie Steele, Sally Willcox, Jane Wildgoose, and Laura Williams. Thanks also to the corporation of Yaddo for their generosity.

Finally, I'm glad to express my profound gratitude to Anne Edelstein.

The Fig Eater
by Jody Shields

A READING GROUP GUIDE

"When I set myself the task of bringing to light what human beings keep hidden within them, not by the compelling power of hypnosis, but by observing what they say and what they show, I thought the task was a harder one than it really is. He that has eyes to see and ears to hear may convince himself that no mortal can keep a secret. If his lips are silent, he chatters with his fingertips; betrayal oozes out of him at every pore. And thus the task of making conscious the most hidden recesses of the mind is one which it is quite possible to accomplish."
— Sigmund Freud in
Dora: An Analysis of a Case of Hysteria

Jody Shields on writing *The Fig Eater*

First there was Dora. Or Dora as a patient described by Sigmund Freud in his *Dora: An Analysis of a Case of Hysteria,* published in 1905.

A teenager at the time of her analysis, Dora was the central character in this celebrated — and deeply criticized — case history, which was one of Freud's resounding failures. The analysis had started well. After his first session with Dora, Freud confidently wrote, "The case has opened smoothly to my collection of picklocks."

Inspired by this observation, I began to imagine Dora's sordid, tangled situation with her family as a mystery that the psychoanalyst would "solve."

I started writing *The Fig Eater* — and soon discovered that Dora was missing from the book. She had been murdered. Unintentionally, I had reversed Freud's case history, and the absent Dora was described by her family and friends.

The Fig Eater was also informed by other books that I discovered by happenstance: The memoirs of a governess who worked for Hungarian nobility. A book by an aristocratic British officer stationed in Vienna during the early 1900s. An account of a journey in Eastern Europe by two intrepid lady travelers. Baedecker Guides and Hungarian cookbooks. Gypsy histories. A photography book supplied visual information, from the surprising profusion of dogcarts on the streets of Vienna to the shape of the topiary trees in the city's gardens. The character of Erszébet, the Inspector's wife, was shaped by one of the few books available in English on contemporary Hungarian folklore, a fortuitous discovery.

A police manual written in 1904, *System der Kriminalistik,* was a random purchase at a flea market. The Inspector, one of the main characters in *The Fig Eater,* employed the investigative techniques detailed in this book. Some procedural information in *Kriminalistik* was completely contemporary; detectives were urged to rely on logic, order, and observation as their tools of investigation. Cutting-edge turn-of-the-century scientific techniques ranged from identifying bloodstains to reading fingerprints and the footprints of one-legged criminals. The manual also featured information on many arcane topics, such as distinguishing the handwriting of a person in a hypnotic state, identifying scoundrel types from their cranial defects, and interpreting superstitious objects left at the scene of a crime.

Kriminalistic was written by Hans Gross, a noted Austrian judge and a professor of criminology. Gross is a fascinating and forgotten figure who should be properly recognized as the originator of modern psychological crime detection. His subtle detective techniques surpassed the exploits of his fictional contemporary, Sherlock Holmes. It is possible that Sir Arthur Conan Doyle was acquainted with *Kriminalistik,* which was published around the same time that Dr. Holmes investigated his first case.

Strangely, everything came full circle: After I'd finished writing *The Fig Eater* I discovered that Freud had actually lectured to Professor Gross's students. And that Gross's son, Otto, had become one of Freud's disciples.

QUESTIONS AND TOPICS
FOR DISCUSSION

1. Why is Erszébet so deeply interested in Dora's murder? What motivates her to undertake her own investigation?

2. How would you describe the relationship between Erszébet and Wally? What role does each play in the other's life?

3. How does Erszébet's approach to crime-solving differ from the Inspector's? To what do you attribute these differences?

4. Consider the many different ways voyeurism is present in the novel.

5. Whom did you suspect of being Dora's killer? Did your suspicions change at various points in the novel?

6. The real Dora, Freud's patient, was seduced by her father's friend Herr K. In *The Fig Eater* Dora is a victim not just of seduction but of murder. Why do you think Jody Shields chose — in a novel that explores women's psychology and sexuality —, to escalate the crime in this way?

7. Are the rules of criminal investigation stated in the *System der Kriminalistik* still relevant? Do today's criminal investigators follow them? Which rules struck you as particularly crucial to Dora's case?

8. Erszébet and the Inspector's marriage has many ups and downs. Discuss the fluctuations in their marriage in relation to their separate investigations of the murder. When are Erszébet and the Inspector emotionally close? When are they distant?

9. Fire is a constant element in the novel. What does it signify?

10. What is the role of food in *The Fig Eater*, particularly as it figures in the characters' relationships? What about hunger?

11. In what ways is sexuality constrained in the characters' lives? How does the repression of sexuality manifest itself?

12. Consider the various ways in which the notion of duality is explored in *The Fig Eater*: the parallel investigations, rational versus mystical, truth versus lies, bourgeois propriety versus sexuality. How does Shields play these off each other?

13. Discuss the significance of Erszébet's research into the history of the edible fig. How did your knowledge (from the novel's title) of the fig's importance to the story affect your reading?

14. Discuss how photographs and photography figure in the novel. What role does Egon play? What powers does he attribute to photographs?

15. What is the significance of the novel's setting: early-twentieth-century Vienna? Think about the mixing of old and new worlds, and the introduction of new ways of thinking.

16. Whom would you cast in the film adaptation of *The Fig Eater*?

Jody Shields's suggestions for further reading

Of the numerous near-contemporary accounts of life in late-nineteenth- and early-twentieth-century Vienna, the most interesting are Arthur Schnitzler's *La Ronde,* Robert Musil's *The Man without Qualities,* and Stefan Zweig's *The World of Yesterday.* Additional background material can be found in Frederic Morton's *A Nervous Splendor* and Jacques Le Rider's *Modernity and Crises of Identity: Culture and Society in Fin-de-Siècle Vienna.*

Notable selections from the vast amount of literature concerning Dora and early psychoanalysis include Hannah S. Decker's *Freud, Dora, and Vienna 1900;* Charles Bernheimer and Claire Kahane's *In Dora's Case: Freud — Hysteria — Feminism;* Hanns Sachs's *Freud, Master and Friend;* and Patrick J. Mahony's *Freud's Dora: A Psychoanalytic, Historical, and Textual Study;* as well as, of course, the original case history, Sigmund Freud's *Dora: An Analysis of a Case of Hysteria.*

Recommended works of psychological interest include Michel Foucault's *The Care of the Self,* volume three of *The History of Sexuality;* Mark Epstein's *Thoughts without a Thinker: Psychotherapy from a Buddhist Perspective;* and Sabine Baring-Gould's *The Book of Werewolves: Being an Account of Terrible Superstition.*

NEW FICTION IN PAPERBACK • GREAT FOR READING GROUPS

Jim the Boy
by Tony Earley

"Rich and satisfying....A novel that perfectly captures the innocence and confusion and wonder of childhood."
— John Gregory Brown, *Chicago Tribune*

"This modest little masterpiece of a book may make you feel like flying." — Mary Ann Gwinn, *Seattle Times*

White Oleander
by Janet Fitch

"A ferocious, risk-loving novel...intimate and epic."
— Mark Rozzo, *Los Angeles Times Book Review*

"Quite simply, *White Oleander* is amazing. It's the kind of book you don't want to put down. It's full-blooded, alive, breathtaking, frightening....This incredible novel is the story of what it is to be extraordinary women."
— Rohana Chomick, *Tampa Tribune–Times*

The Power of the Dog
by Thomas Savage

"A gripping and tense novel....A work of literary art."
— Annie Proulx, in her afterword to *The Power of the Dog*

"Mr. Savage is a writer of the first order, and he possesses in abundance the novelist's highest art — the ability to illuminate and move." — *The New Yorker*

 Available wherever books are sold

Make Believe
by Joanna Scott

"Elegant, rich, and completely spellbinding."
— Deborah Sussman Susser, *Washington Post Book World*

"Wonderful. . . . There are things in *Make Believe* that take the breath away. . . . One cannot help urging anyone who loves writing to read this book." — Nick Hornby, *New York Times Book Review*

Fortune's Rocks
by Anita Shreve

"*Fortune's Rocks* kept me reading long into the night. . . . Shreve renders an adolescent girl's plunge into disastrous passion with excruciating precision and acuteness."
— Katherine A. Powers, *Boston Globe*

"A breathtaking, highly entertaining novel . . . richly rewarding."
— Robert Allen Papinchak, *USA Today*

Evening News
by Marly Swick

"An affecting novel . . . utterly palpable and real. . . . It possesses both the psychological suspense of Sue Miller's bestselling *The Good Mother* and the emotional acuity of Alice Munro's short stories." — Michiko Kakutani, *New York Times*

"A book that lingers in the mind and heart."
— Colleen Kelly Warren, *St. Louis Post–Dispatch*

 Available wherever books are sold